BETTER WHEN HE'S BRAVE

BY **JAY CROWNOVER**

The Welcome to the Point Series
Better When He's Bold
Better When He's Bad

The Marked Men Series
Asa
Rowdy
Nash
Rome
Jet
Rule

BETTER WHEN HE'S BRAVE

A Welcome to the Point Novel

JAY CROWNOVER

WILLIAM MORROW

An Imprint of HarperCollins*Publishers*

BETTER WHEN HE'S BRAVE. Copyright © 2015 by Jennifer M. Voorhees. All rights reserved. Printed in the United States of America. No part of this book may be used or reproduced in any manner whatsoever without written permission except in the case of brief quotations embodied in critical articles and reviews. For information address HarperCollins Publishers, 195 Broadway, New York, NY 10007.

HarperCollins books may be purchased for educational, business, or sales promotional use. For information please e-mail the Special Markets Department at SPsales@harpercollins.com.

FIRST EDITION

Library of Congress Cataloging-in-Publication Data has been applied for.

ISBN 978-0-06-238592-5

15 16 17 18 19   OV/RRD   10 9 8 7 6 5 4 3 2 1

Dedicated to everyone's inner bad girl. That bitch gets to have all the fun! And you better watch out if you dare to cross her.

INTRODUCTION

SOME OF THE THINGS that happen in the Point are outlandish and larger than life, and I love it that way! It's one of the reasons this series is so much fun to write. So as you read, keep in mind that this is fiction. Any liberties I take with police procedure are for the sake of the story, and not because I haven't done the research. So play along with me and allow yourself to get lost in the mayhem, romance, life, and chaos that run rampant in these stories.

When I'm talking about Titus's police station and his office, you might notice it seems outdated. It definitely doesn't have the bells and whistles that most modern cop shops come equipped with. The reason for this is that I am obsessed with *Homicide Hunter* on Investigation Discovery . . . OMG, it is the greatest thing in the world. The show takes place in the seventies and eighties here in Colorado Springs, and all I could see when I was writing was that police station and Joe Kenda's office. So the vision is old and battered, which fits with the overall dreary and ugly feel to the Point. And if you watch the show, you will so be able to recognize the inspiration!

Again thanks to everyone who is giving this series a shot. We all need new blood, a creative outlet, an escape . . . and the Point is mine. I love that I get to write these men and woman with no rules and stretch the bounds of what we see in New Adult and even what we see from me. It's incredibly fulfilling, so I appreciate everyone coming along for the ride . . . and what a ride it's turning out to be! Every single time I think I've gone too far or reached the edge, I always find another corner to turn or another twist to tangle with. Half the time I'm as surprised as you guys are to see where it all ends up. There is nothing more exciting and thrilling for a writer than that. These books are full of dirty fun and I really am kind of like a kid in a candy store when I write them.

We all know a man is so much Better When He's Brave, so I can't wait for you to meet Titus!

Bravery is being the only one who knows that you are afraid.

—*Franklin P. Jones*

BETTER WHEN HE'S BRAVE

Prologue

A T THE BEGINNING OF the end.
  Drip, drip. . .
Splat, splat. . .
Rattle, rattle. . .
Clank, clank. . .
Whoosh, whoosh. . .
Thud, thud. . .
"FUCK . . ."
Groan . . .

I tried to lift my head up after the second time the metal pipe smashed into the back of it, but it was too much. My ears were ringing, and blood dripped down over every inch of my face and splattered on the cold cement floor across my booted feet. I didn't want to think about how deep that puddle was or how wide it was spreading. That was a lot of blood. Too much blood. All of it mine. I couldn't keep my eyes open any longer, so I couldn't see the scattering of men around me as they took turns with fists and whatever else they could find to work me over where I was chained up to the exposed pipe above my head.

I rattled the handcuffs—handcuffs that I used every day to try and keep this city in line—against the pipe, but knew I wasn't getting free anytime soon.

The sound of a metal pipe dragging on the floor as one of my assailants moved closer to me had the last little bit of air that survived the last blow whooshing out of my lungs. The simple act of breathing made me feel like I was going to turn my insides out, so I squeezed my eyes shut as tightly as I could to keep these brutal bastards from seeing just how effectively they were breaking me with fists and metal. My body was slowly crumbling under the torturous onslaught, but my will, my drive to never let a guy like him win, would never break. I would die in this shithole at the hands of these murderers and miscreants, and no matter how much they threw at me, how much they tried to destroy the vessel it was housed in, my bravery, my calling to keep the world safe from people like this, would never be extinguished. I would never cave, never bow down, and never let a guy like Connor Roark win.

I spit out a mouthful of blood, the copper tang filling and coating every raw surface of the inside of my mouth. I managed to crank my neck up just enough to see impenetrable black eyes looking at me. There was no joy in that dark gaze, no victory that he had me exactly where he wanted me. There was no satisfaction. There was nothing but emptiness, a complete void in the place where any kind of humanity should live. I had seen that expression before. My little brother's father had worn it every day for years while he turned this city into a rotting cesspool of lawlessness, debauchery, and mayhem. It was the worst city anyone could choose to try and serve and protect, yet that's what I did with every single breath I took. It was a crumbling ghetto ruled by dangerous men and hard women, but it was my beat and its citizens were my dangerous men and hard women to protect. Many of them were my family and my heart. It wasn't just my job—it was my calling. It was who I was. The Point had no room for heroes, but I was as close as this place was ever going to get to having one. Not that I felt very heroic currently chained up and beaten down, knowing this was the end for me.

I squinted at him through the blood covering my face, twisted my swollen lips into something that had to resemble a gruesome grin, and told him flatly, "Fuck you. You'll kill me before I break."

My harshly spoken words trembled out on the last little bit of air that was wheezing in and out from my obviously injured lung and then I didn't think anymore because another round of beating started, and now someone had found a baseball bat and the way it connected with the outside of my knee made me groan and collapse, so that the only thing keeping me up-right while the thugs tore me apart was my swollen and bruised wrists where they were clamped in the cuffs that were strung up over my head.

In a bloody and misty haze I thought I saw Roark shake his head, and when he spoke, the faint Irish lilt that colored his tone scraped across my broken and bleeding skin like a million shards of glass. He was a murderer, a liar, a criminal tsunami of zero regret and no remorse. He shouldn't have a voice that sounded like rolling green hills and jaunty folk songs. He should come with a tail and horns and his words should smell like smoke and brimstone with every sound he uttered. Connor Roark was as close to the devil incarnate as I had ever come and that was saying a lot considering that I made a living chasing down demons and all other sorts of fallen beings that called my city, my streets, and my own personal version of hell home. I had taken on more than my fair share of villainous masterminds in my role as a homicide detective in one of the most dangerous, corrupt cities in the world. It was a place that was so bad, so dark, so lost in crime and violence it didn't have a name . . . we simply called it the Point. It was the ending point, the breaking point, the point of no return . . . it was simply a place where only the strong survived and anyone else was bound to die trying.

The metal pipe cracked painfully along my already fucked-up ribs and everything went black on the outside of my wavy vision.

I groaned even though I was fighting to keep every reaction they were eliciting from me to a minimum.

"All of this over a girl, over a city that will never repay your blood and sacrifice. Really, Detective King, I thought you would prove to be much more of a challenge. She made you soft. She made you weak. All of the men in this city got distracted by their dicks twitching and forgot there was a war going on. No girl is worth dying for."

I coughed and spit up another mouthful of blood and let my head fall forward as I gasped out a wheezing laugh.

"You can kill me. You can burn this fucking city to the ground. You can do your worst to anyone and everyone that dares to call this place home, but even after you lay waste you still won't have what you want . . . a girl that *is* worth dying for. She'll kill you first."

I gritted my teeth and wrapped my hands around the links on the cuffs so that I could look my captor in the eye as I bit out the stark and brutal truth that I knew would shove him over the edge.

I told him about *the* girl, who was now *my* girl, and how she was going to bring the world Roark was trying to destroy down around him and bury him under it when she found out that I was gone. I got in a few more pointed digs that would drive home the point that I knew what he was up to, understood his real motivation even if it seemed chaotic and unclear to everyone else.

A tick started in Roark's cheek and he took a few steps closer to where I was limply hanging, slowly bleeding to death from inside and out. He stopped when the toes of his boots were touching the blood-covered toes of my own. I felt him put a finger under my chin as he tilted my head back so that we were looking at each other. He had a gaze that was familiar in both its darkness and its madness. Roark came by his insanity and ruthless disregard for human life naturally. There was no getting around twisted genetics.

"*Your* girl?" The accented voice was hard, furious, and I knew I had hit a raw nerve.

I barked out a laugh that sounded more like a dying wheeze, and felt a fleeting moment of satisfaction when some of my blood landed squarely on his face. We were almost the same height, and if I hadn't been hanging limp and broken, we would've been eye to eye. I had a solid fifty pounds on Roark and I knew how to fight just as dirty as the next guy, but what I would never be able to overcome, what would always give men like him the upper hand over guys like me, was the fact that I still had a heart. I still cared. No matter how hard this city continued to kick me in the junk, no matter how many times I had to choose between my family and what was right, no matter how many times I was reminded that I lived in a place absent of justice and light . . . I still cared. I still had hope. I still wanted to be a force that fought for righteousness and the small amount of good that could be found hidden in the cracks and darkness, and I still loved. My heart was protected by a monster that lived deep inside of me, but that beast had kept the thing safe while we scraped by in this awful place.

I loved my brother even though he was a criminally minded hard-ass. I loved my job. I loved my small circle of friends that more often than not were on the other side of the law from me. I loved my mother even though she was a lifelong drunk with no interest in ever trying to dry out . . . and I loved my girl.

The girl. The one I would die for. The one I would fight this war Roark had started for, and if this was the way I was meant to go out, then so be it. I would die for having a heart but at least I knew I was going out for a fucking valiant and important reason.

"Mine." I gave him another grotesque-looking smile as he let my head fall limply back down, my neck too battered to hold the weight up anymore. "She's been mine since the second she flipped on Novak and his crew. She only fell in with you because she wanted me and didn't know how to ask for it. She thought you could keep her safe like she knew I would. How does it feel to know you were nothing to her but a poor substitute for me? Every time you took her to bed it was me she was thinking of. You haven't ever been anyone's first choice, Roark."

I felt him tense up. I knew the girl was a sore spot, a loss that had really amped up his drive to take the Point down in a fireball of vengeance and hate. No way was Roark ever going to let that rejection and slight go, not on top of the others the Point had handed out to him

His hand fisted in the hair on the top of my head and my face was yanked back up so we were once again eye to eye. Mine were starting to swell shut and I knew I was losing too much blood. I couldn't feel much below my shoulders except for my throbbing knee and every part of my exposed skin that I could see was covered in bruises, welts, and open skin, leaking the last of my life force out onto the cracked concrete below where I was dangling. I tried to focus on his face, but it kept blurring and fading into one that looked like another I loved. The metallic burn against my split lips made me gag when the end of a wicked black pistol was sudden shoved between my puffy lips and stopped with the open end of the barrel resting against my teeth.

I saw myself reflected in the absolute void of that black gaze watching me and I knew he was going to pull the trigger.

"She chose wrong. I could have laid this city at her feet."

"If she wanted the city at her feet, she would have put it there herself. That's why you never deserved her, you prick. You never understood she could run circles around you in the misplaced-rage and need-for-revenge department. Only she was smart enough to know that there had to be more to life than that. I'm her more. You were just a means to an end." The words were garbled around the pistol but I had to get them out.

I closed my eyes and waited for it all to end. I wouldn't beg. I wouldn't plead. I wouldn't waver. I wouldn't go out any other way than the way I'd lived my life . . . I was going to go out bravely and there was no fucking way this piece of shit would ever know how scared I was that not only was I leaving my brother behind in this tragic place, but I was leaving my girl . . . *the* girl. When I was gone she was going to unleash hell, and Conner Roark had no clue what a vengeful woman who was far more bad than good could do when she was suffering from a broken heart.

BANG!

Hell is yourself and the only redemption is when a person puts himself aside to feel deeply for another person.

—Tennessee Williams

Chapter 1

Reeve

THERE WERE TWO PLACES in the world that I never thought I was going to step foot in again. One was the crumbling and rotting surface of the city simply known as the Point. The other was the police station that sat in the heart of that city and had just as much corruption and crime inside its walls as the town had on its streets. I hated everything about why I was here and yet I put one foot in front of the other, knowing if I ever wanted a shot at being the type of woman that could live with the person looking back at herself in the mirror every day, I had to do something guided by right decisions for once in my life. I had to do something not motivated by my own selfish desires and my own burning need for payback and revenge against the cruel injustices I knew this place was capable of doling out. Good or bad, we all had a target on our backs if we called the Point home. The city didn't discriminate when causing pain and tearing apart lives.

My hands shook as I reached for the handle on the door. I wasn't supposed to be here. Not in this city. Not at this building. Not in this life that wasn't mine anymore.

I was supposed to be hiding. I was supposed to be someone new, someone that had been handed a chance to start all over. I was supposed to be a girl that didn't know what death and revenge felt like even though they lived so hot and angry under her skin. The new me was supposed to be safe, supposed to be insulated and so far removed from the crime and sleaze that was the lifeblood of the Point, that she wouldn't last five minutes in this terrible place.

Only the new me had never stuck, and truthfully, I had never been a fan of that girl's fragile and soft disguise. Hiding was for the weak, and I knew deep down to the core of who I was that I would never, ever, actually be safe. I had harbored too many demons, made too many deals with devils along the way to ever think I was going to get away with walking out of the Point without doing some sort of bloody penance for my misdeeds.

I was standing on unsteady legs, asking the young cop who was sheltered behind bars and bulletproof glass at the front desk of the station to go find the one man, the only good I had ever seen in the godforsaken place. If I was going to throw my new life away, jump feetfirst back into the fire, Detective Titus King was the only person I was going to trust to keep me safe from the flames.

Some men wanted to watch the world burn. Titus was a man that wanted to put out all the flames single-handedly from inside the blaze. He was the only one I trusted with the information I was holding on to. He was the only one I trusted to help me find a safe place to land after I kicked the new me to the curb and dusted the old me off and put back on her damaged and tattered skin. Lord only knew how long I would last now that I was back, but I knew if I had Titus on my side I would stand a better chance of making it to the finale, to the end, to the place I needed to be in order to right one wrong. One of so many in this hellhole.

The Point was going to war and I was about to become the advantage that the good guys were going to need if they wanted any chance of being able to hold their own.

The young cop asked me my name and when I muttered "Reeve Black" I saw the way his eyes went from appreciating the fall of my long black hair and the way my T-shirt hung against curves that were more dangerous than he would ever know, to speculative and almost disgusted. I had a reputation and it wasn't a good one. Even in this place full of bad people doing bad things, there was still room for the worst of the worst. I was the *worst* and I never pretended to be anything else.

The cop picked up the phone and spoke softly. I heard him say my name more than once and then shake his head. I really, really wasn't supposed to be here, and I knew Titus was going to be anything but happy to see me. He didn't need to be happy, he just needed to hear what I had to say and agree to help me help him.

I pushed some of my hair back behind my ear and willed my hands to stop quivering. This wasn't a time to betray weakness. I wasn't afraid of him. I was afraid *for* him.

Out of the corner of my eye I saw a door that had his name and title scrawled across it in peeling black vinyl letters swing open. I felt my heart quiver a little bit, felt my tummy pull tight as his dark head poked out of the opening. Even across the distance and through all the barriers keeping us apart, I could feel the impact of his outrageously blue eyes and the fury captured inside them as they landed on me.

Yep . . . not happy to see me at all.

He stormed out of the office, eyes locked on me as he made

his way to where I was standing, separated from the rest of the police precinct and the officers milling about, some in uniform some out. Titus never wore police blues. At least he hadn't any of the times I had seen him. No, Titus dressed like a man that had a job to do and that the job was wearing him down and slowly and surely eating away at his soul.

As he stalked toward me I could see the way the knot in his tie hung loose at his throat. I could see the way his rolled-up sleeves tightened on his forearms as his hands clenched into angry fists at the sight of me. I could see the way his dark slacks had wrinkled from whatever bad thing or bad guy he had spent the day trying to set right. When he finally reached me I couldn't stop staring at him. I ended my perusal at the tips of his worn and scuffed-up black boots as he stopped so that he could loom over me. There would never be polished wing tips for a man like Titus King. There would never be pristine tennis shoes used for recreational sports. Nope, Titus would always be a man that needed shoes that could get the job done and handle the muck and mire that he had to wade through every waking hour while he tried to keep some kind of order.

I gulped and fought to keep myself from falling back a step. Titus was a big man and really tall, so it was easy to want to cower under his burning glare, but if I did that I would show him how scared I was and I couldn't afford to start this conversation out that way.

Instead I batted my eyelashes slowly, let out a deep breath that I knew would force him to have to watch the rise and fall of my chest, and kicked the side of my very carefully painted mouth up in a grin that had made more than one man do anything I ever asked of them.

"Detective King." I liked his name even with that title in front of it. He could be the ruler of some ancient barbaric land where only the strong survived.

"What in the fuck?" It was a question and a statement shouted loud enough to draw the attention of both the police and the criminals wandering around the building.

An ironlike hold clamped on my elbow and I was unceremoniously dragged past all the bars and barriers, past the other cops sitting at their desks, past a captivated audience that couldn't help but speculate what kind of bug had gotten up the big detective's ass. Titus was not a man prone to big displays of extreme emotion. He was much more a man of action, so the glower on his harshly handsome face and the force with which he maneuvered me around his coworkers and the riffraff that littered the police station did not go unnoticed. He was beyond pissed at my sudden appearance and doing nothing to hide it.

When we were back at his office he shoved me inside like I was one of his perps and slammed the door behind us with far more force than necessary. I knew the Point was on the verge of burning, but nothing would ever be as hot or as out of control as the wild fury I saw sparking in the depths of Titus's sky-colored eyes. He was pissed like I knew he was going to be, but more than that he was concerned, and I think that made him even angrier. No one wanted to worry about a girl like me. I was supposed to get whatever nasty shit landed at my doorstep. I deserved it. That was how karma was supposed to work, but Titus was hardwired to care, even if the other person didn't earn it or necessarily want it, and that had to make him crazy.

I studied him for a long minute, eyes locked on a muscle that twitched in his rock-hard jawline. He was so beautiful. I had thought so the first second I laid eyes on him when I initially went to him to pour out my heart and seek some kind of re-demption. He was everything a man should be. Everything a warrior needed to be to make it in this wasteland, fighting for things that had long been lost. Sometimes it felt like I was torn between lust and worship where he was concerned.

He was built like an impenetrable bastion. So tall and wide it seemed like nothing would ever be able to break its way inside of him. His body was hard—from the expression on his face to the muscles that flexed and coiled when he did something as simple as lean back on the edge of his desk. His hair was cropped short on the sides and left longer on top; it was almost the same inky black as my own, but at his temple on one side was a startling and shocking snow-white spot. It was a constant reminder of the night the new me had been born and he had watched his younger brother put a gun to his own head and threaten to end it all. Titus also had raven-dark brows and a sexy, dark scruff that slashed across a tawny complexion that had nothing to do with being in the sun.

His eyes were blue, a pretty light blue that should've soft-ened the hardness of his masculine face, but there was some-thing in them, something cold and hard, that made them glitter and shine like a honed weapon, so sharp that they hurt to look at for too long. That beautiful gaze encased by lashes that were too long and feathery for such a hard and unyielding face could do all kinds of damage on its own without the dangerous threat of that strong body behind it. Titus was not a man that anyone would be foolish enough to take lightly, and everything about the way he looked transmitted the fact loud and clear.

He crossed his arms over his wide chest and I watched

shamelessly as the muscles bulged. I shouldn't be here, but while I was, I was going to admire the view.

"Long time no see, Detective."

His scowl got even deeper and I saw the tick in his jaw move to a throbbing vein in his neck.

"We were never supposed to see each other again, Reeve. That's what Witness Protection is all about. You're supposed to be the federal marshal's problem now."

I shifted my weight from foot to foot and nodded my head slowly. "I know, but something came up, and I think you need to know about it."

He swore under his breath and lifted his hands up to scrub them over the longer locks of hair that stood up straight on the top of his head. The wild hair and the look on his face almost made him appear feral. There was wildness in the man and I wondered if he even realized it.

"Look, Reeve." He pushed off the desk and reached out a hand to put it on my shoulder. "You need to get in touch with the marshal in charge of your case. There's been a leak. One of the witnesses that was picked up in the investigation into Novak and his crew was murdered last night. He had just flipped and the fed only had him in WITSEC for two months. Everyone on the case could be compromised, so you being here, back in the city, is a stupid move and far too risky."

I sighed a little bit and moved around his massive frame so I could sit in one of the rickety chairs that lived across from his battered and cluttered desk. I rubbed my sweaty palms along the denim of my jeans and lifted my chin up, hoping he didn't see the way it wanted to quiver.

"Hartman. Hartman was murdered last night."

Murder was such an ugly word. Heavy and unpleasant when-
ever spoken aloud or even thought. The word was made up of
pointy, sharp things that dug into my skin and made my breathing labored. It had the power to hurt, the power to change everything, and it had been haunting me, hanging around my neck
like a stone locket for years and years.

Titus went tense, far tenser than he already was, and his
mouth flattened into a brutal line.

"What?"

I had to look away. He was trying to spear me open with
that glacial blue gaze and I didn't want him anywhere near the
squishy, soft center of the real me.

"I know Hartman was murdered last night and that's why
I'm here. I left WITSEC because I know who did it."

The line of his mouth went from a flat line to a fierce frown that
would have made a smarter woman get to her feet and leave. He
moved so that he was hovering over me and dipped his head down
so that I had no choice but to look directly into his probing gaze.

"What are you talking about, Reeve? Make it good because
I'm about two seconds away from throwing you in lockup and
ordering a Breathalyzer and a tox screen."

I wasn't drunk and I had never touched an illegal drug in
my life. I rolled my eyes and moved the slippery fall of my hair
over my shoulder. He tracked the move with narrowed eyes and
finally took a step back. I breathed a silent sound of relief.

I could take a lot, but Titus might just be too much for me to
handle. There was just so much of him to take in.

"I know about Hartman . . . come on, Detective, look at me."
I waited until his eyes met mine. "I wouldn't give up a cushy
spot in WITSEC and a perfectly manicured lawn in the suburbs,

where people think my name is Jill Parker and where I have a job cutting hair for soccer moms at a strip mall, unless I had a reason to do it. I was safe, Titus. All I've ever wanted since the minute I handed over my soul to Novak was to be safe. I never in a million years would walk away from that . . . but here I am. The war for this city has just started and I know the traitor that fired the opening shots. You need me."

He considered me for a long moment, the tension so thick it was taking up all the air in the tiny room. He didn't want to believe me, didn't want me to be here or to know what was going on and how it was tied to me, but there was no getting around the facts. I was telling the truth. He had the body and the blood to prove it. He fell back to lean against the desk and his thick eyebrows slammed down over his eyes in a scowl.

"Tell me what you know and then I'll decide if I need you or not."

He was gruff. He was rude. He was unflinching. I couldn't blame him for any of that. The Point was under attack and the innocent and not so innocent were becoming casualties. If there was one thing a man like Titus didn't like, it was casualties.

It was a long story, one he only knew the beginning of, and there were parts I didn't want to tell him. Parts like the conclusion, where I had fallen for the traitor. I didn't want to admit that I had been taken in by the general who fired the opening salvo in this battle mostly because on the surface that general reminded me so much of the imposing man in front of me right now.

Conner Roark had swooped in and offered me the one thing I had craved for longer than I could remember. Security. Safety. A shot at a life where words like *murder* didn't have to dangle suffocatingly around my neck. All of that had been the cake and my sweet tooth started to ache, but the icing, the sugar fix that sent me into a full-on rush towards madness, was the fact that he was also tall, broad, had wavy dark hair, dreamy midnight eyes, and spoke with the softest Irish lilt I had ever heard. I couldn't sign up for all of that fast enough and because it was attached to a man with a badge, a man that promised to uphold the law and do right because he had belief and conviction, I couldn't tie my stupid heart up in a bow and give it away fast enough. Not that it was a gift many wanted.

Only Conner Roark was nothing like Titus King. No man was and I was a fool for ever thinking otherwise.

"The marshal that put me in WITSEC . . ." I had to look away. It was hard to admit how easily I had fallen for a cheap imitation of what I would never be able to have. The worst didn't get the best and Titus was definitely the *best* man I had ever met. "Conner Roark. He's as dirty as they come. He sent a man after Hartman once he was out of jail and in a safe house. He wanted Race Hartman to know that taking over where Novak left off is a bad idea."

Titus didn't say anything for a long time. He silently watched me and I could see him turning the words over in his head. "Why? Why does Roark care who takes over the Point? What's it to him and why is it worth destroying his career with the marshals?"

I crossed one leg over the other and tapped my fingers on my knee, pretending to be far more composed than the swirling, uncertain mess I actually was on the inside.

"That I don't have an answer to. He hates the city. He hates the people that live here to a degree that borders on fanatical. I can't tell you why he did it. I can only tell you that he did." I bit down on my lip a little watching Titus try to fit the pieces together.

I finally cracked. My bottom lip trembled and I felt emotion start to claw and scratch its way up my throat. He couldn't decide if he was going to believe me or not, and that hurt. Titus put his hands on his hips and threw his head back so that he was looking up at the ceiling.

"You've got to be kidding me with this."

I slowly shook my head and sank my teeth into my lip. "I wish."

He sighed heavily and suddenly bent forward and put his hands on his thighs like someone had hit him in the gut.

"How exactly do you know all of this, Reeve? Why would a dirty federal marshal let a woman under his protection in on his plan and his crime? Why wouldn't he simply take Hartman out and go about his business? Why does he trust you enough to let you know what he's up to?"

I heard it, the disappointment in his tone, the knowledge that things were worse than he could imagine and more dirty law enforcement was involved. I was right at the center of this particular shit show and he knew that meant I was right. He needed me.

"Why do dangerous and desperate men do anything they do, Detective?"

"Because of love," he said emotionlessly and flat.

I nodded solemnly. "I started seeing Conner almost as soon as he whisked me away from here. After everything that happened with Dovie, I felt awful. I never wanted her to get hurt, but I had to do what I did because of the deal I made with Novak. Conner made me feel loved despite the fact that I betrayed my friend, despite the fact that I'm a horrible person. And he made me feel safe." *I really wanted* you, *but I knew there wasn't a chance in hell of that ever happening, so I settled on what I thought was the next best thing . . .* That part went unsaid, but I knew it was probably there, leaking out of my eyes as we looked at each other.

"This whole story is goddamn unbelievable."

Tell me about it. Even when I thought I was doing something good, it turned out to be just the opposite.

"I can help you bring Conner down, Titus. That's why I left WITSEC. That's why I'm here. I hate the Point. I hate the person I am because of this place, but I owe it to you, and to the people that will never leave here, to do what I can to stop him from doing any more damage. The good guys deserve a win for once." *He* deserved a win.

"How exactly do you think you can help me? All I have right now is your word that Roark is a dirty fed who broke protocol by getting involved with a witness. That can easily boil down to your word against his, and no one likes a scorned lover out for revenge."

I was anticipating that, so picked up my purse and fished around until I found the cell phone I had stolen from Conner the last time he was at my safe house in the burbs. It had only been a day ago but it felt like a lifetime had passed. I handed it over wordlessly and got to my feet. A little zing of electricity zipped down my arm as my fingers brushed lightly across his rough palm.

"This is Conner's phone. Look it over and get back to me. I'm in this now, Detective."

He swore again as I reached out to pull open the door. I looked over my shoulder as he said my name in a much softer voice than he had used up to now.

He was turning the phone over and over between his fingers and looking at me like he was trying to see inside of my head. He didn't really want inside of there; it was a crowded and convoluted place, and I think he would be shocked to see how much real estate he was already taking up.

"You say you don't know why Conner is doing what he's doing, if in fact he is involved, but why are you?"

That answer was looking at me with a mixture of hunger and hate so strong that it very nearly brought me to my knees.

"Because it's the right thing to do and along the way I forgot what that looked like. I don't want to be that person anymore. I can't be her."

I stepped out of the door and almost plowed over the young woman who I had nearly killed with my foolish and selfish actions not long ago.

Dovie Pryce was a sweetheart. There wasn't anything about her that wasn't wholesome and pure. The way her green eyes widened at the sight of me and the way she went even paler under her milky complexion when our eyes met made me feel like the lowest life-form that had ever lived.

"What are you doing here, Reeve?" Her voice was full of worry, which made me feel even worse. She should hate me, loathe me, and yet she was concerned for my well-being. She was too good for me to ever call a friend. She was too good for this godforsaken town.

I tucked some of my hair behind my ear and gave her a lopsided grin. "I just had a little business to take care of with Titus. WITSEC isn't really working out for me." I wanted to grab her in a hug and tell her I was sorry her asshole of a father had been executed by my equally demented and fucked-up boyfriend, but

I figured Titus would do a better job at it than me. Plus Dovie loved him and was *in* love with the detective's hellion of a half brother, Shane Baxter. News like that should come from family.

Dovie made a noise of concern but before she could ask me anything else about my sudden reappearance an elegant looking blond man materialized at her side and put a protective arm around her slender shoulder. I had never met Dovie's older brother, Race, and I wasn't eager to do so now. He didn't know who I was but he surely knew the hand I had played in getting his sister abducted and setting a ruthless gang of thugs in his direction to deliver a beating that he had barely survived. Race Hartman had every right to want terrible, terrible things to befall me. Everyone who had made it out of Novak's final massacre alive did.

That knowledge, coupled with the fact that Conner was going to be after me with a vengeance once he found out I had double-crossed him and sold him out, didn't give me high hopes for surviving whatever fallout followed the events I had just set in motion. Hell, with the way my luck went, it would be a miracle if I made it out of this police station and back to the crappy no-tell motel I was currently calling home.

New me had been a fragile shell. Old me was made of stronger stuff, but even the strongest brick would break when the weight of the entire world decided to rest on it.

Chapter 2

Titus

I T SHOULDN'T HAVE SURPRISED me how well my brother's girlfriend was taking the news about her father's murder. After all, she had never met the guy and he had tried to hire the city's worst and most violent criminal to murder her, but there was something about Dovie that just screamed goodheartedness and sweetness. I often forgot that she had to have a core of concrete, reinforced with rebar, in order to stand toe-to-toe with my thug of a younger sibling and to survive in the Point.

Race was another story. I expected rage, anger, fury . . . I expected anything but the icy indifference that seemed to cloak him as soon as I gave the two of them the news. There was no love lost between Race and his old man. In fact, more than once threats had been tossed around, and had Reeve not materialized out of the blue with her outrageous story, I would have put Race and my brother at the top of my suspects list for the old man's murder.

Neither man made it a secret that they thought Lord Hartman deserved to take a long walk off of a short pier, but Race's frozen expression as he shifted his gaze between me and his sister told me that there was also still a part of him that wanted to grieve the loss of his parent, no matter how awful that parent may have been. Dovie must have sensed it too because she reached out a hand, put it on Race's shoulder, and gave it a squeeze.

"How did it happen? Did Novak's guys find out where the feds took him?"

I rubbed the back of my neck and turned the cell phone I had in my hand over and over so that the corner tapped on the messy surface of the desk. I was dying to open it and scroll through the messages, not just for the information but also to see if the raven haired beauty was actually on the up-and-up. There was something about her, something that stuck with me the first time she walked into the precinct and told me she had dirt on Novak, that she had made a deal with the gangster to kill her sister's boyfriend. I'd never seen anyone so calm and collected when admitting to a felony before. I had never seen anyone so composed when they were pretty much throwing the rest of their life away, and I would never forget how endlessly dark and unreadable her navy-blue gaze was as she candidly admitted to relaying Dovie's location to Novak's goons as repayment for the hit he had carried out upon her request. Reeve was the reason Dovie got snatched off the street and the reason I had been forced to watch my brother, my only family, put a gun to his head with every intention of pulling the trigger to save not only his lady but me as well. Even with that I hadn't been able to stop thinking about the beautiful backstabber since the feds had whisked her off after she agreed to testify against the rest of Novak's crew if they could guarantee her immunity and a new life.

"No, we don't think it was anyone from Novak's crew. I'm looking into it."

Race lifted a gold-tinted eyebrow and the corner of his mouth pulled down. "More dirty cops?"

That was what made Race so dangerous and why he had been the clear choice to take over the long-running criminal enterprise once Novak was out of the picture. He was just so damn smart. He could see the dots connecting before they were even laid out.

"I'm not ready to say that yet. I'm looking into it." I blew out a deep breath. "I called Bax and Brysen. I thought you would want to tell them what was going on in person." The real reason I had called in reinforcements was because I wasn't sure how their reactions were going to play out. Bax would protect Dovie from anything that hurt her, including the news of her father's demise, and now I thought that Brysen was the only person that could snap Race out of the frigid shock he seemed to be encased in. I was a cop. I never underestimated how beneficial backup could be.

Dovie gave a small grin and shook her head at me a little. "You wanted Bax here because you want to make sure he doesn't go off and do something stupid when he finds out."

Race snorted and shoved his hands through his shaggy hair. "How does the old man's murder fit in with everything else that has been going on, Titus?"

RECENTLY, THE POINT HAD seen the working girls scared to do their thing because one of them had taken a beating meant to kill, just as the city's dirtiest, nastiest club went up in flames, taking too many regulars with it as it burned to the ground. On top of that, Race's prized, vintage car had been incinerated right in front of this very police station and bodies had begun piling up for no other reason than to prove a point. Novak was gone and that made the city fair game—at least that was what the initial interpretation had been. Now, with Reeve's revelations and Hartman being taken out, I had a feeling something bigger was at play. Killing Dovie's old man and attempting to kill Race as well didn't do anything for the city. They were motivated by revenge pure and simple. Someone didn't like the fact that Race and his business partner, Nassir Gates, had picked up right where Novak had left off. Burning the club down screwed Nassir and struck right at the heart of what was most important to him, his money and his girls. The same could be said for the destruction of Race's car. He loved that damn car, and even though his dad was a bastard, it was obvious that Race still cared for him. The attacks seemed more pointed now than they had before.

I sighed again and just gave Race a look that he could interpret any way he wanted. He was bright enough to know exactly what I thought without me having to lay it all out in front of him. I got to my feet and walked around where he and Dovie were sitting.

"Let me go give Bax and Brysen the rundown and then you guys can head out. If I don't fill Bax in, I have about five seconds before he comes through the security glass anyway." My cell phone had been buzzing and pinging with impatient messages from my younger brother since he hit the front doors of the station. Nothing, not even bulletproof glass and an army of weapon-packing police personnel, would keep Bax from Dovie if he thought she needed him. "You guys take a couple minutes together if you need it."

I was at the door when Dovie's soft voice stopped me.

"Why is Reeve back, Titus? What does she have to do with everything that's going on?"

I gave her a hard look and pulled the door open. My eyes immediately saw my brother and Race's pretty blond girlfriend. I cringed when I also saw that Reeve's timing had been bad and she was currently being caged in and growled at by Bax. My younger brother had intimidation down to an art form, and I hated to admit that I didn't blame him for the blatant hatred that was pouring off of him as he appeared to be chewing out the slender young woman.

"I don't know yet. I'm trying to put it all together before the city ends up as nothing more than rubble and ash. I have a really bad feeling that I need her."

"You can't trust her." Dovie's tone held old hurt and betrayal. She knew better than anyone just how untrustworthy Reeve could be.

"I know, Dovie. I don't trust anyone."

Race snorted and reached out to grab his sister in a one-armed hug. I could see by the expression on her face that she knew the gesture was more for him than it was for her. "Isn't it already too late to worry about this city burning. The people in it can't help but feed the flames?"

I agreed with him, so I just shut the door behind me and stalked to where Bax was raking Reeve over the coals while Brysen watched with wide, confused eyes. I heard his deep voice bark, "You bitch. I should put your head through that wall after what you did to Dovie. She thought you were her friend." I wish they were just idle words that he was speaking, but Bax didn't make threats he wasn't ready to follow through on. It didn't matter that Reeve was a girl. To him she was the enemy who had put Dovie in danger. He would treat her like any other threat to his woman.

Reeve blinked those unusually colored blue eyes slowly, and I sighed as she went really pale and still under the onslaught of Bax's anger. I hated that somewhere deep in my gut a little bit of pride cheered for her when she refused look away from him.

"No one has friends in the Point . . . at least that's what I always thought. I'm trying to make it right." I reached the little party just as Reeve's voice cracked and her lower lip started to tremble faintly.

I intervened just as Bax was gearing up to lay into her some more. I reached up to pop him across the back of the head with an open palm. I rarely got the drop on my brother, his instincts were honed too sharp, so I took the shot because he was so focused on his prey he never saw me coming and also because I didn't like the way his threatening Reeve had all my protective instincts flaring to life. She was the last woman in the world I needed to feel protective toward, but that didn't stop me from wanting to shove my brother away from her.

"Leave her alone, asshole. She's trying to help." I let both my annoyance and frustration snap at him as he turned around to shift his glare to me.

Reeve looked between the both of us, and was smart enough to bolt while she had an opening. She left without saying anything to either one of us, but I could see the way her hands were shaking as she pulled open the front door to the police station.

"Who on earth was that?" Brysen sounded bewildered and her bright eyes were full of confusion and questions.

Bax retaliated to my smack across his head by tagging me in

the gut with a balled-up fist. He never pulled any punches, so the force made me grunt and double over as I glared at him.

Bax turned his dark eyes to Brysen and bit out, "Reeve Black. She's the person who told Novak that Dovie was on her own the night he had his guys grab her off the street. She got into bed with him over a blood debt and he called it in and used it to hurt Race and Dovie. She should be in jail for capital murder, but she cut a major deal with the feds and went into Witness Protection. She's supposed to be as far away from here as they could put her. I told this idiot"—he pointed at his finger at me—"if I ever saw her again I wasn't going to be responsible for my actions."

"And I told you to stop saying shit like that to me. Remember, I'm a cop." I warned him about his loose tongue and violent temper all the time. My brother had it in him to kill; I didn't need to be reminded of it every time his wild nature slipped the chains he had strapped on it since he fell in love with Dovie.

"Why are we here, *Detective?*" I hated it when he called me that in such a contemptuous tone.

I scowled at Bax and flicked a narrow-eyed look at Brysen as well. I crooked a finger and motioned for them to move closer so that I wasn't spilling secrets all across the station. It sucked that in a place like the Point even the good guys could be bought if the price was right. I trusted no one.

"I got a call from one of the federal marshals handling all the witnesses in the Novak case. Race and Dovie's old man was murdered last night in the secure location WITSEC found for him. Hartman was willing to give the names of major arms dealers, drug suppliers south of the border, where the money was stashed, and all kinds of other information the RICO unit was chomping at the bit to get their hands on in this case. He had a full security detail, was located out in the middle of goddamn nowhere, and someone still managed to get to him."

Brysen made a noise of distress and bit down on her lip. "How are they handling the news?"

I answered as truthfully as I could. "Dovie is a sweetheart, so I think she's mostly worried about Race since he hasn't said too much. Her asshole father tried to have Novak kill her, so I think she's just relieved that that's one threat she'll never have to worry about again. Race just kind of zoned out; I've never seen him like that before. That's not all, though." I rocked back on my heels and put a hand on the butt end of the pistol attached to my belt. "With Hartman being so insulated, we know the hit had to come from the inside. It had to be someone handling his move and relocation." I didn't want to admit that part even to myself, but it was clear there was no other explanation.

Bax swore. "A fed?"

I nodded solemnly. "Probably."

Bax dropped every dirty word he had in his vocabulary. "Not enough we have to worry about the bad guys, now we gotta worry about the good guys too?"

"That's about the shape of it."

"Why was Reeve here, Titus?" It was a sharp change in subject but I knew it was coming. Bax wouldn't be happy that Reeve was back no matter what the reasons for her sudden reappearance were.

"Because she has information I'm going to need if I have any chance of flushing out our dirty fed."

"What kind of info?"

I had to shake my head and I rubbed my hands over my crop of short hair. I told Bax in a flat tone that left no room for any kind of argument, "That's the line where brother and cop cross, Shane. Leave her alone, I need her so I can do my job and I will be seriously pissed if you get in my way." I used his real name so that he knew I wasn't fucking around.

Brysen had obviously gown tired of the two of us trying to out-badass each other and demanded, "Where is Race?"

"In my office with Dovie." I stopped Bax with a hand on the center of his chest as he went to maneuver around me. My brother was big, but I had always been bigger, and I had no qualms about throwing around my weight when I needed to. "Look, I need this girl to stop what is happening in the Point . . . the fires, the beatings, the destruction . . . it's all tied together. She is absolutely necessary. I told Dovie all of this and she gets it, so you need to use your brains and not go off half-cocked, because I will shut you down so fast it'll make your head spin. You got me, Bax?"

Bax didn't say anything, just shoved around me and stomped his way across the precinct house toward a glass door that had my rank and last name stenciled on it in black letters. Brysen went to follow him but I reached out to stop her. I felt like I had to give her a heads-up that her man was having a tough time with the news about his dad but doing his best to try and hide it.

"Race is a good man. He's in a tough spot right now and making some really difficult choices, but he's always been a lot softer at his center than Bax. His dad was a piece of shit, a murderer and a goddamn oily son of a bitch, but when it hits him, when it really settles, he's gonna need a hand working through his old man being gone."

She told me in a haughty tone that she was never going anywhere, as her man, my brother, and his lady all made their way towards us in a somber huddle. I stepped to the side as both the couples embraced, muttered soft words to one another like they weren't in the middle of a very active police station as they made their way to the front door and acted very much like handling things such as murder, betrayal, and deep personal loss was old hat. It made my chest tight because in a place like the Point those things were indeed an everyday occurrence and all of those young adults were far too familiar with them. At least they had all found someone to lean on, someone else to share the burden of all the constant bad news.

Bonds created in the worst circumstances, love forged in the fire, was bound to shine brighter and last longer than feelings that weren't put to the test. Regular people got to love with ease and without thought. People that fell in love in the Point had to do so knowing it was a battle to stay in love. Everything here was a fight, and in a dangerous place full of dangerous people, love was often the only thing people were willing to do the right thing for. My brother was a prime example of that.

Bax's entire life had been one big house of cards waiting to come toppling down. He spent his youth doing one illegal deed after the other, just bidding his time until he got caught. He wasn't a good guy, and he never would be, but the fact that he cared about Dovie, that he loved her, forced him to make smarter choices. He knew that if he went back to jail or if he eventually ran up against someone that was just a little bit tougher or a little more ruthless than he was, it would kill her to have to put him in the ground. Bax had always been dangerous, but now, with the sassy redhead in his life, he was also cautious. I never thought I would see it happen, but the day had arrived when my brother actually thought before he acted.

I went back to my office and settled in. I kicked back in my rickety chair that I was sure was going to give out and dump me on my ass before the year was over and turned on the cell phone Reeve had left with me. I was both curious and slightly sick to see what was on it. I had faced every variety of bad guy there was since I started as a patrol officer in the Point eight years ago. There wasn't much that shocked me, wasn't much that made my skin crawl anymore. Hell, I was the one that snapped the cuffs on Bax and threw his ass in the joint for five years when his luck had finally run out, and I did it without guilt or regret. The idea of a fellow cop, a fellow officer of the law, being the one behind all the destruction and the bodies piling up in the morgue had fury boiling so hot in my blood I was surprised it wasn't burning through my skin. You didn't sign up to serve and protect only to decide that oath was just too hard to keep.

There was a security code on the phone that I couldn't figure out, so I called one of the tech guys up and asked him if he could look at it. I was known as kind of a hard-ass around the station, but I also got the job done, so generally when I called in a favor it got bumped to the front of the line. It only took twenty minutes for the tech guy to show up and another five for him to get me into the phone. By the time he left to go back to his own part of the station, I had already been through ten messages that had my teeth clenching so hard I was lucky they didn't crack.

It was all there. Words upon words that told a tale of revenge and destruction. There were messages back and forth between Roark and someone that had a standing date with one of Nassir's working girls arranging the setup so that the Irishman could get to Roxie, one of the Point's most well-known hookers and a personal friend of Bax's from back in the day.

There were exchanges with someone simply called Zero setting up the entry of explosives through customs. The explosives that had to have been used to annihilate Nassir's club. The fire was intended to punish not only Nassir and Race but also the people that flocked to the heart of the Point in search of bad things. The rage the dirty fed had toward the city was unreal and I couldn't figure out what was behind it. It wasn't like he lived here or had been a victim of the streets like the rest of us that called the Point home had been. His fury and the vengeance it wreaked felt so displaced. I knew there had to be more to it but the phone wasn't giving me that much.

There was another flurry of back-and-forth messages chronicling the plan to grab one of the kids that owed Race money on a football bet and dumping his body as a message to the new criminal elite. More bodies had followed and so had money into the hands of desperate men so they would do ugly things to make sure that everyone knew the Point was never going to be safe, no matter who was in charge. That it was never going to be anything but a forgotten place filled with forgotten people that no one would miss when it was gone.

There was even a picture of Race's classic Mustang as it burned to nothing but a twisted scrap heap of melted metal and rubber.

The guy was vengeful and liked to witness the effects of his handiwork up close and personal. Unfortunately he knew how the good guys worked, so while there was plenty of evidence that he had been present for all these dirty deeds on his end, there was nothing on ours that showed him. Roark knew how to avoid cameras, knew how to blend into the background, and knew enough to keep from getting caught while he pulled strings in the background like a demented puppet master.

I flipped through the hundreds of messages that he had exchanged with Reeve over the last few months. There was nothing unusual in the exchanges. They were flirty and fun. She seemed to really like the dirty fed. She told him she missed him when he had to go back into the city during the week. She thanked him profusely for not judging her by her past actions. She told him that he made her feel special and safe.

He responded with flip answers and easy reassurances. He told her she was beautiful, that she was gorgeous, that she was a prize. While Reeve spoke to him like a woman in the first stages of falling in love, Roark replied like a man with a trophy he was eager to show off and flaunt. His title and his badge had done a lot to win her over, her looks had done everything to convince him to break protocol and take her to bed. I understood the temptation.

It was the newer messages, the ones leading up to the fire at the club, that were the most interesting. Reeve had grown up in the Point and had lost a sister to the vicious and unforgiving ways of the streets. She was not only street-smart but also had keen instincts for danger. She started texting him about where he was going on the weekends and why he wouldn't talk to her about what he was up to. She asked why he was in the Point for reasons that had nothing to do with work. She asked him why his phone was going off at weird times during the night. It wasn't uncommon for a cop but she seemed to know something wasn't tracking. She asked him who Zero was and why had he shown up at her place in the secure location looking for him. It was clear she knew something was off and that Roark wasn't who he claimed to be.

He tried to put her off. He texted that he was in the middle of a top-secret case, that it was high profile, and he smoothly apologized for all the secrecy and double talk. He promised to take her somewhere tropical and warm as soon as the trial for the rest of Novak's crew was over, and when none of that seemed to pacify her he broke out the big guns and told her that he loved her. That shut her down for exactly one day. She told him she loved him back and then went silent.

After the declaration there were no more messages between the two of them but there were several between Zero and Roark. He had his goons watching Brysen and Dovie. He also had eyes on Spanky's, the strip club that was now the de facto operating headquarters for Nassir since the Pit was gone. Spanky's was also where a stripper named Honor danced, and if anyone cared to watch closely enough, they would see that if Nassir had any kind of weakness, it was her. The texts indicated that whatever was driving Roark was amping up to bring the fight right to the heart of those willing to stand sentinel between him and his revenge, and all that could mean was that things were going to get uglier and bloodier before I could put a stop to it.

The texts stopped because it was apparent that the next time Roark saw Reeve she snagged his phone and headed back to the city in order to hand it over to me. She saw his profession of love for what it was, a smoke screen, and had done what she had done since the first time I had met her. She was covering her own ass and I bet Roark was smart enough to know that his cover as a good guy, as a member of law enforcement, was blown as soon as the phone came up missing. I would wager my left nut that the fed had gone into hiding and that I wasn't the only one that would be looking for him. I made a mental note to put a call in to the marshals to see just how much they knew about their dirty agent.

"Well, fuck." I tossed the phone on the desk, curled my hands into fists, and shoved them into my eye sockets. I could feel a headache start to coil around the base of my neck and throb behind the back of my eyes. It felt like a sledgehammer pounding away inside my skull.

I pushed out of my ancient chair and it groaned with relief. The door to my office rattled in the jamb as I slammed it shut behind me and several of my fellow officers stopped to give me questioning looks as I stalked toward the front doors of the station.

Fresh air wasn't something anyone was ever going to find in the Point, but I needed to be outside, needed the freedom to pace back and forth without feeling like a caged beast. I pulled my already loosened tie the rest of the way off my neck and pulled my own phone out of my back pocket. I was about to make a call that I never in a million years thought I was going to make.

It rang and rang on the other end. At first I thought she wasn't going to answer and then I thought that if she didn't I was going to get in my boring-as-hell police-issue sedan and drive every single road of the city until I found where she was holed up. When you looked like her there was nowhere that you could hide.

Finally, when I was at the end of my patience and was just getting ready to hang up and probably throw the phone across the parking lot, her smoky voice came tauntingly across the line.

"Well, that was fast, Detective."

I bent my head down so that I was looking at the scuffed toes of my boots and wondered like I had a million times before why I just didn't walk away from this life. I had the credentials. I had the skill level. I could be a cop in any city, anywhere in America—hell, I could probably go a step further and join the feds if I wanted to. What kept me here was undefinable and impossible to fight. When I was younger I'd tried my hand at a better life, at living on the other side of things up on the Hill. All that had taught me was that bad people and bad things were everywhere. The zip code didn't really matter. I had innocent people to protect here and I was going to do that until I drew my last breath.

"You're right. I do need you, Reeve." And God help us all.

She gave a chuckle that had no humor in it. "You have no idea how long I've wanted you to say those words to me, Titus King."

I had no clue what she was talking about, but I had a bad feeling about what getting into bed with her meant for me . . . a professional bed or otherwise. In either case this girl was trouble.

Chapter 3

Reeve

I TOSSED AND TURNED all night long and it had nothing to do with the fact that Conner had to know I was gone by now and that he must know I was the one that had his phone. I had only had a few seconds left alone with the device before it locked, so I wasn't sure how far down the slippery slope Conner had tumbled, but the few messages I did glimpse laid out clear as day that the man I thought was my savior was actually a murderer and no better than me. When Titus had called and growled that he needed me, his words not only had my panties spontaneously combusting and my heart tripping stupidly, but his words also told me that he had found more than enough on that phone to bury Conner. He wouldn't have bothered with me otherwise.

Titus didn't like me. How could he when he was intimately familiar with all the terrible things I had done in my past? I would never forget the way his pretty blue eyes lightened as I told him my sordid tale when I turned myself in after Dovie was abducted. Most men's eyes darkened, got cloudy and hazy with emotion when they were angry or upset. Not Titus. No, those sharp, intensely blue eyes of his got so light they almost looked silver as I poured it all out. I told him about my baby sister, about how the wrong guy had ruined her. I told him about how the drugs had taken hold of her and how they had led her to prostitution. I told him how it was never enough, so Rissa's boyfriend started to hurt her. I told him how it killed me because she shut me out, closed the door on me every time I reached out to her. I wanted to save her and I was desperate. As my story went on, his eyes appeared lighter and lighter and the frown on his face harsher and harsher.

I told him about the pregnancy and how Rissa's boyfriend had freaked out when she told him. He was so upset that she wouldn't be able to work anymore, that she wouldn't be able to have sex with strangers to pay the bills. I broke down then, starting to sob when I told Titus about the cops showing up at my parents' door in the middle of the night to tell us they had found my baby sister's body naked in a back alley deep in the heart of the Point. I couldn't breathe around the pain in my chest, and I remembered him getting up and coming around the desk so that he could roughly pat me on the back. He wasn't a man prone to gentleness but he tried . . . for me . . . and all that did was make me break into even smaller pieces when I told him the rest.

I explained that I couldn't feel anymore. That I was numb. I whispered that when they put my little sister in the ground they might as well have buried me right alongside her because nothing mattered to me anymore. All I could think about, all I could focus on, was getting back at Rissa's murderous boyfriend. I was consumed by it, obsessed with it. Nothing else mattered to me. Vengeance was what nourished me. Revenge was what woke me up every single day, and eventually I couldn't just think about it anymore. I had to act.

He stopped touching me then. He moved across from me and leaned against his desk, much like he had done yesterday while he watched me. By that time his eyes were glittering like diamonds in his craggy face and the metallic sheen in them felt like it could cut through my thin skin with no resistance.

The next set of words trembled off my lips because I knew I was admitting to a crime that could land me in jail at best and on death row at worst. I told him how it didn't take very long to find someone to point me in Novak's direction. Of course, the way I looked meant his goons were more than eager to bring me to the now deceased crime boss's door. All men liked having a pretty girl owe them a favor and what I was asking meant Novak could own me body and soul for the rest of my life.

I didn't care. Whatever price he asked I was willing to pay. If he wanted me to pay back the debt on my back, I would have. If he wanted me to grind on a pole at Spanky's, I would have learned to dance. If he wanted me to mule his guns and his drugs, I would have taken any and all of those risks just as long as he guaranteed that Rissa's murderer got exactly what he had coming to him. I wanted it to be violent. I wanted it to be bloody. I wanted him to suffer in every single way my sister had suffered, and Novak had given me a smile and promised me the bitter satisfaction I so desperately craved.

It had only taken a couple of weeks and then the cops were back at my parents' door asking if we knew anything about the death of Rissa's boyfriend. My mom and dad were baffled, and all I could do was sit there frozen in shock. It was supposed to make me feel better. It was supposed to make me feel gratification when he was gone. It didn't. I was still angry. I was still hollow and missing my sister, and now all those gaping wounds were filling up with guilt and disbelief that I was responsible for another human being's untimely demise.

Titus growled at me like an animal, and when I braved a look up at him, disgust was stamped all across his handsome face as he got up and put as much space between the two of us as he could. I felt the shame that I made him look like that, felt it all the way to my bones. He inclined his head so that I would keep talking and it took everything inside of me to keep going. I had never claimed to be a good person or woman without faults, but the way Titus was looking at me made me feel like I belonged in a filthy back-alley grave right next to where my sister's final resting place had been.

I explained that Novak hadn't approached me for anything for a long, long time. So long that I thought maybe he had forgotten about me and the favor I had asked. I moved out of my parents' house because I knew I was corrupt, knew I had crossed a line there was no going back from, and went to work in a salon just outside of the District. Strippers paid a lot of money to make sure their hair looked good, and they were awesome tippers since their living was based on the generosity of overly amorous strangers. It was a nice gig and I spent a lot of time convincing myself my actions had been justified, that I had done what any loving, protective sister would do. I wore a mask of normalcy and I kept it on so tightly I almost convinced myself that everything that had happened had been a dream. Then one afternoon Novak's right-hand man showed up and the mask was ripped away, leaving the vicious, hateful girl I really was exposed to the world once again.

Novak was calling in his favor. I was going to volunteer at a group home for kids and befriend a quiet redhead named Dovie

Pryce. I was supposed to learn about her, keep tabs on her, and when the time came, if they needed me to, I was supposed to bring her to Novak with no questions asked.

I thought I could do it. I mean how hard could befriending one shy girl be? Really hard when that girl grew up on the streets and had the same kind of instincts about people as I did. Dovie never let me all the way in, and when Bax entered the picture and I tried to warn her about him, about how bad things were going to get if she didn't walk away, she shut me out completely. Then came the call I was dreading. Novak wanted her and he didn't care how he got her. I debated telling Dovie and just forcing her to leave town. I thought about running myself but knew Novak would just come after us both. At the end of the day I took the coward's way out and called Benny, Novak's right hand, and let him know Dovie was on her own, taking a bus back to some garage where she had been staying. I knew Novak's guys would grab her; what I didn't know was that they were going to use her to hurt Bax, or that they were going to raid the garage and beat her brother half to death and put the garage owner in the ground.

I sweated over my choices until I couldn't handle it anymore and then I went to find Dovie. I had to tell her why I had done what I did. I knew she couldn't forgive me—ever—but I needed her to know my reasons were more complicated than they seemed. I told her I was going to turn myself in and she warned me not to go to Titus. Of course, that meant he was the one I had to seek out. I was ready for the full punishment, and if that included pouring my heart out to Bax's brother for him to do what he wanted with me, then so be it. I deserved whatever the law deemed appropriate, and when I was done speaking with Titus,

I could see he agreed. To him I was nothing more than another criminal doing what criminals did in the Point.

I was prepared to serve hard time, prepared to watch my life drift by while I stared out through iron bars, but then Titus did some something that shocked us both. He called the district attorney, who promptly turned me over to the state's attorney general. He begrudgingly explained what kind of info I had on Novak's operation to the higher-ups, and the next thing I knew I was in a fancy office getting offered a deal if I agreed to testify in the case against the remaining members of Novak's gang in the federal case. They offered me Witness Protection, offered me a way out, and I couldn't jump on it fast enough. Titus might hate me and it was obvious what I had done repulsed him, but regardless, he saved me, and I pretty much knew I was going to love him forever for that. I hadn't seen much good in my life and yet there was a whole big heap of it wrapped up in a towering package of dark masculinity and brooding gorgeousness that couldn't even look me in the eye anymore.

And now he needed me. Which meant he was going to have to look at me, and maybe, just maybe he could see past all the things I had done and all ways that he couldn't tolerate me. It was wishful thinking on my part, but after being so close to him yesterday in the office, after breathing him in and watching those sky-blue eyes heat up and cool off with everything he was feeling, I couldn't stop the longing from crawling all over me. It was so heavy and thick it had kept me up all night. How I had convinced myself Conner was an acceptable substitute for the force of nature that was Titus King was beyond me. One man was a legitimate wonder of this world; the other was a cheap plastic trinket that fell apart as soon as you got it home.

So there I was in the dingy bathroom of the horrible motel room looking at myself in a mirror that was so cracked and so foggy with age that I could hardly see my own face, worrying about how I was going to look when Titus showed up at my door any minute. I knew it didn't matter. He would never see me the same way I saw him even if there was an undeniable pull between the two of us. However, my vanity and my own need to be my best around him still had me fiddling with my hair and trying to fix my face with the meager supplies I had stashed in my purse. When I snatched Conner's phone I hadn't really planned too far ahead. All I had on me were the clothes on my back and what was in my purse, which wasn't much, but it would have to do. I heard the cardboard-thin door rattle as a heavy fist thudded against it, and took a deep breath to steady myself.

I refused to be barefoot on this disgusting flooring, so my slouchy boots made a harsh shuffling sound across the ratty carpet as I made my way to the door. It matched the offbeat stutter of my heart at the thought of being close to Titus again. I peeked out the little hole in the door and pulled back at the ferocity of the scowl that was already on his face. He hadn't even seen me yet and he already looked like he wanted to strangle someone.

I barely had the chain off the door and cracked open before he was barreling that big body through the space. I wasn't the only one who looked like they hadn't changed clothes since our last encounter. He still had on his wrinkled slacks and wilted button-up shirt from the day before and the bags under his eyes made him look far older than his twenty-eight years. He was only a few years older than me, but right now those years looked like decades. He was missing the tie and his dark hair was messy like he had been running his hands through it.

"We found two dead junkies and busted a drug trafficker at this motel not even two weeks ago. This is the best place you could find to hide out?"

As soon as he was in the room I shut the door behind him and fell back against it. He was prowling back and forth in front of me like an angry animal, and all I wanted to do was reach out a hand and try and soothe him. He was coiled so tightly I could see the ropes of tension in all the hard lines of his muscular build and stamped across his face.

I shrugged lightly when that electric-blue gaze finally landed on me. "Conner isn't stupid. He's going to be right on my tail, so I couldn't risk going home. My folks have had a hard enough time with things in the last few years. They don't need to be in the middle of all this."

"Isn't he going to look for you there first?" He moved like he was going to sit on the edge of the bed and then made a face when he caught sight of just how gross the mustard-yellow comforter was upon closer inspection. Instead he crossed his arms over his broad chest and faced off against where I was leaning.

"I don't think so. We weren't close after Rissa died. I was suffering so much and I guess I felt like they weren't suffering enough. I haven't really spoken to them in years."

Titus grunted at me and wrinkled his nose as the people in the room next door decided to start a bout of noisy morning sex that shook the entire wall behind the bed.

"You don't have friends, any other relatives, no one that can give you a place to hide out while we figure out to handle Roark? The state attorney general is going to think you skipped out on WITSEC. You're going to be a fugitive until we catch him and put this all to rights and until I can hand over the proof that he's dirty to the right people."

I let my head fall back until it thunked against the door. "Tell the feds I'll still testify; I just don't want to be in protective custody anymore. They did that for Bax and Race. Besides him being dirty, he slept with me and broke protocol. Why do I have to prove I'm on the up-and-up?" I could see the answer in his eyes. They would believe the best of Conner because he had a respectable job even if he had used it to break the law, and I was just some girl that kept making bad choices.

"Bax and Race weren't involved in a murder-for-hire plot with Novak and his goons."

I cringed involuntarily. "No, but they were involved in his other criminal enterprises. I'm still going to hold up my end of the deal, I'm just going to do it here."

"That's not safe. I saw the texts on his phone. Roark isn't done with his rampage and he's unhinged. He furious about something and it's driving him to do what he's doing. He wants the Point to fall and he's going after everyone involved in holding it up after Novak went down. I'm sure he realizes you're the one that turned him in and took the evidence needed to nail him. Things are going to be really bad for you."

I laughed drily and lifted an eyebrow at him. I wished I had the nerve to walk up to him and wrap him up in a hug. I think we both really could have used one. "Things are always really bad for me. I had a few minutes of peace when I was pretending to be someone else and her skin never quite fit right. This is what my life looks like, Detective."

His eyebrows pulled together and there was a noticeable

tick in his jaw. "You do understand Conner will more than likely murder you when he gets his hands on you for double-crossing him? He burned down Nassir's fight club on a night it was full of people. We pulled ten bodies out of the debris. Most of them were younger than you."

I didn't need a lecture about how cruel and coldblooded Conner was. I knew. The bastard had tossed the word *love* at me like I was an idiot. Like I was some simple girl that hadn't grown up on the streets knowing what a chore it would be to love someone like me. A good man, a man with a purpose and a cause, would never throw the L-word so carelessly at a woman with a past like mine. Right then and there I knew he was up to something I wanted no part of. He thought he could tell me he loved me and I would be malleable and sweet. Instead I lied right back to him and set about really fucking up his plans. Served him right for underestimating me.

"I know what Conner is going to want to do to me if he gets his hands on me, so that's why I came to you."

I looked at him from under my long eyelashes and saw his mouth tighten when our eyes locked.

"You are going to keep me alive long enough to testify, Detective King." He was going to keep me alive long enough that I could take Conner out before he took me, only Titus didn't need to know that part of the plan.

"What makes you so sure of that, Reeve?"

I sighed heavily and pushed off the door. I walked over to him so that I had to tilt my head back and he had to look down slightly so that we could continue to meet each other's gaze. He really was a brute of a man but it worked for him . . . and for me.

"Conner is going to know I'm the one who sold him out. I'm

the reason he can't operate out in the open anymore pretending to be good. He's going to want me to suffer for that, but he's not stupid and he knows all your fancy policeman tricks. This isn't some uneducated thug dealing dime bags on the corner. He's you, Titus, just the evil version." I crossed my arms over my chest to mirror his pose and a small thrill raced through me when he couldn't hide the way his gaze dipped to watch how my shirt pulled across my chest. He might not like me, but there was an attraction there he couldn't always control. There was an inner part of him that pushed against his rough façade when we were within touching distance. That was the part I wanted to snuggle up with and curl around.

"You want Conner; then you're going to need me to dr him out. He's going to come for me regardless of what or wh has to get through to get to me, so you need to put me out and then grab him when he comes for me."

He was silent for a long, tense moment and I saw his apple dip as he swallowed hard.

"Are you asking me to use you as bait? You wan throw you out there in an ocean of sharks when t already full of blood?"

I lifted my hands and pushed some of my hai and let my head fall so that I was looking at th between our feet. The toes of both of our bod touching and everything inside of me longed tiny step closer so that we would be in each o

"If I don't testify against the rest of No deal with the state goes away, and I'm loo rest of my life in jail. I've done some rea can't let Conner pull apart what's left of t

need you to keep me alive long enough to do what I promised to do, and you're going to have to use to me draw Conner out. It's the only way. If he went into hiding you're going to have to give him a viable reason to show himself. He's going to know that not only are you looking for him but so are the feds."

Titus fell back a step and then started pacing again. I could have sworn the white spot in his hair spread a little wider after my declaration. Since I had spent the night in the filthy bed, I was less squeamish than he had been about sitting on it. I flopped down and watched him as he prowled back and forth in front of me.

"Oh, he has a reason for what he's doing, I just don't know what it is yet." His eyes cut to me sharply. "What about going back into WITSEC under the supervision of another marshal?"

I shook my head and leaned back on my hands so that I was staring at the ceiling. There was an unidentifiable stain I hadn't noticed the day before. Ugh. I needed to get out of this place before I caught something.

"No. If I go back into hiding then you'll lose any chance you ave of getting Conner to show himself, plus I already told you at clean and shiny skin doesn't fit me right. I want to be here. I ed to be here." He would never understand that I felt like I not ly owed it to Dovie after the way I hurt her, but I also owed it he city. The Point sucked and there were no redeeming quali- about it, but I felt that way about myself as well and I still ted someone to save me, someone to love me. The city and e so similar I almost felt like I had to save it in order to save lf. If I lived that long. Titus didn't look like he was ready to on board with my plan anytime soon. In fact he looked like about to pass out cold on his feet.

"Did you sleep at all last night?" The question was more personal than I should get with him but the words just slipped out.

He stopped pacing and his head dropped forward like it weighed a million pounds. He lifted a hand to rub the back of his neck and his chest rose and fell in a huge sigh that sounded like it had the entire fate of the world inside of it.

"No. I was trying to figure out what to do with this Roark noise. I was making sure my dumbass brother didn't do something now that he knows you're back in town. I got home and was there for about twenty minutes when I got a callout about a dead hooker in the District. It took me two hours to track down an ID on her. When I went to notify her family I found out not only was she married but also had two little kids at home. She was tricking out because her old man likes to gamble and couldn't hold down a job. That kind of shit is my everyday, so no, I don't sleep much, even when I get the chance."

It made my heart squeeze. Not because the story was heartbreaking or anything unusual in this place, but because he cared so much. He carried those other people's choices and failures around as his own, and in a place like this the weight of that had to be enormous. He was Atlas. He really was trying to carry the world and all its messed-up ways on his back.

Those crystalline eyes cut over to me and then skated over the bed I was lounging on.

"How about you? This place needs a hazmat team to clean it up. Did you sleep?"

"No. I grabbed the phone and bolted. I didn't even grab a change of clothes and I don't even have my real ID. To the rest of the world I'm still Jill Parker. Reeve Black doesn't exist."

"Jesus. This just gets better and better."

"Ohhhh . . . I don't think we've even begun to see the worst of it yet."

He groaned out a swearword and curled his hands into tight fists at his sides. The tick was back in his jaw but there was something working in his eyes. The color was doing that thing where it started to fade into something lighter and brighter. He was molten hot from the inside out. Man, would I sell the fragmented parts that were left of my soul to burn with him.

"How far are you willing to go with all of this, Reeve? What's the limit?"

I didn't understand what he was asking me, so I sat up straighter and leaned forward intently. "There is no limit. What are my options here, Titus? I die or I go to jail, and neither one of those is very appealing. I know I don't deserve a second chance, but I'm stubborn enough and selfish enough to want to take one for myself anyway."

"You know Conner is going to come for you, but have you even considered the other threats? My brother is just as dangerous and just as unpredictable as Roark and you had a direct hand in getting the only girl he has ever cared about abducted and sliced up. And I bet you never even thought about Nassir. That guy is a blackhearted monster. He's mad as hell that his club burned down and that Roark got his hands on one of his girls and worked her over. He's the type that would use you just like you're saying, to draw out his prey, only he wouldn't care if you made it out of the carnage alive or not. You have more than one enemy here."

His words were chilling in their frankness and they brought

goose bumps to the surface of my skin. "I know." It came out sounding shaky and I hated revealing that weakness in front of him.

He moved closer to me so that our knees were touching. He reached out a hand and put a finger under my chin and lifted my head up so that we were once again locked in an unwavering gaze. His eyes were so light now there was almost no color in them at all. It made him look fierce and wild.

"I am the only person on your side and I am there reluctantly."

"Ouch."

I went to lower my lashes so I didn't have to see how he really felt about me shining out of that reflective gaze.

"But as much as it pains me to say it, we can help each other out. In fact I think the only way to do this with minimal casualties is to work together. I want Roark and you want to keep your ass covered, and to do that, we need to be attached at the hip."

I frowned at him as he continued to loom over me. "What are you suggesting, Detective?"

"I'm not suggesting it. I'm telling you that you are suddenly and irrevocably in love with me. You are obsessed with me and we are about to embark on a passionate, out-of-control, unexplainable, and very, very obvious romance. We are going to shove our new relationship so far down everyone's throat that they are going to choke on it."

I gulped and opened my mouth to tell him how crazy he sounded, but he reached out a hand and placed his palm lightly over my mouth. I scowled at him and contemplated sinking my teeth into the meaty part of his hand.

"Seriously, Reeve, it's the only way. Bax will rein it in if he thinks I've got a thing for you. Nassir won't back all the way off, but he'll be less dangerous if he thinks he has to go through me to get to you. Plus, from what you've told me, and what I understand about whack jobs like Roark, if he thinks you replaced him with me, it'll force him to move more quickly. He'll come out of hiding faster if he thinks you moved on without a second thought. If you understand the risks involved, I'm willing to take them with you."

I lifted both my eyebrows up and tapped my fingers on my knee until he took a step back as he gauged my reaction. I don't know what he was expecting but he actually looked nervous as I climbed to my feet.

"What do you think?" His voice was low and he didn't look away as I walked up so that I was standing directly in front of him.

What did I think? I thought there was no "suddenly" about being irrevocably in something that looked a lot like love with him. I thought passionate, out of control, and obsessive about summed up the way I already felt about him and that it would require zero acting on my part. I reached out and put a hand on the center of his chest. He was warm and hard. He felt like security and strength.

"I think you are going to have a much harder time pretending you like me than I will pretending I like you, Detective. Have you considered that?"

He balked a little and lifted a hand to circle his fingers around my wrist. I wondered if he felt my pulse kick at the touch.

"I do whatever it takes to get the job done."

Oh, I bet he did. I smirked up at him and lifted up on tippy toes so that our lips were almost touching. I expected him to recoil, to back away in haste, but he didn't. Instead his tongue darted out to lick across the curve of his bottom lip, and I almost groaned out loud.

"Prove it." I whispered the challenge and then held my breath to see what this scary, sexy man would do once the gauntlet was thrown down.

He didn't disappoint. He never did.

Chapter 4

Titus

PROVE IT.

Those odd, dark blue eyes flashed the challenge at me and I couldn't resist it. Not the challenge or the girl. I didn't like that she got under my skin. I hated that she was right at the center of this mess with Roark, and it really, really grated across my already taut nerves that even with no makeup on and looking like she hadn't slept a wink, she was still the most gorgeous woman I had ever seen. I didn't want to notice that. I didn't want my dick to twitch when she touched me, but it did, which was going to make pretending to be infatuated with her easy and so much harder at the same time. She knew it too.

Prove it.

Okay. I would prove the shit out of the fact that I could do what I had to do in order to make this scheme of mine work. I could pretend to like her, which really was the only thing that would be fake. I couldn't reconcile the way my pulse leaped every time she turned that midnight-blue gaze on me with the fact that she had orchestrated a man's murder. She was beautiful but she was also deadly. She was just as hard as this place we came from, and I'd had enough of the city hammering against my foundation, as it was. Lusting after a woman who had it in her to be just as cold, and just as calculating, as any other criminal I locked up on a day-to-day basis was nowhere for my head to be while I was on the brink of war with her deranged ex-lover.

I was pissed off when I bent my head toward her. I was mad at myself. I was mad at her. More than all of that, though, I was furious that either one of us had to be in this situation in the first place. Every time I turned around, another bad thing or bad person was nipping at my heels. It was getting harder and harder to stay a step ahead. Eventually I was going to trip up and go down and there would be no one left with any kind of conscience in this place, no one left that cared about justice and righteousness.

That anger had my hands shaking as I reached up and used my thumbs to tilt her head back so her mouth was pointed up at me. I didn't have much time to date, didn't have the patience for a woman who didn't understand that I was trying to save an entire city from itself and that my job took up most of my attention and energy. The women I did date were never the right height, or the perfect size, and they sure as hell never looked as luscious and as tempting as this woman did. No one had ever fit me the way she did and that pissed me off even more.

Everything about her was a test of my will. The way her dark eyes flashed when I lowered my head toward her parted lips. The way her hand trailed up my chest to curl around my neck as I got closer and closer. The way she breathed out a soft little sigh that tickled my mouth when I finally touched my lips to hers. It was supposed to prove a point. It was supposed to be an act of defiance, and maybe it was for a split second, but then it was nothing but a kiss and I forgot who she was and what it was supposed to be about. After that half a heartbeat I just wanted to kiss her and keep on kissing her until both of us were naked, and I was balls-deep inside of that perfect, traitorous body of hers.

Her mouth was soft, which was a lie because she was not a soft woman. She tasted sweet, which was also a lie. She might look like a dream and taste like dessert, but I knew there was a lot of tart underneath that pretty outer shell. Her tongue darted out and the very tip of it touched the center of my bottom lip, and before I could consider what I was doing, I was kissing her like I kissed a woman I wanted, not like a woman I was trying to resist.

I had my hands tangled up in her long hair and was using that leverage to back her against the flimsy door in the hotel room. She hit it with a little gasp of surprise and I took full advantage of the way her lips parted to dive right inside. I wanted to devour her. I wanted to eat her up. I wanted to stay in this moment where all I could feel was her heart thudding against mine and her nipples hard and tight against my chest. The way her mouth moved on mine made it so that there was no world that was falling apart around me. There was no city on the brink of ruin that I felt responsible for, there was just this woman whimpering as I forced her legs apart with my knee and stroked her questing tongue with my own.

I felt the bite of her fingernails cut into the skin at the base of my neck. I felt her hips arch up to meet mine when the fullness between my legs lined up perfectly with the softness between hers. It was almost scary how well we meshed together. I wasn't a small guy and often felt like I had to rein myself in when it came to the opposite sex. I didn't want to intimidate or come across as threatening, but with Reeve I didn't have to worry about it. She took everything I was throwing at her and returned it in a way that had me letting the leash I kept on all of my frustration and aggression slip a little. Things deep down inside of me roared and awoke from where they typically slumbered. She didn't even seem fazed that I still had my gun clipped to my belt, where it felt like it permanently lived. She kept her hands up around my shoulders and let me ravish her like she was my last meal and I was a dead man walking. I had never felt starved for anything in my life until my lips touched hers.

I let my teeth bite into the plush curve of her bottom lip and my hands got really rough in her hair as I jerked her head back farther and dove deeper into the hot and welcoming pull of her mouth. My dick was yelling at me to do something, do anything, and my pulse was thundering in my ears so loud I almost missed the way my cell phone was ringing from where it was shoved in my pocket.

I let go of her and stumbled back like she was on fire. We were both breathing hard and both flushed. Her eyes were almost black and I was sure my own were burning white hot with everything inside of me churning. I don't think I had ever felt so good and so bad at the exact same time.

I yanked the phone out of my pocket and put it to my ear with a barked, "What?"

I felt like I couldn't breathe and she just stayed slumped against the door watching me with big eyes. I almost lost it when she darted her tongue out to dab at the moisture and tiny drop of blood I had left on her mouth after my less than gentle kiss. I hadn't meant to hurt her, to cause her pain like that, but her long lashes dipped down a little when she saw I was watching her and it kicked in that she liked it. She liked the edge. She liked the violence. Of course she would.

"I know you just went off shift but I got a DB out on the docks that you might want to look at." I couldn't place which fellow detective the voice belonged to but it was obviously someone that knew that when someone went down for good in the Point, I was the first call that generally went out.

DB was short for "dead body" and I absolutely did not want to go look at it. I had seen plenty of them in the last few days. I shoved my hands through my hair and glowered at Reeve as she finally pushed off the door and wandered back over to sit on the bed. I cringed. It really was too disgusting to touch.

"What makes you think I want to see it?"

"Because she's just a kid. No more than eighteen or nineteen."

I swore and started to pace back and forth. "Yeah, that's shitty but not uncommon."

"Yeah, well, the reason I called you is because she looks a whole hell of a lot like the bombshell that waltzed into your office yesterday. Long black hair, blue eyes. At first glance it could be her but she's younger and worked over in a really personal way."

"Fuck."

"Yeah. Get down here, King, and see what this sick bastard did to this poor girl, and while you're at it find the one that's still breathing and tell her to watch her back."

I hung up the phone and squeezed it so hard in my hand I was surprised it didn't break in half. I looked at Reeve, who was watching me solemnly.

"Grab whatever you brought with you. We're leaving." I didn't ask her.

She blinked at me slowly and her dark eyebrows pulled together. "I already told you I left in a hurry, and that I don't have anyplace to go."

"I have a place that will do for now. A body just showed up on the docks and apparently she bears an uncanny resemblance to you. That means Roark already knows you're here and I think he's letting us know he's pissed about it. Some poor girl got murdered just because she had the same hair and eye color as you, Reeve. Doesn't that tell you how dangerous this is for you? This guy is a sociopath." And I had zero time to figure out what had triggered him, what had started his rampage and how to stop him.

She climbed to her feet and I saw the way her eyes shifted when I mentioned the dead girl. She was capable of regret and remorse. That was good to know and it made me feel a little less like shit for wanting to push her back up against the wall and continue where we had just left off.

"Where exactly do you want me to go, Detective?"

"When Bax got locked up he was staying at this crappy little studio just outside of the District. I didn't know he bought a house before he got arrested. When he got out of jail and hooked up with Dovie, he left the place in the city and took her out to the burbs. Well, I paid the rent on the studio in advance for a few years so that he would have someplace guaranteed to go back to when he got out. It's been empty for a while and it's only about half a step up from this place, but it'll do until I can figure out something more secure." I cut her a hard look. "Besides, everyone knows how Bax feels about you, so no one would ever think you would be anywhere near his place."

She couldn't afford to forget that there were enemies around every corner and all of them would be happy if she suddenly stopped breathing.

"Titus . . ." Her voice was quiet and her eyes bored into mine when our gazes locked. "I came back to help you out. I don't want to be the reason you and Shane end up back at odds. I know how hard it was for you to almost lose him. That's not what any of this is about for me."

Her eyes drifted up to the white spot in my hair that was a constant reminder of how far my little brother was willing to take things. Unlike me, Bax didn't have a cage he kept his wild side locked away in. He did what he wanted, when he wanted, and that made him unbelievably dangerous. That's why she needed me. Bax and I might not always be on the same page and there was still an ungodly amount of tension between us and how we viewed the right and wrong of things, but he respected me enough, cared about me enough that if I could sell the act that this woman mattered to me on some deeper level, he would back off. He wouldn't like it. In fact he would absolutely hate it, but he would still do it.

"Bax is my problem. He always has been and you probably don't want to call him Shane to his face."

She lifted a shoulder and let it fall. "I watched Dovie fall in love with Shane, not Bax. He seems less scary as Shane."

I grunted because Shane and Bax were two parts that made up the entire man. Both were equally scary and equally danger-ous but she didn't need to know that, so I motioned to the dingy room and ordered, "Grab your stuff."

She gave me a lopsided smile. "I don't have any stuff."

She had said that but I hadn't really believed her. What kind of woman could run with literally just the clothes on her back? One that was built to survive no matter what. I answered my own question.

I sighed and walked over to the door. "All right, let's get out of here. I need to get down to the docks."

She nodded a little and went to move past me as I jerked the paper-thin door open. I stiffened automatically when she paused in front of me and titled her head back so that she could look me in the eyes.

"For what it's worth, you are very convincing at pretending to like me, Titus. For a second there before your phone went off, I almost believed you."

She slipped past me out the door, leaving her words lying like bricks at my feet.

IT TOOK A LITTLE bit to get her to the apartment and get her inside with the orders to lay low until she heard from me. Bax's old studio would work for now but I needed to find someplace I could take her that was safe and still visible enough that Roark would know where she was at—where we were at, pretending to be infatuated with each other. My plan sort of fell apart after that, though. I knew I needed to get Roark to show himself, but after he did, I wasn't one hundred percent sure how that would play out. I wanted to be confident enough in myself that I could simply arrest him and take him in without any bloodshed on either side, but the guy was violent and he was pissed, so I doubted that would be the case. Once I had Reeve somewhere safe and secure and the charade began, I would hammer out the rest of the details. The devil always hid in those little fuckers.

The ride to the District was silent and tense. The look on her face when she took in the battered condition of Bax's old bachelor pad was priceless. I assured her Dovie had scrubbed the place down since they stayed there occasionally when Bax worked late at the garage he owned. I promised she was far less likely to get an STD from the bathroom here than she was from the no-tell motel.

She didn't reply and I didn't bother to tell her good-bye, but I did tell her to keep her head down and try not to attract attention. The only way a girl that looked like her could do that was by not going outside, and by ordering pizza and Chinese food. It was a crappy plan but it would have to do. She gave me a hard look, which reminded me that she had taken off with hardly any money and no real identification. With a sigh I had handed over a few twenties that I could see she wanted to refuse. Reeve didn't want to rely on me any more than I wanted to be the only one in a position to help her out.

By the time I got to the docks, I was turned inside out. I was running on fumes and no amount of coffee or fury could fuel me enough to get through the fact that some innocent girl who lost her life for zero reason. The scene was chaotic. There were a lot of cops crawling all over the place and the medical examiner's office was hovering over the body. Well, they were surveying what was left of the body. The poor girl had been through hell and Roark had made her suffering obvious. There was no mistaking that this was a message.

He wasn't just mad at Reeve for turning on him. She was now the enemy and she would be treated as such if he got his hands on her. This guy didn't care who his victim was. Man, woman, or child, his brutality was growing more and more apparent and targeted. This guy took making his point to another level. He was all about the impact and carnage and it seemed like the targets he chose to leave as calling cards were getting younger and younger

The woman had been sliced across her chest much in the way Dovie had been cut the night she was abducted. Only Dovie had survived and had the scars to prove how hard she fought to live. This girl just had the wounds. She also had burns across every surface of exposed skin, a bullet hole in her forehead, and none of that was as gruesome as the things Roark had done to the parts of her that should never be treated with anything but reverence and appreciation. There was rage and hatred acted out upon this girl like I had never seen before and it was eerie because she did bear a remarkable resemblance to Reeve, only much younger and much smaller.

"Is it okay if we take her now, Detective?"

I glanced up at the young tech and nodded. I hadn't been aware that I had zoned out and was just staring at the body like she was going to wake up and give me Conner Roark's name so I could go arrest him with zero hassle. Nothing ever worked that way.

"Yeah. Do we have an ID on her yet? She's just a baby. Someone needs to notify the family."

"Not yet. The only lead we have is that she may have been a dancer over at Spanky's. She was found with a whole lot of cash in her purse and not much else."

Oh, great. Nassir was already on the edge and close to going over because of what had happened to his club. When he found out that one of his girls was in the worst place at the worst time and the same guy who torched the club was responsible, he was definitely going to go over. There were some men that I could care less if they decided they wanted to do battle on my streets. I was tougher, I was faster, I was smarter, and when I had to be, I was more brutal. None of that was the case with Nassir Gates. I wasn't a hundred percent sure what his background was but I knew training and cunning when I saw it. He might try and play himself off as a typical thug but I knew better. Nassir was the Devil, and if he dropped off that thin ledge of civility he was holding on to, the bloodbath that would ensue when he fell would drown us all.

As they put the girl in the coroner's van I stared out over the industrial waterway and felt the weight of one more unnecessary death settle deep into that part of my soul where they collected and filled me up. I lost track of time, trapped in my own thoughts wondering how exactly I was going to fix this particular mess, when a heavy hand fell on my shoulder.

I didn't think.

I reacted and had my gun out and pointed at the offender before my next breath. We both swore as Race took a step back and lifted up his hands in a gesture of surrender.

"Whoa, Titus."

I narrowed my eyes at him and put the gun back in the holster. "What are you doing out here, Hartman? Shouldn't you be off running numbers, or better yet, dealing with all the dark shit that has to be in your head knowing your old man got smoked?"

I wasn't being tactful or kind. I didn't have it in me anymore and I think Race saw it because he just smirked at me and looked as regal and unruffled as ever. He was a different man from the one that had been in my office yesterday. I wondered how much a good woman, a woman that understood him and the life he lived, helped with that. I felt a surge of jealousy that I had to struggle to choke down.

"I live out here. Brysen's little sister heard the commotion and we peeked at the security cameras from the building. I saw you arrive and figured I would wait until the rest of the boys in blue took off before coming down to see what was going on."

"You live here?"

He nodded and motioned to a concrete-and-glass building that looked way too nice to be anywhere in the Point and definitely way too slick to be on these crumbling docks.

"My old man used this place to stash his mistresses. The property owner is shady as hell, so when all that stuff with Brysen's stalker came to a head, I had him transfer the deed over to her name so she had a safe place to go. I like it out here. It's quiet, and when Booker got out of the hospital after he was shot, I moved him into the building to keep an eye on things when I'm working. I like that the girls have someone they can run to if I'm not around. Plus I upgraded the security system so that it's harder to get into the place than it is to get on Bax's good side. No one gets in or out without me or Booker knowing it. There are cameras everywhere."

Noah Booker was an ex-con and an all-around badass. He was a lot like my brother in both of those aspects. Booker was smart enough to know that Race was the one that was going to be running things in the dark and in the back rooms and alleyways now that Novak was gone, so he had gotten in on the ground floor. He had offered himself up as a bullet catcher when Race's girl found herself caught in the sights of a deadly stalker. Booker had almost died trying to keep Brysen and her sister safe, so it didn't surprise me at all that Race had promptly put the man at his right hand and was relying on him for protection not only for himself but for his girls as well.

I rubbed a thumb across my scruffy jaw as the wheels in my head started turning. I lifted an eyebrow at Race and asked, "Is there any open space in the complex?"

He crossed his arms over his chest and his green eyes narrowed at me.

"Why? What's wrong with your place?"

I had a small Craftsman-style house that wasn't exactly out of the Point but it was far enough at the edge of the city that when I did sleep I did so without worrying too much about my windows getting shot out or my front door getting kicked in. It was just a place to store my stuff and crash when I got a few minutes. It absolutely wasn't secure enough to take Reeve, with all the people that currently wanted a piece of her. She would be too isolated and alone if I left her there while I continued to hunt down Roark.

"Nothing is wrong with my place, but I'm in the middle of a situation and I need someplace safe to hang out for a few weeks."

"That situation involves a certain dark haired beauty that's back in town?"

Goddamn, was he too smart for his own good. Well, *my* good, really.

"Yeah, it does, and I don't want to hear anything about it. The guy that torched your car, the guy that worked over Roxie, the guy that tortured the poor girl and left her here on this dock like she was trash, is not only after the Point but he's after Reeve with a vengeance. She gave me his name and she's willing to be the bait we use to draw him out, so I need to do what I can to keep her safe. Help me out, Race."

I could see him calculating the pros and cons of what I was asking him to do for me. Race didn't do anything without weighing all of his options. He knew I was asking him to bring a verified security threat under his protected roof. He understood I was asking him to do something that Bax was going to be totally against. He grasped that I was desperate enough to plead with him to offer shelter to a woman that had not only offered his sister up as a sacrificial lamb but whose actions had led directly to him being beaten within an inch of his life. I was asking him for so much more than he had ever asked me for, and he knew it. And because he was fucking brilliant, he knew that if he agreed it would mean I would owe him huge down the line. Get-out-of-jail-free huge.

I lived my life between very clear black and white lines but lately all the edges had blurred into so many shades of gray it was hard to see through the fog anymore. I believed in right and wrong, in good and bad. I was willing to die for those convictions, but I also wanted the good guys to win occasionally. Lately, it seemed like the way to do that was to play by the bad guys' rules. It made everything inside of me snap and thrash around in anger but I didn't have a choice and I could see Race knew that as well.

"Give me a week. There isn't availability right now, but I'll arrange some things and find you a spot."

I sighed and let my head fall forward so that I was looking at my boots and the worn wood of the dock between them.

"Do I even want to ask how you're going to arrange a vacancy on such short notice?"

He chuckled and it made the hairs on my arms raise up. I remembered him when he was just a lost rich kid boosting cars with Bax. He wasn't lost anymore, and the man he had become was not one to be underestimated.

"Probably not, but you'll both be safe within those walls and

I'll even let you borrow Booker. He can keep an eye on your little rat when you're off trying to save the world."

I snapped my head up to glare at him, but he had already turned away and was headed back toward the fancy-looking condominium complex.

"I would think you would be a little more sympathetic to someone doing whatever they have to in order to survive, Hartman."

I saw his shoulders shrug and he didn't turn around as he hollered at me, "You should remember that no good deed goes unpunished, Titus. She says she's here to help you now, but she told Dovie the same thing right before she set her up. I want the guy that is messing with my life and with my family, and if you think she's the way we get to him, then I want her as close as possible."

I didn't have any way to contradict him because that was the same logic I was using, so I just grunted at his back as he walked away.

Chapter 5

Reeve

A FEW DAYS HIDING out in Bax's tiny apartment made me feel like I was back in WITSEC. I hadn't seen anyone besides the pizza delivery guy. And I hadn't heard from Titus except for the day after he ditched me here when he showed up with a handful of clothes he told me he borrowed from a neighbor and a pay-as-you-go cell phone that he shoved in my hand with a grunt. He told me only to use it in case of an emergency and then disappeared without another word. It was obvious everything about having to deal with me was grating on him, but I didn't have a solution to that problem, so I simply took the phone and collapsed against the door after he stormed away, a cloud of anger and tension hanging thick in his wake.

Every night since I had taunted him into kissing me, goaded him into letting some of that rock-hard veneer he had in place slip, I felt like I was drowning in him. Admittedly my fascination with Titus King was nothing new, but now that I knew, now that I had actual experience with what it was like to be wanted by him, to be the sole focus of that inferno of hot desire, I couldn't get around it. It chased me into sleep. It haunted me when I was awake. I tasted him. I felt him, and when I breathed in and out I could swear when my heart beat it was tapping out his name over and over again.

I should be focused on Conner. I needed to keep my eye on the prize because only the winner of this game was making it out alive. The thought of being in a crazy man's crosshairs was petrifying. He killed a girl just because she looked like me, for God's sake, and he hadn't done it cleanly or mercifully. She had suffered; Titus was brutally honest when I asked about the body that had pulled him away before things had gotten out of control at the motel. She had suffered big-time and we both knew that was nothing compared to what Conner would do when he finally caught up with me.

There was a time before Titus when I would have just run. I was quick on my feet and knew how to make ends meet when I had to. There were plenty of no-name towns in Middle America where I could get lost and never be found again. But now that the surly detective was right in front of me, willing to believe that I had some kind of redeeming quality and was honestly willing to help him, I couldn't do that.

No. It was time to stand my ground and right all my wrongs in the only way I knew how. I was a trap few men could resist, one Conner had already fallen into, and once he came for me I was going to make sure he could never fool or hurt anyone ever again. A showdown was on the horizon. In the real world good didn't triumph over evil because evil didn't play fair. That meant only bad had a shot at taking evil down, and I was just bad enough to get the job done. I wanted Titus to keep me alive, not so I could testify but so that I could put a bullet in Conner before he put a bullet in me or anyone else in the Point. I was going to sacrifice myself for the greater good and the only part of it that made me nervous was the fact that I was lying to the handsome detective about my true intentions. He already thought I was shady and devious; once this came to light, he was bound to think I really was nothing more than a soulless killer.

When someone pounded on the door well after the sun had gone down on the day Titus said he was coming to collect me, I automatically assumed it was going to be him. However, I had lived in the Point way too long to ever just open a door without seeing what was on the other side. When I checked the peephole it wasn't bright blue eyes looking back at me, but instead a forest-green pair set in a face made to make women stupid with lust. It was almost like he could hear what I was thinking because before I reached for the security chain on the door, the golden god smiled at me, flashing a dimple that made my heart trip involuntarily. Race was dangerous in a totally different way from Bax, and I suddenly understood why the two of them together made an unstoppable team.

I pulled the door open and braced an arm on the jamb so that Race would get the hint that I wasn't inviting him inside.

"Titus send you after me?" I hated the sting I felt at the thought of the dark-haired cop palming me off on someone else. I was supposed to be made of stronger stuff than that. I couldn't afford to have my feelings hurt every time I was reminded that Titus didn't feel about me the same way I did about him. I needed to remind myself he *couldn't* feel that way. I was not a good person and Titus deserved the best.

Race grinned at me again and I rolled my eyes. It was easy to see how he got his way with no effort. That smile alone could make someone promise him anything and everything under the sun. The boy effortlessly broadcasted good times and dirty, sexy things.

"No. He doesn't know I'm here and he would probably get all yelly and punchy if he did know. I've been connecting the dots that other people tend to miss, so I figured this is where he would stash you. No one would believe Bax would let you hide out at his place. He hates you and would be happy to hand you over to the highest bidder. Titus is working his tail off to make sure no one knows what's going on with you right now. Bax has been all over his ass wanting information, and I think you're smart enough to know it's not so he can send you flowers."

I bit my lower lip and looked up at Race from under my lashes. "I get it. Bax is spoiling for a fight and he won't care why I'm here or that Titus might need me for his end game."

"If it was up to Bax, you would end up six feet under somewhere and be nothing more than a distant memory for all of us, but he's often shortsighted." Race crossed his arms over his broad chest and I watched the way it pulled his henley across the stacked muscles that lived there. He wasn't as imposing in stature as either Titus or Bax, but there was a severe elegance about him that seemed just as threatening while he considered me silently for a long moment. "I want to know what the end game is, Reeve. What happens once this guy shows up? Titus might think he can dangle you out there and still keep his eye on the prize, but I know him well enough to know that if you're in danger then his focus will be on you and not on taking out the threat. So what's the real reason you agreed to play this game? Keep in mind I'm not a very nice man when my friends or family are threatened. I have no problem making a call and letting Bax know exactly where his brother stashed you if you don't want to be honest with me."

His eyes darkened several shades, and I bit down even harder on my lip. I didn't answer him and I didn't move when he took a step closer to me. He didn't smell like the streets. He smelled good, like something expensive and fancy. It was so out of place in the hallway of this run-down complex right in the center of the inner city that it almost sent me reeling.

Begrudgingly I told him, "I know the guy who was behind the murder of your father. I had proof of who it was, so I brought it to Titus because I want to help him stop him."

Those forest-colored eyes narrowed to tiny little slits and I saw his jaw clench. "Who?"

I rolled my eyes. It wasn't like giving Race the information he was after would change the game at all. Conner wouldn't be found until he was ready. "His name is Conner Roark. He was the fed in charge of handling all the witnesses for Novak's RICO case."

I saw awareness dawn on his too pretty face. Lord Hartman might have been a top-tier bastard, but he was still Race's dad and the fact that Conner had orchestrated his execution would not sit well with the blond Adonis. "You can't stop a man like that with a badge and the threat of bars. The only way to take down a threat like that is with a bullet."

I sighed again because I agreed. I just watched him as things started to shift and move in his gaze as he put puzzle pieces together. When he thought he had it all figured out, he took a step closer to me and scowled while he demanded, "Did you come back here to set Titus up to kill Roark for you, Reeve? Are you playing with people's lives again? Because if you are, I have to tell you it's going to end much worse for you this time around."

I gulped and narrowed my eyes at him. I refused to be intimidated by anyone, even if Race and his words had a cold sweat breaking out across my skin.

"I came back to help. That's it. I don't care if Conner rots behind bars or gets a slug between the eyes. He's a lunatic. I know there are still good men and women here. Titus and Dovie, for instance. I'm trying to do the right thing."

"You think that's enough?"

I pushed off the doorjamb and crossed my arms so that I matched his pose. "No. There will never be enough, but it's a start."

He lifted an eyebrow at me and narrowed his eyes just a fraction. "Well, if Titus doesn't stop this guy for good, there are plenty of people willing to step in and finish the task. I just wondered if you were really conniving enough to know that." He smirked at me again and now that dimple made my tummy go tight. "I think you are. I think you know that Roark has to be put down like a dog and that Titus is too moral, too focused on the right side of the law to do it, but he has enough people that care about him, that want to make sure he keeps his hands clean of the mess the rest of us muck around in, to take care of that problem for him."

I breathed out a heavy sigh and shifted my stance so that my hair slithered over my shoulder. It wasn't exactly a hair toss but it was close. "Think whatever you want, Race. Conner needs to be stopped, and whether you, Bax, or Titus like it, the road leading to him goes right through me."

He gave a bitter-sounding laugh and lifted his hand to rub his thumb along his jawline. He looked like a big golden lion getting ready to pounce on its prey. Too bad for him I had never been on anyone's menu. I was the hunter not the hunted.

"You must be unbelievable in bed, Reeve. You have a good man willing to do bad things for you and a bad man hell-bent on showing you just how evil he can be."

I scoffed at him and lifted one of my own eyebrows in response to his taunt. "How sad for you that you'll never know, Hartman."

I didn't wait for a response; instead I slammed the door in his face and secured the chain. I heard his chuckle through the door as I stomped over to the kitchen to pour myself a glass of water. It made me so mad at myself that my hands were shaking. I had to get my emotions in check. No one was on my side. No one trusted me or my motivations for being here, and I had to get used to that fact. I was not part of the team and I had to stop letting the constant reminders of that get to me. If I let my feelings show, I would give away what I was really planning before it was showtime, and that couldn't happen.

The truth of the matter was I *did* know that the only way to stop Conner was to put him down like a rabid dog in the street. And I also knew that wasn't how Titus operated; in fact I was counting on his strong moral compass to keep him from crossing those kinds of lines. No, what he needed to do was keep me alive long enough, keep me safe enough that I could get close enough to Conner and take care of him myself. As far as I could tell, that was the only way to restore the karmic balance that I had set off kilter when I went looking for Novak all those years ago. When I had wanted revenge, wanted my sister's boyfriend to pay for all the ways he had destroyed her life, I should have been brave enough, strong enough, to take care of him myself and then been properly punished. Having someone else do my dirty work was the ultimate cop-out. I wouldn't ever be that weak or owe anyone that kind of favor again.

Now, when judgment day rolled around, it would be Conner and me face-to-face, and he would know exactly why I was the one pulling the trigger. It was my turn to stop the madness so that men like Titus had a shot, so that Race could take the vices and addictions that were rampant here and put some kind of cage around them, so that Nassir could feed the beast without it having to cannibalize itself, so that guys like Bax actually got a break for once. I understood redemption better than anyone gave me credit for and Titus wouldn't have to get his hands dirty at all. I already had blood on mine, so what was a little bit more?

Conner had tricked me. He made me think he was one of the good guys. That he was one of the fighters for justice and fairness. Sure, I wanted to believe it so badly that I had ignored everything that was screaming at me, that was trying to tell me he wasn't what he seemed. He had pulled the wool over my eyes. The only time I felt secure, had felt like any other normal young woman in her early twenties without an ugly past and a questionable set of ethics, was with Connor and he had faked it all. None of that had been real.

I jumped when the cell phone Titus had dropped off beeped with a text message. I snatched it up and called myself a few choice names when my pulse kicked at just the sight of his name in the message.

I'll be up to get you in 10.

Typical Titus. No mincing words with that guy.

I sighed and cast a rueful look down at the borrowed clothing I was wearing. I had no idea who Titus's neighbor was, but she was much shorter than me and had a thing for bright colors and patterns, where I typically favored a more neutral palette. I cringed inwardly when I thought about how ridiculous the hot-pink short-shorts and stretchy lime-green tank top had to look. I also hadn't seen an ounce of makeup aside from my purse stash since I got back to the Point, and so far the most flattering thing I had come up with for my hair was a ponytail.

I was used to looking good. I was used to being able to use the way I looked to disarm others and to deflect questions I didn't want to answer. I hadn't had that advantage with Titus since he showed up at the motel. He was seeing me at my worst and I didn't like that because he already had such a poor opinion of me. I wanted some kind of upper hand but that wasn't happening, so I resigned myself to suffering his silent brooding and judgment while he moved me from point A to point B. I needed to brace for it if we were going to be spending time together, which we would be if things went according to Titus's plan.

I pulled on a black hoodie that had to belong to him or someone close to his size. It covered my fingertips and reached down to midthigh, well past the shorts I was currently wearing. It wasn't much better than the garish outfit I had on underneath it, but it would do for this journey.

I pulled open the door after his first knock and took a quick step back to avoid getting tagged in the forehead by his falling fist, which was poised to knock again. I sucked in a quick breath that I hoped he couldn't hear as I stood frozen on the spot while his eyes roved over me. The blue was so bright it was like opening the door to the sky. His mouth pulled down on the sides and his eyebrows shot up as his gaze skimmed along the bare length of my legs under the hoodie.

"Do you have pants on?"

His voice was gravelly and rough, much more so than usual, and I had to swallow before I could answer. I was doing a little ogling of my own and it took me a second to realize he was talking to me. Instead of his usual rumpled, button-up shirt and pressed slacks, he had on a black T-shirt that was stretched tight across muscles that looked like they were made of stone. His long legs were encased in faded jeans that had a hole in the knee and one in the thigh. The skin peeking out of the frayed material was a tawny color and looked just as hard as the rest of him. There was no softness to Titus King even when he was off duty. He had on the same boots he wore while he worked but his hair was in disarray like he hadn't bothered to comb it down, and I had never seen the resemblance between him and his younger brother be as strong as it was right then. He looked just as harsh, just as unpredictable, as Bax ever did and it had places inside me quivering in a way that I really needed to ignore so that I could answer him and not sound like a breathless moron.

"Of course I have pants on. It's not my fault your neighbor is a midget."

I stepped away from the door and he followed me inside, immediately making the room feel a hundred times smaller.

"Did I say my neighbor? I meant my neighbor's daughter. My neighbor weighs well over three hundred pounds, but her teenaged daughter is about your size, just shorter. I would've asked Dovie or Brysen, but I wanted to make sure we had a secure place to go before the charade starts. Dovie would have told Bax, and I've had enough of him being all over my ass where you're concerned as it is. Brysen would have been game but I already pulled in all the favors I had where Race is concerned and I didn't want to owe him any more."

"Well, I'm glad no grown woman was trying to wear hot-pink short-shorts as actual clothing." I lifted the hem of the hoodie to show him I did indeed have pants on, and noticed the way silver sparked in the center of his irises. "But I am going to need to get my hands on some real clothes in the near future. If the plan is to flaunt this affair in Conner's face and to get him to come out of hiding, then I need to look like I look normally do."

"How is that?"

He jerked his gaze away from my legs and lifted them up to look me in the eye. "How's what?"

"How do you normally look?" He shoved his hands in the pockets of his jeans and I had to bite the tip of my tongue as the action pulled the top of his jeans down just enough that a sliver of skin was exposed between them and the edge of his T-shirt. Corrugated abs and that vee that was bound to make woman drool danced in front of my eyes. I had to count to ten to keep myself from reaching out and trying to touch the exposed skin that was dusted with just a hint of dark hair. Of course Titus wouldn't be all baby smooth and perfectly manicured like so many men were today. He was too much of a man for that. It was just one more way in which Conner had been a sorry substitution for what I really wanted. He had been polished and primped even more than I was.

"I normally look good. I normally look like I want a man to want me. I definitely don't look like this . . . like I'm not even trying. Conner would never buy that you were suddenly infatuated with me if it doesn't even look like I'm making an effort. How do you think I caught his attention so fast?"

Titus did that guy thing where his lashes lowered and his eyes started at the top of my head and skimmed all the way down to my toes in a way that I could almost feel. I saw his chest rise and fall and his pulse jump a little at the side of his neck.

"You look just fine the way you are. You look better like this than most women do when they put in the effort. You don't need to try, and if a guy makes you think you do, then he's a dipshit. Get whatever you need and let's get out of here."

I might have fallen over or stripped off all my clothes and thrown myself at him if I thought there was a chance he would catch me in either scenario. No one had ever said anything that nice to me in my life. Sure, I had heard I was pretty. I had heard I was more than pretty, but they were hollow words when they came from mouths that spewed lies fair easier than the truth. If Titus said it, then he believed it. There was no hidden agenda, no subterfuge, and there was just something so powerful and alluring about that raw honesty and the lack of artifice.

I gathered my composure and the few things I had left strewn around the apartment and followed him out into the hallway. I dropped my gaze to the gun he still wore clipped to his belt. It was a stark reminder that even when he was dressed down and off duty he was still one of the good guys and I was not. We could want each other all day long, but there was no bridge strong enough or long enough to cross that fundamental divide that kept us separated.

He was alert and stiff as we hit the front of the building. Even though I was facing his back, I could almost feel the way his gaze scanned every single shadow and hidden place that stretched out in front of us.

He stopped in front of a massive, sparkly blue-and-white car that looked just as big and badass as he did. The windows were tinted almost black and the tires didn't look like anything I had ever seen on any other kind of car.

"This doesn't look like any kind of car a cop should be driving." I couldn't keep the disbelief out of my voice as he pulled open the door for me.

"It's not *a* cop's car, it's *this* cop's car. When we were younger Bax and I couldn't manage to spend five minutes in the same room without wanting to murder one another. Our mom had a guy that she saw on the side that owned the garage Bax is running now. Gus put a wrench in each of our hands and told us to figure our shit out. The only time we didn't fight was when we were working under the hood. Bax was always better at it than I was, but I couldn't let my little brother be the only one with a sick ride. I built the GTO after he got locked up. I think it was how I dealt with the fact that I was the one that put him behind bars."

I gaped at him as he walked around the hood and then climbed in on the other side. Everything on the interior of the car was just as pristine as the outside. The gauges were all shiny with chrome inlays as they glowed to life when he cranked the motor on. The car made the entire block shake and I saw a bum startle awake when Titus put his foot on the gas and roared away from the curb.

"You felt guilty you had to arrest Shane?"

His eyes cut in my direction and I instinctively braced my hand on the dashboard as he whipped the monster of a car around a corner with the tires squealing.

"No. I didn't feel guilty about locking him up. He broke the law, he was always breaking the law, and he didn't care enough not to get caught. I felt guilty that I was the reason he didn't care.

I felt bad that I was the reason he was a criminal in the first place. I left Bax to fend for himself with a drunk mother and a mobster father. He never had a chance and I knew it, but I left him anyway. I think failing the one person I was supposed to keep safe was one of the driving factors in me deciding to go into law enforcement. I built the GTO to show him that it mattered . . . the time we spent together before he hated me, before I let him down. Bax is an action guy. The words wouldn't get through, but I thought maybe the car would."

"That's why you paid his rent while he was locked up? You wanted to show him that you cared?"

Titus grunted in agreement and turned his eyes back to the road. I settled back in the bucket seat and watched him as he concentrated on the road. He was driving way faster than the speed limit, and I wondered if he even realized he was breaking one of the laws he was adamant about following. Titus was a complex man and there was a lot more to him than I had initially thought. I knew his relationship with Bax was complicated and that the brothers were polar opposites, but I hadn't known that Titus had demons from his past and from the way he had pulled himself out of the Point that clung to him. It made him seem less infallible, more human. It made me want him even more, which I didn't think was possible.

"Where are we going exactly?" We hadn't left the Point. In fact we were going deeper into it, past the District and all the way out to the docks. No one went to the docks unless they wanted to make a body disappear or they were trying to send something illegal out or ship something illegal in.

"Race has a place on the docks. He's turned it into his own little command center. He has his own muscle and his own security system set up around it since his lady and her sister live there with him. It's almost as good as protective custody, but it's still in the city and visible enough that should Conner want to make a move he'll know where to find us."

I fidgeted nervously. "It's also where he left that girl that looked like me."

Titus sighed. "I know. But it's the best option for what we're trying to accomplish. You'll be safe while I work, and that means I won't have my attention divided between my job and your safety."

A trickle of warmth tried to work its way into the heart I had been trying to freeze up toward him. "I wouldn't think you would care if I was safe or not. After all, I'm the one that got myself into this mess."

I rolled my head to the side so I could look at him and noticed that the tick he got when he was trying to hold whatever he was feeling inside had started to work at his jaw. His big hands tightened on the steering wheel and he bit out, "We can't always control what or whom we care about. Didn't you learn that lesson the hard way with Roark?"

I jerked my eyes back to the road and felt ice take up the spot where the heat had been sneaking in. "You're right. I don't need to learn any lesson more than once. So how did you get Hartman to agree to this setup? If he went to all the trouble of building a castle for his queen and princess, why would he let the wicked witch in the gates?"

He gave me another hard, sideways look. "Because he has his own agenda, and now I owe him. Race is neck-deep in stuff he shouldn't be in, and being able to call in a major favor like this isn't an opportunity a smart guy like him can pass up."

A heavy ball of guilt and something uglier, something dirtier, lodged in my throat. "So you are compromising yourself for me, for this plan of yours? You would never give anyone a free pass otherwise." I didn't want Titus to go against his own code just to get me close to Conner. I didn't want him to change at all. I loved the way he was . . . loved the way he came off as heroic and brave. Knew I could so easily love him with my entire heart if it didn't seem so impossible.

He swore softly under his breath and then wheeled the noisy muscle car down a ramp that looked like it led to an underground garage. He turned to look at me, his eyes almost at bright as the headlights shining in the dark in front of us. He sounded resigned and tired when he told me, "I can't tell the difference anymore between the bad guys and the good guys that are bad because they don't have any other choice in the matter. I'm not compromising, I'm adapting. Isn't that the first rule of survival?"

It was, but I didn't want him to adapt. I wanted him to stay just the way he was, and I would die before being the reason he felt like he had to change.

Chapter 6

Titus

T HIS WAS SOME SPECIAL kind of hell that I wasn't sure I was going to survive.

It had been a week since I moved Reeve into the loft at Race's compound. A week in which I killed myself at work trying to figure out why exactly Roark had declared war on the city. I called the marshals and got shut down because they didn't want anyone else to know they had a viper in the nest, so I was working around them instead of with them. I was also going to the condo at night and pretending not to watch Reeve while she paraded around in clothes that were too tight and too short for my sanity or peace of mind. A week in which I tiptoed around her because the loft was just that: lofty. It was totally open, so there were too few walls and not enough places to hide. The bedroom was just a platform set above the open-plan kitchen, so there wasn't even a door there to shut and hide behind. I heard her in the shower, I saw her kick off the covers in the middle of the night, I heard the sound of clothes rustling as she got dressed and undressed. The noise scraped across my skin, and all of it was making my insides itch and my temper quick to boil over.

It was all a frustrating waste of time and I was almost at the end of my rope.

I gave her the bed and took the couch. I tried to find other places to be so that I didn't have to breathe her in, and pretended to ignore the way every part of my body reacted to her. I was walking around with a constant hard-on, and even if I decided to ignore the pulsating sexual tension between us, Reeve didn't. I caught the way she looked at me out of the corner of her eye. She was waiting, watching. I wasn't sure what she expected me to do, but whatever it was, I refused to give in to the allure of her or the temptation of us together.

We were supposed to be out there putting on a show to draw Conner out, but I hadn't had the time to figure out what was next and I wasn't sure I could pull the game off as wound up as I was. My plan was half developed at best, and until I had a more secure end game in place, I wasn't willing to risk her neck or my own. The condo had floor-to-ceiling windows that went dark and opaque with the flick of a switch on a remote and Race assured me that even if someone could see in during the day, they couldn't send anything through the glass. He had literally built an impenetrable fortress, and I didn't even want to think about where he came up with that kind of cash to sink into those types of security measures.

Every night when I finally went back to the apartment, I had to fight the urge to grab Booker by the throat and throw him out of the loft or into the closest wall. Even with a noticeable scar that decorated half of his face, Noah Booker was a good-looking dude. He was almost the same size as I was but had a much rougher façade. He wouldn't go down without a fight, but the easy way he was with Reeve made it seem like they were both way too familiar with life on the bottom and far too comfortable there. It irked me to an irrationally furious level. Booker knew it pissed me off, so he went out of his way to make himself comfortable in the condo and with Reeve. Every time I turned around he was putting one of his massive paws on her shoulder or nudging her with an elbow like they had been friends for a hundred years. In turn, the raven haired beauty was flirty with him in an effortless way she didn't have with me. I wanted to walk away from this stupid idea of mine and forget the whole thing. I couldn't, but the temptation was there.

I was lying on the couch with an arm thrown over my eyes. It was well past midnight and I had been working the dead-girl-on-the-dock case all day. It turned out she had no one. She was a child of the system. Another poor kid no one wanted, so she ended up on the streets doing whatever she could to survive. It surprised me how furious Nassir was over her situation. Not that one of his girls was murdered by the same enemy that had burned his club down, but that there was no one to claim the body and mourn for her. I silently handed over the information he would need to claim the body and make sure that the young woman was put to rest properly. Nassir never struck me as the sentimental type, but it was a pleasant surprise to find out that he actually did have a heart somewhere under that three-thousand-dollar suit he wore. He cared about those girls more than the income they generated for him, and while I couldn't condone what he was doing, I appreciated that he was doing it with his own kind of good intention.

I was tired. I was more than tired. I was soul weary and there were no reserves left to tap into. I had to recharge and get this plan to draw Roark out into the open moving. I needed an idea and I needed it yesterday. I couldn't handle being stuck with Reeve for much longer, fighting my instincts and my body's urges while trying to do my job effectively.

I heard the covers rustle and heard her mutter something sleepily as the moonlight cut silver shadows through the darkened windows. I bit back a groan and shifted restlessly on the couch. Luckily it was a big leather couch, so there was enough room for me and my bulk, but it still wasn't as comfortable as my own bed or as tempting as the king-size bed up on the platform containing a too-sexy-for-her-own-good Reeve.

"Are you still awake?" Her voice was soft as it drifted down from somewhere above me.

This time I let the groan out so that it vibrated my chest, and shifted so that I was sitting up. I dropped my head into my hands. "Yeah."

"How was work today?" There was a hint of dry humor in her tone. I sighed and threw myself back against the couch cushions and laced my fingers behind my head.

"Really?" I sounded like a dick but I couldn't help it.

It was her turn to sigh. "We've been doing this a week, Titus. Each day that goes by, you get tenser and more tightly strung. Something has to give. We're supposed to be lovers. We're supposed to be unable to keep our hands off each other and making Roark crazy with jealousy. All you're doing is avoiding me. I'm just trying to figure out a way to make this easier for you."

The padding of her bare feet sounded on the stairs. "There is no easy. I'm working a murder investigation where I know who is responsible and I can't even find my perp to question him. It's like all those years hunting Novak while he carved holes in the city only to watch him walk away all over again. I don't want to lose again."

I turned my head when the cushions next to me depressed as

she sat down. I had to bite my tongue to keep it from rolling out of my mouth like a horny teenager. Even in the barely-there moonlight all I could see was miles and miles of long, naked leg and endless amounts of ebony hair. Her shorts and tank top revealed more than they covered and it didn't take X-ray vision to see that she didn't have a bra on. Goddamn, this girl was going to be the end of me. Things big and wild started to swell inside of me.

"The sooner we start to rub this in Conner's face the sooner he'll make his move. Stop tiptoeing around what needs to be done." I flinched involuntarily when she reached out a single finger and gently stroked down the deep frown lines that were etched in my forehead over my nose. "Maybe then you can actually get a full night's sleep. You're going to run yourself into the ground, Detective."

I caught her wrist and yanked it away from my face. Her touching me wasn't a good idea, for either one of us. Rumblings from the things I kept so carefully locked down turned into howls of hunger.

"Tomorrow I'll take you to get some clothes that actually fit, and then we can hit up some really visible places in the Point so that way, even if Roark doesn't see us, other people will and the word will out be on the street."

She pulled her hand free and used it to spear her fingers through her long hair. The motion pushed her breasts up higher, making them strain against the thin material barely covering them and making me grunt as I watched the way her nipples obviously tightened under the weight of my gaze.

"Where exactly are you thinking we should go?"

It took me longer than it should have to come up with a coherent response. With this woman, listening to her breathe was more of a turn-on than anything any other woman had done for me or to me. She shoved all of my common sense and resolve straight into my dick, where it turned into want and desire so thick and heavy it actually hurt as it throbbed behind my zipper. It wasn't just the parts of me long denied that she called to, it was all the parts of me that could desire and want her that listened to her song so carefully!

I wanted to shift a few inches over because I could feel electricity arcing between our bare skin. In hindsight I realized I should have left my T-shirt on when I crashed for the night. Between the two of us there were too few articles of clothing to keep us from feeding off of each other's heat. "I think we need to stop by Spanky's. That gives us the opportunity to be out where the kind of people that need to see us are and it also gives us the opportunity to show Nassir that you're with me. Plus, if for some reason Roark does make a move, we won't be alone. Chuck will be there and Nassir always has armed security staff manning the joint. It won't be an uneven fight if Roark makes a move with a minion instead of doing it alone."

She crossed her legs and I jerked my gaze up to hers to see if she'd done it on purpose. She had. Her dark blue eyes reflected the glow of the moon and I could see that she was just as affected by my nearness and half-dressed state as I was by hers. This was going to explode all over the both of us, and when the smoke cleared we were going to be picking out shrapnel forever. I had a sinking suspicion the wounds we were inevitably going to leave on each other were the kind that never managed to heal all the way through.

"I used to work on the hair of a lot of the girls from Spanky's when Ernie was running the place for Novak. Most of them were really sweet, even the girls that did more than dance. It sucked that once they got in the business there was no way out. Novak owned them."

There was a drop in her voice. She must have felt the same way while she waited and waited for him to collect on that massive favor she'd owed him.

"Nassir takes better care of the girls that work for him than that. He's picky and he makes sure they are protected and taken care of. He won't keep anyone on that isn't loyal and quiet, that includes his clients. I've tried to bust him on solicitation charges more than once, but no one ever comes forward as a witness. He's the one taking care of the arrangements for the girl on the docks, so I think he cares about them in his own scary, silent kind of way."

She hummed a little noise and my balls instantly tightened at the thought of what it would feel like if her mouth was wrapped around my cock and she was doing the same thing.

"They should have someone there to help them when they want out. That's what's so awful about this city. Once you're in, there doesn't seem to be any way out. A girl can get on a stage and be lured by all that money she can make stripping when she's eighteen or nineteen, but what's after that? Suddenly she's thirty and all she knows is selling sex and the streets and what shot does she have for anything else?"

"Are you speaking from experience?" If she ever took her clothes off for money, entire countries would end up broke.

"No. Just from what I heard when they were in my chair and then from watching how quickly my sister got sucked into it all. There is no escape once the Point has you."

She leaned her head back on the couch and shifted her eyes up to the ceiling. I thought I saw a sheen of moisture dance across the navy-colored surface but then she blinked and it was gone.

"It sucks," I said. She tilted her head to look at me. "The way everything went down with your sister, that sucks. But you tried to help her, tried to save her, and that's what you should focus on."

She made a noise low in her throat and shoved up off the couch. She crossed her arms over her chest and looked down at me with eyes that went flinty hard. "It wasn't enough. What time do you want to head out tomorrow?"

The quick change in conversation forced me to switch gears. "I have to work in the morning, so when I get back."

"Are you actually going to come back after your shift tomorrow?"

So my avoidance tactics hadn't gone unnoticed. "Yes. I'll try and be here before five. You really do need some clothes that fit." Brysen had run a few things up after we had been camped out for a couple days and they fit slightly better, but no girl alive seemed to have those ridiculously long legs or the same kind of curves Reeve was working with up top. Brysen's stuff covered her up more than my teenaged neighbor's, but not enough that I didn't get an eyeful every time I looked at her.

She linked her fingers together and lifted her arms up over her head in a way that pulled the hem of her tank top up over the indent of her belly button and lifted the edge of her tiny shorts so high I didn't have to use much imagination to envision what all the secret, soft parts of her looked like. Like I needed any more incentive to keep thinking about her and sex when my mind and attention should be anywhere else.

"I can cover it all up, it's not going to change the fact that you want me and are angry about it."

She twirled on her foot and flounced back up the stairs. If there had been a single door in the loft I knew she would have slammed it to make her point.

She was right. I did want her. I had wanted her from the second she came into my precinct and admitted to me that she had solicited Novak for murder. I wanted her when she tearfully told me about her part in Dovie's abduction. I wanted her when the marshals had whisked her away and I never thought I would see her again. And yes, I wanted her now in the middle of this charade that had life and death woven into the fabric of it. I wasn't angry that I wanted her, lusted after her. She was beautiful, slick, and all kinds of street-smart. She looked at me like she understood what made me tick and didn't care that I acted like it was me against the entire city most of the time. I was fighting a losing battle every single day and that essentially made me a loser, but she didn't seem to see that. There were a lot of reasons to want her, to find her attractive and ultimately irresistible.

There was more than one major reason that every time my blood kicked in response to her, guilt and shame roared to life inside of me. Of course I had an issue with the fact that she was an admitted criminal. She was one of the people I was trying to protect the city from. No matter her intentions, no matter if she was trying to use one bad guy to get rid of another bad guy, she hadn't done it by legal means. But there was also the fact that the monsters of my past, my burden of beasts that I kept buried so deep and dark inside of me that I tended to forget they were there, woke up and started to scream when she was near. There was no more ignoring them and the way they strained against the skin of the man I tried so hard to be.

Being infatuated with a woman that had a history of taking

the law into her own hands would be my absolute undoing, and if I couldn't keep those feelings in a box there was going to be nothing left of me. I would have nothing left to stand against my inner animal, and it would chew me alive from the inside out and I would be just like the rest of the people lost and alone, just waiting for the city to claim them. I couldn't let that happen.

I wasn't angry that I wanted her, I was terrified that I did.

I lay back down on the couch and took one of the decorative pillows and smashed it over my face so I could shout every dirty word I could think of into it. It was already a long night and now it was going to seem endless.

"YOU AREN'T GOING TO try any of that on?" I hated shopping. Hated it. Most men I knew just considered it a necessary evil when they had a woman in their life they needed to keep happy. I only went shopping for myself when I ran out of underwear or needed new shoes and stuff for work. Most of the jeans and T-shirts I wore I had had since the police academy back in the day and that worked just fine for me. Reeve was an anomaly. She seemed to dislike the act just as much as I did.

There wasn't anything close to a mall in the Point, in fact most retailers had pulled up stakes years ago after one too many armed robberies. So we had driven to the outlet shops that were on the outskirts of the city. I braced for hours of torture. Much to my surprise she blazed through the stores like she was on a mission to get in and out as quickly as possible. Her eyes kept darting around like she was expecting someone to jump out of the clothing racks and grab her, and as a result she had an armful of clothing she was marching toward the checkout counter with without having tried a stitch of it on.

She looked at me over her shoulder as the salesclerk started zapping the tags on everything.

"I know what size I wear and I didn't get anything too fancy. Just some jeans and shirts and a couple of skirts that are too short so that anyone looking at us will know why you can't resist me."

I grunted at her and handed over my credit card as the clerk rattled off the total. Reeve thanked us both and then told me she was going to change really quickly after grabbing a pair of the new jeans and darting back toward the dressing rooms. I took the bags the clerk handed over and headed out to the front of the store to wait for her. I scanned the parking lot and kept my eyes on the people milling about while I waited for Reeve to appear.

My phone rang and I hit ignore when I saw my brother's name flash across the screen. I had been doing a bang-up job of ignoring Bax for the last few weeks. He knew I was shacking up with Reeve at Race's place, but I had yet to explain to him why. I was surprised he hadn't stormed the castle yet, demanding answers, but he had changed a lot since Dovie entered the picture. He was a lot less reactive than he had been before.

"Jesus." I jolted involuntarily when a light hand landed on my lower back as I slipped my phone back in my pocket and looked down at Reeve. She shouldn't have been able to get so close to me without my noticing it. It made my spine snap straight and my hands tighten on the bags I held.

She lifted up on the tips of her toes and brushed her lips across my check. I knew it was all for show but the simple and sweet gesture made my back teeth click together.

"Thanks." She curled her hand around the inside of my elbow and looked up at me from under the long fringe of her lashes.

"It had to be done." I started across the parking lot not caring that she had to scramble to keep pace with me. She dug the edge of her nails into my skin, forcing me to look down at her.

"Remember that whole pretending-to-like-me thing. You're sucking at it and we've only been out in public for an hour."

I sighed and slowed my steps to match her shorter ones. I put a hand over where hers were resting and forced a grin across my lips. "Sorry. Being out in the open makes me nervous and I didn't hear you come up behind me because I was thinking that it's odd Bax hasn't shown up demanding answers yet or found me and tried to take a swing at me. I can't afford to be distracted and you can't afford for me to be distracted either."

"You're only human, Titus. There is only so much you can do and only so much you can take responsibility for."

I stopped by the GTO and reached around her to open the door. "Isn't that what I tried to tell you last night?"

She slid past me, her body dragging all the way across mine. I had to suck in a breath when she stopped with the tips of our noses almost touching.

"You're trying to save everyone, I just wanted to save the one person that mattered to me. It's different."

She slid into the passenger seat and I handed over the bags full of her purchases so she could throw them in the backseat. I didn't have an answer to that, so I went around the car and wheeled us out of the parking lot and back toward the city so we could hit up Spanky's.

"What reason are we going to give for being at a strip club? You don't really strike me as the type that needs to slip dollars in a G-string in order to see naked women."

She would be surprised. I hadn't seen a naked woman in a

lot longer than I cared to think about, and I definitely didn't keep my eyes closed anytime I ventured into Spanky's for work.

"I'm going to tell Chuck I need to talk to Nassir about the girl-on-the-dock case. He'll let us in without asking too many questions."

Chuck was the head of Nassir's security. He was a holdover from Novak's days and old-school muscle. He wouldn't let a badge and a gun intimidate him. Luckily he seemed to like me and we generally didn't have to butt heads. I knew that wouldn't be the case if any of the charges I had thrown at the club over the years had managed to stick. Chuck was loyal to a fault and Nassir made sure to reward him accordingly.

"Okay. So what am I supposed to do while you talk to Nassir? Believe it or not, I've never actually been in a strip club."

"We just need to walk in acting like we can't get enough of each other. Nassir and whoever else might be watching needs to think I can't stand to be away from you for even a second. Hold my hand, keep up with the little touches and junk. Just look at me adoringly and sell it. I bet Roark has eyes everywhere, so someone will get the news back to him."

She lifted an eyebrow at me and smirked. "Adoringly. Gotcha."

I grinned and looked at her out of the corner of my eye. "The girls that work there are kind of territorial. They aren't going to love a girl that looks like you waltzing in on their turf, so try and ignore any shade they throw your way."

She snorted softly. "I'm a grown-ass woman, Titus. I can handle myself. No one can make me feel worse about myself than I already do on a daily basis."

I didn't doubt she could hold her own, but years of being nothing more than meat for the hungriest predators the Point had to offer made the girls that danced at Spanky's an entirely different breed of woman. They could be vicious and cruel without a second thought. It was how they protected themselves.

"Just remember why we're there."

She mumbled her agreement and the rest of the ride was silent until I pulled into the parking lot of the strip club. I made sure to park next to Nassir's Bentley. It was the only spot where I was pretty sure nothing was going to happen to my baby. Nassir loved his outrageously expensive car, so I knew he probably had cameras on the spot where it was parked. I didn't want the GTO to meet the same fate that had befallen Race's Stang. Nassir might not give a shit about me or mine, but I left the GTO close enough to his ride that should anything happen to my car, his would be messed up as collateral damage, and the fancy bastard would never stand for that.

I pulled Reeve to my side and wrapped an arm around her shoulder so that her side was pressed tightly all along my own as she curled her arm around my waist and we headed inside. I burned everywhere we touched and I heard her breath hitch at the contact. I pulled open the door and winced as loud music and an overwhelming view of pink assaulted my senses. Nassir had way better taste than the previous owner of the club but he hadn't gotten around to redoing the place. His attention had been focused on his club burning down and finding the man responsible.

Chuck was a giant black man. He was one of the few people I had ever encountered that I actually had to tilt my head back to look in his eyes. He flashed a blindingly white smile at me, which had the gold incisor he sported sparkling at me. I squeezed Reeve when I felt her stiffen next to me.

"What's up, Chuck?"

"Twice in one week, cop. That's not good for business."

"I thought of another question I wanted to ask your boss."

His dark eyes skimmed over me and landed on Reeve. He let his gaze sweep over her and then bounce back to me.

"You traveling with your own talent now?"

I forced a laugh and saw Reeve roll her eyes out of corner of my eye. "Something like that." I hugged her closer and inwardly applauded her when she reached up to put a hand in the center of my chest. She batted her eyelashes at Chuck and gave him that grin of hers that was designed to stop anyone with the Y chromosome from thinking with the head that was located above their belts.

"It was supposed to be date night. He's lucky I'm willing to let him make it up to me later." She played the temptress so well it was no wonder it was all I could do not to touch.

She giggled when I let my hand slip to her ass. She turned the appropriate shade of red as Chuck waved us through into the heart of the club. I wasn't an openly affectionate guy but something about touching her, putting my hands on all of her curves, felt natural. Playacting with this girl felt more right than being with any other girl that I had actually been involved with. That didn't bode well for me or my sanity in the long run.

"Let's go up to the bar. There's less chance of any of the girls getting in your face if you aren't down on the floor taking attention away from them."

She didn't say anything. Her eyes were big in her face as she was taking everything in. There was a lot to see. The naked girls onstage. The lights changing colors as they skipped over bare, glittery skin and drooling customers. The burly security guards that were wandering around keeping an eye on things. The scantily clad cocktail servers that scuttled by on dangerously high heels with trays full of drinks. It was loud and flashy but underneath it was sadness and hopelessness that seemed to permeate every single corner of the club.

I sat Reeve down at one of the black leather bar stools and waited until the bare-chested bartender that looked like he should be on a billboard selling something unnecessary to rich people handed her a drink. I saw the door to Nassir's office swing open, so I bent forward and pressed my lips to the back of her head.

"Sit tight. I'll be back in a second." I stiffened for a second before remembering we had an audience when she swiveled around and touched her lips lightly to mine. It wasn't really a kiss; just a touching of mouths, but it was still enough to have my pulse thundering and my cock tightening.

"Hurry back." Her voice was singsongy and full of amusement. I grunted and made my way over to where the dark-haired club owner was lurking in his office doorway.

Nassir was several inches shorter than me and his build hovered on the slender side but none of that tricked me into thinking he wasn't a threat. His eyes burned a strange bronze color that seemed almost unnatural and there was an otherworldly chill that always seemed to surround him. He was equal parts deadly and sophisticated and I never knew what was going on in his head. He was an ice-cold operator and not someone I would ever trust or be fooled into thinking was on my side. Nassir cared about one thing and that thing was Nassir. He was his own agenda and that made him pitiless and merciless when it came to the way he handled his business.

"How does Bax feel about you cozying up to her?"

He didn't beat around the bush. "I haven't given him the chance to tell me how he feels yet."

"She sold Dovie out. She was in Novak's pocket. How does that work for you, cop?"

"I don't have to like her to fuck her." The words left a bitter taste in my mouth because they were too close to the truth I was struggling with.

Nassir laughed a little and it scraped across my skin like razors. "Yes, you do. There's a reason you're with her and a reason you brought her here. I bet there's also a reason that one of my girls got cut up and tossed on the dock like trash. If I was a betting man, which we both know I am, I would wager it has something to do with the fact she looked a lot like your new piece of ass."

I felt my shoulders stiffen as I glowered down at him. "Why was your girl on the docks that night? You send her out there to meet a client? No one goes into that part of town without a reason."

His glinting eyes shifted up to me and I had to force myself not to look away. He really could be one scary motherfucker.

"I already told you she wasn't working that side of things. She was just a kid. She danced and that was it. Chuck walked her out the night before she was found and he said she got in her car—alone. Just like she always did. You can keep asking and you'll keep getting the same answers. What about you, cop? Why do I think you and this girl mean more than you're sharing?"

"It's not my job to share with the criminal underground, Nassir."

"It is if you don't want to be in the way when I do your job for you. If you can't find the guy, I bet if I got your new girl involved, I could draw him out."

"No one is doing anything." I bit the words out and gave him a hard look to let him know I didn't like him even thinking about messing with Reeve.

"We'll see about that. It looks like your girl is about to get into something all on her own."

I pivoted just in time to see Reeve jump to her feet, sending the bar stool skipping backward with a clatter. She was putting her index finger in the face of the only other woman I had ever seen that was as pretty as she was. Keelyn Foster was as much a part of the Point and Spanky's as my brother was. She had been around a long time dancing under the stage name Honor and she wasn't a woman anyone would mess with if they were smart. Up to this point, Reeve had shown she was very smart and could read people like a book, so I had no clue what she was doing.

Keelyn flipped her auburn hair over her shoulder, flashed a smile that was all teeth, and said something that had Reeve turning red enough that I could see it from here. There was no warning as the dark haired knockout dove for the sexy redhead and they went down in a tangle of arms and legs. Reeve was dressed, Keelyn was not. That was a whole lot of sexy woman-on-woman action happening and the crowd noticed.

Nassir chuckled as I started to move forward in order to break up the catfight.

"What?" I barked it him over my shoulder as I moved forward.

He laughed again. "I would've charged more at the door if I had known you were going to bring that kind of entertainment in with you, cop. When she figures out you're just using her and you drop her on her ass, send her my way if she wants a job. I'll oil her and Honor up every night and make enough to buy and sell this piece-of-shit city a hundred times over.

"Fuck off, Gates."

I pushed through cheering bodies and waving arms until I could get to the spot on the floor where the girls were rolling around. I was assaulted with a chorus of boos and hit with more than one flying beer bottle as I pried Reeve off the stripper. They were both breathing hard and bleeding from various scratches.

"Seriously?" I asked the question as I set Reeve on her feet and watched as she shoved her long hair out of her face. I sighed and grabbed her hand as I started to drag her to the back where the bathrooms that the girls used were instead of the ones that were there for the customers.

"It's fine." Her voice was shaky as I shoved her into the room and hit the light switch.

"It's not fine."

She laughed a little shrilly and then the next thing I knew she launched herself at me so that I had to use both hands to catch her.

"You're right." I wanted to demand to know what she was thinking. I wanted to ask why she had decided to throw down with a stripper, but before my tongue unleashed the words, her mouth locked on mine and then there was no thinking. There was just heat, the tang of blood, and all the sweetness that always seemed to rise above the tartness when it came to this woman.

Chapter 7

Reeve

I COULD TOLERATE A lot of things. I was immune to nasty words and thought very little of the people that slung them around carelessly. I had grown used to hearing that I was a rat. I often heard the word *backstabber* mumbled as people walked by. I had been labeled a sellout, a traitor, but even worse was the disappointment I saw in Titus's eyes every time I got just close enough for him to realize exactly who it was that had her hands on him, what kind of woman it was that made his eyes bleed all their color and burn white hot with craving and need. It stripped little pieces away from what was left of my dignity when he looked that way because the disappointment wasn't directed at me but inward. He struggled with the way he wanted me, fought against big, powerful things that rose up inside him when we touched, and it hurt that he wouldn't give in to them. I wasn't sure he even knew they were there, but I could see them shining out of him and hear them calling to me louder and louder the harder Titus tried to quiet them down. The cop had more going on than his duty to serve and protect, and I wanted to dig into all of it.

Apparently the situation between me and the handsome detective bothered Honor as well. I knew Keelyn Foster and her glittery stripper skin outside of Spanky's. She was one of my regular clients when I worked down here in the District doing hair. She was tough as nails, spoke her mind, and if there was ever a reigning queen of the Point it was her. She was tough and unbelievably beautiful. She was also unabashedly honest and had no problem getting right up in my face and telling me that Titus was a good man, too good for the likes of me, and that I should keep my bloodstained paws off of him. It should have been ridiculous. The words were trite and obvious and she delivered them dressed in nothing but a sparkly G-string and a pair of platform heels that almost made her the same height as me. But it was there in her frosty gray eyes. She really thought Titus was above me, thought I was somehow going to dirty him up and drag him down to the level she and I were at, and she didn't approve. It rubbed me the wrong way, maybe the truth in it, maybe the way I knew she was honestly concerned about what being associated with me would do to Titus's reputation. I only wanted to help him and every time I turned around someone was shoving it in my face that I was going to hurt him whether I wanted to or not.

I told her to back off. I told her Titus was a grown man and could make up his own mind about who he wanted to spend his time with. Key's eyes had narrowed speculatively and she crossed her arms over her naked boobs. She should've looked ridiculous and trashy . . . she didn't. She looked fierce and protective, like an ancient Amazonian warrior, and that just made my hackles rise up even farther. I was worried about Titus just as much as she was. Hell, I was stupidly and hopelessly infatuated with the guy, had a crush built on first impressions that was growing into something so much bigger as I learned more about what was behind his drive to take care of the innocent and good. No one had a bigger stake in how this charade played out with him than I did.

She proceeded to tell me she knew something had to be up, that there was no way the handsome detective would willingly piss off his brother by hanging out with me, that he also wouldn't be so handsy and affectionate because he wasn't that way with anyone. It was the presumption that she somehow *knew* Titus better than I did, that she had intimate knowledge of how he operated, that sent me over the edge. Without thinking, I poked her in the center of her naked chest and told her that obviously he was that touchy-feely, was that hands-on with someone he really wanted. Her eyes had gone predatory, and before I could stop myself I reacted, lunging for her, taking her to the ground before she could get a shot in. The first rule in the Point was to never show any kind of weakness, so I attacked before I could be attacked. It was simple street logic.

There was no hair pulling. There was no delicate screeching. Nope, we went after each other with closed fists and powerful punches. She even caught the inside of my thigh with the edge of one of those lethal heels and the resulting scratch had blood spilling down my leg. It really hurt but so did all of her pointed accusations, which was why I threw myself at Titus as soon as the bathroom door clicked closed behind him.

I wasn't thinking straight. The heat of his hands when he pulled me off the stripper, the blazing silver in his eyes as he looked at my now bloody face . . . it all scrambled my brain. All I could think was that I did want what was best for him, and that despite himself, he wanted me. I locked my hands around the back of his neck where the short brush of his hair tickled my fingers, and sealed my mouth over his as soon as I told him he was right about things never being fine.

I held on tight because I expected him to shake me off, to tell me this was too much and there was no one to put on a show for in here. I expected him to pull away with something haunting and hollow in his too blue eyes.

What I got was completely unexpected from the serious and intent Titus King. Instead of distance, I got backed into the sink so hard that the edge of the counter bit hard into my thighs. Instead of blank space, I got a man returning my kiss just as ferociously as I was giving it to him. I got a rock-hard thigh pressed between my own as my legs were forced apart and an erection that was impossible to ignore even between the layers of clothes pressed up against the tender parts of me that were suddenly every kind of achy and wet.

I jolted as a paper-towel holder got whacked hard enough with an elbow to fall off the wall as Titus lifted one of his hands and clasped it around my neck while the other dived under the hem of the simple T-shirt he had just bought for me. The bathroom was tiny and Titus was really, really not. There wasn't a lot of room to maneuver and yet he still managed to get me up on the counter and my shirt off over my head without breaking anything else or causing either of us bodily harm.

My chest was heaving and I was sure my eyes were wild as I clung to him like he was the last lifeline I was ever going to get and without him I would inevitably drown. I leaned forward and kissed him again, tasting the copper bite of blood and the warm cleanness that was somehow simply Titus. He tasted like he looked, strong, sure, and potent. He tasted like righteousness and honor. Redemption and repentance. He tasted like goodness, and I didn't think there was ever any way I was going to get enough of it.

I twirled my tongue around his. I sucked him in and let him fill me up from the inside. My nails dug into his skin when I felt him tug impatiently at the cups of the new bra I had just bought. The black fabric was no match for his questing fingers and I thought I was going to pass out from pleasure when the pad of his thumb swept over the crest of one suddenly puckered nipple. I gasped into his mouth and he just pulled me closer to that ridge behind his zipper and settled even more firmly into the kiss that was making me see stars.

There had been those who touched me in the past, who knew what they were doing, who made me feel wanted, beautiful, and necessary. But no one had ever made me feel owned and devoured the way Titus did. It was the brush of his thumb back and forth, it was the clench of his fingers at my nape, and it was the pressure from his leg as he pulled me closer and closer. He was everywhere, even where we weren't touching, and I had a feeling there was never going to be a way for me to get around him, which meant I was going to have to go inside of him to find space.

I adored the gruff, far-too-serious Titus that I tormented daily. But the unhinged, uncontrolled Titus was irresistible as he roughly palmed my now naked breast and grunted at me when I snaked a hand between us to fondle that hard length throbbing between us. The wild inside of him when he let it out was the most intoxicating thing I had ever seen and felt, and I knew I better eat every single second of it up while I got the chance. Because once he got his wits back, Titus was going to be furious that he had let the lock off the cage and that his inner beast had been allowed to run free for a few stolen moments in the bathroom of a strip club.

My fingers clawed at the denim that was keeping him from me and I threw back my head with a sudden jerk as his mouth left mine and landed with precision on the nipple he had been torturing with a rough touch. Fire zipped along every nerve ending and something more than passion started to buzz in my ears.

His mouth was hotter than hot and it was greedy. I was stunned and turned on beyond belief that my stalwart detective didn't seem to care about soft touches and gentle caresses. He was all forceful hands and the sting of strong teeth. Titus was rough, and it was un-fucking-believable. I muttered his name and tried to get my hands under his heavy leather belt and behind his zipper but there wasn't enough room. We were too close to each other and he had me trapped while he consumed my sensitive skin with his mouth. I panted and wiggled, wanting to get in on some of the touching action myself, but he wouldn't relent. In fact those thick fingers in my hair tightened and pulled hard enough to make my eyes water just a little bit.

"Stop." His voice was a growl that vibrated against my throat as he abandoned my chest and sank his teeth into the tender skin on the side of my neck, making it tremble under his lips.

"I want to touch you." I sounded whiny and desperate. Two things I had never been before this man.

"No. We are not doing this." He continued to kiss and nibble his way up behind my ear and I wanted to ask him what in the hell he was talking about, obviously we *were* doing something, but then he moved faster than a man that big should be able to and he took a step back and speared me with molten eyes. "We aren't doing this, period, but we are absolutely not going to do it in a strip-club bathroom after you started a catfight, and with zero protection . . ." He trailed off and shook his head at me like we were both crazy. "I've made some questionable decisions since you came back to town, Reeve, but contrary to my recent actions, I do know where to draw the line."

I stared at him. My body heaved, which drew his gaze to my still-naked chest. If I were someone else I would've covered myself to hide my shame. I wasn't someone else, I was just me, and just me had had enough of the hot and cold with him. I narrowed my eyes at him and hopped off the counter where he had placed me. He took a step back but there wasn't much room for him to go, so he ended up with his back against the door as I prowled closer to him, pulling my bra the rest of the way off as I went. He watched me warily until I was directly in front of him. Defiance and passion were warring for supremacy in his still-flaming blue and silver gaze.

I had done a lot of wrong things in my life for the wrong kind of men. This would be the first time I did something wrong for the right man. I didn't care where it was or what was going to come of it, I wanted the part of him he let out to play just for me. Sure, the location left a lot to be desired, but I was taking the part of Titus that was mine and he wasn't going to stop me, not that he really wanted to anyway. Sure, having him fully wasn't going to happen today. He was right that having sex with no protection was a stupid mistake for either one of us to make, but he was wrong about it *never* happening and he knew it. I saw it in the way his dark complexion turned ruddy as I grabbed his bulky belt buckle and pulled the end of his belt through it. It should feel dirty and seedy. It didn't. It felt right and unavoidable.

The leather made a whooshing sound that echoed in the tiny

tiled room. "This is my questionable decision not yours, and I have never paid attention to the lines, Detective."

The belt fell away and the zipper that was straining, hard, sounded twice as loud as I started to pull it down. I wasn't surprised when his hand caught my wrist. I was surprised that he didn't yank it away but just held it immobile, the cotton of his boxers and the heat of his erection burning against the back of my knuckles.

"Why? It won't mean anything. It doesn't change what's going on with us. Crossing that line whether you see it or not doesn't make this act we're putting on any different."

Always the cop with the interrogation and the need for a motive. I cocked my head to the side and he groaned as the long strands of my hair slid across the full curve of my breasts.

"You take care of everyone, always. Maybe I want to take care of you." I lifted an eyebrow and slicked my tongue across my bottom lip. "This *is* happening, Titus. Fight it all you want but you can see it coming from miles and miles away."

We stared at each other in silence for what felt like a solid minute and then he threw his head back so that it thumped against the door with a bang and let go of my hand at the same time. "I usually avoid trouble when it's headed my way."

"Not this kind of trouble."

I got his zipper the rest of the way down, excited about my victory for more than one reason. He wasn't giving in to me for good, but he was giving in to me for now and that was good enough. I laughed a little as I pulled his pulsating cock out of the confines of his underwear. He was impressive *everywhere*. I wasn't surprised. He was the best of the best, so of course his dick would have to fall in that category as well. He jerked in my hand as I rubbed my thumb on the tip where the evidence that despite any reluctance his mind might have, his body and the wild inside of him was loose, leaking out and calling to me.

He grunted in response as I dropped to my knees in front of him. It wasn't my favorite position to be in for any man, it smacked of weakness and submission, but here it felt like power, like taking what was mine. I didn't care about the appropriateness of the time or the location. All of that faded next to the way he burned in my mouth as I sucked him in and played with him. His eyes had drifted to half-mast and all I could see as he watched me was a storm of swirling silver. He was still fighting, he refused to move with me, refused to touch me . . . at least he did until the beast woke back up as I twirled my tongue around and around the aching tip. I was just adding my hands to the mix, curling a tight fist around the base of his erection, when suddenly his hands where in my hair and he was moving into me.

"You're fucking dangerous." His voice was hoarse as he slowly started to give me what I wanted. I hummed in agreement and used my other hand to hold on to the impossibly tight globe of his ass. "Why can't I resist you?"

He sounded angry, but he didn't stop moving and I had to really concentrate on what I was doing because once again he wasn't soft or easy and that was a whole lot of man to try and handle. God, did I want to handle him in a million different ways. I squeezed my hand even tighter and tilted my head back just a little when he guided me with rough hands.

His eyes were open all the way now and they were trying to melt me onto the bathroom floor with their intensity. I saw his broad chest start to rise and fall more rapidly. I felt the way his cock quivered all along my tongue as I hollowed my cheeks and sucked him down as far as I could stand. I felt the muscle I was holding on to flex so hard it felt like stone under my touch and then he swore at me again and it was all over in a hot rush of desire and some more bad words.

We were both breathing heavily as I rocked back and then climbed to my feet. We watched each other like combatants instead of almost-lovers, and I turned around without a word to clean the blood off my face and to get dressed. Caring about this man was hazardous, and if Conner didn't end up pulling the trigger first, the feelings I had for Titus might very well be the end of me.

I pushed my hair back after I got myself situated and looked at him in the mirror, where I could see him watching me as he zipped up his pants.

"I don't know, Titus, but if you can't resist me, maybe you should stop trying so hard. In this place you never know what pile of shit tomorrow is going to hand you, so having something that makes you feel good for even a second needs to be valued."

He shoved his hands through his hair and then reached down by his hip to twist the door open. There was no hiding what we had been in here doing. It was all over him. I was all over him and he was most definitely stamped all over me. I loved it.

"You shouldn't be what makes me feel good, Reeve." There it was. The harsh reality of the way things were between us. Him on one side of the divide and me always on the other.

"But I do, and you're just going to have to learn how to deal with that." I swept past him back out into the strip club, hoping he wouldn't see the way my knees wobbled. I flipped my hair and shoved my hands in my pockets assuming he would guide us to the door. We had definitely made an impression tonight, and if Conner had eyes in the club, there was no missing the way we had just come out of the same bathroom all rumpled and sexed up. Mission accomplished, even if my heart and my ego had taken an equal pounding with Titus's last harsh words.

I was surprised and a little annoyed when he stopped in front of one of the stages where Nassir was standing with Chuck. I saw both men give me a once-over then smirk at the dark-haired cop. The lights suddenly went down and an old, bluesy jazz song started to blast through the sound system. I shifted my gaze to the stage as a burning-white spotlight suddenly hit it and a girl dressed in a way-sexified, old-timey gangster outfit strutted her stuff onto the stage. She had the fedora. She had the suspenders. She had a gun stuck in her garter belt. She even had a lit cigar clamped between her teeth as she sashayed around the stage in platform Mary Janes. I tried not to bristle as all three of the men stopped what they were talking about to watch her as her white button-up blouse hit the floor, quickly followed by her tiny black skirt. She had a great body and she was really working the crowd, but even with the blinding stage lights it looked like she was staring right at where Titus was standing.

I huffed out a breath and turned my head as a body moved up next to mine. Key had gotten dressed and she was now sporting a puffy eye but she still looked better than anyone had the right to. She grinned at me as I glared at her. "You hit like a girl."

I snorted a response. "Those shoes of yours are deadly."

"Why do you think I wear them all the time?" She stuck her leg out and I noticed she did have crazy pointy and tall heels on even though she was now dressed in jeans and a T-shirt. She tilted her head to where the men appeared engrossed in the erotic scene on the stage. I wanted to kick Titus. "You're gonna have to brawl with more than just me for him. You're gonna have to fight Bax, the city . . . hell, you're even going to have to throw down with him if you want him."

I lifted an eyebrow as the music picked up and seemed to get louder. The girl was now down to nothing but her G-sting and she wasn't dancing so much as she was writhing on the stage. She looked like she was making love to an invisible man.

"I've been fighting every single day of my life. Sometimes I think all I have left is fight." If anything was worth the fight it would be any time I had with Titus before things inevitably blew up around us.

She gave me a real smile, not the one she used to con men out of money or get people to think she was just a dumb stripper. It made her look like an entirely different person. She went from a sex goddess to a normal woman, one that just happened to be amazingly beautiful.

"Fighting is all any of us know inside and out. It's exhausting." I muttered my agreement and seriously considered reaching out to pinch Titus in the arm as the girl on the stage acrobatically shifted to her feet and slinked to the edge of the stage. She spit the now stubby stogie out of her mouth much to her audience's delight and pulled the gun she had in her leg band out of the garter. She pointed it out into the crowd. I thought it was a toy, maybe filled with water or those little plastic caps that made cute popping noises.

I was wrong.

Before she pulled the trigger, I was hit by a truck. Not really a truck but getting slammed to the ground with Titus's full body weight sure felt like it. Gunshots echoed through the club, as did

screams of pain from both men and women as the gun continued to go off. I heard Titus scream something at Nassir and then
he was gone, his hands flying to where his gun rode on his hip. I
went to scramble up after him but bodies were everywhere, running for the door trying to escape the melee. I turned my head to
see where Key had ended up and gasped when I saw the bright
red bloom of crimson that was decorating her chest.

On my hands and knees I scrambled across the floor, trying
not to think about how gross that was, until I got to her. Her
gray eyes were wide open and I could hear that she was gasping for air. A few moments ago she had tried to kick my ass and
now she looked like she was dying right in front of me. I put my
hands over the bullet wound and told her, "Hey, you can't go
anywhere. This place needs you." I meant the city, not the sleazy
strip club, and I hoped she knew that. "You get me, Keelyn." Her
eyes drifted closed and I pushed harder on the wound.

Her blood was hot and stick as it leaked through my fingers.
"Key?" No response, so I pressed even harder and hollered, "Honor!"

Her eyes popped open and she snapped at me, "Don't call
me that."

I laughed a little and then was roughly pushed aside by hard
hands. I looked up at Nassir as he sank down on his knees next
to us. Without a word he stripped off his expensive suit jacket
and tossed it to the ground. It immediately got trampled under
fleeing feet.

"You can't die." His voice was harsh as he pulled off his pristine white shirt and balled it up into a makeshift bandage as he
pressed it to the nasty wound. The situation was dire, but even
so I took a second to admire the landscape of smooth, burnished
bronze skin he revealed. Nassir wasn't built like a mountain like

Titus, but he sure was pretty and I'd had no idea the enigmatic club owner had a massive tattoo that covered his entire back. From shoulder to shoulder and all the way down his spine and even into the top of his tailored slacks ink marked his skin. I couldn't make out what the scene was and it wasn't the right time to take a good look at it.

"I can do whatever the hell I want, Gates. You don't own me." Key wheezed the words out as she struggled to breathe.

To which he growled, "I would if you would let me."

I was glad Key sounded like she had some of her natural fight back and now that some of the smoke had cleared I wanted to make sure Titus was all right. I didn't know what was up with those two, Key and Nassir, but it was intense and slightly suffocating.

Titus was kneeling next to Chuck, who also seemed to be bleeding pretty heavily. My gaze darted to the stage and I cringed when I saw the dancer crumpled like a lifeless doll in a heap. I didn't need to wonder if she was dead or not, the steady trickle of blood from the side of her head was a clear indicator. She was too young to meet an end like that. The gun was still clenched in her hand and there was scattered money and the scent of expelled gunpowder everywhere. It looked like a scene out of a Tarantino movie.

I made my way over to Titus and breathed a silent sigh of relief when his eyes darted up to mine.

"I knew something was off. I just couldn't put my finger on it. I kept staring at her, trying to figure out if I knew who she was or if I had seen her somewhere before . . . I thought she might have a warrant out or something. It was the fucking gun. I should've known it was real."

Chuck grunted and asked Titus to help him up. "It's my job, man. I'm the one that should've seen it." His dark eyes drifted over to where Nassir was leaning over Keelyn. "Better get some help for her quick. If that girl dies he will lose his ever-loving mind."

"I already called it in." Titus put his hands on his hips and survived the carnage that surrounded us. "Who was she?"

Chuck was poking at his shoulder and I saw him totter on his feet a little as he prodded the wound. I reached out a hand to steady him and all three of us looked to where the girl had fallen. I wondered if it was Titus who had taken the shot or one of the other guys.

"I don't really know. Nassir hired her on to replace the girl we lost on the docks. She told him she was a student and just needed some extra cash. You know how crazy he is about security. She would have had to pass his background check."

Titus shifted on his feet and reached behind him to collect a kicked-over chair. He shoved it at the big bouncer. "Sit your ass down before you fall over." He scrubbed his hands over his face and narrowed his eyes as he surveyed the scene. "It could be Roark."

I fidgeted nervously and nodded a little to show I agreed with his logic. "The girl he killed looked like me, but she also worked here. He knows how vital Spanky's is to the Point and to Nassir and Race now that the Pit is gone. Conner could have planted her inside here."

He didn't say anything but I could see him considering my words carefully, so I added, "He's handsome and charming. He knows exactly what to say to get you to believe you are the only one for him. She was young and probably was just an innocent college kid. He knows how to pick his targets. Maybe she was supposed to try and destroy Spanky's from the inside out and he heard that we were here tonight, so he upped the game. She was staring at you, Titus. That first shot was meant for you."

I was sure of it, and I was sure Conner had a hand in this and I could see by the stony expression on his face that Titus agreed. Just then the doors to the club burst open and EMTs with gurneys rushed in. Keelyn and Chuck weren't the only ones injured in the cross fire and everyone was watching Nassir like he was a bomb about to go off.

Titus's cop buddies showed up, and all of a sudden I was just the girl he was fooling around with in the bathroom and not the other half of the team that was here to take down a criminal mastermind. I sighed heavily and went over to the bar to pour myself a drink and wash even more blood off my hands.

There was always more blood, always more violence and mayhem, and I hated feeling like my decision to come back had increased the volume and frequency on both those things.

It was good to be home. Sigh . . .

Chapter 8

Titus

I T HAD BEEN A couple of days since the shootout at Spanky's, and once again I was buried in work and avoiding Reeve like she had the plague.

Tracking down witnesses was impossible. It wasn't like the people that spent their off-hours at a strip club wanted anyone to know where their hard-earned money was actually going, and when I found the family of the girl who had been behind the massacre, I was stunned that she was indeed just a normal college girl with a mom and dad who lived in a nice house up on the Hill. Her parents had no idea that she was dancing at Spanky's, and when I told them she had shot the place up and injured no fewer than five people, they were stunned. It was completely out of character for her, and according to them, she had never even seen a gun, so they couldn't believe she was capable of pulling one on a roomful of people. So not only were they tasked with burying their daughter, they also had to process that they really had no clue who she had become or what she had gotten herself into down in the bowels of the Point.

It seemed like Reeve's theory that Roark had sunk his claws into the girl might have some merit. People did crazy things in the name of love. I just didn't have it in me to tell her that she was right. If my head hadn't been spinning, if everything inside of me hadn't been tugging ferociously at the leash to get at her, to get in her, to have her no matter what common sense said, I would've noticed the gun was real. I was watching the girl take off her clothes dispassionately. No naked girl was ever going to compare to the one that I had almost nailed on the counter in Spanky's bathroom and that was just a hard-and-fast fact. But there was something about the stripper that bugged me. I just couldn't place it because my head was still thundering with lust and my nerves were still jangling with want.

I should have spotted the tiny .22-caliber from a mile away, but all I could see was Reeve on her knees in front of me with all of that dark hair of hers tangled in my hands as she turned me inside out with a creative twirl of her tongue and the perfect scrape of her teeth. She knew how to work me over and take such good care of me at the same time. I was trying to keep her alive, trying to keep myself alive, and maybe, just maybe, get both of us out of this situation without broken hearts.

She wasn't helping. I could see it in her eyes when she looked at me. She cared. I didn't think a girl that made the kind of choices she did, who had to look out for herself above all others to survive, could be that empathetic, but it bled out of her and got all over me. She cared a lot. About me. And I wasn't sure what to do with that. I was the one always worrying about everyone, about everything. I had never had someone else in my life that was concerned for me and for my well-being. It made my resolve to stay away from her even weaker than it already was, and goddamn, did I want to see what else she could do with that clever mouth of hers.

I jerked my head up when my office door suddenly opened and an older man dressed in khaki pants and a white polo shirt waltzed in and made himself comfy in the chair across from my desk. He had steely-gray hair and a flinty face that reminded me of Clint Eastwood in *The Good, the Bad and the Ugly*. All he needed was a ratty poncho and a cigar.

I closed the case folder I was going over and leaned back in my chair. I didn't know who the guy was but everything about his posture and the way he made himself comfortable as I assessed him screamed "cop." We tended to be able to spot our own no matter what branch or badge we might carry.

"Can I help you?"

The stranger crossed his ankle on his knee and started tapping his fingers on his leg. "I sure as hell hope so, son, otherwise we're all going to be neck-deep in a bloodbath."

His voice had a quiet drawl, not exactly a southern or even a Texan twang, but there was some country to it, so I put him from somewhere around Virginia or the Carolinas. I lifted an eyebrow at him and waited for him to formally introduce himself. He watched me silently for a long minute before a weathered grin cracked his face.

"Deputy Chief Marshal Otis Packard. I heard through the grapevine you have one of my witnesses in protective custody with no intention of turning her back over to us."

I snorted. "The situation is a lot more complicated than that."

He nodded and narrowed his eyes. "Tell me about it. Out of the four witnesses that we either placed or had plans to move while we were waiting for the Novak case to go before a judge, she's the only one left breathing. Hartman went down first, Ernie Diaz, the club owner, went missing last week, and

Benny Truman didn't even make it out of the joint. Hartman was buried so deep in a shithole town in West Texas there was no way anyone should've been able to find him and Ernie was so scared of retribution that he quit talking to anyone without credentials, so we know he had to have been popped by someone on the inside."

I made a noise low in my throat. "You knew someone was offing the witnesses from your case and you just left her out there unprotected?"

"She took off when we were starting to put it all together. She was quicker than we were. We were planning to go in and get her right after the info on Hartman came in, only she was gone, and so was the marshal in charge of her case."

"You had a fox guarding your henhouse from the get-go."

The other cop considered me thoughtfully for a second and then nodded solemnly. "It looks that way."

"You're looking at Roark for the rest of the murders, right?" "

His jaw started to tick furiously. "We put it together. Too late. Conner has a stellar reputation in our division. He was a marine, and when he got out of the service he worked for Border Patrol. He was always our go-to guy until all this stuff broke loose with Novak. We didn't realize the correlation until it was too late. A few years ago he started taking a real interest in what was going on here in the Point, started asking to be assigned to cases that were here. When you got the feds involved to take down Novak, he was the first one that wanted in on the action."

No one wanted to get involved with the Point. We were a lost cause down here in the gutter. All the warning bells that had been jangling that Roark's motivations were more involved than showing Race and Nassir he didn't appreciate them taking over Novak's business started to ring loud and clear in my ears. "Don't you have to be an American citizen to be in the marshals? Roark's Irish."

"His mom is Irish. Conner has dual citizenship."

"What about his dad? What's the story there?" I knew from firsthand experience with my brother just how important the influence of a father could be. It might be a good place to start digging.

"Not sure. He always said his old man was a soldier from Colorado that had a brief fling with his mom. The guy got Conner every summer, but who knows if it's the truth or not. Turns out Conner is an exceptional liar. Now that we've done some digging, it looks like while he was a member of Border Patrol after he left the military he was helping Novak and several of his associates move guns and drugs across the border. Conner's been dirty a really long time and I feel like a fool for personally assigning him to this case."

I frowned and asked him if he could give me the man in Colorado's name. The older man scribbled a quick note on a loose piece of paper on my desk and shoved it toward me. "Why would a decorated agent suddenly start helping a known criminal move illegal stuff across the border? Money? Did Novak threaten him?"

The older man shook his head. "I don't know. We need to find Conner to ask him that."

I wasn't patient enough for that. I was missing something key, something that would possibly give me the upper hand in dealing with Roark and help me find him. I needed to figure out what it was.

"He burned down the Pit. He beat the crap out of one of the working girls that's been around these parts a long time. On top of murder, he's taking revenge on the people of the Point by hitting them where it hurts the most. Reeve figured out that he was involved with Hartman's murder, and ran."

"Why did she run to you? The evidence seems to point to her and Conner being awfully chummy. Just one more rule that bastard broke."

I sighed. "I don't know. She trusts me. She knows I'm not a dirty cop and that all I want to do is stop him before anyone else gets hurt. He killed a girl just to leave Reeve a message and he had another one shoot up a strip club last night. This guy is effectively bringing the Point to its knees and he's doing it without being seen. He's like a puff of smoke and just as toxic."

"He's good." Begrudging respect colored the older man's voice.

"Too good." I ran my hands over my hair and looked at the empty coffee mug sitting on the edge of my desk. I needed to eat. I needed to sleep. I needed to get laid, and more than all of that I needed get my head on straight. "So why exactly are you here?"

"I'm here because Novak's case is in the garbage. Everyone that had any information we could use is gone. Benny was on the verge of giving us the entire portfolio of suppliers and distributors if we promised him immunity and a brand-new life in sunny Orlando, but like I said, someone got to him before we could make that happen. We need to stop Roark. He's dangerous, and not just because he's skilled and unbalanced, but because he has the training to do serious damage. You already know that the folks keeping this place afloat are a target, but so are you and the girl. Conner isn't going to take being double-crossed lightly."

"Already figured that out for myself." I pointed to the word on the door that said DETECTIVE. "Kind of my job."

"Well, the girl's deal is done. We don't need her to testify anymore."

"So what? You're just planning on throwing her to the wolves and letting her try and fight Roark on her own?"

"No. I think you and I probably have the same idea in mind, son. You know Conner is going to come after her and so do we. We thought we could find him, save the department some embarrassment; turns out he's using our own tricks against us. We want the same thing here, you and I, King. We want Conner brought in."

I grunted. "That was the plan, I'm just not sure how to do it and keep the girl alive in the process. I'm not as eager to dangle her out there like meat and just hope I'm faster on the trigger than Roark is. There has to be a better plan."

"You know you can't afford to lose when it's time to face off with him, and as an incentive you might want to remember that if the girl isn't any use to us, her plea bargain goes away and she's looking at murder-for-hire charges not to mention being an accessory to the abduction for the Pryce girl. We want him brought in; dead or alive is up to you."

I swore and pushed away from my desk. The other man rose to his feet as well, but I still towered over him.

"You left her for dead, and now you would toss her in prison if she's not willing to risk her neck for you? Fuck that."

"She broke the law."

"I understand that, but she agreed to testify against Novak's crew, and when she realized what Roark was up to, she brought that information and that evidence forward. She should still be considered a protected witness."

"She is. As long as she's useful. Make her useful, Detective.

Do what I'm assuming you already have been doing—flaunt her, and show her off. Get Conner to show his hand. You won't be out there alone anymore. We'll put eyes on you and the girl so if he makes a move you have backup. Here's my card. I want to be apprised of any developments in the Roark case. If I was twenty years younger and hadn't been riding a desk for longer than I care to admit, I would handle the fieldwork on this case myself. You remind me a lot of myself, King. I know you will do what needs to be done to take care of business. Like I said, we want the same thing."

I growled at him as he turned to open my office door. I wanted to launch myself over the desk and throttle him. "I wouldn't blackmail a victim to get my own way."

"It's not blackmail. You're already hanging the girl out there as bait. You know Roark is going to charge at her like a hungry shark reacting to blood in the water. I just gave you a friendly reminder of what exactly is at stake should emotion start to interfere with what needs to get done."

"You make it sound like she's expendable." Reeve was driving me crazy, and while I didn't agree with most of the choices she had made that led her to where she was now, she was still a person. She was still a young woman that deserved a shot at righting some of her wrongs. She was trying to help, and trying to do the right thing, and that needed to be acknowledged.

The older cop gave me a hard look. "We are all expendable. We only matter as long as we're doing something to change the world around us, hopefully for the better, but far too often the folks that matter are changing our world for the worse. Good luck, Detective King. You're going to need it."

I watched him wind his way through the chaos of the precinct house and felt my hands clench tightly at my sides. I didn't need luck. I needed a shot. One shot and I was going to bring Conner in and shut him down. I was starting to really resent that the only way to do that was by asking Reeve to offer up her elegant and lovely neck on the chopping block. It didn't seem right even if she kept saying she knew she was doing the right thing, that she was atoning for past sins. If Roark ended up better at this game than I was, paying with her life seemed like an awfully steep price when all she had done was take an abuser and killer off the streets. Using one bad man to rid the world of another bad man suddenly didn't seem like an unforgivable crime. I still struggled with the way she had used Dovie and how her actions had led to what was really one of the worst nights of my life. But everyone used everyone else in the Point so the penance waiting for her shouldn't be any harsher than what was waiting for any of the rest of us.

I took the piece of scrap paper with the name of the man in Colorado the agent had left with me and poked around on the Internet until I thought I found someone that fit the description. It took a little more clicking and two calls to the wrong number before I connected with a man named Alby Jones. He sounded like he smoked twenty packs a day and seemed totally disinterested when I explained that I was a detective looking for information on a possible murder suspect. He was going to hang up on me until I mentioned that I knew he had been in the service; it was the key to opening up the communication door.

He went on and on about his various tours of duty. Regaled me with his heroics and tales of war. I listened patiently because as long as he kept talking I could guide him where I wanted him to go.

I asked if he had ever been married or if he had any kids, and he just snorted, which led to a round of coughing that lasted five minutes. He told me he had been screwed over by a woman once and since then had never trusted the fairer sex again. He explained that he had met a beautiful Irish lass while he was stationed in Turkey. She pursued him, seduced him, and then used him and his status with the military to gain access to weapons she would never have been able to get her hands on otherwise. She used his name and rank to smuggle guns across secure borders, betraying him and ruining his career along the way. He called her a terrorist and then finally, after what felt like hours, mentioned the kid.

A few years after he had been kicked out of the army and sent home disgraced and shamed, the woman contacted him to let him know that he had a son. She wanted money and she wanted his name so that her baby boy could have dual citizenship. The disgraced soldier agreed because despite how she had screwed him, he still loved the beautiful Irish gal and thought raising their son right was the way to win her heart.

Only the boy showed up and the man knew from the start something was wrong with him. He tried to love him, tried to show him guidance, but every summer they spent together the boy seemed to be worse. The man wanted to blame the mother; after all, she was a killer and a terrible person in her own right, but the boy seemed rotten to his very core. He was wild. He was disrespectful. He was cruel to animals and the staff that kept the man's ranch running. He was explosively violent, but what really worried the man was how effortlessly the boy could turn it on and off. He told me when the boy joined the military he thought maybe he would finally turn it around.

Only to his dismay he saw that arming an already unstable young man and teaching him how to kill just made him more violent and dangerous. He told me that his last contact with the man he had always thought was his son was about four years ago. The boy had come home for the holidays right after getting out of the marines and switching to the Border Patrol. The man was looking forward to reconnecting with his son, but what happened had scarred him forever and ripped them apart instead.

According to the man, the boy went missing not long after Christmas dinner. No one thought much about it until they noticed one of the young women who helped take care of the house was also gone. Sure, it could just be two young lovers escaping for a quiet moment alone, but the man knew better, so he went to find his troubled son.

The boy had the girl pinned down in the barn, a knife to her neck and seconds away from ruining her for life. The man pulled the boy off the girl, they struggled, and the man ended up getting a knife to the gut for his troubles.

"I knew you were too weak and pathetic to be my father," the boy said as he stood over the man scoffing. With that, the son kicked him in the ribs and disappeared out of the man's life forever, leaving the poor bastard that had raised him to bleed out where he lay. Only the man was a fighter and had survived the destruction both the mother and son had leveled at him. He was all too happy to tell me all about it.

While he talked my skin pulled tight across my body and I felt a tick start to work in my jaw. All those pieces that had been missing started to land in my lap and I suddenly couldn't see anything but a familiar black gaze dancing in front of my eyes. I cleared my throat and asked the man if he had any idea who the kid's real dad was and the man replied, "Someone just as twisted, brutal, and messed up as he was."

I thanked the man for his time, sat back in my chair, and kicked my desk hard enough that it moved two inches across the floor.

"Son of a bitch!" I couldn't believe I hadn't thought of the connection sooner. Just like Novak had tried to sink his claws into Bax in order to groom him into his own vision, he had done the exact same thing with his other illegitimate spawn out there in the world.

Roark had to be Novak's son, and of course the criminal mastermind hadn't had a thing to do with him until he was old enough to be useful. When Roark joined the Border Patrol, Novak swooped in and got his hands on his already tainted offspring. He had done the same with Bax, ignoring my brother until his skill at stealing cars proved useful. It all clicked into place and it made my heart start to pound.

Roark wasn't trying to exact some kind of righteous vengeance because Race and Nassir were taking over Novak's business; he was paying them back for killing his father. The father—it was now obvious—that he shared with my younger brother. Bax was undoubtedly going to be in Roark's crosshairs since he most definitely had a hand in ending Novak's life. It all had dread settling heavily in my stomach I needed to call my brother ASAP and warn him to watch his back. Just as I was getting ready to dial Bax's number I saw his face light up the screen of my phone. I knew he was going to be pissed about the situation with Reeve, but I needed him on my side and I needed him to know just how careful he would have to be considering he was one of Roark's targets.

"Hey."

"So you're alive. I was starting to wonder."

I rolled my eyes at his tone and could practically see him squinting through the cigarette smoke as I heard him exhale.

"Shit's been crazy."

"I heard. Nassir was more than happy to tell me all about the shootout at the club and the fact you disappeared with that bitch into the back for an unspecified amount of time. I know you put her up at Race's, but I didn't know you were sleeping with the enemy."

I grunted at him as I crossed the parking lot. "Meet me at the diner by the station. I need to eat and I'll fill you in. I have a lot of stuff I need to talk to you about."

"You're done avoiding me?" I could just imagine the way the black star he had tattooed by his eye was twitching in aggravation.

"Listen, I just got you to trust me after everything that went down five years ago. I don't want this girl and what I have to do with her to mess that up. I didn't know how to make you understand that right now she is important and not have you mess with it. Besides, we have much bigger problems on our hands than where I'm sticking my dick."

"She almost got my girl killed."

I sighed because I could still hear how much that tore him up in his voice. "I understand that, Shane. I really do, but sometimes we have to do things we don't like and don't agree with because the end game is bigger than us and our own. Do you get me?"

I heard him exhale again and then a flood of really nasty words hit my ears. "I'll be at the diner in ten. Order me a burger."

Relief hit me hard that he was at least willing to hear me out. Bax and I hadn't exactly been close growing up, but now that we were adults and both in the trenches, albeit on opposite sides, I really felt like we needed each other. I loved my brother and it had taken watching him almost blow his brains out right in front of me to realize how empty my life had been while he was gone. I needed a reason beyond right and wrong to keep up the fight. I needed Bax to remind me that sometimes the bad guys weren't bad because they wanted to be; they were that way because they didn't have any other choice. Bax hadn't had a fair shot from the get-go. Not with our mom being a drunk and his dad being a sadistic killer. Not to mention that I had bailed on him when he needed me the most. It was a miracle the kid had as much humanity in him as he did. It was my job to give my brother options, to remind him that he mattered even if we disagreed, and I would do it until they put me in the ground.

The diner was packed with fellow cops and the only spot available was near the door. It was too exposed and I didn't want to sit there, but my stomach was growling, so I relented and slid into the booth. The waitress hurried over and I ordered the burgers and coffee. The tension that was sitting in my neck was so tight that pain shot up the back of my head in agonizing waves when I reached for the steaming mug she held out to me. The only time that I had felt any measure of peace, felt any kind of relaxation or mindless oblivion, was when Reeve had done exactly what she had threatened to do and taken care of me. I wasn't the kind of guy that got naked and down and dirty in a strip-club bathroom, but it was the only time in recent memory I had been able to let go of everything else I hauled around all the time. There was no Bax. There was no Point. There was no Roark. There was no job that was slowly wearing me down and turning me into a hollow shell of a man. There was just a beautiful woman with dark blue eyes that had everything that made my life and dick hard inside of them and the amazing things she was doing to me. I shouldn't want her, but I did, and the level that want was growing to was really starting to get bigger than me and any reservations I might have had.

I made small talk with a couple of patrol cops that stopped by my table to ask about the shootout at the club. In particular they wanted to know how "Honor" was doing. Keelyn had a place in the hearts of many single and lonely guys in the city, so I told them she was doing okay. She had taken a bullet to the chest and another one had caught her in the shoulder and lodged in the bone. She was a mess and she had lost way too much blood and required surgery, but she was awake now and she was pissed off. According to Nassir, who was blowing up my phone demanding any information I had on Roark, she had quit and told him she was leaving the Point. Nassir seemed to think she was just blowing smoke, but I wasn't so sure. Keelyn had been in the gutter since the beginning. I wouldn't blame her if she was ready for some new scenery, and I saw the way Nassir had freaked out when he caught sight of her bleeding on the floor. She might have been able to stay out of his clutches so far, but eventually he would wear her down. That would mean she was going to be stuck here in this place, with him, forever. I recognized the way he looked at her. He wanted to possess her.

The waitress dropped the food in front of me just as I heard the roar of Bax's Hemi 'Cuda coming from blocks away. That car was a beast. It was louder, faster, and meaner than mine. I totally had motor envy. My little brother was a magician when it came to old muscle cars. What he could do to them was art. The patrol cops nodded in appreciation and got shiny eyes of envy when I mentioned it was Bax's ride making all that noise. It was ingrained in male DNA to get a little bit of a hard-on when a car sounded as powerful and badass as the Hemi did. The GTO was prime but I wouldn't put it up against Bax's ride because my ego couldn't handle getting shown up.

I was spewing facts about horsepower and torque when one of the guys made a strange face and pointed out the window. My heart immediately stopped because the last time someone did that in this diner Race's car was on fire in the parking lot. Another unforgettable calling card from Roark.

"What?"

"I dunno. A garbage truck just went flying up the street. It's not trash day in this part of town and it looked like it was in a hurry."

I didn't hear the rest of the sentence. My ears were ringing as I scrambled out of the booth and pushed past both the uniformed cops who were standing by the entrance. I hit the door just as the sound of tires squealing and the screech of metal on metal drowned out every other sound and made my ears ring. Several of the other diner patrons had followed me out, but I was oblivious to everything but my brother's car, which was crumpled in an unrecognizable heap under the heavy front end of a massive garbage truck.

I heard screaming and the sound of people calling for help, but I didn't realize it was me until my hands hit the metal as I tried to pull the collapsed driver's-side door open to get to Bax.

"Shane!" I was pulling and pulling but the metal wasn't moving and neither was Bax. He was folded over, his shaved head resting on the twisted steering wheel. Blood was streaming all across his face and out of the ear that was turned my way. It didn't look like he was breathing, and I was about to shove my fist through the still-intact window when a set of hands clasped around me and tried to pull me back. The skin on the palms of my hands ripped away and my own blood left gory tracks on the metal as I continued to scream Bax's name, desperate for any kind of response, any sign of life or movement.

I turned around and without a second thought swung at the cop that was trying to pull me back. "That's my brother in there!"

My little brother in a car that looked like a tuna can.

My little brother who was bleeding way too much and not moving.

My little brother who had survived every single shitty thing life had thrown at him and had finally found some good in his life.

My little brother who was finally recognizing that he had people that cared about him, so he needed to care about himself.

I would move the garbage truck with my bare hands if I had to.

"Detective, the first responders have the Jaws of Life. We're gonna need to cut him out."

I slammed my fist into the window and called Bax's name again. He still didn't move. I let myself be dragged backward as the firefighters surrounded the car. While I was trying to bend metal with my bare hands, paramedics and my fellow cops, as well as an entire fleet of firefighters, had arrived on the scene. I started barking orders, telling anyone that would listen to go look for whoever had been driving the truck. I knew Roark was behind it. I had no idea how he knew where Bax would be, or how he had gotten his hands on a massive battering ram like the trash truck, but I knew it was him. And I was going to annihilate him when I finally got my hands on him.

Metal groaned and screamed in protest as they worked to

pull Bax free. I moved forward and kept getting pulled back. It felt like it had taken a lifetime even if only a few moments had gone by, when the car door suddenly popped open and Bax's big body slumped out. He looked worse not surrounded by the protective shell of the 'Cuda. I could see one of his legs was really messed up. I could also see that his chest was indeed moving, but slowly and laboriously. I rubbed my hands over my face and tried not to lose it. I didn't even care that I was smearing blood all over myself from my torn hands.

"I need to call his girlfriend."

Dovie was going to freak out. Rightfully so. With all the dangerous and dirty stuff Bax messed around in, here it was a car accident that was going to have him fighting for his life. It was so unfair I was choking on it and couldn't see around it. I fumed as the paramedics strapped him down and started rolling him toward the waiting ambulance. I had never seen my brother look so fragile or so helpless. That included when he was just a little kid and I had to explain to him that I was moving out, leaving him to fend for himself because there was no other way. He looked broken and it was making everything inside of me howl with the need to do something, to seek some kind of retribution. I never considered myself the vengeful type. I put too much stock in the law and justice for that, but right now all I wanted was revenge. I wanted to bury Roark in a casket of metal and pain just like he had done to Bax.

"His pulse is thready, and he's losing a lot of blood. We're taking him to City General. Time is a factor. They have a trauma unit already waiting for us."

Time was a factor? No kidding. He wasn't moving at all and

there was no color to him other than the black of his star and the red that was covering his face and soaking into his T-shirt. He looked like a corpse.

"You want to ride with us, Detective?"

No. No I didn't want to climb in the back of that ambulance and watch them fight to keep my brother alive, because if they failed I was going to go nuclear and that wouldn't help anyone. My rage and my grief would only hurt the people who were trying to help, and I didn't want that. I worked hard to keep the beast in the cage; letting him out now wouldn't do me or anyone else any good. Reeve had woken that monster up and now putting him back to sleep was getting harder and harder to do.

"No. I need to call his girlfriend and I need to see if anyone has any info on where the driver of the garbage truck went. I'll be right behind you."

The paramedic looked at Bax as they loaded him into the transport vehicle and then back at me. I had seen that look a hundred times before. I had given family members and victims that look myself. He didn't think Bax was going to make it and he didn't want me to miss any of the last moments I might have with him.

"Just go." I gritted out the words between my teeth and took a step back. I pulled my phone out of my pocket and took a deep breath before I dialed Dovie's number. She answered in her usually cheery way and I literally heard her heart break when I told her what was going on. In typical Dovie fashion, she didn't shriek or shout; she just started breathing heavily and asking me a million questions. I could hear her crying, so I told her I would meet her at the hospital and hung up and called Race. I told him to go get her. She needed to be ready for the worst and there was no way I wanted her driving herself. Race handled the news in much the same way his sister did, but after I gave him the limited amount of information I did have, he assured me he would go get her and that he would see me at the hospital.

When I got off the phone one of the patrol guys that I had been talking to before the accident appeared at my side.

"The real driver stopped for gas a few blocks over. He went in for gas and came out and the truck was gone."

"How in the fuck did he know where Bax was going to be?" I muttered it under my breath as the guys from my precinct started to set up to do their standard accident investigation.

One thing was clear. No one that had been involved in bringing Novak down was safe. Even the baddest of badasses like Shane Baxter could be blindsided, and no one was invincible. A son's thirst for vengeance over the perceived wrongs that had befallen his father was a powerful motivator. Roark had hit Race and Nassir where it hurt both financially and emotionally, but Bax . . . Bax he wanted taken out. It was one brother trying to eliminate the other. We all bled the same and Roark was letting me know he wanted to paint the streets red with everyone he held responsible for his loss.

Chapter 9

Reeve

I HADN'T SEEN TITUS in days. I wanted to go to the hospital but Booker wouldn't let me leave the condo, and part of me knew that even though I desperately wanted to be there for him, he didn't need me there. Bax was in bad shape. He hadn't woken up yet and he had been rushed in for emergency surgery on two separate occasions since they rolled him into the emergency room. He almost didn't make it through the second one, and from what I heard no one was sure when he would wake up . . . or if he would. He also had a shattered ankle, a broken wrist, broken ribs on both sides, a dislocated shoulder, and a broken jaw. The ER doctors had scrambled to cut him open and operate on his punctured liver before he bled to death. So even when he did wake up he wasn't out of the woods, but considering he got run over by a twenty-ton truck and was still breathing, everyone was counting it as a win.

Most of my information was filtered through Brysen's little sister, who seemed to have taken up permanent residence in my living room since Race and Brysen were spending most of their free time at the hospital these days. It didn't escape my notice that while the young and stunning blonde appeared to be working on her homework or playing around on the Internet, she was actually watching every move Booker made like a tiny and ferocious hawk. She definitely didn't like the easy camaraderie that I had developed with the brooding and scarred man. Every time I made him chuckle or he reached out to touch me, she flinched and gave me a look like I had kicked her puppy. I wanted to tell her she was too young and too pretty to waste her heart on the kind of man Booker was, but I figured it wasn't my place and lessons like those had to be learned the hard way. All the important ones did.

It was Friday night and I had sent yet another unanswered text to Titus asking him if he was okay and if he needed anything. I wasn't surprised when silence was what greeted me but I was hurt. I still hadn't figured out how to turn that off yet. I was making grilled cheese to feed Booker and Karsen since we were all apparently going to be stuck together for another night when I decided enough time had passed that I could ask the darkly handsome man for the favor I had been working up to since he had gotten saddled with keeping an eye on me. I glanced over at Karsen, who was watching some silly reality show on the flat screen and facing away from us. The last thing I needed was for her to overhear me and rat me out to Race. Not that the golden Adonis would stop me, but I didn't need him to have something else over my head. He already had too many cards in this tricky game that was playing out between me and Conner.

"Can I ask you to do something for me, Noah?"

His dark eyebrows shot up and the scar that cut down the side of his face pulled tight, making him look menacing and frightening. Race had done well to make Booker his right-hand man. He could stop a person in their tracks with that look alone.

"You can ask."

I sighed and turned around to flip the sandwiches. I kept my voice low because Karsen was far more observant than I think he realized. "I need a gun. Conner has shown us that he's ready to make things bloody and I'm not sure how much longer Titus can keep going with this act we're trying to put on. He's barely holding it together as it is, and now with what happened to Bax"—I shook my head and looked at him over my shoulder—"I need to be able to protect myself."

His gunmetal-colored eyes shifted between gray and blue as he considered me silently. The sides of his mouth pulled down in a frown as he leaned on the counter. "You know how to use a piece?"

I snorted and moved the pan off the heat. I tossed my long hair over my shoulder and turned around to meet his steady gaze. "I grew up in the Point. Titus can't know about it and neither can Race." I shrugged. "They wouldn't be on board with you arming the enemy."

He snorted and took a seat as I pulled out plates to shovel the sandwiches and a handful of chips onto.

"You might be their enemy, but you've never done me wrong and I get where you're coming from. I bet the cop has a clearer idea of how powerful a motivator revenge can be after seeing his brother lie unmoving in that hospital bed for the last week. No man can know the trail of revenge and retaliation until he's had to walk it himself."

I bit my lip and set the plate down in front of him. "So can you help me out?" He was my safest option. I had to be ready for Conner, and if Booker told me no, I was going to have to risk hitting the streets to try to find a dealer on my own. That was the last resort but I would do what I had to in order to put an end to this.

"Why do you call me Noah? Everyone has always called me Booker, everyone except for you. It's also weird and you call Bax Shane, which no one else does."

He changed the subject so fast I blinked in a startled reaction as I called out, "Karsen, one of these sandwiches is for you if you want it." The girl turned on the couch and I saw her chocolate-colored gaze skim over Booker as he bent toward me so we could keep the conversation quiet. She scowled and turned back to the TV. "Maybe later. I'm not really hungry right now."

I sighed and looked back at the massive man across from me. "I call you Noah because you've been nice to me. You've kept me company, and even though you're supposed to be protecting all of them from me, you've been protecting me from them as well. You're more than a thug. More than an ex-con, and I see that. I have to see that because I'm more than they think I am too. So you're more than just Booker to me and to her." I pointed over his broad shoulder to where the teenager was obviously sulking and doing it far more elegantly and glamorously than I would ever be able to. "You do know that girl is in the throes of a life-altering crush on you, right? Her heart is in her eyes when she looks at you."

He glanced over his shoulder and then looked back at me with a lifted eyebrow. The way he did it with that scar made him look like a villain out of a comic book. He snorted and picked up his sandwich and took a hefty bite out of it. "She's just a baby. Her heart isn't grown up enough to know anything yet."

I gave a sharp laugh and turned to the fridge to take out a soda. "My sister fell in love with a man around that age. She loved him so much it killed her. Karsen might be young but those feelings feel ancient and very grown up. You need to be careful with that."

He grunted. "I've told Race to put a chain on it. I've told him she's going to get in trouble looking at men that way. She's too pretty and too soft to have that in her if she's going to be part of the Point. She might as well learn that now."

I reached out, snagged a chip off of his plate, and took a swig of my drink. "She's not looking at men that way, Killer. She's looking at *you* that way. The same way Brysen looks at Race and the same way Dovie looks at Shane."

He grinned at me and it changed his whole face. Booker was a good-looking man once you got past all the intimidation and the shock of that imperfection that covered half his face. When he smiled, when his chilly eyes warmed up, it turned him into a heartbreaker, no doubt about it.

"The way you look at the cop."

I lifted a shoulder and let it fall. "I know how it feels when the person you're looking at doesn't look back, so that's why I'm telling you to be mindful. She's a sweet kid and we both know life will kick her around enough without you adding to it. Besides, I don't want to be murdered in my sleep, and she looks like she's on the verge of taking desperate action."

He laughed again and polished off his sandwich. It was the sound of his rough chuckle that finally brought the teenager over. Her dark eyes were narrowed as she put herself on the stool next to Booker and shifted her gaze between the two of us. She really was a delicate beauty. She looked like merely stepping foot on the streets of the Point would dirty her all up.

"What's so funny?"

I pushed the plate in her direction and she reluctantly picked up half of the sandwich. "Booker was making fun of me for having a crush on Titus."

Karsen blinked in surprise and lifted her pale eyebrows at my confession. "Really. Aren't you guys a thing? Why wouldn't you have a crush on him?"

I winced a little. I forgot that not everyone was privy to the real nature of my relationship with the complicated cop. "We're a thing all right, but that thing is often a lot of work and not always fun, so it's good to still have a crush on the person you care about."

I watched her eyes dart to the side and then back to me. "Oh. I see."

I bet she did. This girl was wise beyond her years and she was going to be a handful when she was legal. I had a feeling the wistful looks and covert watching was going to morph into something Booker was going to have a hell of a time keeping at bay once she was old enough to make her own choices.

"Titus isn't as nice as you would think he would be. I mean he's a cop, one of the good guys and stuff, but he's always so harsh and kind of mean. He scares me a little bit."

From the mouths of babes. I shared a look with Booker and had to bite back a grin. Here this little girl was infatuated with a man that had done hard time, that got paid to break necks and smash faces in for her sister's boyfriend, and she thought Titus was mean and scary.

"It's challenging to be a good man in a bad place. He's the odd man out and it makes him hard."

She grinned a little. "Plus having Bax for a brother would make anyone cranky."

It was a somber reminder why the rest of this little group wasn't around on this Friday night. Booker pushed his plate away and leaned over to nudge Karsen with his shoulder. She immediately turned a neon pink, and it was so cute I just wanted to hug her. A pang hit me low in the gut when I thought about how innocent and sweet Rissa had been before the city had gotten to her. The unfairness of it scalded.

"Bax is a fighter. He won't leave Dovie on her own, no way in hell. He'll pull through because there is no way he's going to let a piece of crap trash truck be the reason he goes out. And when Bax wakes up, this Roark asshole is going to be in for a hurting. He just got the 'Cuda running the way he wanted. Now that he has to start all over he's going to be furious." Booker sounded certain and it was oddly comforting.

The mood was somber among the three of us, so I set about cleaning up the kitchen and Booker told Karsen he would walk her back downstairs to her own place. While she was gathering up her stuff and over the noise of the dishwasher, those swirly blue-and-gray eyes of his settled on me and he told me under his breath, "I'll find you a gun, but if the cop finds out about it you're on your own."

He held up his hands and backed away toward the door, where the blond teenager was waiting. The way she was watching him . . . I wondered if he had ever been anyone's hero before.

I waited until they were out the front door before whispering into the empty apartment, "I'm always on my own."

Feeling melancholy and useless, I curled up on the massive sofa and flipped through channels. I wanted to be at the hospital. I wanted to be there for Titus and I wanted to be a good friend to Dovie. She deserved that. And now that I could so easily see what doing the right thing was, I felt like I deserved a shot to be that for her and to be whatever it was that Titus needed. The cop might only need me as bait, but the man . . . the man and the things he kept so tightly controlled inside of him needed so much more. I could take care of all of him if he would just let me.

I feel asleep watching some movie about a bunch of kids thrown into a futuristic battle for survival. I enjoyed it and really loved the girl that was the main character, but something about doing anything to survive, being forced to eat or be eaten, hit too close to home and eventually my attention wandered and I crashed out before I saw how it all ended.

I woke up to the sound of the door clicking closed and the thumping of boots against the wooden floors. At first I was a little bit disoriented because the early-dawn rays of sunlight were drifting though the untinted windows I hadn't powered down when I fell asleep last night. I had no clue what time it was or how long I had slept. There was an aura of unrest circling Titus that had me snapping wide-awake. Everything inside of me went on high alert as he tossed his keys on the counter and then more carefully unclipped his gun and his shield.

He looked jagged and mean. He had passed scruffy and was well on his way to having a full beard covering the lower part of his face. His eyes were too bright and so blistering hot that they gleamed like blue lasers. His mouth was twisted in a harsh frown and the furrow between his eyebrows was so deep it looked like it was going to be a permanent part of his face from here on out. His hair was standing up straight and that white spot that decorated his temple looked like it had doubled in size. He had an Ace bandage wrapped around one hand and some white gauze taped on the other. He looked like a heavyweight fighter that had just gone nine rounds and no winner had been declared.

"Is Shane awake? I wasn't expecting you back anytime soon."

Fury flavored the air as he moved toward where I was still curled up with my legs underneath me.

"He woke up yesterday afternoon. He can't talk since his jaw is wired shut and it's still touch and go because he lost so much blood and hit his head so hard during the impact. But he's awake and he recognized me and Dovie, so the doctors kicked me out and told us that he needed time."

"Oh." My heart squeezed painfully. It would have been nice of him to let me know Bax had opened his eyes. "I tried to text you a couple of times to see if you needed anything or if I could do anything."

He prowled closer, his eyes roving over me like a physical touch. This was not the calm and collected cop that kept the streets safe. This was the wild man that made a deal with a woman he didn't trust and then let her put her hands and mouth all over him because he couldn't resist the pull. This was the beast that wanted, needed, and craved being fed. He was practically vibrating with the emotions that were at war in his blazing gaze. Anger, lust, fear, sorrow, regret, guilt, remorse . . . all of them jockeying for top position as he watched me and prowled closer and closer.

"I chucked my phone at the accident scene. Roark has to be watching. I can't figure out how he knew where Bax was going to be at that exact moment. He's everywhere. I've been at the hospital nonstop since then, so I didn't have a chance to get a new one yet. I only left to run to the garage to grab a shower or to go to the station to see if anyone had anything new on where

Roark might be. I figured Race or Brysen would've told Karsen or Booker what was going on."

"No. No one mentioned that he was awake. It would've been nice to know." I couldn't keep the sharpness out of my tone. Bax wasn't my favorite, but he mattered to Titus, so that meant he mattered to me.

He got to the back of the couch and rested his hands on the cushions. He was towering over me and I knew it should make me nervous with the mood he was in, but this was Titus. He wouldn't hurt me. He wouldn't hurt anyone, no matter how mad or frustrated he might be. He was too good for that.

"I think everyone was so relieved that he finally opened his eyes that was all they could think about. Brysen was worried about Dovie and Race was a nervous wreck. He and Bax are like brothers, so it was hard on everyone to see him like that. So broken and so still. That's not Bax."

I couldn't take it anymore. I had to touch him. I had to try and smooth some of that roughness out of his practically vibrating body. Never had any man needed to come home to a gentle touch like this one did. I lifted up onto my knees and reached both hands up so that they were lying near the center of his chest right over his heart. It thudded heavy and slow under my fingertips, like beating was just too much effort.

"Shane won't stay down for long, and while he and Race might be like brothers, you *are* his brother, Titus. So you're allowed to be just as worried and just as freaked out as the rest of them are. You don't have to hold it together all the time. You're a man, not a machine. Someone needs to be there to tell you that everything is okay every once in a while."

Suddenly it was like his heart woke up and the rhythm under

my fingers started to surge and dance. His bandaged hands came up and wrapped around each of my wrists. I looked down at his grip as it slowly started to tighten.

"What happened to your hands?"

His chest rose and fell with a deep breath and his eyes drifted shut. When the long, black lashes fluttered back open, the color of his remarkable eyes had switched from blue to that luminous silver. My skin tingled instinctively.

"I tried to pull Bax out of the wreck and I cut them on the frame of the car and on the broken glass."

Oh my God, he was amazing and fearless. How could one man care so much about everyone else and not see the damage that it was doing to him? He couldn't be responsible for the entire world. It would kill him.

"Titus . . ." My voice got caught on the emotion that welled up.

I didn't have to add to it because he simply shook his head and told me quietly, "Tell me everything is going to be okay, Reeve."

There was no hesitation as the words fell fast and furiously from my lips. "Everything will be okay."

I met him halfway as he lowered his head toward me. The setting was different and far more appropriate, but the way he put his mouth on mine wasn't. There was still the raw and brutal edge to it. Still the harsh scrape of teeth and the urgent twist of his tongue as it twirled all around mine. His lips were hard and eager. His breathing got jagged and uneven as he let go of my wrists and put his hands around my waist.

In a show of pure strength he lifted me up from my kneeling position and lifted me onto the edge of the couch. I thought he was going to settle me into that position once my legs were coiled around his waist but he didn't. He put a hand under my ass and held me up, walking toward the wall of windows until my back hit the glass, his mouth moving over mine, devouring me the entire trip.

Once he had me secure between his big body and the glass behind me, he started pulling at my clothes. The soft cotton of my T-shirt and the delicate satin of my bra were no match for his questing and impatient hands. Between one gasp as my aroused nipples hit his chest and another as his heavy thigh forced its way between that notch in my legs that was getting damp and heated under his attentions, he had me mostly naked and was steadily working on getting my pants open. Things were moving fast, too fast. He was in some kind of frenzy and I could feel it as his lips and hands raced haphazardly across my skin. This was all about want and had very little to do with need, at least on his part, but I was greedy enough, gone enough over this man to let him take . . . for right now.

The button on my jeans proved to be very little deterrent as without warning, his hand and his very nimble fingers were all over me and unerringly finding all the places that would welcome him even if my common sense was screaming at me that I should put a stop to this right now. The bandage across his palm was rough on delicate skin and the brush of his fingertips even more so as they dipped inside of me. I moaned in response and my entire body jerked against his where he had me pinned. He pulled his mouth off of mine and we both sucked in a much-needed breath. His eyes burned and all I could do was smolder and move with him as he started to stroke me with firm, steady motions. Nothing about the way he touched me felt reverent. It was frantic and wild. The urgency made it all the more exciting and hot.

"You're so gorgeous. You feel even better than you look. Do you know that?" There wasn't a lot of room down there since I still had my jeans on and his hands were big, but his words made me clench around him and move even harder on his swirling fingers. The pleasure was tight, so tight and so full it felt like it didn't fit inside of my body. It needed to get out.

I curled the fingers of one hand into the corded muscles at the base of his neck and locked the other in the hair at back of his head. It was surprisingly soft. Probably the only thing on him that was. I threw my head back so that it thumped against the window when his thumb suddenly landed with precision on my clit. Every nerve in my body went tight and I felt my blood start to rush around between my ears as desire started to bleed from every pore.

"Titus." His name was a plea to give me more or give me less. I needed one or the other if I was going to make it out of this alive.

He moved his leg higher into the apex of my legs and the motion shoved my breasts even tighter against his chest. He still had his T-shirt on but the friction of the cotton against the aching peaks was enough to make me gasp his name again. He grinned at me and it wasn't very nice. His eyes were hot enough to brand scars where they raked over me, and I thought I was going to pass out when he added another finger to the sexual games he was playing with my body. The walls of my sex clenched in automatic response against the fullness and I knew I wasn't going to last much longer under the sensual assault.

"Are you done, Reeve? Is this as much as you can take? I always want more, there is always so much more."

His voice sounded like sandpaper as he lowered his face and

sank his teeth into the skin at the side of my neck. It felt amazing and the scrape of his beard across my tender skin made it even better. I wanted to know what it would feel like lower. I lowered my hand from his hair and put it on his cheek. I waited until he lifted his head up and met my gaze. He turned his wrist at the same time and I almost shattered under the sensation. I wasn't sure what kind of battle of wills we were engaged in, but I knew if I didn't hold out for the rest of what he had, I was never going to get all that was Titus King.

So I simply told him what he needed to hear. "It's okay, Titus. Give me all you got. I want more."

It was the green light he needed. Suddenly he was every-where. His mouth biting, sucking each aching nipple into his mouth. His hands working feverishly to get the rest of my clothes out of his way without separating us. I had to admire the sheer strength it took to hold me up and pull my clothes off at the same time. I heard the leather of his belt slip free and suddenly a heavy wallet was in my hand. I looked at it in confusion while he wrestled his shirt off over his head with one hand. I couldn't make words work anymore.

"Condom. Find it."

"What?" Seriously I was struck dumb by the sight of him. He was beautiful. He was a warrior. He was a man made to fight, to win. He was big and hard. He was cut and defined. He was powerful and massive in a way that made me feel unbelievably delicate and feminine. He was all that a man should be and then some and there was never going to be anyone that would ever compare. He was going to ruin me in both the good and the bad ways.

"I bought a couple of rubbers last time I was at the gas station because I can't get you off my fucking mind, and I like to be prepared. Find one."

He sounded like a caveman and I kind of liked it. I also liked the light brush of his happy trail as he pressed his pelvis into mine. The long length of his cock rubbed against me as he pulled his zipper down and leaned farther into me. I found the foil packet and tore it open with my teeth after tossing the wallet to the floor.

"Hurry." He sounded like he was on the brink, so I grasped the heavy shaft and rolled the latex down. He jerked at my touch and the power of that was so intoxicating I leaned forward and sealed my mouth back over his. He responded by wrapping one of his bandaged hands around my breast and squeezing it tight.

It wasn't until the tip of him slid in, stretched me, burned a trail that felt like heaven and hell combined that I realized I was bare-assed and the tint on the windows was still turned off. Anyone looking close enough up at the complex would get a clear view of the debauchery currently happening between me and the hot cop.

"Titus . . ." I wanted to tell him we had to move. That we needed to stop for just a second, but he just grunted and thrust his hips hard so that we were joined all the way together, our pelvises aligned so there was no him and there was no me, there was just us. And we were so in tune with each other, so hungry for one another, I forgot what I was going to say.

He put a hand under my backside and tilted my hips more toward him. He nuzzled his face in the curve of my neck so every grunt, every pant, every whispered curse drifted through my ear like a promise. He put his other arm on the glass over my head for leverage and then proceeded to fuck me into oblivion.

Our chests rubbed together. Our bodies writhed and grinded against each other. I felt him tense and flex inside of my own and I felt the way my body responded to him. I was flushed and sweaty. I was wet and burning. Everywhere we touched felt fused together and I never wanted it to end. Suddenly the hand he had been using to hold me up vanished from my ass and showed back up between my legs. How he knew just where to touch, how he knew just how much pressure to add, I would never know. But he worked me over like a pro and it felt so good it hurt too much to hold back anymore.

I broke apart. Shattered like glass and he watched me the entire time. When I was stuck, captured and panting, he ran his fingers, wet from my own desire, up the center of my chest and used them to wrap lightly around my throat. It made me open my eyes wider and he just grinned at me. I had told him I wanted it all, but he didn't squeeze, didn't tighten his grip. He just left his fingers there as he pounded into me, rutting and thrusting like the beast he had released.

It only took a few more minutes for him to reach his own completion, and when he did, it again made me dumb. His muscles all locked, his eyes scorched everything they touched, and the look of relaxation that finally dotted his hard features was like a miracle. I wanted him to look like that for me all the time.

He bent his head so that he could put little butterfly kisses all along my collarbone as he pulled out and let my legs fall to either side of him. Our clothes were a mess and we both definitely looked like we had been frantically screwing each other's brains out.

"You didn't give me a chance to hit the control for the window. The people in the building across the street probably just got one hell of a show." It was really early in the morning, but still.

He pulled the condom off and situated himself back inside his pants. He ran a hand through his hair and looked at me with eyes that once again looked summer-sky blue. "I wouldn't have let you hit the tint. I want the people watching us to see." He said it so matter-of-factly that it left me stunned. He knew exactly what he was doing. He wanted Conner to see what we were up to, wanted my ex to see us together like that. It hadn't been about us at all. He told me he needed to take a shower, but I couldn't really hear him over the sound of my heart yet again blowing up because of this man.

I was never going to learn. Or I would learn, but it was going to be too late by the time the lesson took hold to keep it from breaking me.

Chapter 10

Titus

I FELT LIKE A stranger had taken up residence in my body. He was doing things, saying things, making choices I would never make. I wanted to chalk it up to being tired, to the stress of almost losing my brother, to the frustration of figuring out too late who Roark was and exactly why he waging war on my city. But the truth of it was that I had grown up on these streets, had fought my own fight to survive and become the man I was, so there was just as much dirt and grime under my fingernails as the next guy's. The rough parts of who I was and how I had become him had always been buried deep down inside of me, covered by my sense of honor or my drive to make the world around me a better place for the innocent and unprotected. The layers that covered up the darkness and brutality were getting thinner and thinner, and what was starting to get exposed was the heart of the man I really was.

The soul of that man had no qualms about getting in as deep and as far as he could with Reeve. She made the edges that poked at him less sharp. Those navy-blue eyes brought the calm, and that mouth, the things she did with it, made the buzzing from

every bad thing that followed me home go quiet for a few minutes. She was like belladonna. So pretty and soft on the outside,
so delicate to the touch. But once she was on the inside, once you
had any part of her, you knew she was strong enough and deadly
enough to kill you. She was just as dangerous on the inside as I
was, and I was pretty sure after that round of purely animalistic
sex in the living room, I no longer cared. I didn't have any desire
to search out reasons and logic to stay away. I liked being with
her. I liked that she wanted to make sure that I was okay. I liked
that she looked at me like I was everything and then in the next
blink dared me to give her all that I had. I was done trying to
make myself feel bad for the attraction that pulled me toward
her. I wanted to feast on it instead.

I was always careful during sex and not just with protection.
I knew I had a tendency to get intense, to forget that my partner
didn't need the escape, need the oblivion in the same way I did.
More than once, sex had ended badly when I let the leash slip and
the act turned into more than the girl could take. Reeve didn't
care. She didn't just tempt the beast that lurked inside of me, she
poked the needy bastard with a stick and demanded he come out
and play. She called to the parts of me I often forgot existed. She
demanded more and more.

It was that same beast on the inside that demanded that I
show Roark exactly what he was missing. I wanted her, and I had
known that I was so exposed, so unsteady with emotion after
Bax had finally woken up, that any kind of sympathy or kindness
on her lovely face was going to have me climbing all over her.
It was an added bonus that I got to cram that fact right down
Roark's throat. It was crude. It was classless and she and I both
deserved better than that, but the second she told me everything

was going to be okay, I lost it. I may have taken it too far, lost my mind with hunger and need, but the end result would've been the same. I would have taken her. I was bound to lose myself in her whether Roark was watching or not. It was an added bonus that the stab of revenge felt good. I just hoped she wouldn't hold it against me. I planned on explaining it all to her and clarifying my moment of insanity and lust once I got a few hours of sleep and my brain didn't feel like it was made of cotton candy.

I got out of the shower, rubbed a towel over my head, and wrapped another one around my waist. The bed that lived on the massive elevated platform looked like heaven and I could hardly keep my eyes open as I stumbled toward it. I was so tired I didn't even notice that Reeve was sitting on the end of the mattress until I flopped down and almost kicked her. She had changed into a pair of skintight black pants and an oversize sweater that fell off of her shoulder and bared way too much creamy skin for my liking. Her hair was pulled up into a ponytail on the top of her head and for all the world she looked like any normal, hot chick on her way to work at some trendy salon for the day. Nothing about this woman was normal and all the things that made her so complicated were the things that made her so tempting.

"Where do you think you're going?" My voice sounded sluggish and heavy to my own ears.

"I need to run an errand. I'm going to have Booker take me. I need to get out of here for a few hours."

She had been cooped up the entire time I was at the hospital. She was probably going stir-crazy. She was following orders and laying low. I was such an asshole for not thinking to borrow a phone or to even use the landline in Bax's room to let her know what was going on. She deserved a break and a chance to get out of the loft, but selfish bastard that I was, I wanted her to stay with me. I wanted her to tell me it was going to be okay over and over again and I absolutely didn't want her anywhere near Booker after what had just gone down between us in the living room. If I was functioning at full capacity, I might have been able to put all of what I was feeling and struggling with into words she could understand. Since I was only at half capacity I reverted back to the guy I always seemed to be around her, the one that was unhinged and greedy with want and need. The one that took without asking. The one that forgot to be civilized.

I levered myself up so that I could get my hands around her upper arms and pull her with me as I fell back on the bed so that she landed mostly on me. I rolled so that I was on my side and her back was pressed firmly against my front. The towel had been lost at some point but I was too exhausted to care and her rigid posture as I held her to me indicated she wasn't the least bit interested in the fact that I was naked and holding her close. I didn't care. I felt my heartbeat start to settle, felt my limbs start to get heavy and lax. I buried my nose in her hair and inhaled her flowery and girlie scent. Nothing in the city smelled that good.

"I need to sleep. Stay with me for an hour then I'll take you wherever you need to go. I need to head back to the hospital anyway." I sounded sleep drunk and I wasn't sure the words made it out or if I just thought them as darkness started to pull me under.

She wiggled a little against me until I squeezed my arms even tighter around her and put a hand on her flat belly to keep her still. I made sure every inch of her was pressed up against every naked inch of me. That was what a real-life dream felt like.

"You'll sleep better if you have the bed to yourself." She whispered the words but I heard them loud and clear.

"No, I won't. Everything seems to be better with you close by. Just give me an hour, Reeve. Please?" I inhaled her and knew there wasn't going to be any fight left in me as soon as I exhaled. I always seemed to be asking her to give me things, which was so against my character. I never took for myself—at least I hadn't until she came back to town.

I couldn't stay awake any longer to see if she agreed to stay or not, but when sleep finally claimed me I went under thinking about a peaceful meadow and a sky that was about to turn midnight blue.

When I woke up the loft was dark and it was well into the afternoon. I had definitely slept more than an hour according to the digital clock next to my wallet, gun, and badge on the nightstand. I woke up alone. It shouldn't have surprised me after the way I had manhandled her and been all over her like a maniac. She was tough but every girl needed a little bit of finesse and I had given her none. No matter what she may have done in the past, or the choices she made that kept us on different sides of the law, she still deserved what every other girl that was willing to give of herself deserved, and I had given her nothing when she deserved everything for taking care of me.

Swearing at myself, I threw an arm over my eyes and tried not to think of every single thing I had done wrong where Reeve was concerned. It all started when I turned her over to Roark to begin with. I shouldn't have let a badge automatically lead me to believe he was one of the good guys. I knew better than that. It had been dirty cops that had dragged me beaten and bloody to Novak. Cops that had been on the crime bosses' payroll since before I had even made detective. The good guys were getting harder and harder to come by and yet I had been so blinded by revulsion at her actions, so outraged that such a pretty girl had done such ugly and illegal things, that I wanted her out of sight and out of mind. I thought with her in the marshal's hands the desire that kicked at me when I looked at her would stop warring with my head screaming at me that she was bad news. I wanted her to be someone else's problem because I felt guilty for wanting her. I thought she was bad news but that didn't stop me from admiring her bold honesty about the pretty messed-up things she had done. The push and pull of my feelings toward the troublesome beauty had me shoving her off as quickly as I could before I did something foolish like take her to bed or fall in love.

I heard the front door open with a quiet snick and then the click of shoes on the floor. I could tell she was trying to be quiet in case I was still asleep, so I called down to her, "I'm up."

She didn't reply but I heard her steps change direction as she headed up the stairs. "I didn't want to wake you up. You looked like you needed the rest." Her head cleared the landing and her eyes skimmed over me before a flush worked into her face.

I looked down at myself and had to smirk. I was still on top of the covers and still very naked. All it took was her being in the same room to have my dick twitching in interest.

"I did. I wasn't thinking very straight. Did you take care of whatever you needed to do?"

I could have sworn something that looked like guilt danced across her dark eyes, but then her attention landed on what was happening below my belly button and her expression shifted to something else.

"I did. Booker took care of it for me, and I also stopped and got you this." I grunted a little as she pulled a small box out of her purse and tossed it in my direction. It landed on my chest with a thump. I picked up the cell phone and lifted an eyebrow at her.

"You got me a phone?"

She shrugged and took her purse off her shoulder. It hit the floor with a thud and she winced a little. I frowned at her and shifted so I could swing my legs over the edge of the bed. I wasn't used to having anyone do anything for me, and every time I turned around she was doing something thoughtful and kind like that.

"Thank you."

"Well, you said you didn't have one and I figured you needed a throwaway since Roark is probably tracking everything you do. It's no big deal." She bit down on the lush curve of her lower lip and my cock went instantly hard. There was no pretending I wasn't paying attention to every little thing she did now. I was stripped naked in more than one sense and she could see it all. "Wanna get dressed and go see Bax? I'll tag along if you don't mind. I kind of want to check on Key."

I rubbed a hand across the fuzzy lower half of my face and cranked my neck to the side. The popping noise it made was loud enough that she heard it from where she was still standing at the top of the stairs. "Key?"

"Keelyn . . . Honor, whatever you know her as. She used to come into the salon I worked at before . . ." She trailed off. Before and after always seemed to be such important indicators. "Anyway, she's never had it easy and she doesn't have many friends because she's kind of a bitch, but I've always liked her. I think she might like seeing a friendly face."

"Friendly? Weren't you trying to beat the crap out of each other last week?"

She shrugged again and moved a little closer. She licked her lips again, her gaze locked firmly on the erection that was now standing tall and straight between my legs.

"There are only a few shades of difference between friend and foe in the Point. Sometimes the same person plays both roles."

The tension between us popped and cracked like it was a living thing. Electricity arching and bouncing from me to her and back to me.

"Reeve, come here." My voice dipped low and heat started to pool thick and dense in my veins.

She cocked her head to the side and narrowed her eyes at me just a fraction. "I don't think so. I gave you your hour, Titus. I don't think I'm up for giving you anything else right now. I know you want Roark to make his move. I know you're furious he almost killed Bax, but no one wins a game like this if everyone playing is a pawn."

Shit. I knew she was pissed about the windows, and even with that she had stayed with me while I slept. That made me want to grab her and put her under me forever.

"You aren't a pawn, but I am an idiot. Look, when I walked in that door I had so much stuff going on in my head . . ." I trailed off and took a deep breath. "I was barely holding on waiting to see if Bax was going to make it, and then he opened his eyes. I had to explain to all the people that matter to me that Novak's legacy is still fucking with our lives. I had to tell Bax he has another half-sibling out there besides me, and this one wants him dead." I shook my head slowly at her. "All of that had to go somewhere and that somewhere was you. I wanted you, Reeve. I came here to you instead of going back home or to the apartment in the city. I screwed up, but what happened between us is very much about you and me and has nothing to do with him."

She wrinkled up her nose like she was considering the validity of what I was saying to her. So I held out a hand in her direction. "Come here and I'll prove it to you. The windows are dark. There is no one in this room but you and me. I want you whether we have an audience or not. I'll show you if you just come here."

She was wavering. Her eyes told me she wanted to take those few steps that separated us but the way her body was stiff and the way her hands involuntarily curled into tiny and fierce fists told me she wasn't completely buying my assertion that our previous interlude had been based on lust and overwhelming passion rather than macho pride and bitter vengeance. That made me feel like an utter tool bag. Now that I wasn't sleep-deprived and strung tight with too many emotions to name, I knew that in this moment I absolutely wanted her more than I wanted revenge for what Roark did to my brother.

I asked her softly, "Have I ever given you reason to doubt me before this morning?"

Her fingers finally relaxed a little and she took one step closer to me. "No, but we haven't really known each other very long."

"I don't have any kind of hidden agenda here. You know I want you and that it's complicated because I need you to get at Roark. I can admit that neither one of us was really playing pretend when it came to acting like we were attracted to each other and that something between us was bound to break loose. Now that it has, I'm done trying to stop it. You want me, you got me."

She took another step closer and reached out her hand so

that her fingertips brushed mine. "It's not the want that's the issue, Titus. It's everything that's more than that."

She wasn't wrong but I couldn't think about that until Roark was off the streets. That was a different battle that was going to have to be fought and I didn't know what kind of shape the warriors were going to be in when it was time to fight or throw up the white flag. Since she was close enough to touch now, I snagged her wrist and pulled her so that she was standing between my legs. My dick twitched happily in her direction, and I put my hands on her hips and leaned my head forward so that it rested right below her breasts. She tunneled her fingers through my hair and nothing had ever felt so nice. She was trying to soothe me, but I wondered if she knew that the gentle way she handled me had the opposite effect. It made me want to eat her up, which is exactly what I was going to do.

"I can't do more right now, Reeve, so this is all we've got. It's this or nothing." I reached around her and pulled her closer with a hand on her ass. When she was as close as she could get, I started working my hands up underneath the back of her loose sweater. She didn't seem to have anything on under the flimsy material. There was no bra to get in my way as I smoothed a palm up the delicate divots of her spine, taking the fabric with me.

She let go of my head and brushed her hands over my shoulders. Her touch made me shiver, and once I had her top all the way off of her, I clasped her to me and pulled her back on the bed so she was sprawled over the top of me. I needed to get her as naked as I was, so I flipped her over so that she was on the bottom and went to work on her pants before she even gave me the green light. Her tummy sucked in as she breathed in deeply when I started to pull the stretchy fabric down her mile-long legs.

"I guess it's this." Her voice was husky and kind of smoky-sounding as I tugged her boots off and then crawled back up over her prone form so that I was hovering over her, my erection rubbing enticingly against the soft skin of her stomach. She always felt so good even when I wasn't really touching her.

I looked down at her and promised with everything I had in me, "I will make *this* worthwhile. I will make *this* enough until we can tackle more. *This* matters, whatever it is, and for now *this* is everything, okay?"

She regarded me solemnly for long moment, long enough that my dick got impatient and moved against her like it had a mind of its own. That made her lift a dark eyebrow at me and everything inside me surged when a sweet half grin lilted up the sides of her mouth. "Okay. *This* with you is more than *more* was with anyone else anyway."

She was going to be my downfall. She was going to be my corruption and my vice. She was going to be my addiction and my compulsion and I was still going to fall headlong into her knowing the landing was going to be rough for both of us.

I kissed her hard on the mouth. A sharp, biting kiss, but I didn't linger. I could get lost in kissing her and the way she met me bite for bite, let me lick her and nibble on her like she was a sweet treat. She let me kiss her until neither of us could breathe, until it hurt us both, and I loved it. I loved that she just let me have at her with no hesitation and no fear, but that wasn't what I wanted this time around. She was always giving; this time it was my turn. Just me and her and all that I could give to her. All that I wanted to give to her.

I made a place for myself between her legs and started to work my way down her body. I kissed her on her throat and felt her heart thump against my lips. I kissed her in the center of her chest and watched as the simple touch of lips made both of her velvety nipples peak. I moved over to suck on each tip. Made love to each point with my lips and my tongue until she was writhing underneath me and digging her fingernails into my skin. I left her nipples wet and glistening and moved down so that I could lick across the flat plane of her stomach. It shivered and pebbled up in pleasure as I continued my way down. She gasped just a tiny bit when I dipped the tip of my tongue in the little indent of her belly button and she whispered my name when I got to the apex of her already damp folds. Her legs shifted restlessly on either side of me and I grasped her knees and pushed her legs open wider and I moved to kneel before on her the floor.

Shiny. Pretty. Secret. Forbidden. Elusive. Mysterious. She was all the things that had led men to break the rules I'd followed since the beginning of time and she was laid out before me like a banquet fit for the gods. This was supposed to be about giving not taking, but when she looked at me with those midnight-blue eyes over her heaving chest, there was no way to deny I was getting just as much as I was giving. The equality of it, the rightness of it, settled around me in a way that was startlingly comfortable. It was like *this* was exactly how it was supposed to be between two people and I had never experienced anything like it.

I wanted to touch her but I wanted to taste her more. The way she glistened beckoned me closer. I leaned into her, used the pad of my thumb to rub over her slippery folds, and found that little nub that was bundled tight with nerves and desire. The first swipe of my tongue across it had her arching her back up off the bed. The second had her pulling at me frantically and tossing her head from side to side. Her eyes were squeezed shut and she was breathing like she had just run a marathon. She looked turned on and hot as hell as she moved in time with the stroke of my tongue across her most sensitive parts.

I added the scrape of teeth and shifted so I could add a finger or two to the equation. She bent her legs up next to my head and dug her heels into the edge of the mattress. Her inner muscles were grasping at me, pulling at me, and it made my own arousal pound inside of me. I could feel her winding up, feel the way she got tighter and more liquid the more I worked on her. I could happily bury my face between her legs for days on end, but I wanted her to come, wanted to watch her go over. I lifted my gaze up and groaned into her, which made her bark out my name.

Her eyes were open now and she was watching me. A bright pink was riding high in her cheeks and spread across her chest. She had her hands on her tits and she was rubbing her fingers lightly over the raised tips. Fuck, was she perfect, so perfect. Her eyes were nearly black with druglike passion and I could see her teetering on the edge of her orgasm. So beautiful, and she tasted that way across my tongue and felt that way across my fingers.

I added a little pressure and another finger, and that was it. She practically levitated into my mouth and her wash of desire consumed me. As she shivered and quaked around me I pulled back just enough to brush a kiss across the inside of her thigh. I needed to shave still, so I left a trail of moisture wherever my mouth touched her. I thought it was sexy as hell.

I leaned to the side until I could get hold of my wallet, thanking the Lord for small favors that I had listened to that nagging voice that told me I was going to need more than one condom if I was going to be around her. I dug the sucker out and handed it over to her while she looked up at me with hazy eyes and a flushed face. I bent down and kissed her how I really wanted to, with lots of tongue and no give. She didn't waste any time grabbing hold of my straining erection and maneuvering it so that she could roll the condom down the rigid length. My eyes crossed a little when she snuck her hands between my legs and gave my sensitive and tightly drawn sac a playful squeeze. She didn't have limits and I think that was my favorite thing about her.

I put my hands around the base of her head and used my thumbs to tilt her head back as far as her position and the bed would allow. I bent my head so I could nibble on the taut arch of her throat and nudged her legs out of my way so I could slide inside of her welcoming heat. Even through the latex she scorched me. So hot. So wet. So greedy, as her inner muscles pulled me farther and farther in. Everything inside me was clawing at me to drive home, to bury myself as deep as I could go and assuage the need hammering at my insides. This was supposed to be about her, about showing her *this* was something, maybe not something more, but something nonetheless. I had finesse goddammit, and I would use it even if it felt like it was going to strangle me.

Her hands slipped up my back and then wrapped around my shoulders. She brought her long legs up on either side of me and then I felt the bite of her heels in my ass, urging me closer and closer. Without a thought I let my teeth sink harder into her tender skin and she moaned in response.

"Titus, move!" It wasn't a sigh or a sweet nothing, it was an order, and it was fucking hotter than anything had ever been.

She arched against me, clamped down on me, and moved against the sharp edge of my teeth. Her fingernails scratched against my back and the burn of it was enough for the reins to slip. I grunted and did what she commanded. I moved.

I pulled her legs up even higher and plowed into her. There was no finesse. There was no care. There was no elegance or romance . . . there was only me taking her and her letting me have her over and over again.

It was sweaty. It was aggressive. It was noisy and almost brutal in the way our hands grabbed, the way our bodies fought to get closer and take more. It was the single best sexual experience I had ever had in my life.

I forgot that my face was covered in stubble and it tore her soft skin up as I ate at her neck and her mouth over and over again. I got a hand between us and captured one of her nipples between my thumb and forefinger and pinched until she called out as pleasure turned to pain. I would've apologized, but I felt the way she liked it as pleasure coated the surface of my cock as it moved in and out of her at a fevered pace. It was so good. Everything about her, everything about doing this with her, was so unbelievably good and it was going to turn me inside out. I felt it racing up my spine. I felt burning in my balls. I felt it as my dick drove harder and deeper with every thrust.

"More. I want more."

Her voice cracked and that was it for me. I couldn't give her the more that she wanted, but I could give her this.

I lifted her hips up and pounded into her hard enough that our pelvises banged together in an almost painful way. I sank my teeth into her lower lip and sucked on it hard. That was all it took to shove her over again. She screamed my name into my lips and I felt her body flutter and spasm around me. I was close myself, so as soon as those dark blue eyes locked on mine and shined up at me with pleasure and completion, I let go. It all raced out of me and rushed into her, and like she had done since she came crashing back into my life, she caught it all without a complaint.

I collapsed on top of her, breathing heavy and covered in sex and sweat. I panted into her throat as she glided her hands up and down my back. I felt boneless. I felt weightless. I felt like all that mattered in this moment was me and her, which is exactly why I couldn't give her more. She already had too much.

"This has to be good enough for now." I said the words but I could hear they lacked the strength they needed to make my point.

"For now. Let's get cleaned up so you can go see your brother."

I muttered an agreement and rolled off of her so she could get up. I didn't want to tell her now was all the time we might have if I couldn't get a handle on Roark before he got a handle on me.

Chapter 11

Reeve

THERE WAS A TANGIBLE shift between the two of us as we raced across town in his badass car. It went beyond sex. It went beyond wanting what we shouldn't. There was a simple acceptance now that it wasn't "him" and "me," it was "us," whether that was good or bad. We were finally in it together no matter what the outcome might be. We were a team.

The engine roared in my ears and so did the fact that any legal deal I had with the feds was gone, considering they were closing the Novak case and they no longer needed me. Titus laid it out for me in bare bones terms, and I knew good and well that meant I could be looking at jail time if I didn't manage to help him bring in Conner. My purpose had been served and I was of no use anymore, at least as it applied to the feds and Novak's crew. The feds thought the same thing Titus did. Conner would come for me and that would be the only chance anyone had to snatch him up. I had no intention of letting Conner go anywhere without a bullet in his head, so that meant I was going to royally screw up any chance I had of skating out of all of this without seeing the inside of a cell.

I didn't say anything to Titus while he tried to tell me it would all work out once he had Conner on lockdown. He tried to tell me that I was the one risking my neck and that even the straitlaced feds had to know that came with some give and take. I just muttered a noncommittal response and thought about the Glock that was sitting heavy and loaded in the purse at my feet. Everything came with give and take, and when I was done taking it would be well past time that I gave something up. If that something had to be my freedom, then so be it. It was a price I was willing to pay after setting everything back to rights.

Once we got to the hospital I thought we would just go our separate ways since Bax was still in intensive care and Keelyn was on another floor in general recovery, but surprisingly Titus wanted me to walk with him to his brother's room. I was hesitant because I knew Dovie and Race were floating around and I didn't want any kind of ugly confrontation. I mean, before I was sleeping with Titus I was sleeping with Conner, and Conner was the reason Bax had nearly died. If the situation were reversed I would have had a lot to say on the subject myself. However, as Titus clasped my hand in his and pulled me along behind him as our shoes squeaked obnoxiously on the linoleum floor, I didn't really have the right words to object, so I just followed him silently.

Bax's room was easy to spot. There were two armed police officers standing on either side of the door and a rumpled red-head pacing back and forth in front of them. Dovie looked haggard and worn out. She had purple shadows set deep under each green eye and her typically creamy pallor was splotchy and red. She looked a mess and agitated as we approached her. Her gaze flew up to Titus and without a word he dropped my hand and scooped her up in a rib-cracking hug. Immediately giant sobs started to shake her lithe body. Titus made soothing noises and stroked one of his big hands up and down her back. It made my heart swell just a little. He was always there to take care of everyone else, always. He had to put the beast away and be the guy that fixed everything so often that it was no wonder that when his own monster got loose he had no idea what to do with it.

"He can't even talk and he told me to leave. He told me he doesn't want me here." Dovie's voice sounded like she was dying. Like everything she had ever loved had just been taken away from her. She was shaking so hard it was a wonder she didn't break apart. "I kept telling him how ridiculous that is. I'm wherever he is, but he just kept telling me to go. How can words hurt so much when they aren't even spoken?"

Titus swore and then set her away from him so he could put his hands on her shoulders. "You look like hell. He can see how much you're hurting, and he can't do anything about it. It's no different from when he got arrested after Novak got shot and he refused to see you. He's trying to keep you from suffering with him. Have one of these officers take you home. Take a shower. Get something to eat and then come back and ignore whatever idiotic thing he's trying to tell you. He wants you here. He needs you here and you both know it."

She blinked her watery eyes and took a deep breath. "He almost died, Titus, and the person that almost killed him is his brother!"

I saw Titus dip his head in acknowledgment. "I know. But he didn't die and that's what matters, okay? As for Roark, just because they share half of the same blood doesn't make them brothers. You leave him to me."

She squeezed her eyes shut and then visibly collected herself.

When she opened her eyes back up they were dry and there was no longer a tremble in her lips. "Okay."

The big cop bent forward and placed a tender kiss on the center of her forehead and it almost had me melting into the floor. He was so good with his own. They were unbelievably lucky to have him. Titus gave her a lopsided grin and moved around her to reach for the door. "Maybe he's just cranky since he can't smoke with his jaw wired shut. Bax without a fix is a total nightmare."

Dovie rallied enough to smile back at him. "Maybe it'll force him to quit."

Titus chuckled and told her drily as he disappeared into the darkened room, "I wouldn't count on it."

Once the big man was gone from the hallway, her eyes landed on me. She had every right to hate me. She had every right not to trust me. But Dovie, being Dovie, just looked at me with a contemplative expression on her face as she took a step toward me.

"You need to be good to him, Reeve. I don't know what is going on between the two of you, but I'm telling you right now if you hurt him, betray him in any way, you won't have to worry about the boys. You'll have to worry about me."

A chill raced up my spine because it wasn't a threat. She was just laying it out there as a statement of fact. If I screwed Titus over she was going to make me hurt. I didn't doubt her. You didn't keep a guy like Bax or survive in this life successfully without knowing how to get down and dirty.

I gulped a little bit and shifted uneasily from foot to foot. "He needs someone to care for him. All day, every day, all he does is give himself to everyone else."

She lifted a coppery eyebrow at me. "Are you that someone? You're going to care for him? Weren't you screwing the guy that killed my dad and just tried to kill my man? Did you care for him too?"

I wasn't scared of the truth, so I told her flatly, "I thought Conner was someone else, and yes, the man that I thought he was I cared for."

She snorted at me. "Who did you think he was?"

I sighed. Admitting how wrong I had been, how easily I had been suckered in by a façade, was still hard for me. I was supposed to have more street smarts than that. "I thought he was enough like Titus that I could fall for him and make it work. I thought he was a good man, but he isn't. He's great at being who you need him to be, but it's all a lie. As for being the someone to care for Titus, for now it's me." Because he couldn't talk about more, and until he could, this would have to be enough.

She sighed back at me and lifted her hands up to rub them over her obviously tired face. "No one is like Titus. No one is that strong, that secure, that hard. He is his own law and his own army. Bax is never going to like you being anywhere near his brother. He won't ever trust you."

"I know that, but I'm sure Race didn't like Shane being near you and eventually he had to come to terms with it. Shane doesn't have to trust me as long as his brother does. Right now Titus and I need each other, so no matter what anyone else thinks or feels, we are a package deal."

She considered me silently before giving me a tight nod that had her tangled red locks falling forward.

"I've got my hands full with my own stubborn and danger-ous man. I don't have it in me to worry about what another one

is doing. Titus knows what you're capable of, so if he's still willing to dive neck-deep into the mire with you, who am I to question it? You should know that if you cross him, though, he has it
in him to be just as bad, just as wicked, as Bax. He's not all good
guy. He hides it well but there is bad in there."

"I know." I stepped around her. "He doesn't try and keep his
bad hidden from me. Probably because he knows I won't ever
judge him for it." I had more than my fair share of bad fueling
me every single day, so why would I bat an eye at Titus having
shades of it come to life within him from time to time? Dovie
just nodded at me and we walked our separate ways.

It took me a minute to find Keelyn's room, and when I did I
was surprised to find her sitting up on the edge of her bed, fully
dressed and looking like she was about to head out shopping or
to run errands. It wasn't until I called her name and she turned to
look at me that I saw her arm was in a sling and she had a thick
bandage peeking out of the collar of her loose-fitting top.

"Hey. You're already up and about?" I couldn't keep the surprise out of my voice.

She blinked her wide gray eyes at me then slowly nodded her
head. "I'm declaring myself well enough to leave. You actually
have perfect timing. You can help me get downstairs, where the
cab I called is waiting."

I frowned at her and put my hands on my hips. "So you aren't
actually cleared to go anywhere?" Now that she was facing me I
could see she had a really gray cast to her normally flawless skin.
Her mouth was also pinched in a grimace of pain.

"The doctor thinks I should stay for a few more days, but I
need to get out of here. I made them discharge me."

"You need to get out of the hospital? Why? What's the rush?"

"I need out of this city. I can't do this anymore, Reeve. Look at me." She waved a hand at her immobilized wing and bandaged chest. "I have twenty stitches in my chest and half of that in my back. I look like a character in a video game. No one is going to pay money to see a washed-up stripper covered in scars take her clothes off. All of this is just so tired and sad. I'm exhausted and I don't want to do it anymore."

I closed the door behind me and walked into the room. I set my purse down on the floor and winced at the heavy thud the gun made when it landed. I was going to need to get used to that or Titus was going to get suspicious.

"You've been in the Point as long as I have. Where else would you go?" I had seen the suburbs, thought I could make that work for me, and had been so wrong. I wondered if Key had been anywhere but the Point.

"Anyplace where no one has ever heard the name Honor. I want to bury her. I don't want to be her anymore. I don't want her life. I don't want to want what she wants." She shifted and used her good hand to push some of her dark red hair over her shoulder. Only she could be shot up and bedraggled and still look so perfect. "There was this girl that danced at Spanky's for like six months a few years ago. She was kind of a gypsy, not one to settle any one place for too long. She was young, but smart and ambitious. She ended up in Denver, I think. I heard she reconnected with an old flame and has a kid on the way now. We keep in touch here and there, so I was thinking maybe I would head that way. She says Colorado is the most beautiful place she has ever been. Nothing like the Point. Fresh air might be just what I need to get my shit together."

"It's not that easy," I told her quietly.

"What's not?"

"Leaving this place behind. The scenery changes, the people are different, but you'll still be you and that means you'll always have a huge part of the city in you. You can't just leave it behind; you can try and fool yourself into wanting something different, but it doesn't work." I would never settle for an imitation again.

She scoffed a little and then struggled to her feet, forcing me to scramble and help her as she wobbled unsteadily.

"I can try. Now, will you help me outside or not?" She sounded so surly and disgruntled I had to chuckle at her.

"Yeah, I'll help you." What choice did I have? "So are you planning on telling Nassir where you're going or that you're leaving?"

I put a hand on her waist and let her lean on me as we shuffled to the door. I pulled it open and she grunted in discomfort as the action jostled her.

"I already did. He didn't believe me."

The nurses looked up when we hit the hallway. They scowled at Keelyn but she just smiled sweetly as we slowly made our way to the elevator. She lifted an eyebrow at me. "They don't like me, for some reason."

I snickered at her and reached out to push the button with my free hand. "Because only you can get shot, operated on, and still look like a goddess. It's not fair."

She rolled her eyes. "I paid a lot of money to look this good."

I'd bet she did. "I saw Nassir when you went down. He wasn't happy, like really not happy. There is something there with him and you, isn't there? That's why he thinks you won't really leave?"

She slumped back against the elevator and closed her eyes.

She was obviously hurting and from more than the bullet wound in her chest.

"Nothing makes Nassir Gates happy. He is a coldhearted bastard and the only thing he cares about is Nassir. What he wants, he takes, and I have had enough of being taken by men to last me a lifetime. He would destroy me." Her voice cracked on the last part of her sentence, and when she pulled her lids back up to look at me, I saw an expression that was all too familiar. The longing, the yearning, the burn for a man that you shouldn't want.

"He's very intense."

"He's a killer. There is no good or bad with him like there is with Bax and Race. There's just this void where he exists in his own world and operates under his own rules, and anyone that doesn't want to comply is going to be collateral damage. He's ruthless and the only side that matters to him is his own. He's all smoke and mirrors and what's under the reflection of sophistication and humanity is a nightmare. He's the devil in an Armani suit."

"I see."

"Do you? Do you really see, Reeve, because most people I talk to about him only have a vague idea about how dangerous he really can be."

There were undertones there that spoke to something deeper between her and the exotic-looking club owner but I couldn't question her about it because the elevator dinged as we hit the ground floor and I put my arm around her waist so that I could almost drag her toward the front doors. She was moving really slowly and I think she was in much more pain than she was letting on. I gave her a little squeeze and told her softly, "I think I see very clearly, Key. You think you can run. You think space, time, and maybe even a different man will get him out of your system because he's not who you should want. You think that maybe, just maybe, you can be a different person, leave all the shit and mess here in the Point, and be someone you always thought you should be. You think you can replace him, lose him, and I'm going to tell you from firsthand experience it's not that easy. Just like the city is in you, so is he, and you will always be you, so that part of you that hungers for him, aches for him even though you know he might be the end of you, it'll still be there."

A battered yellow cab was waiting for her, so I pulled open the back door and helped her into the backseat. The cab smelled gross and looked like it had bullet holes dotting it, but that was pretty typical for a taxi in the Point. She looked up at me with a scowl.

"Thanks for the hand, but you're still a bitch."

I shrugged. "So are you. Good luck chasing down a new life."

She bit down on her lower lip. "Promise me something." I lifted my eyebrows up at her and waited to see what she was going to ask of me. "If you see me back here in the next six months, promise me you won't say 'I told you so.' That'll really piss me off and I might have to swing at you again."

I smiled at her and grabbed hold of the door so I could swing is shut. "Good luck, Key. I wouldn't want to be you when Nassir finally catches up to you, but I promise not to rub it in when he brings you back."

The cabdriver took off as soon as metal touched metal and I crossed my arms as I wandered back inside. I really didn't want to go up to Bax's room and intrude on the brother's time together, so I went to the snack bar and got myself a bottle of water to bide some time. I didn't need Bax in a worse mood than usual trying to give me hell for getting my hooks into his brother. He was injured and needed to focus on getting better. I took my water and found a waiting area to sit in for a little bit, flipping through old magazines until almost an hour went by. I figured Titus would be wondering where I had gotten off to by then, so I headed back to the elevators to take me up to the intensive care unit.

When the doors opened I ran immediately into a broad chest and had strong arms wrapping around me and moving me backward the way I had just came. Titus wore a thunderous expression on his face and looked mad enough to spit nails. It was amazing to me how much emotional damage Bax could do confined to a hospital bed and unable to speak.

"Are you okay?" Those heavily muscled arms tightened a fraction around me.

"No. My brother is a dipshit and reasoning with him feels like beating my head against the wall."

"He really doesn't want Dovie here?" That was sad and wrong in so many ways.

"Oh, he wants her here, but not until he gets rid of the armed guard outside of his door and gets to take a shot at Roark. Bax thinks once Roark hears that he survived the crash, he'll come after him. He wants me to get him a gun."

"Oh no. He didn't really ask you that? He had to know you would say no." I shivered at the uncanny way Bax's plan echoed my own.

"Of course he knew. It was just his none too subtle way of telling me what he has up his sleeve so I'm not surprised when it all goes to hell. And you know what sucks? Of course I told him to fuck off, but Race won't. If Bax asks Race to help him set this up, he will. Goddammit. Everyone I love has a death wish."

He put his arm around me and tucked me into his side, and

I wrapped an arm around his lean waist. It was such a normal, couple-y type thing to do it made my heart thump a happy beat and I immediately chastised myself. Stuff like that most definitely fell into the category of *more* and Titus wasn't there yet. And if he knew what I was planning, knew that this was going to end with me dead or behind bars, *more* wouldn't even be an option, so why couldn't I stop myself from asking for it, from chasing it every time he touched me? Good thing he wasn't even close to loving me, or I would just be one more person he cared about playing a dangerous game of chicken with fate.

"Did you tell him what you and I have been up to?"

He grunted and paused next to the sparkly-blue car. I was stunned when he bent his head down and gave me a hard and searing kiss. It made me tingle all the way to my toes.

"I told him that you and I have a thing. I told him he doesn't have to like it, but it is what it is. He was surprisingly quiet on the subject, well quieter than he was about other stuff. He told me not to get my dick shot off."

I cringed and ran my hands up his chest. I loved the way he felt so solid and hard. I liked to think of him as unbreakable, bulletproof, even if it wasn't true. I curled my hands around the back of his neck and drew him down so I could kiss him much softer than he kissed me.

I teased his lips open with my own, ran my tongue along the seam of his mouth, and dipped inside when he finally opened up. I licked across the curve of his lower lip and darted inside to twist my tongue around his. He tasted like coffee and a faint hint of toothpaste. He tasted real and clean. He tasted like everything that made life worth fighting for.

In typical Titus fashion he only let things be soft and sweet for a second before he took over. One of his hands found my ass as he jerked me closer and bent his head closer to mine so he could devour me. When he finally pulled away we were both panting and had dirty, sexy things floating around in our eyes. I could see my own rumpled, anticipatory expression shining back at me in the translucent silver of his eyes. It was a good look for me. It was a better look on him.

He pulled open my door for me and I slid in, making sure to drag my fingers across the front of his jeans and the straining hardness that I knew was waiting for me there.

He got behind the wheel of the car and gave me a hot look out of the corner of his eye. "Did you see Honor?"

"Keelyn," I corrected automatically. "Yeah, I saw her. She's having a hard time with getting shot."

"Anyone would."

I nodded absently. "She's looking to make some changes."

"Nassir mentioned that she told him she was leaving. I didn't think it was a serious threat. I didn't think he would let her leave. He has women crawling all over him, but for some reason she's the only one he treats like an actual human being. Typically he treats everyone like they are just a nuisance and a waste of his time."

I fiddled absently with my hair as the graffiti-covered buildings and broken sidewalks flew by in a blur. If you squinted just right it was almost pretty, like abstract art. Almost.

"I don't think he'll know she's gone until it's too late. She knows he wouldn't let her leave and she would let him convince her to stay. She needs to see what it's like out there. She needs to see that nowhere is like the Point, and that isn't always a good thing."

He reached out a hand and settled it on my thigh. Again it

was the normality, the simple gestures between us that were tearing me apart and making me crave more. I took my index finger and traced the heavy veins on the back of his hand around the clean bandage I had wrapped around it after our sexual acrobatics on the bed earlier. He was lucky the stitches hadn't pulled open, as aggressive and handsy as he tended to get when he let loose.

"Is that what you figured out in WITSEC? The grass isn't always greener?"

I gave a bitter laugh and rubbed my finger across his cut-up knuckles. "I had never even seen grass until WITSEC. I wasn't one of those girls that chased boys on the Hill. I wasn't trying to date outside my class. I had no desire to be some Point trash that got used and abused. I was always the one that was doing the using. I learned grass is hard to keep green and you need a lot of idle time and disposable income to even try and grow it. I'm not comfortable with either of those things, so I'll take the concrete and the asphalt any day. You don't have to keep it alive, you just have to hose it off."

He let out a low whistle between his teeth and turned his head to look at me. His eyes were that oh so pretty blue that I could just stare at all day. Keelyn might want Denver for a breath of fresh air, mine was right there in those penetrating orbs.

"That's a pretty bleak view on life, Reeve."

I just shrugged. "It's the way it is. I think it's important to make the most of what you have. Before you know it, all of it can be gone and then all you're left with is regret."

"Are we talking about your sister?" His tone was soft but his fingers tightened on my leg.

"We could be, but we could be talking about anything really. Why did you leave Bax when you were younger, Titus? Was it because you wanted more instead of appreciating what you had? What did it leave you with? Regret that your brother fell in with a bad crowd? Regret you weren't there for him? Is that why you're saddled with the overwhelming desire to protect everyone innocent and unassuming, because you couldn't do that for the person that mattered most? I'm not judging you; I'm just saying that not accepting where you're from and how that shapes you isn't good."

He lifted his hand off my leg and I immediately felt the loss of his touch. His hands curled around the steering wheel until the knuckles turned white. I had struck a chord with him, but I wasn't going to apologize. I had stopped apologizing for myself a long time ago.

"I know exactly where I come from and how that plays into who I am now. It was why I left in the first place." He growled out the words in such a rough way I practically felt them scrape across my skin.

"And where is that? Where do you come from?" I knew the answer was more than the Point or the Hill, but I didn't know if he was going to share it with me.

I held my breath to see what he would do, and felt crushing disappointment when he looked away from me and muttered, "That falls into the *more* category, Reeve." Effectively shutting me down and out with minimal effort. I wished it didn't feel like he was reaching inside of my chest and squeezing my heart with his fist every time he did it.

"It doesn't matter to me, you know? I don't care where you

come from. I care about who you are now. I see it in you, Detective. I see the parts you try and lock away and keep hidden. The parts that make you wild and rough. I see them and I don't care because they're part of the entire package."

That's what I had been searching out when I fell prey to Conner. Someone that would see all the parts of me, all the things that made me who I was and love me anyways.

"You see too much." He was gruff.

"Only because I'm looking."

We hit an impasse and the rest of the ride passed in heavy silence. I thought when we got back to the condo we would each take a separate corner of the loft and take a time-out. The tension was thick and rolling between the two of us and I hated it.

Apparently Titus hated it too because before the front door was even closed behind us he had his hands all over me, his mouth over mine, and he was efficiently stripping both of us and headed toward the bed. It wasn't talking. It wasn't letting me in. It wasn't giving me *more,* but it was something, and the something it was felt so good, felt so right, I couldn't stop him if I wanted to, which I absolutely didn't.

Only an idiot would say no to those melted silver eyes, that talented mouth, those impatient and heavy hands, that body made to punish and please, and I was a lot of things, most of them pretty unpleasant, but an idiot wasn't one of them.

Chapter 12

Titus

WHERE I WAS FROM was something I never wanted to talk about with anyone, ever. It had nothing to do with Reeve or the fact that letting her into that deep dark hole was going to cement me even more solidly to her. I might be a man that had a purpose now, but before I was just like every other punk kid running the streets, and I hated those memories. I hadn't been handed a way out; I made my own, and the way I went about it still left a dirty taste in my mouth all these years later. I had as much bad blood circulating in my veins as Bax did, maybe even more when it came right down to it. It was that part of me that I fought every waking minute of every day to keep buried under honor and duty. That tainted blood, that nasty past, followed me, haunted me, which was why I never had any room in my life for the gray. The fog of the past was full of monsters that feasted on my soul, so I kept them locked in the dark. Usually they wallowed there, starved and angry, but ever since Reeve blasted her way through my fortress of protection they were climbing to the surface and demanding attention.

So far they seemed content to feed on her attention and her

luscious body. They drank in the acceptance and understanding in her navy gaze like it was ambrosia, but I knew eventually she wouldn't be enough to keep those animals at bay. My carefully constructed life was liable to fall victim to the wreckage they would cause if they escaped. That's why I crawled out of bed every single morning before dawn and went to work, leaving her sprawled on the other side of the bed, naked and marked up from my teeth and hands. Every night she let me have her without complaint and every day I woke thinking she deserved better than what I was giving her. Two weeks that felt like forever while I climbed all over her and let her sink deeper and deeper inside of me. Her pretty skin had angry red marks from my face rubbing all over her, and instead of wincing in regret that I had damaged something so beautiful, messed up such perfection, I wanted to beat my chest with pride and declare myself the winner of the world's greatest prize. It was a dangerous way to think because she wasn't a prize, a trophy, and I had done nothing to win her, so I left her there every single morning and went hunting.

I hit up every back alley I could find. I popped into every underground bar and rattled the owners in a hope I could make them talk. I waltzed into every drug den I had on my radar and demanded answers. Anyplace Novak was known to haunt back in the day . . . I showed my face there asking about his wayward son. I even stopped the girls that worked the street corners, the ones that didn't want Nassir's protection and preferred to tough it out in the wild on their own, and asked them about Roark. It was the same story from every lowlife I encountered. The elusive man with an accent had made his presence known. All the criminals and miscreants knew Roark was in town, hiding in the shadows, making those he deemed responsible for his father's death pay. No one seemed to know where the Irishman was, but they all told the same tale. He was watching and they were afraid of him.

Honestly, so was I.

Seeing Bax broken like that, watching Nassir hover over Keelyn as blood pumped out of her chest . . . it all hit too close to home. I was used to having to juggle the law and people I cared about. I mean I had locked my brother up for five years, and I was just waiting for Race to do something stupid enough for it to be his turn to sit in a cell. But the kind of outright warfare Roark was launching at the people I loved was an entirely different ball game, and I hated knowing he had the upper hand. When the bad guy knew all the good guy's tricks, it made trying to catch him twice as hard as it should be.

I was already feeling defeated and disgruntled after hours of hitting the streets when I got called to an armed robbery with a fatality. The liquor-store clerk was dead at the scene and two of the customers that had been waiting around to buy beer were also shot and en route to the hospital. It wasn't an uncommon scenario in the Point, but for some reason, when I got to the scene and saw that the kid that was hooked up in cuffs and sitting in the back of the patrol car couldn't be any older than twelve or thirteen, it almost made me turn around, get back in my boring sedan, and not stop driving until I got to the station to turn in my gun and my shield. All the violence and unnecessary waste of life just seemed like too much to keep wading through every single day.

I pulled up the knot on my tie and tried to smooth the wrinkles out of my slacks as I climbed out of the car. The uniformed officer that was talking to a group of people gathered on the outside of the crime-scene tape saw me and started over in my direction. The kid in the back of the patrol car looked up at me and I could see that he had tear tracks on his face. Shit. He should be playing football with his friends not out committing felonies.

"Anybody see anything?"

The uniformed cop nodded and pointed at the kid with the end of the pen he was using to jot down witness statements.

"The guy behind the counter was the owner. His wife was in the back doing inventory when the first shots were fired. She saw her husband go down and said the kid just kept shooting and shooting. She gave us a positive ID on him."

I grunted and frowned as the coroner's team rolled a gurney out of the store with the body covered in a heavy, black plastic body bag. I heard gasps from the crowd at the sight, and sighed.

"How did the kid get caught so fast? Have his parents been notified?" He might be a killer but he was still a minor, which meant we had to do things by the book.

"He went back to school. Guess he didn't know what to do when things went south. One of the teachers saw him slipping back inside the building and noticed he didn't look right. When she approached him she noticed the blood spatter all over his clothes and shoes. She had a school security guard detain him and the principal called us. We brought him down here and got the ID from the wife. He ditched the gun, so we're still looking for it, and there are no parents. Mom is in prison for manufacturing meth and there is no father. According to the kid, he stays with an 'uncle.'" The cop made quotes around the word in the air. "But it sounds like the guy is a freak show. The kid said he was trying to rob the place so he could buy a bus ticket and get out of town. Said he was tired of his uncle hurting him. The gun is the so-called uncle's, by the way, so we sent a unit over there to grab him as well."

"Jesus." I ran a hand over my face. "It never ends, does it?" It was all such a vicious cycle with no end in sight.

The other cop sighed and looked at the kid. "No. No, it doesn't."

"If the other two victims make it through surgery, be sure to get statements from them. Make sure the kid has someone from Social Services with him when you process him in since he doesn't have a legal guardian. You want to make sure every *I* is dotted and every *T* is crossed because I bet they try and prosecute him as an adult."

"Can't say I disagree with that. This is a pretty adult-size fuckup he landed himself in."

It was, but the kid never stood a chance, and all I could think was how easy it would've been for Bax to do something just as stupid when he was struggling to feed himself and survive because no one else was there to take care of him when he was that age.

"Sometimes it feels like the only choice you have is the worst choice there is. Too many kids these days end up getting put in that position. We just have to do our job and do it to the best of our ability in order to keep everyone else safe from those terrible choices and the people forced to make them."

"You speaking from personal experience, Detective?"

I didn't bother answering. When you were a cop in this city—or any city, really—for any length of time, you saw it all. Killer kids. Druggies that were practically zombies from their addiction. Women doing whatever they had to do in order to feed their families or themselves. Families living on the street because a backroom poker game was more important than paying the mortgage. Men forced to bend the law rather than work inside it because someone had to be the bad guy and they figured it might as well be them. So we all had personal experience with why things happened the way they did here, and I didn't need to spin sob stories about my own drunken mother and my mass-murdering father, or my car thief of a brother, to showcase just how much experience I had with how dark the Point could be.

I grabbed the surveillance tapes, had a quick chat with the inconsolable wife, took the notes I would need for the report, and then drove across town to the elementary school where another patrol unit had found the gun hidden inside one of the tube slides in the elementary school playground; that was just a block over from the middle school the kid had attended. The weapon was still loaded, with the safety off, and we were all silently thanking whatever god was watching that day that no other little hands had run across it and caused even more of a tragedy. I was thinking about what a mess it all was and how deeply sad it made me. I felt the waste of that young life all the way to my bones, and yet I knew there was nothing I could do about it. It was the impotence of not being able to fix that poor kid's life, of not being able to help him before he got so desperate, that killed me. No living being should be driven to those lengths, yet it happened every day here.

I was packing up the scene when one of the patrol officer's radios squawked. A callout for a bomb threat at a charter high school a few miles away. Kids called in bogus threats all the time, but ever since Nassir's club had been blown up and burned to the ground, we tended to take them more seriously. The officer responded and we all climbed in our respective vehicles and headed over to the school. It looked like most of the teachers and kids had already been evacuated. There were a lot of bodies milling about in front of the building and on the street. As I climbed out of the car I frowned hard because all the kids were dressed in a very familiar-looking navy-blue-and-khaki uniform. I saw that same color combo every time I passed Karsen Carter when she was coming and going from school.

The hair on my arms danced upward and tension had my spine snapping straight. I let my eyes scan the crowd looking for a familiar white-blond head and didn't see one. I didn't see Race or Brysen either, which made me breathe a sigh of relief. The school would've had to call Brysen to pick her sister up once the kids got released.

"What's the status?" I looked over at another detective as he came up beside me asking the question.

"I don't know. It's not my scene. I was working the armed robbery downtown and was just a few miles away, so I drove over. I think they're just waiting for the bomb squad to go in and make sure that it isn't a real threat."

He grunted in response and I took a few steps toward where I saw the kids gathering to wait for their parents to pick them up. I was hoping to find someone that had seen Karsen when a harried-looking woman clutching a cell phone rushed up to me. Her eyes took up most of her face and she was panting like she had run a mile. She thrust the phone at me and bent over to put her hand on her knees as she struggled to catch her breath.

"Are . . . you . . . Detective . . . King?" I looked at the phone in my hand then at her. A chill of apprehension slid down my spine as she panted and shook in front of me.

"I am. Who are you?"

"Debbie Granger. I'm the principal. The man on the phone said to find you. Told me to give you the phone."

I scowled at her and put the phone up to my ear. I wasn't surprised at all when the voice that greeted me had a lilt to it.

"Hello, Detective."

My teeth gnashed and my heart rate kicked into overdrive. "Roark."

"I thought it was about time I let you know that I very much remember the hand you played the night my father was murdered. I saw you there, Detective."

My spine snapped straight and my hand curled painfully around the phone. "What are you babbling about, Roark?"

"The night my father was killed . . . you were there. I saw you when we raided the club. Beaten and useless. You did nothing to stop my brother from killing our father. He still had the smoking gun in his hand when we made entry into the building. I've been slowly corrupting the one thing you care about most, Detective, and you haven't even seen me doing it. And if you think you can just swoop in and take my girl, you are sadly mistaken. I will not let any of your actions or her betrayal stand."

I forked my fingers through my hair and swore. "What do you mean you've been corrupting what I care about most? Are you talking about Race and Bax? Are you talking about hurting my family?" My head was spinning and the more time that went by without me seeing Karsen the more certain I became that she was inside the building, possibly with him, possibly sitting on a powder keg getting ready to blow.

The accented voice cackled and it made the hair on the back of my neck rise. "You'll figure it out. In fact you'll figure it out as you stand there in front of that school and do nothing while you wait on pins and needles to see if I harmed the pretty little blonde." He clicked his tongue at me and his voice got hard. "You step foot inside the building and the girl dies. If I see a single cop head toward the front of that building, I'll take her out and she won't be the only casualty. Do you understand what I'm telling you, Detective King?"

I gritted my teeth and bit out, "The apple didn't fall far from the crazy tree with you, did it, Roark?" He had me over a barrel and it was killing me that he was close enough to watch his handiwork unfold, but not close enough for me to get my hands on.

"One man's crazy is another man's brilliance. We'll be seeing each other soon enough. Tell Reeve hello for me. She looks like she's enjoying the limited time she has left on this earth fucking your brains out."

I forced myself to hand the phone back to the principal and stared up helplessly at the entrance of the school. There was no doubt in my mind that Karsen was trapped somewhere inside and everything inside of me was screaming at me to go save her. That's what I did—saved the innocent from the violence of the Point—and now Roark had effectively tied my hands, and it was making me furious. I started shouting at my fellow officers and anyone that would listen that they had to wait before they went inside. I wasn't sure what kind of threat Roark had in place but I was in no position to push him. When my colleagues looked at me like I had lost my mind, I told them we had to wait for the bomb squad. It was the simplest excuse I could come up with off the top of my head. They didn't like it but they backed down as I paced back and forth, never taking my eyes from the door.

She was just a kid, a really good kid at that. She deserved better than to be drawn into Roark's deadly games. I clenched my hands into tight fists at my sides and looked at the cop that I had spoken to when I arrived on the scene. "The parents are starting to show." He nodded his head in the direction from which cars and people were starting to stream in. Parents hysterical as they spotted their kids and the kids looking bored with it all. I was trying to figure out a way to sneak inside the school or a way to get some idea of what was happening on the inside when I heard a shrill voice call my name.

"Titus! What's going on?" My heart immediately dropped into my shoes when I saw Brysen jogging up to me, her superblue eyes wide with fear. She wasn't with Race, which was surprising; instead Booker was keeping pace with her, looking like he was going to murder anyone that got in his way.

"There was a bomb threat."

"I was in class and I got a call saying the school was evacuated and they needed me to come get Karsen. Where is she and why are you here?"

"The students are all with the teachers over there but I haven't seen Karsen with them." I wasn't ready to tell her that her little sister was currently a pawn in a very dangerous game and that I had no idea how to help her.

Booker lifted an eyebrow at me. His look downright menacing with that scar distorting his face. "Why don't you tell me why you aren't in there looking for the girl because we both know she isn't over there with those teachers."

I let out a long breath and lifted my hand to rub the back of my neck. I looked down at the tip of my boots in shame and defeat. "Roark just called me. He said if I go in the school after Karsen, he'll kill her. He told me to keep all of law enforcement out of the building or there will be fatalities. I'm just trying to buy time until the bomb squad gets here so we can get eyes inside and I can see what we're dealing with."

Brysen lifted shaking hands to her mouth and I saw her eyes pop to an unnaturally large size. "You think he's in there with her?"

I didn't want to think anything, but if this was another one of Roark's salvos then anything was possible. I was going to open my mouth to give the pretty young woman my typical platitudes when Booker stepped around me and took a striding step toward the front of the school. I reached out a hand to grab him and got pulled off balance as he jerked to a stop. The guy was built like a mountain and it wasn't often someone could match me in the physicality department.

"Where do you think you're going? I told you no one goes in until the building is clear. We can't risk it."

He shook me off and his eyes went flat and hard. I knew the look well. It was the same look Bax got when he was getting ready to tell me to go fuck myself because he was going to do something I didn't like.

"I'm not a cop and all Roark said was keep the cops out. Race pays me to take care of those girls, so that's what I'm going to do."

There was no point in arguing any further because aside from tasing him or putting a bullet in him, the guy was going to do whatever he wanted anyway. And honestly, I wished I was the one that was just saying to hell with it all and storming inside the building to look for the missing teenager. Booker flipped off a couple more cops that tried to stop him and even pushed one over that was stupid enough to get directly in his path. I sighed because now he was looking at charges for assaulting an officer even if he skated around whatever charges I could find to throw at him for ignoring a direct police order.

"What if she's hurt or something worse? How can I live with that? It's my job to keep her safe." Brysen's voice was weak but she was holding herself together surprisingly well. She wasn't crying, at least not yet, and she was wrong. The safety of Karsen and the rest of the kids that hadn't been tainted by the city yet was my job.

It hit me like a ton of bricks. So heavy and hard it almost took me to my knees. Roark had been going after the thing that mattered most to me from the very beginning. I cared about the people that still had a shot at making it out of the Point. I fought for the innocent and the young because I often felt like no one else was going to. Every person that Roark had hurt, had twisted, had infected in his quest to exact his revenge had been someone I'd sworn I would protect and keep safe.

It started with the kid whose neck he snapped and ditched outside of the Pit. Just some dumb jock barely in his twenties that liked to gamble, but he was just a kid and deserved a better end. Then it was the club. Before it burned to the ground, Nassir had been deliberately lured away and all the victims were just kids out looking for some trouble and fun. They lost their lives doing what kids all across the country did every single day. After that it was the girl on the dock and the armed stripper at Spanky's. Two girls too young to be caught up in that kind of life and too young to be dead. Two girls I should've been able to keep safe. And lastly there was my brother. Sure, Bax was far from innocent, far from having a shot at a good and law-abiding life, but he was still my only family, my blood, and even if I had let him down in the past, I took my duty to keep him safe and keep him out of trouble to heart now. Killing Bax would have served the dual purpose of exacting revenge on the man who Roark thought was responsible for his father's death and rubbing salt into the wound I would suffer for being unable to protect him.

The realization of how insidious and malicious as well as how fucking brilliant in his evil machinations Roark was had me shaking so hard I almost missed Brysen's words as she whispered "Someone needs to stop him; he can't be allowed to go after anyone anymore."

I blew out a breath and tried to steady myself. "I'm trying."

She narrowed her very blue eyes. "Try harder."

No wonder Race was sprung on her. She looked like a doll but had the bite of a barracuda. She was his perfect match in that way—all golden and glossy on the outside but made of stronger, more resilient stuff on the inside. If Roark did have Karsen, I sure hoped the younger Carter was as tough as Brysen.

Just as the big, black utility vehicles with SWAT team members and the bomb technicians rolled up to the scene, the metal front doors at the front of the school clanked open and Booker came striding through with his arm wrapped around an obviously shaken and upset Karsen. The teen looked so tiny and fragile next to the giant man that it had murderous rage toward Roark thumping heavy not just through my heart but the heart of the beast that was wide awake in my chest and hungry for retribution.

Brysen let out a shout and took off running toward the duo. I should've stopped her considering the building still wasn't secure and I still had no idea where Roark was lurking, but I didn't have the heart to keep her away from her sister. The two blondes hugged and then they were both crying as Booker was ripped away from the teen and slapped into cuffs by the same cop he has shoved over only moments before.

Karsen started yelling when the cop began to haul Booker away, but Brysen shushed her and guided her over to where I was still standing. I watched curiously as the guys dressed in black tactical gear unloaded a robot that looked like something from *Star Wars* and used a computer to guide it toward the front of the school. I was dying to know if they were going to find anything or if this had all been some elaborate ruse Roark had staged only to show me he had me right where he wanted me.

"Are you okay?" The teenager was crying big, fat, silent tears but she looked unharmed. She nodded and looked in the direction where the cops had taken Booker.

"Why is he getting arrested? He was the only one that came and looked for me." Ouch. That accusation burned hot across my skin.

"He pushed a cop. They tend to take offense at that. Why were you still inside the building, Karsen? What happened?" I didn't want to press her too hard because she was obviously pretty shaken up but I didn't have any time to waste either.

She frowned and leaned her head on her sister's shoulder as Brysen stroked her fair hair. "Yeah, why were you still in there?" Brysen sounded mad.

Karsen swallowed hard and looked up at her sister with wide eyes. "They announced that we all had to evacuate over the PA system. We do drills all the time, so it was no big deal. My whole class got up and headed to the door like usual. Well, Mr. Kline, my math teacher, stopped me and told me that I had to wait for a minute. I thought it was weird, but then he told me that he had to have a witness to verify that the room was totally empty, so I stayed." She blinked her eyes like an owl and looked between the two of us. "I knew something was off. I was getting ready to bolt for the door when he grabbed me and shoved me back into one of the desks. He kept rambling about how he has a family and that he was so sorry. He locked me in the room. I couldn't get out."

Brysen said every dirty word that had ever existed and glared at me over her sister's head. "Tell me you are going to do something about this?"

I nodded. "Karsen, is the teacher still here?" I asked the question just as the bomb-squad guys hollered an all clear and stormed the front of the school, finally making their way inside the building. It hadn't been a real threat. It was all a distraction. Unease and something stronger, scarier, raced up and down my spine.

She gave a cursory glance to where the crowd was thinning out and shook her head in the negative. "No. I don't see him. This is because of that guy, isn't it? The guy who burned down Nassir's club and who burned up Race's car and killed his dad."

I didn't see any reason to lie to her, so I was going to tell her yes, but, like she had conjured him out of thin air, Race was suddenly there looking beyond furious and ready to take on the entire police force and anyone else that might be in the way of him getting to his girls. He wrapped them both up in a hug so tight it had them squeaking, and glowered at me over their heads.

"Seriously? A kid is getting dragged into all of this? It ends now, Titus."

I couldn't agree more but I wasn't sure what any of them expected me to do. I was already dangling the carrot in front of Roark; he just hadn't bitten at it yet.

Karsen pulled herself out of Race's suffocating embrace and looked up at him with pleading eyes. "Booker was the one that came in the school and found me. I heard him calling my name and pounding on all the doors until he found the right one. They arrested him. You have to help him, Race."

There was more in her tone than concern for her savior. Oh, boy, I didn't envy Race or Brysen having to deal with a crush like that on a guy like Booker. It was just asking for all kinds of ugly heartache.

Race gave me another hard look and I just shrugged. "This is my job, Race. Booker decided to ignore police orders and went in even though we didn't know if the scene was clear. He could've been putting Karsen at greater risk. He got handsy with a cop when they tried to stop him, so they hooked him up."

His green eyes flashed to black with fury and his mouth pulled into a hard, tight line. "What if there *had* been a bomb, Titus? What if she was just stuck there waiting to die because some madman has daddy issues?"

Deciding that things would just get nastier with Race because I didn't have an answer to his questions, I asked Karsen to give me the teacher's full name and promised her I would do what I could to get Booker out of lockup as soon as possible. The poor kid had been through enough for one day.

I called Dispatch to get an address on the math teacher and decided I better call and check on Reeve since she was on her own. My hackles lifted straight up when the phone just rang and rang. She was supposed to be at the loft, and she was too smart to venture out into the city on her own knowing Roark was winning this deadly game hands down. I tried to remind myself of that as the phone continued to ring unanswered. She wouldn't willingly put herself in harm's way knowing what the stakes were. I also tried to keep in mind that if she had left the condo, the feds were supposed to be keeping an eye on her per our deal, so she wouldn't be out there in the war zone alone.

The teacher lived in that weird in-between neighborhood where Bax had bought a house. It was nice enough not to need bars on the windows, but still close enough to the city that you could feel the grime and the dirt under your feet. The teacher had a simple ranch-style house that was well maintained and looked about as lower middle class as one could get. There were no signs of anything that would indicate that he was somehow mixed up with Roark, but I knew looks could be deceiving. I shot Reeve one last text demanding that she tell me where she was before climbing out of the sedan and walking up to the front door.

I raised a hand to knock and almost fell into the house as the door swung open under the tapping of my knuckles. The interior was dark, and before I even took a step over the threshold, the metallic and iron scent of blood hit my nose.

I swore under my breath and walked into the house expecting the worst. I got it.

The middle-aged teacher and his wife were sitting on the couch, each with a perfectly round bullet hole in the center of their foreheads. They were still holding hands.

A teenaged boy that couldn't be any older than Karsen was a few feet away, facedown on the carpet and missing the back of his skull. It looked like he had tried to make a run for it and not gotten very far. I pulled my phone out so I could call the murders in and saw that I'd missed a text from Reeve. I ignored it so I could call the station, explaining that I thought the multiple homicide was directly related to the bomb threat at the school. I wasn't sure how to explain Roark, so I just told Dispatch that it was all part of an ongoing investigation. One more kid I hadn't gotten to in time in a pool of blood. Roark really was eating away at the very foundation of what I did and why I did it.

I went outside so that I could go talk to the neighbors and see if anyone had seen anything. As I stepped outside I remembered to look at Reeve's text. I tapped the screen to open it and frowned at her terse message.

I had to go home.

What in the hell did that mean? She was still at the loft? She had to go back to her place up north where WITSEC had stashed her? She had to go back to her place she had in the city when things went to hell? I wasn't sure what she considered home and I didn't like that at all. I shot her back:

WTF does that even mean? Call me NOW! Tied up at work. Triple homicide most likely Roark.

I thought that would get her attention, and I would hear back from her in a split second, but all I got was silence. I didn't like it, but I had a job to do, so I started knocking on doors. The first neighbor hadn't seen or heard anything. Of course not. The second took great pleasure in telling me all about what a delinquent the son was. Apparently the kid had a drug problem and had been caught trying to break into various neighbors' houses.

Two houses down, an old lady that had to be in her eighties swore she saw a big silver truck that didn't belong in the neighborhood pull up in front of the house. She also thought Clinton was still president of the United States, so I jotted the info down without much hope of it leading to anything. Finally, when I spoke to the young couple that lived across the street, I got something that might actually be helpful.

They said they saw a bald guy with a goatee talking to the kid. He had been around a few times when the parents were gone, and the couple agreed he didn't give off a good vibe. The kid's drug problem was well known around the neighborhood, so they thought he might be a dealer. I told them thank you and made my way back across the street as the crime-scene crew arrived. I was getting really sick of those guys and the ones with the body bags.

Roark had a full head of hair and was clean-shaven. He looked like a lot of retired military men look. Hard and battle weary but still stuck on the regimen of being clean cut and straightened out. I wondered if the bald guy with the goatee was the infamous Zero, who had shown up on Reeve's doorstep asking after Roark. It sounded like I had a description of the man Roark had doing his dirty work for him while he pulled the strings safely hidden away.

Once I was done at the scene I started blowing Reeve's phone up and tried to fight down panic when there still wasn't any answer. I knew she was smart, but so far Roark had proven smarter than all of us. She knew that all of her protection was tied up at the charter school with Roark's carefully crafted distraction, and she wouldn't have left the safety of the loft unless she felt like she absolutely didn't have a choice. I needed to figure

out what "home" meant and I needed to figure it out right now.
I called Otis, the marshal, to see if his guys had eyes on her and
they could guide me in the right direction.

When he told me where she was off to, my heart dropped
and I knew I needed to get to her. She had been taking care of me
since the moment she stepped foot back in the Point. Now it was
time for me to return the favor.

Chapter 13

Reeve

WHEN BOOKER TOOK OFF after a panicked call from Brysen, I had planned on settling in for the rest of the day and doing nothing. I was getting real sick and tired of doing nothing. I had never had the opportunity to just sit around idle while someone else took care of me, and I didn't care for it at all. Especially since I woke up alone and bereft every morning knowing that Titus was purposely putting space between us during waking hours. We needed to figure out a way that I could be out in the open that seemed like I was on my own without actually flying solo. I needed to be someplace where Conner could get closer to me. This condo was like a fortress and there was no way he could get his hands on me if I was cloistered behind the impenetrable walls.

I was messing with my hair in the bathroom mirror because I was that bored when the cell phone Titus had given me rang. Only two people had the number, Titus and Booker, so I froze when neither one of those names came up on the display. I thought I knew who would be on the other end, that a deadly and lyrical Irish lilt would hit my ears when I answered the call.

I was so surprised to hear a voice I hadn't heard since my family was whole that I actually went weak in the knees and had to sit down before I fell over.

My mom sounded so much like Rissa over the phone it was like talking to a ghost. I was shaking so badly that I was having a hard time holding on to the cell and her words were getting lost in the rushing of blood through my head.

She said something about a federal agent stopping by the house and letting her and my dad know there was new information on Rissa and her boyfriend's murder. She told me the agent had been so nice, so handsome and polite. She told me that he thought she should be the one to call me because it was information the entire family needed to know. My mother hadn't had that much life in her since my sister's body went into the ground. Her words stabbed through me like broken and jagged shards of glass. She asked me to come home. I hadn't been home to see her or my father in almost six years. Too much time and such a huge secret kept me from going back to them, and now Conner was manipulating the situation so I had no choice.

He wanted me to tell them what I had done. He knew that admitting to my parents my part in what had happened after Rissa's death was my worst fear. He was using things I had told him, shared with him, when I thought I was in love, against me. He was pure evil and really tricky. It didn't escape my notice that he was guiding me away from the security of the condo while both Titus and Booker were away. I wondered if he had yet to pick up on the marshals that were supposedly keeping an eye on me from the background or if he just didn't care.

I promised my mom I would try and make it home soon. She cried, and when I hung up I knew without a doubt the phone would ring again. I don't know how Conner got the number, but I was done questioning how he managed to always be a step ahead. Instead I needed to focus on luring him closer.

I would never understand how such a terrible man could have such a beautiful voice. It was without a doubt one of the greatest weapons he had in his arsenal. His accent just a shadow under his hard words as he said my name.

"Reeve. Pretty, pretty Reeve. It's a shame it had to go this way. I had such big plans for you."

I stared at the phone like it might bite me. His words coiled tight and threatening around my throat.

"Because you loved me, Conner? You had plans because you loved me?" I sounded bitter and scorned, and I kind of was. I hated that he had fooled me so badly. I hated that he had just brought more bad into my life when all I wanted was good. I hated that I was going to kill him, and this beautiful thing that was unfurling between me and Titus would wither and die.

"I love you about as much as you loved me, Reeve. One user can usually spot another from a mile away. I thought that's what we were doing . . . using."

I scoffed at him. "I thought we were starting a relationship. I thought you were something different."

"That makes two of us. I thought you would understand why I'm doing what I have to do. I thought we spoke the same language of revenge, of doing what had to be done to right a wrong."

I flinched at the word *revenge* and how powerful it could be in the wrong hands. I shoved my fingers through my long hair. "Why did you go to my parents' house, Conner? What are you trying to do to them?"

He laughed, and it made my stomach turn over and over. I wrapped an arm around my waist and bent over. I felt like there was a good chance I might get sick.

"I'm giving them the truth. Don't you think they deserve to know the role you played in bringing their daughter's killer to justice? Don't you think they should be proud of you, admire what you risked?" He laughed. "I'm helping you face your fears, my dear. Don't you think it's time you came clean, laid the burden down? You went back to the Point to end me but forgot just how many of your secrets still lived there. There are a lot of ways to make someone suffer, Reeve, and I think you should experience them all before we meet again."

He wasn't trying to do anything to my parents or for them. He was trying to do it to me. I'd left because things hadn't felt right. I hadn't felt right knowing what I had done and not feeling an ounce of guilt over the choice I had made. I couldn't stay there and lie to my parents' faces, so I left, and now he was forcing me to go back. He was going to blow up my family once again, using me and my past choices as the dynamite. I squeezed my eyes shut. He was right: there *was* more than one way to make someone suffer. I felt the pain well up inside of me.

"You expect me to tell them what I did. You want me tell them I went to Novak."

"I don't expect it, I know it. If you don't do this, the next call will be from your new boyfriend because he's on the way to their bodies. Do you understand me?"

"You'll kill them anyway. It's what you do." And even though my parents and I weren't really close, I still couldn't let him do that to them. They were innocent in all of this, their only crime being that they were related to me. Their deaths would be my fault, and even though I was strong, the weight of more guilt and more bodies would cripple me.

"I haven't killed anyone who didn't deserve it." That voice was so seductive, just begging me to believe him.

"Oh yeah? What about the girl on the docks? You want me to believe you didn't have your hands in that? She looked just like me."

He laughed a little bit. "She had your smart mouth as well. I might have taken a personal interest in her and gotten a little overzealous in trying to teach her what happens to pretty, mouthy girls. It's time to go home, Reeve. Go alone. If the cop shows, it won't end well for anyone."

I whimpered a little bit. "He's going to want to know where I'm at. He won't just let me drop out of sight." Titus was going to be pissed that I was leaving the condo in the first place. When he found out why, he was going to call me every kind of idiot for falling into one of Roark's traps.

"Well, you better buy yourself some time, then. This little reunion has been a long time coming and your new boyfriend isn't going to mess with my fun. I have another call to make but I'll be seeing you soon, Reeve." It sounded like he blew me a kiss over the line before he ended the call. After hanging up the phone I just sat there staring at it for a long time. I didn't get my head together until I realized I was crying and big, fat teardrops were hitting the screen. Going to see my parents was a stupid risk to take. I could take a cab to their house, explain what I had done, and Conner could still send Zero after them, but if I didn't go, they were dead for sure. There was no winning in this scenario, and as usual, at the end of the day I came out the loser. Figuring I didn't really have a choice, that a homecoming and a come-to-Jesus talk with the people that had raised me was long overdue anyway, I called my mom back and told her I would be home for dinner. I was surprised at how excited she sounded to see me, and the lure of new information, of some kind of closure when it came to her daughter's death, had her practically giddy. It made my heart hurt.

I put on some makeup, deciding I needed it like war paint to psych myself up, and then called for a cab. Titus tried to call me, once and then again, but he didn't leave a message and I knew if I tried to talk to him, tried to explain what I was doing and why I had to do it, he wouldn't let me go alone. Hell, part of me hoped that it was all an elaborate ploy to get me to leave the fortress castle so Conner could grab me. I had the Glock in my purse and that confrontation was one I was prepared for. Far more than I was prepared for this new one with my parents. I had had a hard enough time telling Titus about the murder-for-hire plot when I turned myself in; I couldn't imagine trying to find the right words to justify my actions to my parents.

Conner wasn't just evil, he was twisted and cruel. He knew that telling my parents that I had arranged for a murder, that I had sold my soul to Novak, would effectively end any feelings they had for their surviving daughter. This wasn't about hurting me so much as it was forcing me to rip their world apart once again, effectively making me as bad a person as he was. He wanted to remind me how alike we were, which was also a way of reminding me how different Titus and I were. That wounded. It burned and festered inside of me. I didn't want it to be true but there was no denying that it was.

I called a cab and decided to turn my phone off. It wouldn't keep Titus at bay forever, but it would hold him off long enough for me to get the dirty deed done. I figured if the marshals were still following me around looking for Conner, they would fill him in on the fact I was on the move. I sent Titus a text telling him I was going home before killing my phone, hoping it would give him a vague idea of what I was up to. I knew he would have a million questions once he caught up to me, but for now I couldn't let him or his rightness flavor the discomfort and unease I was tasting as I headed toward the outskirts of the city.

My parents still lived in the Point. They had a town house behind a strip mall that had long been abandoned and left to rot. The side of the building where they lived was covered in graffiti and all the windows had vertical bars running across them. My parents didn't have a drug problem, and neither one had ever gambled a day in their lives. They had been two young kids that had fallen hopelessly in love, had a baby way too young, and never managed to get ahead enough in any job to invest in their future. My parents were the working poor, they always had been, and the Point fit them like a comfortable old shoe. My mom worked as a waitress, had since she was a teen, and my dad was a janitor for some big building on the Hill. He tended to jump from job to job, and while there had never been anything extra growing up, there had always been enough.

As I looked at the faded paint on the front door memories flooded in. All I could see was my sister. All I could feel was the loss and the emptiness that always lingered when it came to Rissa. I had to fight back more tears when I lifted my hand to knock on the door.

When my mom pulled it open I guess I expected her to look older, still drawn and ravaged with grief. She didn't. In fact she looked so much like she had before Rissa was murdered it made me fall back a step. The distance between us didn't last long as she reached out and wrapped me up in a hug. I was so shocked by the contact I didn't even hug her back. The warm reception stunned me and made the reason I was here after all this time even harder to choke down.

"You look so pretty. It's been so long." She led me through a familiar hallway littered with pictures from my youth. Picture after picture of me and Rissa growing up. The memories knocked me sideways so hard I had to put a hand on the wall to stay upright. My mom gave me a concerned look and took my elbow to guide me the rest of the way into the tiny and cluttered living room, peppering me along the way with questions about where I had been and what I had been up to. My father was lounging in his easy chair watching TV. He looked so normal, just like my mother did, that I practically fell into the couch when the backs of my legs hit it. How had life just gone on for them? How had they battled down the grief and sorrow without doing something about it? I shifted my gaze from one to the other in shock. This was not the family I had left behind. This was a family that had healed and moved on without me.

I gulped as my mom patted my knee.

"It was lovely to hear your voice today, Reeve. Your father and I missed you. We wonder how you are doing every single day." There was so much kindness and love on her face that I wanted to fold over and clutch my stomach because I felt like I had been kicked in the guts.

My dad grunted his agreement and turned back to the television. I took a deep breath and curled my fingers tightly into my palm.

"I missed you guys too. It was just hard to be here. Too many memories." I was going to have to tell my mom that I nearly suffocated on them and ask her how she hadn't.

"Well, the memories are all we have left, so we try and hold on tight to them."

Conner knew just what he was doing. This was going to kill me more effectively than a bullet to the brain or a knife slipped between my ribs. He was killing my soul, murdering my spirit, and the bastard knew it. I was going to tarnish the remaining good my parents held on to from Rissa and from me. Those memories would be forever tainted once I told them the length I had gone to, to exact vengeance against Rissa's killer.

"We were so excited when that handsome agent knocked on the door and told us there was new information. We just knew Rissa wasn't into all that horrible stuff they said she was when she died."

A cold sweat broke out across my skin and I had to blink slowly and force air in and out of my lungs. "That agent lied to you, Mom. He doesn't have anything new on Rissa. She died because her boyfriend was a drug dealer and a pimp. She died because she loved a bad man and he hurt her. She died because she made really bad choices for herself and she was just as messed up as he was at the end."

My mom gasped and lifted her hands to her mouth. My dad shot a look at me from his reclined position but he didn't get up. So it began.

I sighed and told my mother, "The agent came here to see you because he knows secrets about me. Ugly, dark secrets, and he wants me to tell them to you so you can know what kind of person your surviving daughter really is." I had to take a deep breath because the look of horror that flashed across my mother's face was almost enough to make me stop talking. "He wants me to tell you what I did when I found out Rissa was dead. He wants me to confess that I went a little crazy, got so lost in the need for revenge and in grief that I made my own bad choices. He's not even a marshal anymore, I don't think he ever really was. He had a badge but he just used it for his own ends, not to help anyone else. He's a bad man and he's trying to hurt a lot of people. He forced me to come here and hurt you."

My mom got to her feet and started pacing back and forth in front of me. "What are you talking about, Reeve? None of this makes any sense." She still had hope. I could hear it in her voice. If I hadn't been planning on killing Conner already, I would be now. I hated having to be the one to take that hope from her.

"I knew Rissa's boyfriend was the one that killed her, and I knew he was going to get away with it. Too many people die in the Point for one young girl to matter, even if she was carrying a baby. It was too much. Too much hurt, too much pain, too much injustice. I decided that he needed to learn a lesson the same way he taught it, so I went and talked to Novak."

My mother gasped and jerked her gaze away from me. She looked at my dad with wide eyes and he finally climbed to his feet. He lumbered over so that he could put an arm around my mom's shaking shoulders.

"I promised him anything. I would have given my soul, my body, every dime I earned from then to eternity to stop feeling all the anger and hurt I was feeling. He told me he would take care of the boyfriend and he did." I lowered my head so that my hair fell over my face and I felt my nails break the skin on my palms just enough to release a tiny trickle of blood. "Rissa's boyfriend died because I needed him to. It was the only way I could keep on living."

I heard my mother muttering under her breath and then shuffling as she left the room. When I finally looked up it was just me and my father, and he was looking at me like I was a stranger.

"We raised you better than that. All life has value and you are not the judgment maker. We didn't turn our back on Rissa when she fell into drugs. We didn't stop loving her when she turned tricks for that boy. We still valued the good in her. How could you do that, Reeve? How could you make a deal with a monster like Novak? Where is there any kind of good in that?"

"I felt like I had to. Rissa deserved better than she got." How could he not want the man that had hurt Rissa so badly to pay? Why was I the only one that thought that way?

"Did it make you feel better after it was done? Did it bring you peace?"

All I could do was shake my head in the negative. He sounded disgusted by what I had done. I wasn't surprised, but it still cut to the bone. "No. Nothing has."

"Because there is no cure for grief. All you can do is wait it out, and day after day, little by little, you come to terms with it. But what you did"—now he was the one shaking his head at me—"even time can't fix that kind of mistake. You will always be tied to a killer, Reeve, and we've had so much death and loss in this family. Why did you come here? We were doing fine. Why did you think we had to know that?"

I swallowed hard to keep his words from hitting me like blows from a fist.

"I didn't have a choice. The agent that came to the door is trying to take his own kind of revenge against people he feel has wronged him and I'm one of them. He threatened to hurt you and Mom if I didn't come clean about what I had done. He might hurt you anyway, so you should really be careful. Revenge can make a person go crazy." I know that's what it had done to me and I wasn't nearly as demented and deranged as Conner was turning out to be.

"Hurt? That isn't the right word to describe what you've done here today, Reeve. We lost one daughter to her vices and her love for the wrong man. We're losing another to her own selfishness and impulsiveness. You shouldn't have come here. If this is what you had to bring home with you, you should've stayed far, far away."

"I had to." I really did. This was the reaction I expected, but it still tore me right down the middle.

"Just like you had to make a deal with a terrible man so you could seek out retribution. 'Had to' and 'want to' are very different creatures. I think you should go."

"I'm sorry."

I got to my feet and stumbled to the front door.

"You should be." My father's voice was harsh and shaking throughout the entire exchange. I had rendered my mother nearly catatonic but he had enough in him left to tell me, "Don't come back, Reeve. We were healed, had moved on without you."

They had healed because he was right: it was only time and the acceptance of the loss that led to healing, to moving on. I had yet to accept my sister's death. I was still stuck in the moment, watching dirt cover Rissa's casket and smoldering like a live ember with fury and rage. I was never going to be whole.

I pulled the door open and burst onto the crumbling cement stairs that led to the door. I tripped a little over my own feet because I was weak with rejection and disappointment, but hard hands were there to hold me up. He seemed to be there catching me every time I fell these days. I didn't even look up, just leaned into his chest and started crying. Titus didn't ask any questions. He just folded me into his strong embrace and took me to his car. The GTO stood like a beacon of freedom, of justice, in this worn place, and once I was inside it, I completely fell apart. The sobs racked my entire body as the motor roared to life and Titus pulled away from my parents' house. It felt like I was leaving my entire past behind.

"Don't turn your phone off again."

I hiccuped a little at his stern tone and blinked the water out of my eyes to see where we were going. The city was behind us and we were cruising at lightning speed around the Hill and up into the mountains. I had never been up that high. I was a born and bred city girl, so the closest I got to nature was walking across the grass when I was in WITSEC. The landscape was dark and imposing and also beautiful.

"I had to. If I spoke to you I knew you would talk me out of going or insist on going with me. Conner told me he would kill them if I didn't go alone. Besides, you didn't need to hear me explain what I had done again." Shouldering my father's disgust was hard, but seeing it on Titus's handsome face again would have killed me.

"Roark might go after them anyway."

"He might. But it was more about ripping me apart than it was about them. He figured my dad was going to look at me like he never wanted to see me again, and he was right. I had told him that telling my parents what I had done was the one thing I could never do. Admitting it to them was always one of my biggest fears. Turns out I had a reason to be terrified." I leaned my forehead on the cool glass of the window and asked, "How did you find me?"

He snorted and the wheels spun as the gravel turned to dirt, kicking the back end of the powerful car out to the side. "I called the feds. Though I'm feeling slightly annoyed at myself that I couldn't figure out where 'home' was from the instant you sent the text."

I hummed a little acknowledgment. "Where are we going?"

"To the top of the mountain. We used to race down the side for money and pink slips. Bax had a hell of a winning streak when he was sixteen that sort of put everyone off of doing it anymore, but it's still a nice place to have a quiet minute."

"I don't know that quiet is good for me right now." I felt cold and numb all over. "But thank you for coming for me."

He swore and the car fishtailed again but he didn't seem that interested in slowing down. His voice was smoky and thick as it washed over me.

"My mom is a drunk. She had a bottle in her hand the second I was born and hasn't put it down since. She was never very interested in being a mother, but she was beautiful and had an uncanny ability to attract very dangerous and powerful men."

"Like Novak."

He nodded in the darkness and I could see how rigid his jaw was as he talked to me. "Novak and my dad, Elias King."

I couldn't stop the shocked gasp that fell from my lips. The life of Elias King was a horror story parents told their children to get them to come home early at night and to keep them on the straight and narrow. His was a name whispered in fear when his awful misdeeds were tossed out as a warning to young girls. Elias King was a serial killer. A rampaging murderer that had raped and murdered more woman than I had fingers and toes. Not to mention when they finally arrested him the guy had been sitting on enough black-tar heroin to feed all the junkies in the entire state's habit for years to come.

"No." There was no way on earth that this man, this marvelous, amazing, law-abiding man, came from a horrific miscreant like Elias King. Titus had monsters inside of him but I couldn't believe he was born of them.

"Yes. I think my mom knew what he was up to; that's what started her drinking in the first place. She learned her lesson, though, and when she got knocked up with Bax she knew enough not to saddle him with a killer's last name. I've had a mass murderer following me everywhere I go my entire life."

"Oh my God, Titus, I had no idea."

"Not many people do. It's not something I advertise, and King is a common enough last name that people rarely make the connection. My mom was pregnant with me right before he went away. I've never even seen him in person. I only know what the rest of the world knows through the news and media. He's slated for execution but the date keeps getting pushed back."

"But still . . ." I trailed off, still trying to work my way through his major revelation.

"When I was fifteen I had this friend named Jordan. His mom used to bring him by Gus's shop and we would dick around with cars. He was from the Hill but I didn't really think anything of it until one day his mom told him not to talk to me, not because of my dad but because of where I was from. Seriously, I came from murderous genes, but because I was poor and from the Point, that was why she didn't want us to be friends? It was so fucked up, but it made me realize that was what my life was always going to look like. It was bad enough I had a killer's last name, but I was also from the wrong side of town to ever be of use to anyone."

I was breathing heavy and my heart was thundering in my ears. I couldn't believe he was giving all of this to me. Letting me inside the cage that held his monsters.

"Well, turns out Jordan's mom was at the shop a lot and it wasn't because she had car problems. She was there because she was sleeping with Gus. I told her if she didn't let me come to the Hill with her, if she didn't give me a shot to get out of high school and into college so I could make something of myself, I would tell her husband everything. Gus being Gus agreed to help me if she didn't bend."

"What did he do?" I barely breathed the words, fascinated by this other side of him.

"There was a video. Gus wasn't the shy type. She moved me into her mansion, got me into a fancy Hill private school, and let me stay there until I graduated. I blackmailed my way into a future, and I left my little brother behind to fend for himself while I did it. I wish I could tell you I did it all so I could go back and help Bax and my mom, so that I could take care of them, but I did it because I wanted to be more than a broke kid from the inner city. It wasn't about the money; it was about the way people looked at me. With a uniform I got respect, and it didn't matter if I was on the Hill or in the gutter of the Point. I mattered. It was in my first year on patrol that I realized I could actually make a difference. I could stop kids like Bax from getting sucked into the criminal underground. I could help young girls have something more than a corner to work on. I could make a difference and matter in a way that actually counted for something while being a better man and placing myself as far away from the legacy of Elias King as possible. I wanted the innocent, the people that still had a chance to make the right kind of choices, to have a shot. My reasons for being a cop didn't start out anywhere near as altruistic and noble as most people think, and I have to live with that. That's why I work so hard, why everyone out there in my city—good or bad—matters to me. Everyone has choices to make, Reeve, and they aren't always going to be the right ones. Sometimes they're the necessary ones. Just because you do bad things doesn't automatically make you a bad person. There is a gray area there that I have a tendency to ignore because I don't want to be reminded that I spent plenty of time there myself. That isn't fair to you."

The car finally skidded to a stop in a shower of gravel and dust. The headlights illuminated the drop-off in front of us. The moon was high in the sky, forcing its way through smog and clouds to shine silver. It was the same color as Titus's eyes when he was turned on, when he was buried deep inside of me.

"I haven't had my parents in my life for a long time, so I shouldn't feel like I lost them. But I do."

"I felt that way when I locked Bax up. I knew he wouldn't understand that I had to do my job, and when he got out, the first time I saw him he punched me in the face. He hated me." He turned off the car and reached out a finger to twist a piece of my long hair around it.

"Don't let Roark win. Once everything is settled, go back to them and make them understand."

I turned to look at him. He was fierce in the shadowy light. He was what heroes were supposed to look like no matter the path he had taken to become one.

"I don't even know if *I* understand. At the time it felt like my only choice. Now I'm not so sure." I leaned across the space separating us and brushed my knuckles across his still-bristly cheek. He was almost in full beard mode and it looked so good on him. "Lately the only thing I understand is you, Titus."

He lifted one of his dark eyebrows at me and asked, "What is it that you understand about me, Reeve?"

"That you make everything better. You make me better, and I might never be good enough for you, but you make me feel like I can get close."

One of his hands slid down to my wrist and the next thing I knew he was guiding me over the console and the emergency brake so that I was straddled across him with my back to the steering wheel. I hadn't been in a car like this with a boy since I was a teenager. I kind of liked it. More than kind of.

"You make everything better too, Reeve, and there is no good enough because *this* with you is the best there has ever been." And then his mouth was on mine and I didn't get a chance to tell him we had left *this* behind and were now firmly venturing into *more*. Knowing that Titus was flawed, that he had made some questionable choices on his road to becoming the man he was today, made me love him even more. Where he was from was even uglier than where I was from, and that was beautiful to me. So was the way he was pulling on my clothes and kissing me along my throat.

I pulled back a little and met those glowing metallic eyes. "I tame your beast all the time, Titus. I think after that scene with my parents you need to try and soothe mine. She can use some petting and some coddling." I wanted to do to him what he did to me but in a different way. I wanted to manhandle him with softness, rough him up with tenderness, love him up until he was breathless and boneless under light touches and barely-there kisses. I wanted to kill him with kindness. We both had had so little of it in our lives we could get drunk on it and forget about the rest of the world for just a little bit.

His eyebrows shot up to his hairline and he lifted both of his hands off of my skin.

"Give her to me."

Once I did, he was going to have to keep her. My beast made of gentleness and compassion was made to fit perfectly against his beast made of hardness and fight.

Chapter 14

Titus

I COULD COUNT THE number of people I had willingly talked about my father with on one hand, and I shared blood with two of them. I never talked about my parents, about where I had come from or how I had ended up where I was now. I didn't like to think about it. Those memories made me feel like a fraud, like a fake, like a phony. It didn't matter how dedicated to the law I was, how focused on helping others, or how much of myself I devoted to trying to make a difference in this godforsaken place. Underneath it all I was no different from Bax or Race. Hell, I was actually just as cold and just as manipulative as Nassir when it came right down to it. I hurt others to get what I wanted, and I did it without remorse, because the truth of the matter was I would do the exact same thing over again if that was the only way out I had.

Reeve talked about the beast inside of me and she was right. The basic parts of who I was still had huge chunks of that angry kid with a killer for a dad and a drunk for a mom making me the man I was today. There was still a little boy that was hungry because there was never any food and scared because he had a little brother he was never going to be able to take care of properly. And while I tried to hide it, tried to keep it all locked away, the more time I spent on the streets, the more time I spent with this woman who understood the darkness and despair, the closer to the surface those angry memories climbed.

She was sitting on top of me, one of her hands hard and insistent in my hair as she pulled me closer to her mouth. The other was yanking on the already loose knot of my tie and violently tugging at the buttons on my shirt. I never knew impatience could be such a turn-on.

I didn't touch her. This was her show. Her turn to take what she needed to take, and I would gladly give it over. Even though the front seat of the GTO didn't offer enough room to do the kinds of things I would really like to do with her. She had thus far shown no fear, no stopping point, no edge of hesitation when we came together. That just made me want to push her more and more. It was an addictive element to sex I had never experienced with anyone else. Granted no one I had ever been to bed with matched me the way she did. No one took everything I had to give and then asked for more. I think she was the only human being that had ever seen the real me. He wasn't very attractive in all his greedy, insatiable, and grasping glory, but she never once looked away.

Just like she wasn't looking away now as each of her hands grabbed one side of my shirt and pulled. Little plastic buttons pinged off every interior wall of the car and bounced off the glass. She wrestled the fabric out of the top of my pants and ran her hands over my stomach where my abs contracted as she switched and used the edge of her nails to lightly scratch the skin.

"I love how strong you are." Her fingers climbed upward

and tripped lightly over my chest and across my collarbone. I sucked in a breath as she used her index finger to scrape over the flat of my nipple, and wondered if this is what it felt like when I went after her. "You seem unbreakable."

I sat as still as stone as she switched her attentions to the other side. I could feel my blood getting thick and starting to pool below where she was sitting across my lap. The interior of the car felt like it was a million degrees and all I could see was the endless dark of her oddly colored eyes. She leaned forward and her hair slid like dark satin across the skin she had exposed.

"Everyone has a breaking point."

I sounded gruff and really had to concentrate on getting the words out because she leaned forward and her lips hit right below my ear on my rough jaw. Her teeth started to nibble and her tongue lapped a long wet trail all the way up behind my ear where she breathed, "I would love to see you when you reach yours."

She curled a hand around the back of my neck and rubbed her cheek against mine. When I let my monster have at her, it took in giant mouthfuls, gobbled her up, and tried to burn as fast and as hot as the pleasure would allow. She wasn't kidding when she said hers needed to be soothed. Every move she made was deliberate, erotic. We touched everywhere and somehow it was more intimate than all the times I had been inside of her over the last month. She brushed her chest against my own and I decided the playing field needed to level out a little, so I hooked my hands under her shirt and lifted it up off over her head. Her hair fell back down around us like a dark curtain and I grabbed her face so I could kiss her. She blinked at me with big eyes and smiled.

"You are the only one that sees it, over and over again. You were the breaking point from the moment you walked in the door to tell me you helped Novak grab Dovie. I wanted to be disgusted, to hate you, but I didn't. I thought you were beautiful and resilient. You seemed so misguided and lost, and even then I wanted to get you naked and fuck you on my desk."

Her face lowered to mine and our lips touched just a tiny bit. One of her hands skated down the center of my chest and landed on my belt buckle. I reciprocated by popping the clasp on the back of her bra and pulling it out of my way.

"You should've tried. I would've let you." The words danced across my lips and somewhere in the center of my chest an animal howled in delight. That was what was missing in my life. Someone that appreciated all the sacrifice, the hard choices I had made to become the man I was, but who could also appreciate the fucked-up kid I had been.

I was still letting her set the pace, so as she sat there and breathed me in while she worked on my belt buckle I simply ran my hands up and down her ribs, across her back, and under the lush curves of her breasts. I wanted to roll each puckered tip between my fingers. I wanted to shove my tongue between her teeth. I wanted to grind my throbbing cock up into the heated center seated on top of it. I wanted anything I could get, but she was moving, touching, playing like we had all the time in the world, and it was torture.

She got my belt open and had me lift up a little so that she could get my zipper down. In the confined space every movement felt amplified, felt erotic and overly sensitized. She put her hand in the opening she created and wrapped her hand around the shaft. She slid her grip up and down until I was ready to buck her off of me. I panted against her still lips where they rested against my own as we watched each other like predators deciding who the ultimate winner of the standoff was going to be. She glided her palm over the head of my cock and took the moisture that was pooling there with her as she continued to work me over.

I felt my face heat up. I felt my breathing get labored and heavy. My eyelids drooped down a fraction and I squeezed my hands so hard around the curve of her waist that I wouldn't have been surprised if I left marks behind.

"Thought I was supposed to be calming your beast, Reeve. This feels like the opposite of that." I was about to come in her hand and she was still mostly dressed and unkissed. "You're supposed to be taking what you need."

She laughed a little against my mouth and finally gave me a soft little peck. "I am. I like you this way. You're never soft, never gentle, but for me you are. That soothes something inside of me. I like being the one that can make you come to heel. The leash is always pulling, always tugging, but right now it's not." There was power in those words. By soothing her inner wild, my own had quieted down. The need to mark and mar was nowhere under her featherlight caress. It was different with her. It always was.

"I'm gonna be really soft in like two minutes and then you're gonna be shit out of luck if you want to use that for anything."

I pointed purposefully to the hard-on she was still working up and down. It looked angry and massive in her tiny fist. Her gaze drifted downward too and her dark eyes got wide. It was an incredibly sexy sight watching her watch what she was doing to me. I saw the tip of her tongue dart out to touch the center of her bottom lip and watched as her pulse fluttered as I jerked in her hand.

Suddenly she grabbed hold of the tie that was still around my neck and pulled me to her for the kind of kiss I wanted. Teeth knocking, tongues tangling, breath mingling, air being stolen. Her naked breast rubbed wantonly against my chest and I took it as my cue to go ahead and start trying to help her get naked. There was no room and she had stupid long legs, so it probably looked like a ridiculous game of twister. It didn't feel that way. Everywhere our skin touched was electric. Everywhere her mouth landed and sucked or licked, scorched. Everywhere my hands touched felt precious and irreplaceable.

I got her pants out of the way and decided I wasn't going to waste time with the underwear. They were just little scraps of lace anyway, so I pushed them to the side and pulled her down over the top of me. She didn't have anywhere else to go with the steering wheel at her back, so she slid down on my cock and we both groaned as she stretched around me and let me all the way inside. There was none of the frantic tug and pull that we usually had when we had sex. This was different. This was *more*.

She kept one hand fisted in my tie and the other one wrapped around my shoulder. I hand a hand under her ass helping her as she rode me up and down and the other I curled possessively around her breast. Every time I used my thumb to circle her nipple I felt it when she involuntarily clenched around me. I let her kiss me. Soft and sweet while we climbed higher and higher. The scrape of fabric combined with the smooth glide of her soft skin as she rose and fell was enough to have me cross-eyed and incoherent. Nothing in my life had ever felt so certain, so absolutely mine.

When she whispered my name I whispered hers in return and let my head fall back on the leather seat of my car. The windows fogged up and it almost made me laugh at how cliché it was, how cliché she and I were. The cop and the sexy criminal with a heart of gold. It was laughable really, but that didn't stop me from prying her clenched fingers off my tie and dragging them between us so that she could touch herself . . . and me.

She moaned at the contact when her fingers found her needy little clit. I moaned when the back of them rubbed enticingly along every single ridge and rise in my dick as we moved together. Between her seductive buildup earlier and the double stimulation, neither one of us was bound to last much longer. All my muscles were vibrating and I could feel hers getting loose and warm around me. Her body quivered from the inside out, and when I moved her back just a fraction so I could get my teeth on her nipple, that was the end of it. I pushed her over the edge and she took me with her.

We came on a sigh, eyes locked and hearts beating in time to each other. It was easier sex than we typically had, which was odd considering how much more was inside of it.

She blew out a long breath and then moved the hand that was around my neck so that she could rub her fingers along my scruffy face. She was just staring at me and I was just staring at her in the quiet and in the dark. I don't think I had ever known such a soft and peaceful moment with another human being. It was made even more profound by the fact that we were still as closely connected as two people could be.

She gave me a little half grin and went to move off my lap. The drag and pull of tender flesh against flesh as she moved had both of us freezing. No wonder everything felt better, felt like more, felt like forever. There was nothing between her and me literally or figuratively. I sighed and leaned forward so that my forehead hit her in the center of her chest.

Her hands came up to brush through the hair at my temples. She stopped on the side with the white spot and traced it.

"You know when I left WITSEC I didn't take anything with me, right? That includes birth control."

I nodded. "I know." We had been having enough sex lately that it hadn't escaped my notice that latex was a necessary evil when we did it.

"Ummm, okay. We can hit up a pharmacy or something. This isn't a reason to freak out." She sounded so calm, so okay with anything and everything I did to her that it hit me square in the gut and maybe in the heart, though I wasn't ready to admit that yet. I ran my hands up and down her ribs some more and pulled back so I could look her in the eyes. They were swirling blue and black like midnight.

"*This* just turned to *more* and we'll deal with it accordingly. If you want to stop somewhere back in the city, we will, but if you don't, I'm okay with that too."

She looked surprised and tentative at the same time. "Titus?"

I sounded like a lunatic. We were so not right for each other and here I was trying to tie her to me forever.

I pulled her to me in a hug and gave her one of those soft kisses she apparently liked. I lifted an eyebrow at her and lifted her up so I could set her back in her own seat so she could wiggle back into her clothes.

"I already told you I will do what needs to be done. Always."

She still seemed a little lost, so she shook her head and started pulling her pants back up her legs.

"I've never set out to ruin your life." She said it so quietly that if the car had been running I wouldn't have heard her. "I just want to help you. I want to do the right thing."

I tucked myself back inside my slacks and pulled my destroyed shirt the rest of the way off. I reached out and pulled on a lock of her dark hair and gave her a lopsided grin.

"The right thing for us might not be the right thing for someone else, and you didn't ruin anything. In fact you might be fixing parts of me I didn't realize were broken. Now, are we stopping or not?"

I shouldn't push her. Hell, I wasn't sure why it mattered. I should demand that she take the morning-after pill, but I didn't want that. I absolutely didn't want that. It felt wrong. I felt like I was supposed to be building something with this girl that understood me, got all the parts of me, and wasn't scared of any of it. I don't think I had ever been whole until she started pulling the beast out to play.

Oh so slowly she shook her head no without looking at me. Her gaze was trained on her bag between her feet and she was white as a ghost. Since I'd gotten the answer I wanted, I didn't push her. I think we were both crazy, and I hadn't decided yet if it was the good kind or the bad kind. Only time would tell.

Chapter 15

Reeve

I knocked on Race and Brysen's door an hour or so after Titus left for work. I kept waiting for Booker to show up, and when he didn't I figured I better go find out where he was. I needed to give the gun back. I couldn't do it. Couldn't let myself fall back into the trap of trying to make decisions like who should live and die because I thought I knew the right answer. Not after the way things had shifted between me and the cop.

He brought me back to the loft and took me to bed. His tie got put to much more interesting use throughout the midnight hours, and being tied up, held down, and worked over by him, albeit more carefully this time around, had made me realize I couldn't lie to him, couldn't keep the secret agenda I had from him anymore. Not if I ever wanted a shot at the thing between us being real. He woke me up when he had to leave, took me into the shower with him, and kissed me good-bye when it was all over he was on his way out the door. The simpleness in that, the way it felt like a real relationship, made me hastily get dressed and pace back and forth while I waited for Booker to show. When an hour or so passed I got impatient and went downstairs.

Race opened the door wearing nothing but a pair of low-slung jeans and a grumpy glower on his too pretty face. His golden hair was messed and his green eyes looked dark and tired. He propped a shoulder on the door and leaned, crossing his arms over his smooth and defined chest. Boys that looked like him shouldn't be threatening, but he was and I felt the warning zip along my nerves.

"Hey. Do you know where Booker is? I borrowed something from him and I really need to give it back."

I was trying really hard to keep my gaze focused on his, but that was a lot of exposed skin, and really, I was only human.

Race lifted a tawny eyebrow at me. "He spent the night in jail. It was a pain in the ass to bond him out but he should be home soon. He was released this morning."

I frowned. "He usually comes by as soon as Titus leaves for work. I haven't seen him."

He lifted a hand and ran it across his jaw. "I don't know where he is, then. I'm not his keeper. After everything that happened yesterday, Bry and Karsen are staying home, so maybe he figured he deserved a day off."

Booker didn't seem like the type that needed a day off, but I didn't share this opinion with Race. I took a step back and told him, "Well, if he does pop up, can you send him my way? I'm sorry about what happened to Karsen yesterday. Conner doesn't have any limits."

"No, he doesn't, and he crossed a line there is no going back from." The threat was there plain as day. I gulped a little.

"I agree. In fact I was just thinking I needed to figure out a way to be more visible, to be out there more so that if Conner wants to make a move, he can. You did a great job of making this place safe and secure. No one can get to me in here."

He cocked his head to the side a little bit and considered me thoughtfully. He looked at me like I was a puzzle piece and he was trying to figure out where I fit in the grand scheme of things.

"You're really willing to risk your neck like that?"

I gave a bitter-sounding laugh and tilted my chin up defiantly. "I am, and I kind of don't have a choice. The feds are dropping the case against Novak's squad. Conner blew it apart, so they don't need me. The only way I'm useful is to bring Conner down. They haven't said anything yet but the feds already told Titus my deal goes away if I don't help bring Conner in. I can't do anything from inside this stronghold. Someone needs a shot at him and I don't think you'll argue it doesn't matter who takes it."

He nodded slowly. "So what, you still want someone to cap Roark for you or do you want Titus to do his job?"

I flinched and lifted my arms to cross them over my chest. "I've decided it's not up to me to decide that. Conner is an awful person who will continue to do awful things, so I ultimately only want for him to get what he deserves. I don't want anyone else hurt in the process."

Race pushed off the door and tunneled his fingers through his blond hair. The golden-tinted locks had nose-dived from shaggy into longish. Surprisingly it worked for him. The look made him all the more pretty. "If you don't care about the outcome, then my advice is to hit up Nassir. Go ask him for a job at Spanky's. Tell him what you have planned. Let him know that you'll bring Roark right to his front door as long as he keeps you breathing. Nassir won't hesitate. He'll agree to anything to get his hands on Roark. Whether or not he'll keep up the end of the deal that keeps you alive is questionable. It's not smart to trust Nassir." He laughed a little and pointed at me. "Even though there's no way in hell Titus is going to let you do that. Even with the feds watching your back, he won't like your main line of defense coming from a gangster and a pimp."

I gulped a little and squeezed myself tighter. "He's not going to have much of a choice. Eventually the feds will force his hand, and I'll end up out there on my own anyway. I think I would rather take my chances with Nassir. At least he'll shoot first and save the interrogation for later."

Race made a noise of agreement and looked over his shoulder as a feminine voice called his name.

"Give me an hour and I'll go down to the club with you since Booker is missing in action. Nassir might not hear you out, but if I go in with you, he'll take five minutes to listen to the tale you have to tell. You need to tell Titus what you're doing, though. I don't need him banging on my door in the middle of the night looking to kick my ass from here back to the Hill."

I reluctantly agreed to his stipulation and made my way back upstairs. I stopped at Booker's door on the way and pounded on it just to make sure he wasn't home. I needed to ditch the gun. Just having it in my possession made me feel guilty and dirty.

When Titus had told me that he was good with whatever happened after our reckless bout of unprotected sex, I thought I had heard him wrong. Bringing a kid into this world, especially with things as unpredictable and uncertain as they were now, was a horrible idea. It was foolish and totally not something I would have ever considered before him. But if he was willing to do whatever it took, then so was I, and that meant no more lying, no more subterfuge, and no more wishing I was anything more than I was. I wouldn't ever be perfect and I had really screwed up, but after he let me in and let me see that he had flaws similar to my own, I no longer felt like I had to be a better version of myself to deserve him.

Nibbling nervously on my lip I called his cell phone and waited anxiously for him to answer. I was secretly hoping it would just go to voice mail and I could leave a rambling, incoherent message explaining what my new plan was, but no such luck.

"Hello?" His deep voice came across the line and instantly my tongue got stuck to the roof of my mouth.

I had to clear my throat before I could begin. There was the sound of sirens and the noise of traffic and voices in the background.

"Hey, are you busy?" Of course he was. I could hear how busy he was, but he shouted something and then the background noise faded away.

"Yeah, but I have a minute. What's up? Is everything okay?"

I laughed a tad hysterically. I couldn't believe he stepped away from his job for me, even if it was just for a second. What he did was such a huge part of who he was that the significance of the gesture wasn't lost on me at all.

"Everything is fine, but what I'm about to tell you isn't going to make you happy."

He swore. "What's going on, Reeve?"

I twisted a piece of hair around my finger. "I'm going to go talk to Nassir. I can't keep hiding out in this condo. Conner needs his hand forced and the only way to do that is if he can get to me. I'm going to see if Nassir will put me to work in Spanky's. Race seems to think he'll be game for anything, including keeping me alive, as long as it lures Conner out into the open."

I expected an immediate argument. I expected him to yell and to blow his top. I expected him to question my sanity and whether or not I had a death wish. Instead he swore softly and asked, "You're going to strip at Spanky's?"

I was telling him I was going to put myself directly in the line of fire and he was worried about me getting naked in public? It startled me so much I laughed. "No. I have no rhythm and no desire to get pawed at by sweaty and drunk strangers. Plus G-strings go where no article of clothing should ever go. I'll ask him to put me behind the bar or something. I'll figure that part out later. You aren't mad?"

He sighed. "I don't love the idea. It leaves you really exposed."

"You understand that if Nassir gets a shot at Conner, he isn't going to sit him down and have a drink while he waits for you to show up and cart him off to a maximum-security prison, right?"

"I know exactly how Nassir works, Reeve. I know what'll happen if he gets close enough to Roark to do any kind of damage."

I breathed out. "Okay."

He grunted and I heard what sounded like someone tapping on glass. I figured he must have retreated to his car so we could talk.

"I gotta go. A junkie broke into a bank and tried to rob it with an assault rifle. It didn't end well."

Good Lord, his job was disheartening. I don't know how he did it day after day. I let loose the hair I was playing with and tucked it behind my ear. "Take care of yourself, Detective. Or better yet, get home in one piece so I can take care of you."

"No one has ever wanted to take care of me before. That makes being careful all the more important. For you too. Stay safe."

He hung up the phone and I couldn't believe the amount of relief that washed over me. Honesty like that was unheard of in my life. I looked at my purse and thought about how deceitful I had been with him from the beginning, planning a murder under his nose from the second he dragged me into his office. Maybe I needed to come clean about it all, tell him that I was still thirsty for retribution, and that taking out a bad man with a bullet was still something that made sense to me. Maybe he needed to know what my plan had been from the beginning now that I knew I couldn't go through with it. I didn't want to be a killer. I wanted to be someone he could love. I sighed and tapped the edge of my cell phone against the center of my forehead. Only I could get my hands on something I wanted so badly and be prepared to mess it all up in the next heartbeat.

I fancied myself up a little while I waited on Race. I had seen the girls that Nassir put to work, and none of them were anything to sneeze at. Sure, most had the hard, worn look that came from being part of the Point, but under that they were all stunning, like Keelyn. She might have man-made boobs and an attitude that even a rabid hyena would be afraid of, but there was no denying she was a stunner and that most of it was God-given. I figured it wouldn't hurt to throw a little sex appeal Nassir's way while I was asking him to keep me alive.

Race knocked on the door exactly an hour later. He had put on a pair of pin-striped pants and a black sweater with the sleeves pushed up to his elbows. His boots were black and looked expensive and foreign. The only thing out of place in his polished look was the edge of the white wife beater peeking out under the collar of his shirt. He looked like he was on his way to work in a financial firm or at a law firm not to a strip club in the middle of the day. Race Hartman was an odd character, and I knew it was in my best interests to never underestimate him.

His gaze skipped over me from my curled-up hair and heavily made up face down to my legs that were bare under the hem of a simple sundress. Before Titus, I would have donned a miniskirt that showed more than it covered, and found the most revealing top I could find, but now I knew the subtlety in sex could be an effective weapon if used correctly.

Race's mouth kicked up in a grin as I closed the door and started down the hallway with him hot on my heels.

"He's going to ask you to dance. With those legs you would make a fortune."

I wrinkled up my nose even though he couldn't see it. "No way. I already told Titus I wouldn't do that. He's begrudgingly rolling with this plan as it is. I'm not going to give him a reason to pull the plug on it before it even begins."

"Nothing wrong with dancing for a living. Honor made more money than Bax did when he first started working for Novak by taking her clothes off."

I gave him a look over my shoulder. "Keelyn. She might've made a lot of money but she lost herself doing it. Why do you think she left?"

His eyebrows dipped down into a deep vee over his evergreen-tinted eyes. "I thought she left because Nassir wouldn't let up on her. He's been circling her forever. I think that's one of the reasons he doesn't like me. She and I used to have a thing when we were younger." He smirked at me as we hit the elevator that led to the underground garage. "Granted I used to have a thing with half the city back in my heyday. But she was always one of my fondest memories."

I rolled my eyes at him and poked the button to take us down a little more violently than was necessary.

"One of your fondest memories and you don't even call her by her real name, just her stage name? How do you think that made her feel?" I sniffed a little and tossed my hair over my shoulder. "I'll tell you how it made her feel. Like she was nothing more than a body, a sex object, like she was only good enough for sex and the fantasy, nothing more."

His smirk fell away and I could see the gears and motors that worked his powerful mind start to fire. He leaned back against the wall of the elevator and a frown pulled at his handsome features.

"She never said anything to me. Before or after."

When the doors opened into the garage he grabbed my elbow and held me still so that he could lead the way out. He moved with an alertness and a tenseness I was getting used to in the men that kept this place alive. He was vigilant and moved with purpose, so I let him guide me along.

"Why would she? You had sex with her. You called her by her stage name and then you moved on. When you started making money, started to make a name for yourself when you took over Novak's action, did you ever think to ask her if she wanted more? Nassir too. He took over the club from Ernie and he just let her keep dancing on that stage. He never offered her anything more. If he had, she would have handed herself over to him without question. All she wants is someone to value her."

He grunted and popped the locks in a sleek and modern sports car. It was so different from the old-school muscle I had been cruising around in recently that I almost made a face at it. Boys took their toys seriously, though, so I stopped myself just in time. Green eyes locked on me over the top of the car and

Race's voice was contemplative when he asked, "How do you know that's what she wants? I thought you two didn't like each other. Nassir said you tried to kick her ass a few weeks ago when Titus took you to the club."

I blew out a breath that had some of my hair lifting and falling back toward my face.

"I know because I am her. We're from the same place. We're made of the same stuff. We've had to fight the same battles, and I know all I wanted was someone to value me, all of me."

"Titus." It wasn't a question.

I lifted a shoulder and let it fall. "He doesn't approve of some of the things I've done in the past, but those things give me the ability to see all of him, so we have to accept each other. Plus, where I come from gives me enough fight to try and hold on to him when he wants to break loose."

I pulled the door open as Race gave a dry laugh. "I always knew big brother had more going on than anyone really knew. Bax was so angry at him when we were younger that he made him out to be a monster. I always trusted Titus with my life, but I knew underneath the surface there lurked something else. None of us that survive here gets the luxury of being one thing. We all have our hands in different cookie jars hoping that at the end of the day we don't get caught in any of them."

The car stared with a low purr, far quieter and less angry than the noise the GTO made. Race and I were silent on the rest of the way to the club, and when he parked around back he leaned across from me to pull a gun out of the glove box in front of me. I recoiled a little because I was still jumpy about the one in the purse at my feet. I needed to get rid of it like yesterday.

"I don't usually carry a gun, but something tells me hanging out with you might make it necessary." The weapon disappeared behind his back and under his sweater as we climbed out of the car and headed into the overly pink building. It was so much worse in the daytime. It just screamed debauchery and degradation. It was so gaudy and ugly it hurt to look at. I couldn't believe someone with as much style and class as Nassir hadn't changed it yet. And I told Race that.

He made a noise of agreement as he punched a security code into a pad and a massive metal door swung open.

"Nassir doesn't care. He ended up here by default after the Pit burned down. He's only here until he rebuilds his club."

"That's dumb. He takes care of all those girls, he invests in them. He should give them someplace they can be proud of. This still feels like it did when Novak used it as a brothel and a betting house. Nassir should put a little bit of the money those girls make him into it and turn it around." I mean, it was always going to be a strip club, but I didn't see why it couldn't be a nice strip club.

Race led the way to the office and lifted his hand to knock on the door. Before his fist connected he shot me a hard look. "Remember not to trust him. Nassir has his own agenda in everything he does."

I lifted an eyebrow. "So do you."

"Damn straight. So does Bax, so does Booker. We all do. In fact the only person you should rely on being up front with you is Titus. He's the only one of us that is trustworthy."

"I do trust him." I more than trusted him, which meant he could break me so very easily if we weren't careful.

Race nodded just slightly, some of his blond hair flipping into his eyes. "Yeah, well, he trusts you too, which is the scary part. Don't let him down, because that isn't a gift lightly given."

Ugh. Stupid, handsome genius. It was like he was looking right through my skin and seeing the guilt lurking there about still having the gun and about my own original, deceitful plot. I didn't have to respond because Chuck pulled open the door and ushered us inside.

Nassir was sitting behind a rickety metal desk that looked like it was going to fall apart. He had a MacBook open in front of him and a glower on his sinfully handsome face. Nassir was a hard guy to read but he was making no effort to hide the fact that he was frustrated and on edge. Chuck gave me a wink, flashed his gold tooth, and leaned against the door we had just come through. It was meant to look like a casual gesture, but there was no getting out of the office without going through him, and that made me feel slightly trapped.

"Have you seen Booker since he posted bail?" Nassir's voice was smooth and smoky but there was always a razor-fine edge that laced through it.

Race snorted and shrugged. "No, and I'm not sure why everyone seems to think it's my job to keep tabs on him. I don't have the guy microchipped. He can come and go as he pleases."

Nassir's caramel-tinted gaze switched over to me. It was hard not to flinch under the intensity of it. This guy was scary, and it had me wanting to rethink this hasty plan.

"What are you doing here?" There was only annoyance in his tone as he spoke to me.

I cleared my throat so I could speak without my voice cracking. It was never a good idea to show fear in front of a predator. "I want you to find me something to do in the club so that Conner will make a move. All this waiting is getting us nowhere and he's escalating. I'd rather you go toe-to-toe with him than the feds, which is the next option. They pulled my deal off the table."

Nassir didn't say anything for a long moment. His tawny eyes shifted between me and Race and then one of his pitch-black eyebrows shot up on his forehead. "This was your idea?" He asked the question of Race.

The blond man shook his head in the negative and hitched his thumb in my direction. "All her, and she even cleared it with the cop."

The second eyebrow winged up to joined the first on Nassir's face. "The cop knows if the Irishman comes anywhere near me he isn't going to walk away breathing. He would never agree to that."

"Desperate times." I couldn't really explain Titus's motivation in agreeing to this new scheme, but as long as he was supporting it, I wasn't going to tempt fate by digging too deep.

"What exactly do you want to do? Get up onstage?" His eyes rolled over me and white flashed as he gave me a lecherous grin. "I could work with that."

I crossed my arms over my chest and narrowed my eyes at him. I refrained from elbowing Race in the ribs as he muttered, "Told ya," out of the corner of his mouth.

"No, I don't want to dance. I told Titus that wouldn't be part of it. Can't you put me behind the bar or something?" I didn't ask about cocktail serving because even those girls had to work topless, and while I wasn't shy, I wasn't okay with having my lady bits within grabbing distance of drunken hands.

"There isn't room behind the bar. And that job is murkier than getting naked onstage. The cop would have a fit if he knew you were messing around with dirty money."

Both Race and Nassir looked so suave, so clean cut, that it was easy to forget they had their hands on piles and piles of illegal cash from running the city's underground. All that dirty money needed to get clean somehow and running the bills through the bar at a strip club was obviously a no-brainer.

Race agreed and then grinned at me. "You know how you're focused on building yourself a new club and always complaining about how you don't want to be here? Put Reeve in charge. She thinks Spanky's is butt ugly and was just telling me how someone needs to show it some love. Why not let a woman do it? The dancers would probably like having a softer touch around here. She thinks they need something to value as their own. She thinks that would've kept Honor around."

"Keelyn." Nassir and I barked the woman's real name at the same time and eyes that were the color of spiced cider switched from annoyed to speculative.

"What do you mean, give them something to value?"

I lifted a shoulder and let it fall. "You hire the prettiest girls you can find. You give them a degree of security they wouldn't have out on the street, but they are still getting naked for strangers and that can be demeaning. Class the joint up. Get rid of the pink everywhere. It's gaudy. Make this place feel expensive and worthwhile and the girls won't just work here, they'll own it. Plus you can charge more and bring in a better class of loser. This place feels like a throwback to harder times, and after that shootout . . ." I shrugged again because he wasn't stupid and knew exactly what I was talking about. "You need to breathe new life into this place just like you're trying to do with Novak's other old businesses."

Nassir muttered something in a language I didn't understand

but it sounded exotic and sexy. No wonder Key ran. Having all that smoldering intensity and sexy appeal focused solely on her had to be nearly impossible to resist.

"You think a new coat of paint and some new decor would have kept Key here?" He sounded skeptical.

"No. I think she had to go so when she comes back she can do it knowing she'll probably never leave again. That's a hard pill to swallow. I think if she knew she was more than just tits and ass and a pretty show you would've gotten a lot further with her."

He grunted at me and sat down in the chair behind the ugly desk. He looked at something on the computer and then over my shoulder to where Chuck was still standing as a silent sentinel.

"What do you think? Is this a crazy idea?"

The giant African American man barked out a laugh that had me jumping a little. "No way. It's fucking brilliant. The regulars are too comfortable and you have too much on your plate. Let her tear this place apart and fix it up. Let her make it as pretty as she is. No one will know what hit them."

I shot Race a look out of the corner of my eye and then shifted my feet nervously. This wasn't what I had expected at all. "Uh . . . I can't play around with laundering money. The feds already have me on their radar and Titus will kill all of us after he locks us up if he thinks any of that is going on."

Nassir flicked a look to Race then back to me and he folded his hands together and leaned back in the chair. He looked like a devil sitting on a tattered throne.

"That's one of the reasons I need to finish rebuilding my club. We always tried to keep Spanky's clean. Right now just the bar is handling anything we need filtered through legitimate means. We can find another avenue for that while you're here, but only if you take up the reins. Unless you agree to do this, then the only other place I have for you is up on that stage, are we clear? And you have to see the job through to the end, not just until I put a slug in the Irishman."

I fidgeted nervously. When people called Nassir ruthless they weren't kidding. He had a way of maneuvering people and situations so that he got the exact outcome he was after. I felt like there was zero wiggle room for me if I agreed to do this. There was far more responsibility involved than I had been expecting when I planned on asking him to put me to work. I didn't know anything about managing a strip club or how to work with fierce strippers forged in the fire of this brutal city. I didn't know how Titus would react to me working for Nassir. He made it clear he wasn't a fan of the guy's business practices and ability to skate around those pesky little things like laws and regulations. But then again, it wasn't like I had any other option on the horizon. I was just waiting for the showdown with Conner, so I might as well help some other ladies out until judgment day found me.

"If you can keep it legal, *all* of it aboveboard, so that Titus doesn't have any reason to doubt me, then I'm in."

Race chuckled and patted me so hard on the back I almost fell over while Nassir studied me hard.

"The cop's opinion matters that much?"

I tilted my chin up and made sure all three of them could see how serious I was when I replied, "It's the only thing that matters."

Chuck laughed from behind me. "Welcome to the family, pretty girl. This should be interesting."

Interesting was probably the simplest thing it was going to be. No matter what I did I just seemed to sink deeper and deeper into the grip of this city. At least I was smart enough to know struggling against it only made the hold tighter. Like Keelyn was soon going to figure out, once you came back here you did it knowing you were staying forever, and there was a weird kind of peace in that knowledge. I was going to die trying to protect my home or my home was eventually going to kill me. It was the same for all of us, which made us exactly what Chuck said—a family. The most dysfunctional one ever, but still we all had the same fate that tied us together.

Lucky us.

Chapter 16

Titus

I JERKED AWAKE AS my fist, which was propping up my head, slipped away from under my chin. I had drifted off while sitting in Bax's hospital room after having a fast and furious text argument with him since he couldn't adequately tell me to fuck off through the pins and wires still holding his jaw shut. Dovie hadn't left his side since the night he had forced her to go home. The reason I was there now was that she needed to run home and clean up the house a bit because Bax was getting released tomorrow. He was supposed to have been released two weeks earlier but had had a setback when one of the multiple screws holding his shattered ankle together had broken and he developed a nasty staph infection. He ended up requiring more surgery and more time laid up in recovery. He demanded that Dovie spend the night in a real bed, that she rest, and when she went to argue he agreed to text me and ask me to stay with him until he was sprung loose the next day. It was kind of cute, my ultra-badass brother acquiescing because he cared so much about the spunky redhead. Dovie didn't want him to be alone, so he texted and I showed up to stay with him. As soon as she left Bax proceeded to chew me out for not helping him keep her away. It took me a second to recognize that he was scared, really scared for her well-being and thought she would be safer away from him and me and the whole mess with Roark. He was trying to push her away for her own protection, but she was too smart and too stubborn to go.

We went back and forth, back and forth, until he wore himself out and fell into a fitful slumber. After he was asleep I watched him for a while, stunned at how different he looked. Bax had always been big and built like a truck; now he almost looked frail. His face had thinned out dramatically, the black star inked by his eye now looking huge and ominous on the suddenly sharp planes of his face. His collarbone protruded under the neck of his hospital gown and all the bulk across his shoulders and arms had drastically thinned out. If it wasn't for the tattoo on his face and the perpetual sneer that twisted his mouth even in sleep, he'd have looked like any other starving kid from the streets. He hadn't been so close to being "Shane" instead of "Bax" since he was a little kid. It made me realize that he wasn't just scared for Dovie, he was terrified he wouldn't be able to take care of her in his current condition. He was terrified of failing her, so of course he was trying to get her to go. Thank God she never would.

I took a seat next to the bed and turned it all over in my head. Bax was trying everything to keep Dovie safe, even if she wasn't playing along. The opposite side of that coin was the way I had dangled Reeve out in front of Conner from the very beginning. It made me cringe to think about the way I dropped her right into the lion's den every day when I took her to Spanky's and left her out there in the Point to fend for herself. She kissed me good-bye, swung those long legs out of the car, and pranced into the strip club like she didn't have a care in the world or a giant bull's-eye painted on her back . . . and I let her. What kind of man did that make me?

I knew I cared about her, knew this thing between us no longer had a rapidly approaching expiration date and was going to last beyond a showdown with Roark. She was in me. Deep down inside the same cage where I kept the monster and she seemed happy to be there, so how could I live with myself knowing I was willingly putting her at risk every single day? How had my little brother that never cared about anyone but himself turned into an honorable man trying to do right by his woman and I ended up the opposite? When had my world turned upside down and how come I hadn't done anything to stop it?

It made me slightly sick. Reeve was too good for that. Beyond her bad choices, which had been fueled by grief, she was an amazingly good woman. She had a hard heart with a soft center and she deserved better than what I had given her so far. She deserved someone willing to risk as much as she was risking. She deserved to be coddled and protected the way Bax coddled Dovie, sheltered the way Race, in building a fortress, protected Brysen. She deserved more than me.

I pulled out my phone and sent her a text asking how her night was going. She freaking loved that filthy strip club. True to form, she took something downtrodden and broken and had added her street savvy and sharp style to it. She had taken a bunch of jaded and life-weary dancers and given them a purpose. I hadn't been inside the club in the week she had been there, but already on the outside it looked like a totally different place.

The graffiti was power-washed off the walls, the neon-pink sign that flashed GIRLS-GIRLS-GIRLS was long gone, the parking lot was lit up like a beacon, and the ridiculous sign declaring the place SPANKY'S was nowhere to be seen. Instead an old antique sign that looked like something from the Moulin Rouge shone with soft lights and directed people to the newly minted EMPIRE. It was sleek. It was sexy and it was fitting. Those girls had built an empire on naked skin and gyrating hips. Reeve was giving them their own kingdom of sex and power to control and I could see how empowered she was by it every time I looked into her shining navy eyes. She loved that she was helping women she identified with, and I think in that she felt like she was making up for her little sister getting torn up and spit out by the Point. She wanted to make sure no other young girl suffered that same fate.

I'm headed home. See you soon.

I stared at the text and frowned. Booker hadn't shown back up since making bail, which had everyone wondering and questioning where he might be, and leaving Reeve to fend for herself with just the feds and Nassir to keep an eye on her when she wasn't with me. I hated the idea of her out on the streets alone. I was doing a terrible job of keeping her safe.

Like she could read my mind, another message came through.
Chuck is going to drop me off. Don't worry about me.

I swore out loud and sent her back a message telling her I would be home in the morning since I promised Dovie I would stay with Bax. Reeve sent back a frowning face and I felt my heart kick. She didn't want to go to bed alone any more than I wanted to let her. I needed to step up my game, needed to make sure she knew I wanted her safe every single second she was risking her neck. I couldn't let Bax show me up. My competitive nature and the fact I really did care about Reeve in a deep and powerful way wouldn't allow for it.

I told her to think of me while she fell asleep and she shot back that if she was thinking about me while she was in bed, the last thing she would be doing is sleeping. I groaned out loud into the quiet of the hospital room and tapped my phone against my forehead. She really was perfect, just the right blend of good and bad, and I couldn't get enough of either part of her.

I settled back into the too small chair and gratefully watched Bax's chest rise and fall until I drifted off at some point listening to him breathe. It wasn't comfortable and I never slept deeply anyway, so I was wide-awake as soon as my chin slipped off my hand. I shook the fog out of my head to clear it and squinted into the dark to try and figure out what time it might be. I climbed to my feet stretching my arms over my head, making every vertebra in my spine pop painfully. I was too big to try and curl up for a catnap. I rubbed a hand over my short hair and was scrolling through e-mail on my phone when the door snicked open and a familiar shock of red hair appeared.

Dovie tiptoed in, silent as a cat until she saw me wide-awake and watching her. She blinked slowly and shrugged without guilt.

"I don't go to bed without him."

She moved toward the hospital bed and reached out a finger to brush it across Bax's star.

"He's worried he can't keep you safe." It was a rough whisper but she heard it and nodded. She kicked of her canvas tennis shoes and hopped up on the edge of the bed.

"I know he is, but I can keep both of us safe until he gets better. And he's just going to have to get used to it."

Bax muttered something in his sleep and instinctively reached for her. She gingerly lay down next to him and put her hand on his chest that was concave and thinner than it had ever been. "We take care of each other. That's what love in this place looks like. You have each other's back."

She sighed softly as Bax turned his head and rubbed his nose in her wild hair. Neither one had ever looked so removed from the grime and grit of their everyday. They just looked like a couple united and in love. It twisted something deep and hard in my gut. Bax had gone through hell to get to this place. It was a victory hard won.

"I'm gonna take off since you're here with him. Call me if you need any help getting him home. He might be more of a handful once he isn't tied to a hospital bed."

She giggled a little bit and waved me off in the dark. "I like it when he's a handful. It's my favorite when he makes me work for it."

"You guys are perfect for each other."

"No, we are so not, but we aren't right for anyone else, so I guess that means we're stuck with one another until the end of time."

Bax made a noise in his sleep and moved his broken wrist toward her. She whispered soothing sounds to him and continued to rub the pad of her finger over that black star. Like I said, that was what love in the Point looked like and I couldn't be happier for either of them.

I closed the door quietly behind me and pulled my phone out so I could text Reeve that I was headed back to the loft after all. She didn't text me back, so I assumed she was already asleep since it was the middle of the night. I was pulling out of the hospital parking lot when my phone starting ringing. I thought it was Reeve calling me back to let me know she was awake and ready to play some after-dark games once I got home. My blood froze when the unnaturally calm voice of one of my fellow detectives came across the line.

"Detective King, we just got called out to those high-rise condos on the docks. Shots fired and one reported fatality. One of the witnesses on the scene demanded that we call you. Said you've been staying there."

I had to concentrate on breathing after my lungs seized and my heart dropped into my shoes. "The fatality, is it a male or a female?"

I heard the typical background noise that went along with a crime scene and practically put the gas pedal through the floorboard of the GTO as I raced across town.

"Male suffering multiple gunshot wounds to the head and chest. Looks like a break-in and attempted sexual assault. The victim said she shot him in self-defense. She told the female officer on the scene that she's your girlfriend and asked us to call you right away." The other cop coughed. "Pretty girl. Looks like she took a nasty beating before she pulled the trigger. She won't go with the paramedics until you get here."

A nasty beating? What exactly did that mean? My mind was racing with every worst-case scenario I could think of. I couldn't believe Reeve had shot someone. Where had she even gotten a gun from and how had someone gotten past all the high-tech and extreme security measures Race had in place at the condo? None of it made any sense to me, but all that mattered right at the moment was that Reeve was okay and that whoever had tried to hurt her was the one not breathing anymore.

When I pulled up in front of the condo, it looked like a scene out of a bad TV cop show. Flashing sirens, worn-down docks, bored bystanders waiting to see the bodies rolled out to the coroner's van, patrol cops and tired-eyed detectives keeping the scene secure, and sure enough, a lovely victim dressed in practically nothing sitting in the back of an ambulance while a paramedic fussed around her. Reeve was wrapped up in a rough-looking blanket. Her dark hair was snarled and sticking up all over her head like someone had been using it to scrub floors or something. She was talking to another cop and the spinning red and blue lights cast harsh shadows on her pale face. She looked calm. She looked composed. She looked like a miracle and it wasn't until she caught sight of me and turned to look in my direction that I saw the damage the other detective had described.

She had white Steri-Strips over one of her dark eyebrows. She already had a black eye starting to form around one of those dark blue orbs. Her chin was split open and sporting spidery black stiches, and as she got up and started to move toward me I could see the scratches and bruises that decorated her soft skin. An angry and bright red slash decorated her throat, and it made me clench my fists. All she had on was a tank top that was being held up by one strap as the other one dangled torn and useless off her shoulder. She also had on those too-short shorts she liked to sleep in and I could see that her knees were torn open and raw like she had been dragged across the floor.

I let out a soft little "oomph" as she hit my chest and tucked her head under my chin. She started crying as soon as my arms closed around her. She cried and cried. Her body shook so hard I thought she was going to fall apart. I stroked my hand over her messy hair and muttered soothing words to her as the other detective meandered over to where we were standing. He looked at me and then at Reeve and lifted his eyebrow.

"I still have a few more questions to ask."

I narrowed my eyes at him as Reeve shook even harder against me. I wasn't used to being on the opposite end of this conversation and I couldn't say I cared for it at all.

"Give us a minute."

"All right, but I'd like to get back to bed before the sun comes up, so a minute is all you get."

I wanted to punch the guy in the face but Reeve needed my attention more, so I bent my head and put my lips to her ear.

"Roark?" I had to know if the mouse had finally turned the table on the cat. She shook her head in the negative and her wet cheek touched my lips, so I pressed light kisses on it.

"Who?"

"Zero. I'd just gotten out of the shower. I was getting ready for bed and he was just there all of a sudden. I recognized him from when he showed up at the safe house looking for Conner. He had a knife."

She pulled back and looked at me with wide, fear-filled eyes. "He was going to kill me."

I shushed her softly and pressed my mouth to hers. "But he didn't. Where did the gun come from?"

She looked away and started shaking again in earnest. It made me scowl and squeeze her a little harder on her arms where I was holding her. "Reeve . . . the gun?"

"That's my question too, Ms. Black. That's an unregistered firearm with no traceable serial number. Where did it come from?"

She looked at me then quickly looked away. She pulled away

from me and wrapped her arms around herself. She wouldn't pull her gaze up from the ground as she whispered, "He brought it in with him." It was a lie. I knew it right away and it made my skin feel suddenly too tight.

I opened my mouth to call her out on it but then looked at the other detective. He was watching her and watching me and I knew that saying anything would lead to more questions that couldn't be answered.

"Finish up with her while I go wake Race up and ask him how in the hell someone bypassed his security. I'll be right back." I knew I sounded angry and far less sympathetic than I should be but I couldn't help it. She was lying and still making choices that put both of us in a tight spot legally. She was still walking in the gray and I hated it. It made me want to shake her when she looked like all she needed was a hug.

Turned out I didn't need to wake Race up. Brysen answered the door with wide eyes and told me that he was with his tech guy in the security center of the building trying to figure out how Zero had gotten inside the fortress. She gave me directions to the basement and I went to find Race and his so-called security expert. The door was open when I got there and I was immediately confronted with an entire wall of live camera feeds. There was the front of the building, the garage, the hallways on each floor, the elevators, the roof, all of them showing the activity currently happening.

"What in the hell happened tonight?" I barked the question and neither Race nor the other guy jumped. The other guy looked at me over his shoulder behind the frames of his black Buddy Holly–style glasses and frowned. He should look like a computer geek the way he was pounding on the keyboard and tinkering with knobs and dials that made up the surveillance system but he didn't. The guy was as tall as me and almost as ripped. He had tattoos over every visible inch of skin and a hard glint in his eyes that let me know he wasn't scared of my size or my fury that was filling the room.

"What happened is someone turned everything off and then opened the front door for that fucker. He waltzed right in."

"What?"

Race turned to look at me. He appeared as angry as I was and I realized his girls were just a few floors down from Reeve, so a stranger in the compound was as much of a violation to him as it was to me.

"Stark has this system set up so that no one can mess with it. It's constantly recording and feeding into servers so we have a visual on everything at all times. Someone literally pulled the plug on it tonight, and once that was done they let the guy in. There is no footage of him going up the elevator to the loft, nothing. He kicked the door in and attacked Reeve, but since Booker is normally the only other person on that floor, no one heard her screaming. Someone called the cops when they heard gunshots and then all of a sudden the feed comes back to life like it got plugged back in."

"All this fancy equipment and a single plug undid it all?" I knew I sounded incredulous but I couldn't help it.

"It's a computer. Computers need power to work." The tattooed guy, Stark, snapped the reply and went back to messing around with the laptop. "There is a fail-safe that keeps everything recording to an external server after the power gets pulled, but that takes a little while to fire up. Plenty of time for someone to use the blackout to their advantage."

"So who knows it's here in the first place? Who would know where the plug was to pull? Not Roark, and not his minion."

Race shoved his hands through his shaggy hair and shared a hard look with the computer guy.

"We're playing earlier footage to find that out. Only a handful of people know where this place is located in the building and even fewer have the code to get in the door."

Something flashed in his eyes like he already had the answer and was just waiting for confirmation. I lowered my voice and asked him, "How did Reeve get her hands on a gun?"

His green eyes went dark. "You're a detective, Titus. Detect."

I blew an angry breath out through my nose like a bull as a familiar face suddenly decorated the monitor at the entrance to the building. "Booker."

"Exactly." I realized Race was answering my question about the firearm and not seeing what I was seeing on the screen.

"No, Booker is at the front doors and fuck him if he's the one that got her the gun. He's out on bond; I'll throw his ass back in jail."

Race turned around and I saw his entire body go stiff. Booker walked through the front doors of the complex, looking right at the security cameras the entire time. He got on the elevator and I saw Race visibly flinch when he hit the button to the basement level.

"Shit."

"I thought he was your boy." This from Stark as Booker hit the lower level of the building and the cameras followed him right to the door of the room we were in right now. He paused and looked at the camera one more time before punching in the code. The door opened and then everything went black.

Race swore and Stark rocked back in the chair, blowing a whistle out between his teeth.

"You got a rat, boss."

Race clenched his hands and looked back and forth between me and the computer guy. "He likes Reeve. Why would he set her up like that?"

"It was weird. The way he kept his eyes on the cameras. He knew you were going to see him doing it."

Race shook his head. "I don't get it."

I grunted. "I don't have to get it. I see him and he's getting locked up. She was almost raped and killed tonight."

Race lifted one of his gold eyebrows at me and asked, "Then I guess it's a good thing someone gave her a weapon to protect herself with, isn't it? This story could have a much sadder ending, couldn't it, Titus?"

We glared at each other, neither willing to give an inch. The tension was broken by Stark clearing his throat.

"Guys, same team, remember? Maybe you should turn all that posturing and anger toward the dude that let the bad guys in the door."

I was the first to look away. I shifted my eyes to the monitor, where it felt like Booker was looking right at me through the glass.

"If I find him first he's going back behind bars."

Race's mouth pulled tight. "If I find him there won't be anything left of him to put behind bars. This is the one safe place in this entire city and he took it away from me, away from my family. There is no explanation on earth that will make up for that."

I used to tell him not to say stuff like that to me because I was and always would be a cop. That made his actions premeditated. Now I just told him, "Don't get caught," and turned around and went back to Reeve.

She was sitting in the passenger seat of the GTO. Someone had gotten her a sweatshirt, but even before I got behind the wheel of the car, I could see that she was still shaking like a leaf. I asked the detective in charge of the scene if she was clear to go. He just grunted at me and told me she was one lucky lady.

When I got in the car I noticed she was still crying big, fat silent tears.

"Are you okay?" I was still mad at her for lying to the cop, for being dishonest with me, but it was obvious she need a kinder touch than I wanted to give.

"Fine. Where are we going? We can't get back into the loft until they clear the scene."

"My place." It wasn't as secure as the condo, but look at how well that had worked out.

"Okay." She sounded so defeated, so broken, I couldn't resist the urge to reach out and put my hand on her knee. It made my teeth clench when she jolted and jerked away at the contact. She cut a look at me and more tears fell. "Sorry."

I swore softly. "Don't apologize. It was a rough night. We can talk about it later. All of it."

"What if I don't want to talk about all of it?" Some of the iron that fortified who she was threaded back in her tone, and pride at her fight licked up my spine. My girl had the tools to take care of herself, the fight to keep herself safe, and that made the way I risked her every day feel less like a dick move.

"You don't have a choice. That's what *more* is, Reeve. You and me and all of it. But that can wait until tomorrow."

She looked away from me and leaned her forehead on the passenger window. "Tomorrow is another day, but I'll still be the same girl, Titus. You aren't going to like what I have to tell you."

"The story has a man hurting you and me nowhere around to stop it. It has you alone and scared while fighting for your life. Damn straight I'm not going to like what you have to tell me, Reeve. The rest of it I'm going to listen to and we're going to work through because you have to trust me enough not to lie to me anymore."

"I have always trusted you. It's you trusting me that I'm adjusting to."

"Then we'll adjust together."

I hoped they weren't just empty words I was handing to her because she needed reassurance. I wanted to believe that we could indeed figure out something other than the strict black and white that ruled my life and the hazy gray that filled hers. This time when I put my hand on her knee she didn't flinch or move away; instead she covered it with her own and squeezed.

Chapter 17

Reeve

TITUS'S HOUSE WAS A little bit like him. It was a tidy little Craftsman on the outside, with a perfectly mowed yard, but on the inside things were kind of messy and all over the place. It was easy to see from his decor that he was a bachelor and that he lived alone. There wasn't a lady's touch anywhere and the little furniture he did have was heavy and dark, covered in discarded items of clothing and dotted with empty beer bottles and empty takeout containers. Titus was sloppy in his own space, and I would have never believed it if I hadn't seen it with my own eyes.

I was tired and I hurt all over, so instead of jumping into the showdown I knew was waiting for me, I asked him if I could use the bathroom to clean up a little bit. He told me to wait a second and I heard him banging around as he was rushing to clean up a little bit before I saw even deeper into who the man behind the badge really was. It took him twenty minutes or so, but when he was done he came and got me, led me to a bathtub filled with steaming water, and waited while I crawled inside. He watched me as I sank my sore body into the heat and told me he would get me something else to wear since the stuff I had on was either trashed or borrowed. I nodded and watched as he walked stiffly out the door.

He was mad and trying to hide the fact while he struggled to be gentle for me. He was mad at me for lying and mad at himself for not being there when I needed him, and wasn't sure which of those things had him more fired up. I also wasn't sure that he was going to be able to look me in the eye after I told him why I had the gun and what my initial plan had been to do with it. He said we would work through it but I was going to let him down again, and I wasn't sure his innate sense of morality was going to be able to handle me admitting I was fully intending to be part of another person's death. It was a lot for anyone, especially a man with such a strict code of right and wrong, to have to muddle his way through.

I wasn't supposed to get the stitches in my chin wet, so I submerged myself up to the top of my shoulders and did my best to scrub the raw wounds on my arms and legs. My hair floated out like a dark cloud around me and I had to concentrate really hard on my breathing so that I didn't start shaking and crying all over again.

Not much scared me. I had seen a lot, lost a lot, suffered a lot, but being blindsided by Zero in a place that had felt so safe was enough to make me feel like I would never be secure again. He was just *there*, in my face and everywhere, without a sound and I knew he was there to kill me on Conner's orders, but the look in his eye told me he would make it hurt and make me suffer for his own pleasure.

He was a brutal-looking man. I recognized him right away with his bald head and tightly trimmed goatee. He smiled at me when I screamed and I saw the knife flash out, and it caught me across the fleshy part of my arm before I realized I should be fighting back. Only I was in the bathroom, in my pajamas and completely unarmed. I was as helpless as I had ever been in my life. It wasn't a fair fight by any stretch of the imagination, and just as I realized I should make noise or try and run he lashed out with a closed fist and punched me in the face. It was a hard enough blow that I fell immediately to my knees.

He put a hand in my hair and jerked my head closer to his crotch as he brought his knife down and touched the tip to my cheek. "No wonder Conner has such a hard-on for you. You're even better up close and personal."

The sting of the blade and his crude words were like a slap across the face. I had no clue how he had gotten inside the condo, but I knew only one of us was walking out the front door.

"Conner is a lunatic. He's ruining lives because of a man that was a sociopath, a man that didn't claim him as his own until he needed him!" I didn't think, I just threw my head forward until my forehead connected solidly with the vulnerable parts of his body hidden behind his zipper. It was enough of a shock that he doubled over, giving me enough room to move around him. I scrambled on my hands and knees out the bathroom door, leaving a sizable chunk of my hair in Zero's fist. He swore and dove for me, but I was faster, and as soon as I cleared the bathroom I got to my feet and made a mad dash for the stairs.

The Glock was still in my purse. No one had seen Booker and I wasn't ready to admit to anyone else that I had it, and right in that moment I was so glad I hadn't gotten rid of the weapon.

When I was halfway down the stairs I was hit from behind hard enough to pick me up off my feet and send me flying through the air. I didn't hit any more stairs and crashed to the ground floor with all of Zero's weight on top of me. My teeth tore into my bottom lip, my chin cracked into the hardwood with enough force to make me black out for a second, and my palms and knees lost the first layer of skin as I hurriedly tried to find any kind of traction on the floor to get away from the oppressive weight on my back.

He swore at me, called me filthy names, and flipped me over so that he was straddling my waist. The knife glided across my chest as I swung wildly at him with my fists and tried to claw at him with my fingernails. He just laughed at my struggles and used the blade to cut the strap of my tank off of one of my shoulders. I screamed at him as he told me all the disgusting things he was going to do to me as the knife dug into my chest. I screamed until I had no air left but that just seemed to egg him on as he leaned down and bit the exposed slope of my breast where the fabric of my shirt had been torn away. He swatted my hands away and used his free hand to wrap around my throat.

All I could taste was panic and blood and he applied pressure and continued to nick at my skin with the blade. I kicked my legs uselessly under him as he went on and on about how hot Conner told him I was in bed, about all the obscene and awful things he'd been doing to himself while watching me for the last few months. It was gross and far more violating than the way he was sitting on me and the way he was choking me.

I was starting to see spots around the edge of my vision. I needed air, but no matter how much I pried at his hard fingers he didn't loosen them an inch. I heard my phone ring from somewhere in my purse. It made him laugh as he moved his lips over my own where I was gasping like a landlocked fish for any kind of breath.

"Is that the cop? Imagine how fun it will be for him to find you like this. Broken, ripped apart. Covered in filth and another man. I only wish I could be around to see his face. Conner will love that."

I had to do something, and since fighting wasn't getting me anywhere, I decided to stop. I let my arms fall to the floor next to his legs. I stopped kicking and jerking my legs and hips. I went stone still and lay under him like I was already a corpse. I saw triumph flash in his beady eyes and he pushed his grotesque mouth to my own again.

"I like it better when you fight, but this works too." I forced myself not to move a single muscle as he loosened his hold around my throat and started to rub the edge of the blade along where I was sure my pulse was hammering. Before I could change my mind or evaluate the risk involved, I lifted my head up off the floor just a little bit like I was going to kiss him back and sank my teeth into his lip. I felt flesh rip, felt blood surge, but it was enough to once again throw him off balance so that I could wiggle out from underneath his bulk. The knife raked across my skin with a stinging burn as I got myself free, but I couldn't stop to think about how bad the cut might be. Instead I ran for my purse and almost started crying on the spot when my fingers touched the chilly metal of the gun.

He was close again. I could feel him. So I released the safety and turned around already pulling the trigger without aiming. I fired and fired, each shot louder than the previous one. I fired until the clip was empty and my shoulder felt like it was dislocated from the recoil. The entire loft smelled like blood and gun-powder as Zero slumped over in a heap on the floor at my feet. I hadn't hit him with all the rounds, but enough had made contact that he wasn't a threat anymore. The knife now sat useless and covered in crimson on the floor next to his lax form.

I called 911 only to be informed that units were already on the way to my location due to reports of shots fired. I told the dispatcher there was a dead body on the scene and then Race and Brysen were suddenly there hustling me out of the apartment and asking me a million questions. No one heard me scream-ing, but they sure as hell heard the gun go off. Before I could even start to process what they were asking or the fact that I was bleeding and probably going into shock, the cranky detec-tive was all in my face asking more questions, and all I could tell anyone was that I wanted Titus.

I just wanted *my* cop.

Speaking of, the bathroom door swung open and his big frame was suddenly filling the space. "Are you okay in here?"

Without my noticing it, the water had gone cold, and I was just sitting in the tub crying. I lifted my hands to rub at my cheeks and went to stand up.

"Yeah. I just needed a minute." I was always fighting. Fight-ing someone, something, fighting myself. I wasn't used to being the victim, to being weak and out of control.

I never got to my feet. Before I could stand up, his strong arms were around me and under me and he was cradling me to his chest. Soaking himself and the bathroom floor in the process. I didn't argue. I just wrapped an arm around his thick neck and let him take me to his bed still dripping wet and teary-eyed.

He had obviously spent the time I was soaking cleaning up

his bedroom. There wasn't a stray shirt or sock in sight and the bed was made with obviously clean sheets and blankets. I rubbed my sore cheek against his pec and sighed against his heartbeat.

"I can't believe how messy you are. I never would have guessed."

He grunted and shifted me a little so he could pull the top blanket back and put me in the center of the bed. He stared down at me for a long moment before he started pulling his clothes off. That was a show that would make me millions if I charged other woman to watch it. Too bad I was greedy and wanted the flex and bend of all that hard muscle and tawny skin to be forever for my eyes only.

"The only person that ever sees it is me, so I guess I never really bothered to take very good care of the inside of the place. I'm not here a lot."

Again it reminded me of the man himself. The only one who ever saw into the darkness where his heart actually lived was Titus. The beast was lonely, and I was the only one he had ever let inside the cage. It needed me. I just hoped he could still see that after I told him the last of my dirty secrets.

Once he was as naked as I was, he reached over, turned off the lights, and climbed into the bed next to me; even though it was early morning and the rest of the world was just starting to wake up, we were going to bed.

He curled an arm around me and drew me tightly to his chest. "It's tomorrow."

I knew he wanted to talk, but I wasn't ready for it yet. "It'll still be tomorrow when we wake up. Let's just rest for a minute." I needed it. Oblivion had never sounded so nice.

I felt his lips brush across the top of my head and his palm skimmed over the battered and raw surface of the arm I wrapped around him.

"Okay. We can rest. By the way, I'm proud of you. You're one hell of a fighter, Reeve."

I could only pray he felt that way when I opened my eyes and told him my tale. Between my own emotions being drained and stripped to nothing and his warmth and the security of finally being in his arms after my nightmare, I couldn't keep my eyelids open anymore. Sleep and a tiny reprieve was one thing I wasn't going to fight against.

I WAS HAVING THE most amazing dream. It was full of questing hands. Tender kisses. The brush of soft hair against my skin. My name was whispered between lips that I loved and I had never been in a more secure or happy place.

But then it changed and I was being chased. I was running for my life and I woke up with a scream stuck in my throat and tears silently running down my face. I sat up in the bed and looked down at Titus. Bright blue eyes were watching me carefully, full of sympathy and rage. I pushed my hair out of my face and put a hand to my racing heart. He lifted his hand up and brushed his knuckle across my damp cheek. It was an achingly tender gesture and it was so unlike him that it started me shaking all over. Titus had looked at me with a lot of different emotions since I burst back into his life, but I refused to have pity be one of them. I understood the risks . . . all of them . . . and he needed to know that.

I leaned over and gave him a stinging kiss on his frowning mouth. "I'm fine. At least I will be."

I saw his eyes skim over the cut on my neck and the tender

and bruised skin around my eye. "You are not fine." He sounded like a cop, and not the very naked and very sexy man that could so easily replace all the bad memories with much better ones.

It might not make sense but I wanted his hands on me. I wanted my heart thundering and chasing itself around my chest for him and not because I was scared and shaken up. Everything that was bad, everything that was tragic and senseless, Titus was there to give meaning to. He was the good and I needed all of that in me.

"I will be. Make me fine, Titus."

He scowled at me in the early morning light but he could never hide the way his eyes shifted, and since we were both naked, there was no missing the way his body reacted. I kissed him again and this time he curled his hand around the back of my neck.

"I'm not sure that's a very good idea. You had a rough night."

"You and I together is always a good idea. I need this." I knew he would never deny me when I told him I needed him. He was too giving to say no.

With a sigh he kissed the battered side of my face. His lips touched the side of my neck where my pulse thudded heavily in a mixture of anxiety and desire. His scruffy face brushed across my tender skin as he moved steadily downward across my bare chest and along my quivering tummy.

My skin was humming with tantalizing pleasure and my heart was sprinting to catch up to the way my body moved against the one that was pressing it down into the soft mattress under my back. I was caught in the middle of a cloud, floating on love and sex. It really was the best cure for any kind of bad dream or awful memory ever, and as cold air hit that hypersensitive place between my legs and the covers shifted away from the tangle of naked limbs, I was ready and aching for a kiss that was far more intimate and far more serious.

"Titus . . ." Just saying his name made me feel better, stronger.

He chuckled against my most sensitive place and it brought my hips up off the bed. I tugged on his hair to let him know he was headed in the right direction and he squeezed my ass in return.

His head disappeared between my splayed legs and I gasped as he used his clever tongue to distract me. His fingers tickled the back of my knee as he started to devote his attention to all the slippery and needy flesh in front of his face. He licked. He sucked. He bit. He chuckled again the more anxious I got and the harder my hands grasped his hair. He used his hands and mouth in tandem until I couldn't see straight, and when I was a quivering mass of nothing but pleasure and completion under him, he started all over again.

After the second orgasm I was sure I would never move again. Titus let my legs slide back to the bed and then stopped to kiss his way along every scrape, every cut, every bruise, every mark or imperfection that hadn't been there before I tangled with Conner's man. The sweetness of the gesture got me all choked up, and once he was braced over me, his biceps straining as he held his considerable weight over me, I couldn't stop from wrapping my arms around him and pulling him down so that he covered me like a sexy security blanket.

He kissed my chin and my black eye. He kissed his way across the angry red mark the knife had left at my throat. He nuzzled his nose into my ear and whispered, "I'm so sorry I wasn't there."

I could feel the remorse in his massive body. I could feel the way his regret and anger made his muscles tight. But honestly, I cared more about whether he'd stay once I revealed what I'd been planning for that Glock than I did that he wasn't there to protect me from Zero. I rubbed my cheek against the roughness of his, held him close to me so that our hearts jumped and leaped to touch one another through our chests, and told him, "I can take care of myself and take care of you, Titus. No one should underestimate me."

He sighed into my ear and it made my hair flutter. He curled his arms underneath my shoulders and shifted so that his lean hips settled into the cradle of my own. We were touching as much as two people could touch. I had never felt so much a part of another human being in my life. It seemed like I would die if he were ever to be torn away from me. So much of Titus was now woven into the fabric of who I was and who I knew I deserved to be.

He lifted his hips and let them drop back down, rubbing his erection between my swollen and sensitive folds. It was a breathlessly sexy tease that had me pulling my legs up along his sides and lifting my own hips to follow his movements.

"I never underestimated you. I overestimated myself. I thought I could play this game, let you risk everything for the end goal, but I was wrong. You are more than more to me, Reeve. You are everything right now."

If his light caresses and reverent touches hadn't been enough to make the tears spill over again, those words and the way they were growled at me out of the man and the beast's mouth were. They were both staking their claim and I couldn't have been happier.

"I'm embarrassed to admit how long you've been everything

for me, Titus. Any risk was worth it to end me up right where I am with you right now." And God willing it was enough to keep us together like this after the truth came out.

He slid along the crevice again. Making sure the tip of his cock hit my clit with each thrust and retreat. It was enough to have me tugging at him impatiently to just get inside. Sex with Titus had always been a full-contact sport, and while I liked the soft and sexy stimulation, I was needy and really wanted that sense of fullness and being owned that came with him entering into my ready heat. He was making an effort to be nice and thoughtful, considering what I had been through the night before, but I didn't want the reminder. I didn't want any of that to ever have a place here between us, so I locked my legs around his lower back, dug my ankles into the rock-hard globes of his ass, and impaled myself on his turgid cock.

The way my body devoured him made us both gasp. I clawed at him with my fingernails and threw my head back so that I could look up at him. His eyes were luminous with silver heat, and a high red flush decorated his cheeks.

"You already made it all better and kissed all my boo-boos. It was sweet, but now I need you to fuck me like you normally do, please." I batted my eyelashes at him and nudged him again with my ankles, hoping he would get the hint.

His eyebrows dipped over his glowing eyes and white flashed on his face as he grinned at me. "Did you just ask me to please fuck you?"

"Yes. Now, will you move?" I wiggled my hips impatiently, which made his dick twitch inside of me. I squeezed it back and he muttered a dirty word.

"Well, since you were so polite about it . . ." He shifted his leg just a little so that my hips tilted upward and then began to ride me the way I was practically begging for. Our hips ground together. My breasts were flattened against his chest. Our breath mingled as we breathed each other in and out instead of kissing. His hands pulled on my shoulders, which would hurt after the tumble I took earlier, but I loved it. I needed it. I craved this sort of wild and unhinged kind of give-and-take with him. It was mine. I was the only one he gave it to, so there was no way I was going to let him hold it back from me.

He growled some more, pushed my legs up even higher along his ribs, and grabbed a pillow that was next to my head. He shoved it under my backside, forcing my hips to lift up even more off the bed and then got to his knees as he continued to pound into me. He watched me from his elevated position. His eyes locked on mine and he drove us both closer and closer to the edge of orgasm. I loved the way he started to sweat, started to glimmer like a polished statue all hard and strong. It was an unbelievable turn-on, so I couldn't help but rake my hands over my nipples. I stopped to play for a second, which made him move even faster and his eyes shine even brighter. When I felt his fingers dig deeper into the skin of my hips, I knew he was close.

Since I was still reeling from the gifts he bestowed earlier with his mouth, I was further behind. I brushed the tips of my fingers over my abdomen, stopped to circle my belly button, loving the way he watched me the entire time. It felt nice to touch myself but it felt even better to know that when I did it, it made Titus lose his mind. He was breathing like he was running a marathon and his steady rhythm had turned slightly desperate and frantic. I paused at the apex where we were joined, let him brush against the tips of my fingers as he thrust in and out.

He groaned loudly and demanded, "Touch yourself. Let me see it." So I did. I smiled up at him. Scooted around a little bit so I could get my fingers on my own little center of pleasure. I made sure the angle was right for him to see the way I circled the little nub. The way I tapped it. The way I brushed it in time to his motions. It felt so good, and as soon as he barked my name and collapsed on top of me, I followed him over the edge and fell with a much softer landing. It was perfect. He was perfect. We were perfect.

I massaged his spine as he pulled the pillow out from under me. He finally gave me a kiss and then locked his arm around me and rolled so that he was on the bottom and I was sprawled across the top of him. My knee hit a very obvious wet spot on the sheets and I had a moment of panic. We weren't careful again, and this time I wasn't sure he was going it be all in once he heard what I had to tell him. I took a deep breath and talked to his heart since that was here my head was at.

"When I came back to the Point I was planning on killing Conner. I knew you would keep me safe and I needed to stay alive long enough to get close enough to have a shot at him. He's a monster, Titus, and he's smart. He'll never see the inside of a jail, and we both know that. I was hoping you would agree to my plan so that I could be the one to pull the trigger. From the beginning I knew it was jail or a shallow grave, and I figured jail for righting such a major wrong all those years ago was a fair trade-off. I knew you would never approve, so I didn't tell you that I had Booker get me a gun or what I was planning. I didn't want you attached to yet another crime. I lied. I lied from the very start, and I'm so sorry, but after you told me you were all in with me in the car, I knew I couldn't risk it, or you. I knew I needed to be better, do better, so I was fully intending to let Booker take the gun back and let Nassir or even Race do the dirty work. Please try and see why I made the choices that I made."

Really I wanted to plead with him to love me the way I loved him. I wanted to beg him to forgive me for being desperate and rash. I wanted him to see me for who I always would be, a woman that had a good heart but often made bad choices. I was human. Flawed and broken, but so was this place I called home and so was he. I wanted him to see that we fit right in as a couple on these damaged streets.

He stiffened under me and I bit my already trashed lip because I thought he was going to push me away. He didn't. His fingers raked through my messy hair and massaged the back of my neck.

"I figured all that out when you lied to the cop about the gun. And just so you know: Booker is the one who let Zero into the building."

It was my turn to stiffen. "What?"

He sighed and moved his head so he could kiss my forehead. "Booker let the guy in and disabled the security cameras so no one could see him coming up to the loft. None of it makes any sense."

I was dumbfounded. I knew Booker was a thug and an ex-con, but I also thought he was my friend. We understood one another.

"What about the rest of it, Titus? I screwed up again." I was giving him proof that I was never going to be as good as he was even if he came from a place that was as dirty and tarnished as I was.

He blew out a deep breath and curled the arm that wasn't

holding me up around the back of his head. "You can't be the judge, jury, and executioner if we're going to be together, Reeve. You have to understand the difference between a bad choice and a choice that has consequences that are undoable and forever. If Dovie had died, if you had succeeded in killing Conner . . . where would you be at the end of all of that? Buried under guilt and remorse just like you have been since you asked Novak to take care of your sister's boyfriend. I need you to trust me to do my job, and you have to trust the process. I know Roark was a dirty cop, I know there are more of them in this city than there are good ones, but I'm not one of them. You have to give me the opportunity to do what needs to be done."

I nodded slowly. "I know that."

"Now."

It was my turn to sigh. "We didn't start out as a united front, Detective. I was on the outside looking in. I was trying to do what was best for everyone. And just so you know, Race thought I was trying to set *you* up to kill Conner for me. He never trusted my motives."

I saw his teeth flash in a grin. "Race is smart but that doesn't mean he knows everything. I knew from the beginning you would never expect me to compromise myself no matter how vicious and violent Roark made this fight. You told me too many times how much you admired and appreciated my dedication to doing the right thing. I kind of figured you had a plan. I just didn't put it together until you lied about the gun."

"I don't want you to regret being with me, Titus." I could hear everything my heart felt for him in my voice.

"There is no regret, Reeve, and there is no choice. Right or wrong, you are it for me. You get all the parts of me. You make me feel like I can just be me, not a cop, not a big brother, not a hero, not a savior . . . just a man. A man that has his good and bad parts. I'll never be perfect but for you I will always be real, and you can always be just who you are with me. Even if that is a girl that thinks she can solve her problems with a bullet. I just need to keep reminding you there are always other options and that we have too much to lose if we don't think things through. We're both a freaking mess, so who else would want to bother with us anyway." He kissed me to show me he was teasing with the last part. "I've wanted you from the beginning. I should've known from the start this is where we would end up."

It wasn't a declaration of love. He didn't even ask me to be his girlfriend, but him saying I would always be the one that got all of him, all of who he really was, felt just as important as those three little words.

I was going to thank him and smother him with my relief and with more kisses and definitely more sex, but his eyes got flinty and he suddenly bolted up in the bed and pulled at his hair.

"Son of a bitch!" He didn't apologize for the interruption to our intimate moment; instead he swung his long legs over the edge of the bed and reached for his pants. I saw his shoulders tense, which made me sit up and ask him, "What's wrong?"

He looked pissed off and extra wild as he started pulling on his clothes.

"It's the beginning. All of it has been about the beginning. It started with Novak."

"So what?" I didn't understand what he was talking about but he was making me nervous. This was the first time I had seen both the cop and the beast loose at the same time. He was frightening in his ferocity.

"I didn't see the connection when Roark started messing with Nassir and Race. I totally blew the relationship between him and my brother. It took a bomb threat and too many dead kids for me to see the way he was hitting at me where it hurt me the most, but now I see it all. It's been about paying us back by using our weakness against us, and the only weakness Roark has shown is his bizarre obsession with his old man. I looked everywhere in this damn city for him except for the one place where he would feel closest to his father." He swore some more and I shivered as he clipped his gun on his belt.

His train of thought sounded ominous and I had a really bad feeling about it. "You think Conner is at Novak's old warehouse?"

He just grunted and dug a card out of his wallet that he tossed in my direction.

"I don't know if he's there or not but I need to go check it out."

I picked up the card with the marshals' logo on it and curled my fingers around it. "Don't go alone." My voice was barely a whisper. I couldn't stand the thought of him in danger even though I knew it was his job.

Titus bent over to kiss me hard on the mouth and told me to trust him and to believe that he could do his job. He told me he would call for backup and that if I didn't hear from him in an hour to call the marshals. I knew exactly where Novak's old spot was located. If he didn't call me in an hour I was going after him myself; I just didn't tell him that. So I kissed him back with everything I had and told him I would do exactly what he had asked me to do. As I watched his broad back disappear out the door I asked any higher entity that might be listening to keep this man that held this world up safe. I didn't want to live in this place without him.

Chapter 18

Titus

I was surprised when the big, lifted-up truck rolled to a stop next to the GTO where it was parked up on a hill overlooking the battered and long-abandoned warehouse that Novak and his now defunct crew used to work out of. I had been standing there for a while, just waiting and watching, kicking myself for not putting the pieces together sooner, which seemed to be how I handled everything dealing with Roark. Sometime the bad guys were just better than I was. When the driver climbed out of the beast of a machine, some of the surprise wore off and I figured I should've known he had to be lurking around waiting to make whatever move he was planning after the attack. The way he had watched those video cameras so that we couldn't miss seeing that he was tied into Roark's plans was telling. The entire way Booker had acted when he was in Race's building had hinted that something was up, that he was maneuvering pieces around the game board we couldn't see. It was just like an ex-con to make up his own rules and forget to clue the rest of the players what they were.

If I was surprised to see him I don't think he was at all shocked when I was on him before his feet hit the ground. I wanted to rip his head off and spit down his throat for the danger he had put Reeve in. I was happy I hadn't called in for backup yet. I couldn't drop-kick him across the Point if I had witnesses.

He thumped against the side of the truck as I barreled into him but we were evenly matched in the size and bulk department, so it wasn't long before I had a fist in my ribs and we were both rolling around on the asphalt exchanging heavy blows and grunting with exertion. He got in a good shot to my cheek and I was pretty sure I broke his nose when I slammed my forehead into the center of his face. I took an elbow to the sternum, which knocked the wind out of me, so I retaliated with a kidney punch that finally had the other man rolling away from me. We both staggered to our feet, bloodied and furious, as we continued to circle one another like fighting dogs.

"She could have died, asshole." I spit a mouthful of blood toward his feet, making him step back and swear at me.

"She has a gun and she knows how to use it. It was the only way any of us were going to get close to Roark. Someone needed to get in on the inside and the only way to do that was to give him something he wants."

"Reeve's corpse?" Just saying the words made my blood heat even more and I took another threatening step toward the other man. Booker held his hands up in front of him in a gesture of surrender and shook his head slowly.

"No. He wants you, but in order to convince him that I was trustworthy, that I would follow through, I had to show him how far I would go. Why do you think I let the cameras catch me? I know every fucking blind spot in that building. I wanted you guys to see me. Race is smart and it's your fucking job to figure shit out. I wanted you to know something was up."

"The bastard cut her, almost raped her. It wasn't worth the risk. She isn't yours to play with like that."

"We don't have a choice. Sacrifices have to be made because so far Roark is winning and we're all just dangling on the end of his string waiting around like a bunch of dumb shits to see who he goes after next. I believed Reeve could take care of herself and it got us exactly where we needed to be. I followed you when you left the house so I could talk to you, even though I knew you were going to take a crack at me. Roark won't show himself, but he will let me bring you to him now that I've proven myself to him. He'll think I took you down just like he believed I wanted to let Zero in the building. It's the only shot we have at getting close, Titus. He's too smart. He knows the way this shit works from the inside. He's better at it than we are and more people we care about are going to get hurt. We can stop it if you trust me."

I crossed my arms over my chest as he let his hands fall. "Why does he want me?"

Booker heaved a deep breath and lifted a finger to wipe at the steady trickle of blood leaking out of his nose. My side was aching and my jaw throbbed. We had done a number on each other. "Because the girl loves you. It's obvious to anyone that sees the two of you together. He doesn't want her gone, he wants her to suffer. In his own sick and maniacal way he really did care about her. He thought the two of them were a match made in heaven when she told him about how she asked Novak to take care of the sister's boyfriend. He thought she was as brutal and as violent as he was. He thought revenge would tie them together forever. I think she let him down by proving she has a heart and actually cares about other people, and he wants to make her pay for it. She disappointed him, so she deserves to feel that same kind of pain."

"Zero tried to kill her, Booker."

The scarred man shook his head and I winced as it sent blood flying. "Roark is malicious and devious, Titus. Zero didn't know she was armed, but Roark did. He sent the guy in after her knowing she was going to fight back. Knowing she would pull the trigger. Why do you think the guy only had a knife? Roark wants her to be like him. He wants her to be a killer. He sent his man in there to die by her hand."

"The gun was downstairs. Zero could've stabbed her the second she got out of the shower. He surprised her and she had to fight. She fought hard to stay alive. There are too many what-ifs in that scenario."

"It's win-win for Roark. She kills his guy and he feels like he has proven to himself that she is exactly what he wants her to be, or she ends up dead and she's out of the way while he continues to torture the rest of us. Like I said, he's better at this than we are, so the only way to stop him is from the inside. I told him that I could get to you, that I would arrange to have you meet me, and that you would show just to take a chunk out of my hide for betraying the family by letting Zero in. I told him you would do your job and the opportunity to take me in for violating my bond and disappearing couldn't be passed up. I told him I would take you down and bring you to him. He believed me . . . only *after* I let Zero in the building.' "

"How did he contact you in the first place?"

Booker wiped a hand across his face, smearing more blood

and glowering at me as he poked his swollen and quickly bruising nose. "Zero was waiting for me when I got out of jail. Literally right outside of the police station. He asked if I needed a ride back to the condo and made it clear the only answer I had better have was yes. He asked me about Karsen. He knew I went into the school after her. She's just a kid, dammit. She should have no part in anything that goes down in this place. She has a shot at having a normal life. I told him to leave her alone and he mentioned that Roark was always looking for good help. It was very 'come to the dark side.' He made it sound like they would leave the kid alone if I did what they wanted, so I told him there was always a right price for things, and that's when he told me about getting into the building to go after your girl."

I growled because I couldn't help in, and my fist flew out of its own accord and smacked into his cheek. His entire head cranked to the side and he took a step toward me vibrating with rage as I shook out my now throbbing knuckles. "What's the rest?"

He worked his jaw back and forth and lifted his fingers to poke at his now red and swollen cheek.

"As soon as Zero was in the building, I got a call from a blocked number. I knew by the accent it was Roark. He told me he always rewarded a job well done. He offered me three hundred thousand for letting Zero in and another ten thousand if I agreed to lure you to him. I told him it was a deal."

"Were you supposed to bring me here?" My mind was already spinning. I needed backup. I needed more firepower. I needed to calm down because I had to do my job when all I wanted to do was shoot first. I couldn't believe Roark was finally close enough to touch, and I really wanted to knock Booker around some more.

"He didn't say. He gave me a number to call once I had the package secured." He lifted an eyebrow at me. "You're the package, cop."

I snorted. "I figured that. So what? We pound the hell out of one another and then you throw me in the back of the truck and take me to some secret location? What's to prevent Roark from putting a bullet in both of us the second we arrive? That's what I would do in his shoes."

Booker shook his head again. "I'm telling you he has a majorly sick and twisted thing for your girl. He wants you to suffer and he wants her to know you are suffering because of *her*. As for me . . . that's just a risk I'm gonna have to take."

I snorted again. "It's a stupid one. If he kills you, then you aren't a threat and he doesn't have to pay you. You're a dead man."

"So be it. It's the only way to end this."

"I need to call for backup. We can't try for a takedown alone." I was regretting not calling the station the second I left the house. Part of me had to make sure I finally finished the puzzle. Finally had all the pieces in place before I called. I was tired of being a pawn. It was time to be the king.

"No more cops. If he knows it's more than us, he'll just sink back underground and we'll never get a shot at him. Remember, he was a cop. He doesn't play by the rules, so he'll know what to expect. He has the entire police station wired. He's been watching you guys scramble around to find him and he's laughing at all of you. Video, sound . . . he knows every move you make. He's fucking everywhere. We're all fortunate Novak didn't hand him the reins . . . I think he knew the guy would've killed him off just to be number one. He's insane."

"So we just roll in like Butch and Sundance? You know

they died at the end of that movie, right? This is a terrible plan, Booker. You think you're gonna get a shot off before he does?"

"Well, it's the only plan I got and I only need one shot to make it count. You need to let me kick your ass some more, cuff you up and toss you in the truck. Your phone has to go since it can be used to track where you are. I'm supposed to toss mine too after he gives me the location. I'm telling you the guy thinks of all the angles. He even told me to disable the LoJack in your GTO so that it couldn't be tracked."

I swore, dropping every dirty, ugly word I could think of while trying to come up with some kind of a plan. Nothing was clicking. Booker was right, Roark was too good at this game. I shoved my hand through my hair. I had asked Reeve to offer herself as bait since the very beginning of this game. It was now my turn to hang myself out there like a worm on a hook. If she was strong enough to do it, brave enough to risk her neck time and time again, then I could be too. I could do it for her, to prove I was worthy of her strength and her bravery. "Fine. Let's go get shot. But I need to call Reeve and tell her what's going on. If we don't make it back from this . . ." I trailed off. If I didn't make it back she was going to wrap herself in vengeance and the need for blood. She was going to go back to where she had been before she came to me, and feel like it was her sworn duty to take Roark down to avenge me. I couldn't let that happen. She'd just gotten her soul back where it belonged. I couldn't be the reason she lost it again.

She answered on the first ring sounding breathless and scared. "Hey. It's me." I didn't let her speak before launching into what I was doing and the role Booker played in it all. I could tell she was crying by the time I was done talking.

"That's a terrible plan." Her voice was husky with tears.

"I know, but what choice do I have?"

She was silent for a long moment. "You can give me to him instead."

I barked out a laugh that had no humor in it. "No. I can't." She was crazy if she thought that was still an option after everything we had fought through to get to *more*.

"You have to be okay, Titus. I can't be here, I can't be someone good without you." That made my heart feel like it weighed a thousand pounds.

"Don't be good, then. Just be you, Reeve. Don't worry because you know what they say, you can't keep a good man down." She was crying in earnest now and I could almost taste every single tear through the phone. "It has to end, you know that."

She sniffled a little. "I should be the one to finish it. I'm the one he really wants to hurt. I should be able to take care of you, Titus."

"You already have, so much better than anyone else ever did." I should tell her I loved her but it felt wrong, cheap. She needed to hear the words when there wasn't a very strong chance that it was the only time I was going to be around to say them. "Trust me, and my initial order stands: if you don't hear from me in an hour, call the marshals and tell them where I'm at."

I hung up as she was sobbing my name. I took the battery out of my phone and handed it to Booker. He dropped the device to the ground and smashed it under the heel of his boot. I unclipped my gun from my belt and handed that over as well. He pointed to my ankle and stood there watching me while I bent down and released my backup weapon. I pulled my badge off my belt and tucked it into my pocket.

"Let me disable the antitheft device on the car and I'll grab my cuffs from the glove box."

I didn't want anyone else to put their hands on my baby. I just hoped that whatever happened, someone got her back to Bax in one piece. She deserved better than being left abandoned in this wasteland. I scooted under the frame and tugged on the wires that would send out the location signal should I need to find her if the pretty machine ever went missing. I also fished my handcuffs out of the glove compartment and handed them over to the other man. He tossed them up and then caught them with his hand with a smirk.

"Never been on the other side of these bad boys before." He lifted an eyebrow, which pulled at his scar. "Remember it has to look real."

I was going to ask him what in the hell he was talking about when the first blow landed on my cheek. The metal from the cuffs made Booker's fist feel like it was encased in steel. I shook my head to clear the ringing in my ears when another blow landed on the other cheek. I lifted my hands in automatic defense but he moved around them and landed an uppercut under my chin that had my teeth splitting my tongue open. I grunted at him and all it got me was another blow with the hand wrapped around the cuffs. I was having a hard time staying on my feet. I wobbled a little and was seeing spots as darkness started to swirl around my vision.

"Hey, cop."

"What?" The word was gasped out from lungs that felt taxed and from lips that were broken and rapidly swelling.

"I'm really sorry about this." I didn't have a chance to ask what he was talking about because the next thing I knew his forehead connected with my own and everything shifted and I went down to my knees. I was barely conscious and sure to have a concussion after the force of that blow. Something itchy and coarse fell over my head, making it harder to breathe and impossible to see. I struggled out of pure instinct as Booker hefted me up and shuffled me harshly to the truck.

"Take this thing off of me." I wanted to pull the hood off but my hands were yanked behind my back and secured with the chilly metal of my own cuffs.

"Can't. That was part of the big bad's orders. I think he might actually be a little afraid of you. The cuffs and hood were required." I felt him put something in my back pocket. "That's the key if by some miracle you make it out of this alive."

I heard him take a deep breath and then all I got was his side of the conversation as he called Roark.

"I got the cop. Yes, he's unarmed and secured . . . Yes, he's still breathing, but the fucker broke my nose." A forced laugh and then, "Where do you want him?"

A thump against the side of the truck. "Of course I'm coming alone. Bax can hardly move. Race wants to kill me and the cop is trussed up like a pig."

A litany of swearwords. "Yeah, I'll ditch my phone. I already told you I would. Look, I just want you to leave the girl alone. We already went over this. I don't give a shit about the rest of them."

I shifted around trying to determine if I could see anything through the fabric of the hood. It was no use. I was practically helpless and getting ready to ride right into the belly of the beast. It was the dumbest and bravest thing I had ever done. I wanted to kick my own ass for not having any other solution that didn't seem so hopeless and so desperate.

It was Booker's turn to snort. "You've got to be kidding me. Okay, I'll be there shortly."

"He's in Novak's warehouse, isn't he?"

I sounded garbled and suffocated from behind the cloth covering my face.

Booker thumped the side of the truck again. "Yeah. He said it seems fitting that it's the last stop for you since you spent so much time trying to take his father down. No one has been there since the feds seized it. It's been government property, and since he used to be a marshal and worked the case, he knows that."

I thumped my head back against the flatbed. "I fucking knew it."

"Showtime, cop." I heard the second phone crack and shatter on the asphalt and the plink of metal on metal, which I could only assume were my weapons as they landed in the truck bed next to me.

The truck fired to life and we were rumbling through the city. I was trying to keep panic and fear at bay. I was trying to remind myself that I had tangled with really bad men before and had always won. I gritted my teeth and reminded myself over and over that there was too much at stake for me to not come out on top.

It might have been ten minutes, but it felt like five seconds. There was only a sliver of time between theory and practice, and now I was about to come face-to-face with the man that had waged war on my city, hurt my brother, scared and harassed my woman, and personally challenged everything I stood for.

There was no way the Titus that wore the badge could do this and survive. It was time to meet Roark monster to monster and mine was long denied, long suppressed, and far hungrier than his would ever be.

The truck rumbled to a halt and I heard the door open. I heard Booker shuffle out and then, "You have a present for me?"

That lilting Irish brogue. I wanted to chew him up and spit him out.

"Yeah. You got some money for me?"

"Oh, Booker. You think I don't know about that sweet Ruger you have tucked into your waistband? You think I don't know you have a weak spot in the shape of a pretty teenage girl? Men that care about something that fragile are so predictable. Just like Detective King. I knew he would come with you no matter what the circumstances were, thought having him all wrapped up in a bow is a nice touch. Thank you."

I heard a gunshot and then another. I heard someone grunt and then the sound of deadweight hitting the ground. The iron scent of blood filled my nostrils and the next thing I knew I was being hauled out of the truck by grabbing hands. I went to struggle but it was no use. There were too many of them, and with my hands bound and my head covered there was no way to fight. Hard hands locked under my armpits and dragged me across gravel and God only knew what else. My legs and feet flailed for purchase.

I knew we had entered the warehouse once my struggle started to echo against the cement and steel walls.

"Too bad for Mr. Booker that a man with training will always be faster on the trigger than a common street thug. He was close, surprisingly close. He knew he was going to die but he took the chance anyway. Who says criminals have no honor?"

My arms were jerked high above my head and I felt something hard slide against my wrists as my feet dangled, barely touching the ground. I was stretched out like a side of beef in a cooler and I knew this wasn't good. Booker had been counting on getting a shot in, and now he was down and I was strung up like some kind of sacrifice. This was exactly where the plan fell apart. Just call me Butch Cassidy.

The hood was ripped off my head and I came face-to-face with the man that had turned my world upside down.

Conner Roark looked much like he had when he first came to collect Reeve for WITSEC. Tall, handsome, similar enough to Bax that it made hating him just a tiny bit hard. His ebony eyes glimmered with evil glee as he walked back and forth in front of me.

"Can I tell you a funny story, Detective?" That voice, so soothing, so deceptive about the evil it held captured between the melodic tones. I strained against the cuffs to no avail.

"You can go fuck yourself."

He lifted an eyebrow at me. "How uncouth. Trust me, Detective, this is a story you will want to hear. You see it involves the woman that we both can't seem to stay away from."

I didn't want to hear him say Reeve's name. I heaved again, muscles flexing and straining, while he just watched me like I was an animal stuck in an exhibit at the zoo.

"When I saw her that day after she turned herself in, I knew I had to have her. Beautiful, soft, but with an edge. She was perfect for me. Revenge, the need to make others pay for the way they had wronged her. It was music to my ears. She was everything I had ever wanted and I thought she hated this place, the things it had done to her. I thought she would stand with me and watch it burn because she understood."

"She thinks you're a sociopath. She saw through you, Roark. She's good like that. She has X-ray vision."

I heard something dripping in the background and could hear Roark's men shifting with anxiety to get their shots in. I was a life-size piñata and they couldn't wait to tear into me. I told myself I had to wait an hour. I could survive an hour before the cavalry showed, that was if Reeve did what I told her to do and didn't try something foolish like taking matters into her own hands. Realizing that struggling against the cuffs was getting me nowhere, I went lax and instead wrapped my fingers around them and just dangled there. Roark wandered a few steps closer to me.

"Maybe she did, but she never saw through the man that made me. You really believe Novak would be so selfless, or even slightly altruistic enough to take out a man that killed his hooker girlfriend? You think Novak cared about anyone else enough to get involved in their petty drama? The answer is no. He was a businessman and Reeve was a pretty girl. The boyfriend owed him money for a stash he blew by snorting it up his own nose. He wouldn't pay up, so he got taken care of. It was just coincidence that Reeve showed up begging for retribution. The guy was a dead man before the girlfriend was even in the ground. Novak was a clever man. He knew Reeve might prove useful down the road, so he let her believe for years that she was the catalyst . . . that she had it in her to be a killer. He kept her on a string and it was beautiful. I thought she could be my doll too."

He leaned closer and I saw my chance. I used the leverage my hands had on the cuffs and wrenched my entire lower body up from the waist. I kicked my legs out so that I could hook them around the Irishman's smug neck and started to squeeze. He punched at me, struggled, but I just closed my thighs tighter and tighter. I was going to choke the life out of him and I didn't care if I took a bullet in the back.

"People aren't toys." I huffed the words out and just as Roark was turning purple, and really looking like he was going to go down to his knees, something cracked across the back of my skull hard enough that it made me go immediately limp. My head fell forward and I felt blood start to run down the back of my neck in an untamed river.

Something dripped. Something landed with a splat. Something rattled. There was a clank and a whoosh. I faintly heard a thud and all I could do was silently swear and groan as my brain throbbed hot and heavy in my skull. The beating had begun in earnest.

"Fuck you. You'll kill me before I break."

"All of this over a girl. Really, Detective King, I thought you would prove to be much more of a challenge. She made you soft. She made you weak. All of the men in this city forgot there was a war going on when they got distracted by their dicks twitching. No girl is worth dying for."

I coughed and spit up another mouthful of blood and let my head fall forward as I gasped out a wheezing laugh.

"You can kill me. You can burn this fucking city to the ground. You can do your worst to anyone and everyone that dares to call this place home, but even after you lay waste to the whole city, you still won't have what you want . . . a girl that *is* worth dying for. She'll kill you first." I hoped it didn't come to that but I knew she would if he pushed her to it.

"No matter what you do to me or to this place, it won't change the fact she chose me and the Point over you. You're just as twisted and messed up as your father and you sure as fuck weren't ever good enough for my girl."

"Your girl?" The accented voice was hard, furious, and I knew I had hit a raw nerve.

"Mine."

"She chose wrong. I could have laid this city at her feet." He sounded almost like a lovesick lad, a character he was trying to portray instead of the murderous asshole he really was.

"If she wanted the city at her feet she would have put it there herself. That's why you never deserved her, you prick. You never understood she could run circles around you in the misplaced-rage and need-for-revenge department. Only she was smart enough to know that there had to be more to life than that. I'm her more. You were just a means to an end." I should've just kept my mouth shut because my heated words were what had him shoving the gun in my mouth and the metal clicking warningly against my front teeth. He looked at me coolly, with victory and insanity shining out of his dark eyes, and I saw his finger twitch on the trigger. It was time to end things.

The world exploded . . .

BANG!

I saw Roark jerk violently as bullets started to fly all around the cavernous warehouse space. His eyes stayed locked on mine as he fell to his knees in front of me, the gun in his hand falling harmlessly to the side. Roark's guys started to scatter as the room was suddenly swarming with guys in tactical gear and other guys wearing black jackets embellished with US MARSHAL across the back. I ducked my head uselessly as a bullet pinged against the pipe above my head, and looked around at the chaos that was ensuing. A familiar face appeared as a man dressed in a polo shirt covered in Kevlar dashed into the fray and stopped at Conner's body. He kicked a guy aside as he bent down to check Conner's pulse and frowned. He looked up where I was dangling and then maneuvered around his men and the bodies of Roark's crew where they lay.

"You got a key for those, King? You look like shit, by the way."

"In my pocket." He started patting me down as I continued to watch him. "That's some good timing you got there, Packard." Not that I wasn't happy to see him, considering I was about to eat a bullet.

Roark's old boss lifted his gray eyebrows at me as I collapsed in a heap at his feet once my hands were free. I wasn't sure if it was broken, but my kneecap felt like it was made of Jell-O, so there was no way I was walking out of here on my own.

"I got a frantic call from Reeve Black. She said a man named Noah Booker abducted you and was taking you to Roark. She told us to hurry. She said you told her to wait an hour but that was too long. She called us the second you hung up the phone. I pulled my guys off of her and moved them to go after you. Gotta say the timing couldn't have been any closer. The guy in the parking lot almost bled out but the paramedics seem to think he'll make it if he gets into surgery quick and gets a blood transfusion. He was still conscious when we rolled onto the scene, so they took that as a good sign and the bullet missed anything major. Lucky bastard. Looks like you would've been in pretty bad shape if we had been even a minute later."

I didn't know if Booker would agree that he was lucky. This was the second time he took a round in the chest in less than six months. Even if he did have as many lives as a cat, they were starting to run out.

"I'm glad she ignored me and called you." Hell, I was stunned she hadn't tried to ride to the rescue all on her own.

"Yeah. Told someone who she was and was screaming something about trusting the system and doing the right thing. She also said if we didn't send someone after you, she was calling in the not-so-legal backup. I didn't realize you had your hand so deep in the cookie jar, Detective. Can you walk?"

I shook my head in the negative and he hefted me up while wrapping an arm around my back. We both looked at where Roark lay still and lifeless, a bullet hole decorating the center of his forehead.

"Seems anticlimactic after everything he put you and the people of this city through."

I disagreed, but I had just spent the last hazy moments getting beaten with pipes and fists. "He died on the ashes of the empire we took from Novak. Seems oddly appropriate."

Packard snorted as we hobbled toward the door. "I'm just glad it's over, and though I'll never officially admit it, I'm glad I'm the one that fired the shot. I screwed up with Roark. Evens the scales back a little in my favor."

I sighed. This was the Point. It was never over and our scales were always out of whack in the opposite way anyone wanted. I shuffled, jumped, and stumbled with his help out of the warehouse to where I could hear sirens wailing. We were headed toward the back of an open ambulance when I heard my name. I saw her dark hair in the crowd and growled at Packard when one of his guys grabbed her to keep her back from the chaos and crime scene.

He ordered the fed to let her through and she ran at me like the hounds of hell were chasing her. She hit my chest hard and almost took all three of us to the ground. I was covered in blood, not all of it my own, and she didn't seem to care. She kissed me all over my face and helped Packard get me the rest of the way to the ambulance. She was talking a mile a minute, her eyes wide and shiny with relief and unshed tears. I slumped down and grabbed her cheeks so I could hold her face. I kissed her to shut her up and because I had to. I was alive. She was alive. The good guys were battered but victorious.

"You didn't wait."

She wrapped her arms around my neck and buried her face in the curve there. "I've been waiting for something good and right in my life forever, Titus. I wasn't going to wait for it for another hour. I couldn't risk it. I couldn't risk you."

"Thank you. I'm so proud of you for knowing what to do, for taking care of me."

She nodded against me. "I wanted to do the right thing. I wanted you to see that I do trust you, trust the system. I wanted to show you more. I wanted to take care of you the right way."

I squeezed her and winced as she brushed my knee. That sucker was shot. It looked like a basketball and was the same color as her dark blue eyes.

"Any choice you make to take care of me is the right choice, Reeve. I love you."

She hiccuped against the side of my neck and I felt the tears start to fall. "I love you too."

I ran my hand up under the heavy fall of her hair and

wrapped it around the back of her neck. I gave her a little squeeze and whispered into her ear as a uniformed paramedic started to make his way over to us. "I need to tell you something."

"Anything."

"You never had anything to do with your sister's boyfriend getting killed. He owed Novak money for drugs. He already had a target on him. Novak manipulated you, used you like he did everyone else in the Point. You've never been a killer, Reeve. You aren't a bad person. You can go make things right with your folks and let go of some of that responsibility you let control you."

She pulled back and looked at me stunned. She fussed at the paramedic when he asked her to move away so he could get to my injured leg.

She slowly shook her head and took my hand. "No. I'm still the same, Titus. Regardless of whether I had a hand in it or not, I'm glad Rissa's killer is dead, and I would've killed Conner. I still want to now seeing how badly he hurt you. I won't make that choice again, I know I can't and still keep you, but I still want to. I don't think it makes me a bad person. I think it makes me a survivor. If it's me and someone I love or a bad guy, the bad guy is going down and I won't feel guilty for that anymore."

I leaned over and kissed her. "You are a lion tamer." Fearless and always willing to dance in the dark with the monsters and animals that wanted to eat her up. No wonder my beast loved her. She wrinkled her nose at me.

"Can't it be Beauty and the Beast? I think I like that better."

I wanted to laugh but I groaned instead as they told me they needed to move me to a gurney. It really hurt but it was tolerable because my girl was there to take care of me.

Like she always was. I might bleed for everyone else. Fight to the end for this town and those that I loved that lived here, but this woman . . . she would bleed for me and never ask for anything in return. There was nothing more than that. This is what my love looked like in the Point: a girl that could take care of herself and anyone else she cared about . . . and God help anyone that got in her way.

Chapter 19

Reeve

THE GARAGE WAS BUSY when I walked through it. It was noisy and smelled like oil and gasoline. I got a few curious looks from the different guys that had their heads buried in engines or that were working on various other parts of the car but I didn't pay any attention to them. They all knew I was with Bax's brother, and as long as they wanted to keep breathing or stay out of jail, they kept their opinions to themselves.

I knew Bax was somewhere in the cavernous compound. I had called Dovie earlier to ask her where I could find him. She told me he was going nuts sitting at home, and since the contraption holding his jaw in place had been removed, he went back to work. She sounded frustrated and I knew exactly where she was coming from. Though Titus's injuries were less serious than Bax's in the grand scheme of things, he was still laid up with a broken knee and some busted ribs. The cop was a terrible patient and he was making me insane with his bad mood and surly attitude while he thumped around the house in his cast. My personal opinion was that the rest was good for him. He deserved some time off after everything he had been through, but Titus wasn't the kind of guy that unwound. He stayed coiled tight, listening to his police scanner and constantly on the phone with his fellow cops talking about work and unsolved cases. Even hobbled and banged up, the guy was a force to be reckoned with, and the same could be said for Bax.

He was sitting behind his big, metal desk in his office. His wrist was still in a heavy plaster cast but he had his broken ankle up on the edge of the desk and it was encased in a bulky, black walking boot. He was still too skinny and the sharpness in his face made his glower all the more intimidating as I took a seat across from him without asking. He still emanated badass and don't-mess-with-me even though he looked like he had been on the losing end of his last fight.

Dovie had given me the codes to get into the compound and through the massive gates in the first place since there was no chance in hell I would ever be invited. I wasn't welcome and the fact was evident on Bax's hard features.

"What are you doing here?" He tapped his fingers on the knee of his lifted leg and I glanced around the office. I was trying to figure out what seemed different about him besides the weight loss when the old smell of cigarette smoke snuck into my nose.

I lifted an eyebrow at him. "You don't have a cigarette in your hand."

The vein by the star inked on his face twitched in annoyance. "I have enough shit trying to kill me every day. I figured I didn't need to help matters along. It was a bitch to try and smoke through all the wires and shit that were holding my face together until a couple of days ago. What are you doing here, Reeve?"

I pushed some of my long hair over my shoulder and cleared

my throat. "I know you don't like me, that you don't trust me and want someone else for your brother."

He didn't say anything but his chin dipped down in a barely-there nod. "None of that is a secret."

I locked my fingers together in my lap and forced myself to meet his dark gaze and the animosity that lived deep in the depths. "Look, I know I screwed up with Dovie and she got hurt, but I saved Titus's life, so that has to count for something. I'm not going anywhere and you know you can't do anything about it without hurting your brother. I want some kind of truce, Shane. Like it or not, we're part of the same family now."

He didn't say anything. He rocked back in his chair and steepled his fingers in front of him while he considered me. It took every ounce of self-control I had not to wiggle and fidget under that heavy and deep look. It was like the entire night sky was landing on top of me.

"What are you going to do with Titus in the long run, Reeve? He's always going to be a cop and you're always going to be a chick with one foot on either side of the law. Are you going to make him choose between you and who he is, what he has always been?"

I shook my head slowly. "I'm going to love him and take care of him like he has always done for you, Shane. He needs someone to care for him and I promise that I won't ever compromise him. I told Nassir that when I agreed to stay on at the club. Everything is aboveboard and legal, and it stays that way or I walk. Maybe it's not the most morally pristine job for a cop's lady to have, but it pays well and I like being able to take care of the girls. Strippers are mostly good women just doing what they have to in order to survive out here. I understand that better than Nassir or Race ever will. It's not like you can judge anyway. I know what all those cars sitting on your lot are for. Out of the two of us, you're the one that tests his resolve to be who he is, not me." I got to my feet and put my hands on the edge of the desk. I leaned forward a little so Bax could feel my own heavy and deep gaze as it landed on him. "And he wasn't always a cop. He was a kid stuck just like you were. He is a man that has had to make the hard choices just like you. Don't force him to make another one, Shane. Find a way to make peace with the fact I'm here and I'm here to stay."

I wouldn't beg him. I had too much pride for that, but I would fight him if he made me. Titus needed both of us in his life and I wouldn't let Bax reopen the gap that had separated them for so long. I pushed up off the desk and turned to head back out the door. Bax's gravelly voice stopped me just as I was pushing the lever to open it.

"When you say 'here to stay,' are you talking babies and a ring? Traditional shit that makes no sense in this place?" He sounded baffled by the concept.

I just shrugged my shoulder. What happened next hadn't exactly come up in conversation with the cop, but he didn't seem at all concerned that birth control had gone out the window. Well, once the feds had officially cleared out and there was no longer the threat of possible jail time hanging over my head, birth control had fallen by the wayside. Babies and the Point didn't really mix, but when the mother was willing to do anything, and I do mean *anything*, to keep them safe and happy, I think Titus and I realized bringing a life into this messed-up world was a risk we were both willing to take. And as traditional and serious as the man was about family, I had no doubt that at some point in the future he would want to make all the *more* between us official.

"I'm here for all of it. Whatever it is."

He swung the bulky contraption holding his ankle off the desk and got to his feet. He crossed his arms over his chest and we had a stare-down. When I didn't look away he gave that tiny little nod again and let his mouth twist up into a smirk.

"We're fine for now, Reeve, but if you ever hurt anyone I care about again, there won't be a place far enough away that you can hide to get away from me."

"We care about the same people, Shane. I won't make those kinds of mistakes again."

I walked out before he could say anything else. It was a shaky truce at best, but it would do for now. Bax was never going to be my biggest fan, but as long as he tolerated me and understood I would never let anything hurt Titus, I was a happy girl.

I had one more quick stop to make before going back home to my cranky cop. As nice and modern as the loft was, it didn't feel like a home. I didn't want to be locked up in a fortress and I didn't want to be lifted high above the streets that were my home. I liked Titus's messy little Craftsman. I liked that once it was cleaned up and actually had some things inside of it to make it feel lived in and homey, it automatically felt like a home we had built together. He hadn't even asked me to move in. I just did it as soon as he came home from the hospital. I knew he was going to need help since he could barely walk and still had more reconstructive surgery to look forward to, but he didn't say anything about all my stuff overrunning the closet and overtaking the bathroom counter. I assumed he was happy with the situation since he never complained or batted an eye even if I did harp on him to pick up after himself. I never knew any one person could leave such a tornado of mess behind them wherever they went. He was lucky I loved him because the man was a straight-up slob.

I found the room I was looking for when I got to the hospital with minimal effort. I had wanted to come by sooner, but between the cops questioning him and the feds wanting a piece of him, Booker was a busy guy. Not to mention he had required three separate operations to keep him alive and to dig the bullet out of his chest, and was just now awake and lucid enough for visitors.

When I pushed the door open I wasn't surprised at all to see that he wasn't alone. Big brown eyes looked up at me guiltily as Karsen took a startled step back from the bed. The teenager flushed and bit down on her lip.

"Hi, Reeve."

"Hi, sweetie. Does your sister or Race know you're here?" The teenager flushed even hotter red and I knew the answer was no. I sighed. "You better go, then. You don't need to get the brute in any more trouble with Race."

She nodded and whispered good-bye to Booker before scurrying out the door. I shut it behind her and went over to take up the spot she had just vacated by the bed. Booker was looking up at me with weary blue-gray eyes and he had all kinds of tubes and wires coming out of him.

"You really do have a death wish if you think Race is gonna let you get your hands on that girl, my friend."

He wheezed out something that sounded like a laugh. "You still pissed at me too?"

At first, when Titus explained why Booker had betrayed us

all, I had been so burned, felt so violated, that I was sure I never wanted to see the man again. But I was a master of knowing all about drastic choices made in the vortex of desperation and frustration, so when I calmed down I knew I couldn't stay mad at him. Booker was playing the only hand he had been dealt just like we all did. We all gambled with fate and chance every single day, so we were bound to lose every now and then.

That's why I was here. I knew all about screwing up so bad that you felt like you were all alone and no one would ever be able to forgive you. I needed Booker to know that even though his actions had hurt me, had been dire and foolish, I got it and I understood what made him do it. The two of us were an awful lot alike, and in this place it was hard to find people that you not only liked but could relate to. I wasn't going to cast him out and I wanted him to know that.

Race wasn't as quick to forgive as I was. His fortress had been breached from the inside and that made him feel like he couldn't keep his girls safe. I wasn't sure what the future held for him and Booker and their working relationship, but with Karsen still sniffing around the much older and much harder man, I knew the road bumps were just beginning for Booker.

"No, I'm not pissed anymore. I understand why you did what you did, but that's only because I've been there. The guys . . ." I turned my hand back and forth in a so-so motion. "They can only see you putting their women at risk, so they want to go caveman on you. Give it time. Race will see the entire picture sooner or later."

"What about the cop?"

I shrugged. "He doesn't love that I got beat up, and he doesn't love that you got me the gun, but he's proud of me for taking care of myself. I think he gets that you were desperate and grasping at straws. Someone had to do something and maybe it wasn't the right thing, but in the end your actions brought Conner down, and that's all that matters. Titus said you're still going to get probation for skipping on your bond, though."

He wheezed again, which I think was a laugh. "He let you keep the gun?"

I nodded a little. "No. But he got me another one. This one is licensed." I was still doing me and living my life, I was just doing it with more clearly defined lines than I did before. It was actually pretty fun when I had my own sexy cop around to enforce the rules.

"Good. I don't want you to lose your edge." His eyelids started to droop, so I reached out and squeezed one of his hands. Despite it all, Booker's heart had been in the right place even if he might have gone about everything all wrong. That was something that was painfully familiar to me.

"Those edges just smooth out naturally when they end up rubbing against the person that is your rock, my friend."

He grumbled something and let his eyes drift closed. "I don't need a rock. I'm hard enough on my own." I didn't say anything, but I did think of the doe-eyed teenager that had just snuck in to see him. Sometimes rocks were tiny pebbles tossed around in a storm, battering endlessly against a much bigger boulder, slowly, silently chipping away at the surface.

I slipped out of the room and went down to the GTO so I could get back to Titus. He didn't throw the L-word around a lot . . . in fact he had only said it to me twice. The day after Conner was hauled away by the coroner and the day he finally came home from the hospital when he was still stoned out of his mind on pain pills. It didn't bother me because the next day he had handed over the keys to that Liberty Blue muscle car and told me I could use it until his leg was out of the cast. If that wasn't a full-on declaration of love and devotion, then I didn't know what was. The keys to the GTO were better than any diamond ring he might give me.

I parked the car in the alley behind the house and made my way through the back door. The kitchen was a mess, obviously the leftover remnants of Titus trying to make himself lunch. I sighed under my breath and threw my purse on the table. It took me fifteen minutes to put stuff back in the fridge, rinse off the dishes, and wipe down the counters. I was irritated when I went to go find him. I wasn't his maid for goodness' sake.

When I got to living room he was easy enough to spot. Somehow he had managed to push all the furniture to the edges of the room and he was laid out on his back in the center of the room doing sit-ups. His shirt was off, showing the Ace bandage that was still wrapped around his bruised ribs and all he had on for clothing, if you wanted to call it that, was a pair of black boxer briefs, since getting anything on over his cast took both of us and a lot of tugging and swearing. He must have been at it for a while because all his muscles were pulled taut and a slippery sheen of sweat dotted all of his naked skin. He was breathing hard enough that I could hear him from across the room and it was louder than the heels of my shoes clicking on the hardwood floors as I made my way toward him. He turned his head as I approached but didn't stop curling up and down until I plopped myself down right on top of him. He fell back to the floor with a grunt and put his hands on my waist. Fortunately for me, I had worn a skirt when I went out to run around town, so all his hot and sweaty skin brushed enticingly along my bare thighs as I straddled him. He always felt better than anything in life ever had.

I rubbed my fingers on the white spot in his hair. It seemed to have stopped spreading and now was the size of an Oreo cookie, stark and brilliant against the rest of his black hair. It was one of my favorite features of his. One of the other ones was coming to life under my backside as I leaned forward to kiss him soundly on the mouth.

"How did you move all the furniture? You're supposed to be taking it easy."

His hands moved to my thighs and started pushing the filmy fabric of my skirt up my legs. The roughness of his palms made me shiver as he kissed me back just as hard and just as forcefully as he always did.

"Taking it easy sucks. I want to go back to work as soon as this stupid thing comes off. That means I need to stay bigger and badder than the guys committing the crimes."

I put my hands on his rock-hard chest and dug my nails into the unyielding muscle that lived there. "Sitting around and watching TV for a few weeks isn't going to turn you into an out-of-shape blob, Titus. You deserve to relax."

His eyebrows shot up as his fingers dipped into the edge of the panties at the very top of my thigh. I was already getting wet and ready.

"I do relax." His fingers danced under the fabric closer to the heart of me.

"When?" The word came out in a breathy rush and I leaned forward even more, giving him more access to the places I wanted him to touch. My hair fell around us like a curtain blocking out the afternoon light.

"When I'm inside of you." I gasped at him as his fingers found that perfect point of pleasure and began to trip across it.

I narrowed my eyes at him and put a hand on his cheek. "I'm going to cut you off from sex if you don't start picking up after yourself. Seriously, how hard is it to throw a plate in the sink?" The threat would have held more weight if I wasn't riding his fingers as he slipped them inside of me.

"You can't say no to me, Reeve. You want the beast just as much as he wants you." He kissed me again and I whimpered a little as he pulled his hand away from me and out from under my skirt. I was going to pout at him when he told me, "Take those off and turn around. We can relax each other." He wiggled his eyebrows up and down as I apprehensively did as he asked, proving that he was right. I would never say no to him.

Naked, I sat back down on top of his ripped abs and looked at him over my shoulder through my lashes. "Now what, Detective?"

He chuckled low and it vibrated through my entire body. "Now we take care of each other." His big hands grasped my hips and pulled me backward so that I was on my hands and knees, hovering over him, with all my private and secret places opened and in front of him. I was about to ask him what he thought he was doing when his tongue darted out and licked across me from top to bottom. The searing heat made me gasp in shock, and when I looked down I realized I was right above his cotton-covered erection. Take care of each other indeed. I braced myself with one hand on the floor next to his cast and carefully worked his straining flesh out with the other. The velvet-soft head brushed against my lips as I brought it closer to my mouth.

He said my name and it made my clit tingle against his lips. I was trying to concentrate on what I was doing and I bent down to engulf his cock in the wet heat of my mouth, but what he was doing to me with his mouth was making it hard.

I took him down as deep as I could and then bobbed back up. I tried to time it with the tricky flick of his tongue and the delectable thrust and retreat of his fingers, but it was impossible. His rhythm was fast and hard, I liked mine to be slow and torturous. He wanted to wind me up and make me shatter, I wanted to slow him down and fill him up with so much pleasure that he overflowed. It was the sexiest war ever fought.

He added another finger as he continued to lick and fuck me. I added my fist around the base of his erection and squeezed as I continued to suck him and play with him. My head was swimming with the combined arousal, mine and his, and when he reached between us and got his clever fingers around the hurting tip of one of my breasts, I knew I wasn't going to be able to hold out any longer. I hummed around his staring arousal and darted a hand between his legs so I could rub my fingers across his taut balls. It made his entire body bow up off the floor.

"Let me inside, Reeve." I sort of loved it more than anything when he gave orders like that, so I released that delectable hard flesh with a slick flick of my tongue and lifted myself back up onto my knees over him. I didn't bother to turn around. That would've just wasted time. I scooted down to his waist and lifted myself up so that he could align himself with my glistening opening. Once I felt the tip of him touch my damp fold, I sank all the way down, making both of us sigh. He put one hand on my hip and lifted up his good leg, which forced my legs farther apart on either side of him. It stretched me out and made the drag and pull of him inside of me even more noticeable as I started to move up and down in a steady rocking motion.

I looked over my shoulder, wanting to make sure he was feeling all that I was feeling, but he wasn't looking at me. That passion-hot gaze lit from the inside by silver fire was locked on the place where we were joined. He licked his lips and his fingers got tighter and tighter every time my body took his in. That was the look of possession. It was the look of the primal things that he kept hidden coming up to the surface and taking what belonged to them. It was the look of love and the fight that it took to keep that love. It was a look that was enough to have me erupting and breaking apart all over him.

I leaned forward with a sigh and rested my cheek on his good knee as he lifted his hips a few more times and pumped into me until he found his own completion. I almost purred as he rubbed his palm up and down my spine.

"See. Nice and relaxed." I would've rolled my eyes at him if I had any kind of energy left.

"That still doesn't make up for leaving the kitchen a mess." He twisted his hands in my hair and pulled me back so that I was lying all over the top of him and we were staring at the ceiling. "I'll take care of you forever, Titus, but I'm not going to clean up after you like the hired help."

He laughed in my ear and put his arm across my breasts. He couldn't be comfortable with the floor at his back and me on top of him, but if he wasn't going to complain, I was in no hurry to move.

"I'm sorry. I'll try and be better about it." I could only sigh because that was what he always said. "And I didn't move the furniture, Nassir did. He stopped by to ask me for a favor, and while he was here I asked him to help me get it out of the way."

I stiffened automatically. I couldn't think of any kind of favor I wanted my too slick and too ruthless boss asking my man for.

"What did Nassir want?" Titus's free hand started rubbing in slow circles across my belly and I wondered if he was thinking about what was inevitably going to happen in there if we kept having uninhibited sex without protection. I shivered a little when I realized he was tracing invisible hearts across my skin.

"He asked me to track someone down for him."

I put my hand over his and whispered, "Keelyn?"

Titus grunted his affirmative. "Yeah. I told him no."

I couldn't believe the relief that swamped me. "Why?"

"Because he's going to find her with me or without me, and when he does we both know she'll end up back here. She's your friend . . . sort of . . . so I don't want any part of bringing her back to this place if she had a chance at making it somewhere else. Nassir gets it, but he left here and went right to Stark. That guy will have a location on her in two minutes. Especially since we all know that she's in Denver already."

I sighed again. "Nassir named the new club Lock and Key. That can't be coincidence." It wasn't open yet but already the city and the streets were alive with noise and anticipation to see what the prince of sin and darkness could offer to them.

"No, it's probably not. Love can look really strange in the Point. In fact, if you aren't paying attention you might miss it altogether because it doesn't look like love at all."

I tilted my head so I could kiss him. "Well, I'm glad not much gets by you, Detective."

He kissed me back. "And I'm glad you fight for what you think is right, Reeve."

That's what it took to not just survive but to thrive in the Point.

Love and fight.

Good thing we had plenty of both.

To be continued with Nassir's story . . .

ACKNOWLEDGEMENTS

R EALLY MY BIGGEST THANKS in the whole world goes to all of you that made it to this point (pun slightly intended). I can never tell those of you that are willing to try something new—willing to let me tell all kinds of stories, willing to follow me as I build all these new worlds, and willing to invest your time and trust into these intense, complicated, wild characters— how grateful and appreciative I am of you. You are readers and book lovers after my own heart. I adore that you took a chance on something different and I can only hope that I didn't let you down. I always hope the risk is worth the reward because as most of my readers know my entire career is based on taking a risk and trying something new. Honestly, the Point is a total manifestation of that kind of do-or-die attitude and maybe that's why I have more fun than any one person should have when I write these books.

I have so many ideas, so many stories floating around in my head that without you being here, I think I might just explode. Creativity is a hungry beast and it needs more than one kind of food to feed it. So thank you for the support, the love, and the journey. Thank you for being brave. ☺ I wouldn't be here without you and neither would any of these amazing characters you've given me the opportunity to bring to life. My readers are everything . . . never doubt that.

Thank you blogger nation for all that you do. Thank you for getting the word out. Thank you for loving books and sharing that love with the rest of the world. Thank you for being hard working and selfless. Thank you for being honest. Thank you for being real.

As always, the hot cop would not be all he could be without my editor Amanda and he wouldn't get as much love out there in the world if it wasn't for my killer team over at HarperCollins/ William Morrow. Jessie, Molly, Caro, Elle . . . all you girls make this entire big bad world of publishing just slightly less terrifying and always make me feel like me and the boys are where we are meant to be . . . even if I thought A was trying to kill me this go-around. Oh don't mind Jay over in the corner curled up in the fetal position when revisions come in . . . that's just par for the course now. But seriously, thanks team, for well . . . being my team!

I can't live without KP Simmon in my life! That's all there is to it. She's not only a marketing and publicity guru, she is also an amazing friend, a kind human being, a caretaker and a force to be reckoned with. Life, both business and personal, will always be just a little sweeter with some KP in it.

Stacey Donaghy, thanks for always being my guiding light and for always being able to roll with my crazy. Some days I know it can be a lot to handle but you always manage to do it and never let me go over the edge. Not an easy feat.

Melissa Shank and really the whole Shank crew, thanks for being wonderful, loving and strong. Thanks for being family and so full of love and life that it makes me happy every day that you're a part of my life. Mel, you know I couldn't get through half of the chaos that I create without you, and really, just thank you for always TCB without me asking. You're the best and I have endless amounts of love and gratitude to heap on you forever and ever.

Vilma Gonzalez, Denise Tung, and Heather Self—thank you for being my girls! Thank you for putting up with endless texts and PMs. Thank you for reading all of the bazillion books that I write and giving me your unvarnished, raw, real feedback. Thank you for making me better at what I do. Thank you for being amazing, strong, funny, delightful women that make every day just a little bit better. Ha, and thank you for letting me send you endless parades of hot dudes while I'm searching for a cover guy . . . right . . . being my friend is hard sometimes. ☺ I love you ladies and I really, really hate that you're both so far away from me . . . blurg.

All my book peeps—Jen, Jen Mc, Jenn, J4, Tiffany, Cora, EK, Emma, Kristen, Jamie, Kimberly, Laurelin, Sophie, Monica, Tucker, Amy, Tijan, Lo, Karina, Chelsea, Crystal, Carolyn, Ali, Debbie, Denise, Renee, Stephanie, Damaris, Courtney, Christine, Danielle, Teri . . . you guys kick so much ass and I just want to squeeze you all and smother you in so much love.

Anyone that follows me on social media or has come out to meet me at an event knows there is a good chance my folks will make an appearance. I love my family and I have really been blessed with a set of parents that are everything. My mom has always been my best friend and my dad has always been the coolest guy I have ever known. One of the great joys writing has brought into my life is that I get to experience all this excitement and all these dreams coming true with them. So thanks mom and dad for being around to see all this and thank you so much for coming on the ride with me. Thanks for always bringing me a Bud Light so that I never run dry. Oh, and thanks for being so much fun—people at signings would rather hang out with you two than me!

As always, mad love to my pack (my furry family is the best thing in the world to come home to) and the man that loves them for me when I'm on the road. Thanks for being so dope Mike Maley! And I'm serious about an invite to the Renaissance festival this year!

As always, I'm easy to find if you want to holler at me and have me holler back:

https://www.facebook.com/jay.crownover

https://www.facebook.com/AuthorJayCrownover?ref=hl

@jaycrownover

www.jaycrownover.com

http://jaycrownover.blogspot.com/

https://www.goodreads.com/Crownover

http://www.donaghyliterary.com/jay-crownover.html

http://www.avonromance.com/author/jay-crownover

BUILT

Sayer Cole and Zeb Fuller are as different as two people can be. She's country club and fine dining, he's cell block and sawdust. Sayer spends her days in litigation, while Zeb spends his working with his hands. She's French silk, while he is all denim and flannel.

The differences between the two of them don't stop Zeb from dropping every hint he can think of that he would like to get to know the lovely lawyer on a more personal level, but Sayer seems oblivious to his interest. To Sayer, a manly guy like Zeb, someone so good with his hands, could never be interested in someone as reserved as she is. She's never been with anyone that was hot enough to melt her icy exterior, but something tells her Zeb might be the guy to finally thaw her out.

When Zeb gets the surprise of a lifetime in the form of a kid he never knew he had, getting Sayer into bed takes a backseat. He desperately needs her professional help to get custody of his son before he ends up lost to Zeb forever. Somewhere between bringing broken, battered homes back to life and making sure a family stays together, these two opposites realize that on the inside they are exactly the same. As much as Sayer needs Zeb's heat to melt the ice around her heart, he needs her cool head just as much—to win the most important fight of his life.

Available Winter 2016

BOOKS BY JAY CROWNOVER

THE MARKED MEN SERIES

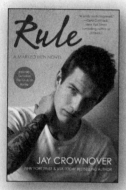

RULE

JET

ROME

NASH

ROWDY

ASA

Available in Paperback and eBook

Visit www.BetweentheCovers.com

BOOKS BY JAY CROWNOVER

THE WELCOME TO THE POINT SERIES

BETTER
WHEN
HE'S
BAD

BETTER
WHEN
HE'S
BOLD

BETTER
WHEN
HE'S
BRAVE